Pra

Winner of th

All cover quotes from beta readers.

"[A Cactus In the Valley] will change you. It's full of love, heartache, salvation, and survival. I cried and laughed and was on the edge of my seat. I am so in love with this book," - Craig Perkins, book blogger

"A Cactus In the Valley delivered a sort of raw passion that I have yet to see again in its genre. Wyatt and Terra's story catches you from page one, and when it's done, it leaves you wishing the book hadn't ended," -Maddyson Wilson, author of *Doubt the Stars*

"This book had me feeling so much: hope, fear for the characters, pity, happiness, sadness and about a thousand other things. Bennett truly has a gift for storytelling. From the first page, I couldn't stop reading," -Paige Anderson, book blogger

"A wonderful, beautifully written story about the issues teenagers face in our society today that need to be discussed," -Michael Evans, author of *Control Freakz*

"A Cactus In the Valley is a novel of thrill, romance, action, self-knowledge, and exploration of not just the Arizona desert, but of inner conflict. Bennett's descriptions pull you into the scene. This novel needs to be on your reading list ASAP," -Brittney Kristina, author of *Forsaken* and *Fifty Days*

Ages 14 and up.

All cover quotes from beta readers.

ISBN-10: 1548231401

ISBN-13: 978-1548231408

Cover photo: Anton Foltin

Cover design: Olivia J. Bennett

Author photo: Shailey Heuermann

Dedication

This story is dedicated to my parents. You did a lot wrong, but you also did a lot right. I don't think this story would be as impactful as it is without you two. Thank you for showing me the beauty in dysfunction.

All glory be to Christ, to whom I owe everything.

A Cactus In the Valley

Olivia J. Bennett

Winner of the 2018 Scholastic Gold Key Award

CHAPTER ONE: Shattered Glass

Day 1 - Terra; August 5th, 2015

I breathe. For an entire second of reality, I am not able to exhale. Just the swollen, toxic air eating at my lungs. When I finally am able to breathe out, it's like fire, ravishing every inch of my insides. My stinging eyes finally come into focus, but still, the world's colors swirl in front of me.

I breathe, the soupy air getting caught in my throat again. My voice echoes, the throaty heaves piercing the metal walls of the plane.

Sensations flow through my body as I become aware of myself for what seems like the first time. Smoke collects in my lungs, tearing fissures in the delicate tissue. My heart squeezes in my chest, vibrating as the panic rises within me.

Something warm and wet dribbles from my hairline onto the soft part of my eyelid. Still, my eyes are clouded over as my head swirls in my skull, like a spoon chasing the last bits of cereal in the milk. My knees jam against the cushioned chair in front of me, so hard that I can feel the metal skeleton deep within.

Ringing. High pitched and whirring. Close and emanating from inside of my skull. As I struggle to push myself up against the airplane seat, the tendons in my neck scream at me and oppose my movement. The hissing of fire crackles in my ears. I frantically search for an armrest, still half-blind.

My hand claws on the leather beside me, grasping for something concrete in a world of senses. I can feel the smoke infiltrating my bloodstream, making a buzzing in my lungs.

7

I grasp onto strands of hope as my vision finally returns. Heaving, my estranged cries still crowding out the cabin of the plane, I see. The broken front seat, coated in worn, beige leather. The shattered windshield of the plane, the edges piercing like diamonds in the white hot sun. The smoke rising from the nose of the plane. And the way that the lonely desert wind blows the heat right into the cabin of the Cessna 310.

Suddenly, my throat thrashes in my neck, releasing a cough into the still, silent air. The sudden, almost painful movements jar the fuzzy edges off of my consciousness, and I become strikingly aware.

I breathe. Shuddering, I push my bangs out of my eyes and run my hands over my face, my wavy hair caught in my simple stud earrings. My hands come back coated in blood and dirt.

My abdomen contracting with boiling panic, I assess myself, making sure to move every joint and squeeze every muscle. Something active and hot buzzes through my body, and I can't stop shaking.

I find myself thinking one pulsating thought.

I have to get out of this plane.

My mind launches into its default position. While the electricity does not cease to flow in my veins, I can focus. And this gives me a lens in which to create order.

And I can work with order.

Grasping onto the front seat, I gaze into the open windshield. Almost no shards of glass remain, other than some stragglers on the edge. The hood of the plane still smokes profusely, warping the air coming from it.

No luck there.

Yet again, I can feel the pulsing of emotion inside of me, threatening to break through. But I breathe, taking in the familiar scent of the plane, the heavy smoke, and the arid desert.

I just breathe. And in the stillness, noise floods my mind. I'm alone . . . I'm alone I'm alone I'm alone I'm alone.

The door.

Hell, why didn't I think of that first? My head whips around to face it, but my head wobbles in the fluid of my skull and my neck tightens, threatening to choke me. Note to self: don't do that again.

My eyes rapidly scan the door to find that it's badly dented - inward. The leather-covered wall juts toward me, where the door should slide smoothly out and then open. But the handle is jammed, silver and stuck in the wall like a sore thumb.

I run my hands over the perimeter of the door. Sunlight peeks in through the warped edges. Straining, I push against the outer rim, and nothing but a low, hollow creak ripples through the plane.

I breathe, sucking in air through my nose and out my mouth. The voice in my head screams at me to get out. Encroaching claustrophobia floods around me, licking at my neck and rising up inside of me. I am an empty aluminum can, and the world is a garbage crusher.

In one panic-fueled second, I lurch out of my seat - only to be jerked back by a strange force around my torso. I look down to see the seatbelt tangled around me and I reach down to unbuckle. Easy enough.

But when I try to move again, another force to my side holds me down. Frustration now buzzing within me, I look down to see the edge of my cardigan lodged in between my seat and the indented door, pressing into my side.

9

With trembling hands, I grab onto my jacket nearest to the door and tug, but nothing moves. My heartbeat pounds under my fingernails, and a haunting, fluttery feeling rises in the hollow of my stomach.

I give the stupid thing fast and ferocious tugs, but there's nothing. Nothing. My arms burn and my throat screams at me.

Suddenly, like lightning, I am thrust from the tug of war I play and shoot back onto the seat next to me. And onto something warm and supple.

And human.

Shivers striking up my back like spiders, I leap off of the seat next to me and onto my own, my body electric with terror.

A boy about my age sits in the seat next to me, unconscious. However, he is slumped to the side of the plane. I reach out to touch him, but don't. Something inside me pulls back.

Stretched out in the small crevice of the plane, I stand on the seat, petrified because something even more caustic swells inside of me. Confusion.

I stare at this boy for a while, sifting through blurry memories as I try and remember this boy's name - who he is, why he is here, sitting next to me.

But when I come up empty handed, I sit back in my seat, relaxing and still heaving from the shock.

I stare at him again, and suddenly, as if thrown in my face, there it is. His name is Wyatt.

About the same age as me, 16. No last name appears to tack onto the end of his first name, and I assume he's just above the rank of a stranger to me. I gather that he and his family (whom I have no memory of) were customers at my family's lodge and touring business: "Lombardi Lodge and Desert Tours."

During the renovation, I was against keeping the name.

And then it all comes to a slamming halt. My memory goes blank of every reason why I am on the plane, why he is here, what happened before . . . Maybe my brain is eluding me, hiding this from my consciousness for the better.

Sighing in the lull of events, I look back over to the unconscious Wyatt. Swallowing hard, I reach out and nudge his shoulder. Stiff and supple - he's not responsive.

But then my eye catches on something stark and red - the thick plane window is utterly smashed. He slumps awkwardly to the side, towards the window, and a good portion of his head actually juts out of the window, his skull resting on the sill. Pieces of shattered glass linger in his curly dishwater-blonde hair.

Reeling, I turn away from this most likely dead boy - only to bang the top of my head on the low ceiling of the plane. *Shit.*

Curling up to stifle the impending scream boiling inside of me, I bite my bottom lip until it bleeds. My eyes flick to the ceiling, ready to get mad at this stupid plane for holding me in here like a prison cell.

But I stop. I see something that might be my last hope - the sunroof.

About two and a half feet in width, and maybe two feet in length, and covered in a thick layer of glass. I remember that the glass is single pane and an inch thick - no easy way out. How much do you want to bet that I can fit through the hole?

Crouching in the cabin, I stand on the floor, suddenly struck with terror that the floor itself will give out from under me. Steadying myself on the seat, I inspect the sunroof. Black rubber surrounds the edge, and I pick at it with my fingernail.

Maybe if I could get that off, I could somehow disconnect the mechanism from the body of the plane . . . like with something sharp, because my fingernail is not going to cut it.

11

Inspiration bubbling inside of me, I take my bag off of my back and take out my keys - this should work.

The keys make for lighter work than my fingernails would have, but once I get a good enough chunk off, I can take the rubber and peel it off from the perimeter of the sunroof.

I run my fingers through my hair and get it caught in the tangles around my back. Dissatisfied, I push it out of the way.

There's nothing useful for me under the rubber - it only covers the frayed fabric stapled to the metal crevice that holds the sunroof.

Since that didn't work, I have to break through it - something hard, something resilient.

Sighing, I take out my metal water bottle. The belt hook and porcelain charm of a cat jangle against the coated metal.

Blunt force works like shit - all I get is a dented water bottle and scratches in the paint job. But the sunroof remains resistant to any and all effort.

Sweating, I lay back down in my chair, stretching out. White-hot frustration makes my fingers tremble. Swallowing hard, the malleable tissue of my throat gets stuck together and I pat my dry tongue on the top of my mouth. Trembling with a new ferocity, I twist off the cap and throw the top to the side.

Gulping down the still cool water, I lick off the condensation. But then my eye catches on something - something broken, at the boy's unmoving feet. The painted cat charm, given to me by my brother, Nick, lays on the floor in shambles.

But I have no time to be sentimental - my hands fumble over the shards of ceramic, testing my finger on each one. When a particularly large and sharp one draws blood, I prepare to throw.

I lay on my back, in between the seats. I tuck my knees up to my chin. My head rests on my seat, my bottom and legs on Wyatt's seat, and my back on the plastic divider.

I suck in one last breath of air before closing my eyes and throwing the piece of ceramic straight up onto the sunroof.

For a brief second, all I hear is a plink and I fear that I have done nothing to the glass at all. But then a high-pitched, intense crash rings out and shattered glass rains down, tearing holes in my pants and opening gashes on my arms that now cover my face and head.

Elation and glee burst within me, but I refuse to move. Fragile tinkling noises continue around me as the glass settles. And the breath of fresh air that leaks into my nose tells me that I've broken through.

I ignore the pain and warm blood that seeps from various places of my body because I stare up at the brilliantly blue sky with delight.

"Woo hoo!" I shout, springing up and brushing the glass shards off of me. Standing up now, I use the edge of my bottle to break off the larger chunks that still remain on the outer rim of the sunroof. This works surprisingly well.

Taking a deep breath, I put one foot on the seat of my chair and the other on the seat of the unconscious boy's chair, being careful not to touch him.

Licking my textured lips, I pause, staring down at Wyatt's unconscious figure.

I should check and see if he's got a pulse, if he's still alive. My hands itch - I don't really want to touch him. If he's alive, he'll come around eventually.

Sighing, I poke my head up, unsure of what will meet my eyes.

Immediately, the wind blows my brownish-auburn hair into my face. Nearly gagging, I take the hair tie from my wrist and pull it back into a ponytail.

But this is one of those rare times when I wished my hair was still in my face, and I still couldn't see because what meets my eyes and the terror that follows is something I will never forget.

I am truly in the middle of nowhere.

~

The Sonoran Desert takes up a good portion of Arizona; the rest is the Colorado Plateau in the north, also known as the Grand Canyon. But I'd rather be there than here, because there, I wouldn't be stranded.

I swallow hard. The great scale of everything makes my insides collapse in on themselves. In the Grand Canyon, the land shifts and bleeds and moves. Here, it can be flat for dozens of miles. Stagnant and littered with rocks, pebbles, and boulders like pimples on a freckled kid's face.

The wind dances across the sand, and into my eyes. It varies from a copper to a deep rusty red to a rich tan. Hard packed and not moving much, the Sonoran varies from the deserts of Africa in its percentage of life, weather, and sand.

Tough brambles and bushes spring up, trying not to lose themselves in the chaos of the desert. Dull and hardy, the green plants here always seem to be weathered with time, no matter how young they are. Every twenty feet or so, a Saguaro cactus will jut up into the air, making its regal presence known as the king of the desert.

The diversity of cactuses is interesting, actually. I've read about all of the cactuses in the Sonoran and seen most, but seeing the sparse chorus of them popping up and down all over the horizon, trying not to be overtaken by the hard, sedimentary rock, a terrible encroaching feeling rises up within me. This is nothing like looking out my bedroom window and seeing the tame yet skittish wildlife and the nearly rolling hills of sand. This is the wilderness, and it is unforgiving and unrelenting and utterly wild, and it won't change its ancient ways for me.

Hot tears running down my face, I squint into the distance and see small peaks rising from the hard packed sand. The foothills of the Rocky Mountains.

My heart beats inside my chest with rising intensity, under my fingernails, in the hollows of my temples - I can feel it in there, buzzing and whirring around like it has no place to go.

Like me.

The immense and simple beauty of nature cannot be overwhelmed by my swelling anxiety. Flying in a plane over it is different than being dropped down into the wilderness, capsized by the uniformity of it, where I can't spot the Phoenix afterglow at night or even the resort in the distance.

Where I can't spot the resort. The phrase rings cold and true in my head, and I whip my head around, no matter how much my neck protests. My heartbeat permeates my ears and my breathing clips short without my consent.

I squint into the bright distance, looking behind me, hoping that my eyes will make out the Phoenix skyline or even a cluster of black dots that indicate buildings.

But there's nothing.

I breathe, my palms boiling against the white metal of the plane. The only thing the sun barely silhouettes is the Rocky Mountain range off to the west. West . . . yeah, that's west. I look toward the mountains and scan the sky, looking for the sun. I know I've met it when the blue fades and my eyes sting. It's about three-fourths high in the sky, meaning it will set by the mountains, right? Then that means east is directly opposite of that. But how can I know where Phoenix or even my house is? I don't know how far off track the plane flew, so there's no way to know. Hell, I don't even remember what route we took.

Heaving, I close my eyes and try to imagine the events leading up to the plane crash. But all I can remember is the emotion that bitterly lingers: fear. Intense, rapid fear. Then, the impact.

Then, nothing.

My eyes fly open, and as soon as they do, a painful breed of disorientation sweeps over me, where I lose myself entirely. A hard, succulent panic that flutters in my chest and blossoms like a poisonous black rose. Tears sting my eyes, but my skin is a shell, containing the nuclear amounts of emotions I have within me. Sinister thoughts download and run on a treadmill, burning energy and causing friction, but gaining nothing.

I'm lost. I'm alone. I'm hurt. And I'm going to die.

I halt my mulling thoughts because I have stopped breathing. Swallowing panic washes over me. Pressure builds around my lungs, collects around my chest. Suddenly, I'm terrified that the perimeter of the sunroof is shutting around my ribs like a vise because that's what it sure damn feels like.

A scream vibrates in my throat, and I push off the seats, springing myself upward. I lean forward, so my chest presses against the hot metal of the plane. Clawing at the metal with my almost non-existent fingernails, I frantically grasp for purchase. Unwilling to fall back into that god-forsaken plane, I kick at the air for momentum.

"Damn it," I hiss, still swinging like a pendulum, balancing half of my body on the plane and my legs jutting into the cabin.

Grunting, I push up with my arms. I pull up my leg onto the top of the plane, breaking open the fabric and skin as a shard of glass grazes my calf.

But I've made it. For a split second, like atoms slamming together, I grasp onto the boiling metal roof of the plane and tell myself that I'm going to be okay.

I tuck my leg up and plant my feet on the solidity of the roof of the plane, which now I realize is tilted at an awkward angle.

Adjusting my bag on my shoulders, I jump about seven feet or so to the ground. Reddish dust clouds around me, and I brush myself off before turning around to look at the plane.

Half of the nose of the plane is embedded into the soil, as is much of the underbelly, at about a thirty-degree angle. One of the propeller spokes is bent and pressed up against the nose of the plane, sticking out of the dirt. My eyes travel to my door. Now I realize why I couldn't open it - a huge boulder lays embedded in the mangled metal, pressing into the cabin, right where I was sitting. I swallow hard. Another few inches and I would have been crushed.

The plane also seems to be tilted to its side, with my side down. The wing next to me is still smoldering and split in half from being jammed into the ground.

Questions rise to the surface like boiling water: But how did we crash? Why did we crash like this?

I shut my eyes and open my mind's eye, but I am met with nothing of value. Fragments, flashes, sounds, and images all come back to me, but none of them make any sense.

But then, I hear a deafening hum - one that drills into my bones and vibrates in the hollow cavities of my skull. It comes distinctively from my left. Then - a scream.

After that, I'm looking out a window. The wing of the plane with its happy little propeller drifts by.

Then it explodes.

I flinch, dropping to my knees. I remember shouting something up to the pilot. For a moment, my mind draws a blank on who that could be. But then common sense kicks in and says: Come on, Terra. There are only two people who could be piloting that plane. My father or my grandfather are the only people who are pilots for our business. But grandfather retired to the California border seven years ago . . .

My eyes shoot open. "Dad."

And in that single moment, that split second of realization, I get it. I connect the dots. It all comes flooding back like a hurricane carrying me away. Nothing physical is stopping me from breathing, but I can't release my constricted throat to breathe in, for fear a horrible, painful sound will tear into space.

I slowly turn around to face the plane. Terrible images fill my head, knowing vaguely what's coming, and my mind races, filling in the blanks. I don't know how I didn't notice it before, but I know that I will never be able to forget the next few minutes of my minuscule life.

~

I see the pilot's side door, smushed into the ground like the wet stain of a bug under a shoe, buried in the sand.

And I see the shattered side window, cracked beyond repair.

And as I move closer and closer to the smoldering plane and its wretched remains, the more and more that I see.

And the more I wish I could unsee.

With each breath, each heartbeat, I recount the way that every Friday, we would ride our bikes into Phoenix just to get large chocolate brownie shakes and then, end up complaining about our stomach aches as we rode back.

With cold hands, I grab the latch and pull.

But as the door flies open, a gummy, wooden arm flops down, it's purple fingernails grazing the sand.

And with it, I am thrust back onto the hard-packed earth. Rocks poke into the soft flesh of my back. My eyes open to the bright sky, pain blossoming in my chest.

But I stand, regardless.

The first thing my eyes meet is a dull, silvery glint. Less than a millisecond passes before I know it in my soul: these are my father's cold, dead eyes.

Heavy with lead but buzzing with electricity, my chest pulls apart and slams back together, heaving. Without my consciousness having any say in the matter, a shrill scream erupts from deep within me and expels out of my throat, like a volcano made entirely out of sound waves.

Even in the midst of horror, a release of terror comes spilling out, like throwing water on a fire and the sizzling that follows. And when my knees give out and I fall back onto the ground, I can breathe again.

Groveling and pushing up on my knobby elbows, I flip my head up. My father's eyes still shine with that bluey-silver that they always had, but now they have deteriorated to slushy gray, and I cling to the pleasant memory of those vital eyes, for their life is being sucked out before my eyes. They turn a bit downcast, just grazing at my feet.

It takes me a moment to absorb the scene fully. I keep myself propped up, my hands pressing into the rocky sand, my body undulating with heaving breaths, in a crab-like position, ready to skitter away if anything moves that shouldn't. Since the plane crashed on our side, nose down, the engine was pushed back into the cabin of the plane when it crashed, crushing my father's legs. Other than the zentangle of cuts and scrapes that tear into my father's waxy skin and boiling burns from the fire, he should have been fine.

He should have been fine.

He should have been fine, but he's not. My father, half of myself, is crushed between his own seat and his own vehicle, the yoke pressing into the supple and unmoving flesh of his stomach.

And here I am, living and breathing and crying and living.

Why?

~

I wonder if he died instantly. I wonder how long my father had to suffer as he slowly bled out, turning the vibrant hues of the sand the color of death, trapped under his own airplane. How did he feel in those last, fleeting moments before death? Was he angry, feeling unjustified as he knew this was how he was going to go? Was he at peace, knowing that the powers in the sky were greeting him with open arms? Was he ashamed, felt that all of this was his fault?

I find myself standing, slowly walking over to the airplane, the pilot's door still wide open, my father's hand still in the swollen, clutched position that fell off of the door handle. Tears have suddenly been sucked from my eyes, and a pinprick of fear whistles inside of me, but I keep walking, this disconnect keeping me breathing.

As I approach the plane and my father's body, squished like a bug under the footsteps of life, I find myself at a shameful loss of words. Everything I've ever wanted to say to my father, my dad, every 'I'm sorry,' every 'I love you' burns on the tip of my tongue, but no matter how hard I try and push the air from my swollen vocal chords, nothing comes out. A pressure squeezes inside of my chest, growing from the inside out, but I have no external emotional reaction as I crouch by my father.

I feel the panic swirling inside of me because I want to feel; I desire the pain and the suffering to come and then to leave. The heaviness of survival mode hasn't set in yet, but it seems that while I have closed my eyes, my humanity has seemingly already been taken away from me.

That's when I get it. That's when the light bulb shatters in a crack of electrons. My subconscious is forcefully shutting down my emotions so the 'left side' of my brain can function, can let me live on.

Even when I don't want to.

As I begin to step back, I realize that I'm not sure which side I want to believe. It might be less painful and conflicting if I was being ripped apart limb from limb, medieval-style.

I find my hand drawing back from my father's face. His facial expression strikes me with unsettling confusion. My father's death tears away at the dust cloths of my soul, arousing something ages forgotten. Sometimes, people are found, no matter their circumstance, having a peaceful look on their face. Satisfaction, almost. Everyone accounts this to the saying of 'They're in a better place,' but I have always despised that. How do you know that they're in a better place? Bullshit, there is no way to know.

But what truly disturbs me is the expression plastered onto my father's face. It's not calm or peaceful, stripped of any human pride. It looks defeated, conquered, overcome, and even while deceased, in pain. How can someone who's been dead for an indefinite amount of time have the slightest hint of pain scarring his face?

Every time I blink, I see my father's gray eyes gleaming of silver, branded into the back of my mind. They fade in brilliance each second they stare at the ground. So, without words, I reach forward with a trembling hand and press two of my fingers up against my father's eyelids, shivering at the coolness of his skin in this sweltering environment.

And the moment that they close is the second a loud bang comes from inside of the plane, then a crash explodes from the opposite side.

Fear jerks through me, sending the blood in my veins to solid concrete for a full second. Something clatters to the ground, and I send cracks through my back as I duck down to see.

The side door.

Everything inside me screams DANGER, and another, terror-filled scream erupts from me against before I can clap a hand over my mouth.

Scampering back silently, I regret it with every cell of my being, my hot and shaky breath passing between my fingers. Relief drowns me because I can hear the echo of my terror shooting out into the vast desert. I keep my breathing steady until I can no longer feel my heartbeat against my fingernails.

Something moves slowly behind the plane - I can see only a flash of it as it bends down to pick up something. Even though I can no longer feel my heartbeat in the tips of my fingers, it still thuds in my ears and pumps through painfully constricted blood vessels in my head. Someone might as well be pounding on my sternum with a drumstick.

I slowly back away, making sure not to crunch the gravel and sand beneath my boots - until I trip backward over another damn rock and fall back onto my ass again. No matter how hard I bite my lip, a pained squeak still escapes.

My mind has no time to worry or ponder about what is around the body of the plane because the tall, lanky figure treks around the smoldering nose of the plane and rests his hand on the metal. It clanks with a hollow wince.

Wyatt. He's . . . alive.

I feel my jaw go slack, but it is now that I can fully take in the wholeness of this strange boy. Athletically built, but looks the opposite of a jock. Gangly, almost. His clothes hang limply over his still maturing teenage frame. A crisp, yet slightly ill-fitting, henley shirt, with the stripes in navy blue, canary yellow, and white adorns his top.

Under first impression, the formality surprises me and not at all something that a boy of his demeanor would wear, but when my eyes travel down to see the loose-fitting, light-wash jeans with shreds and holes and Converse sneakers, the picture looks more complete. With that light dusting of freckles and pimples on his face, he could pass as your average teenage boy.

But getting lost in his appearance also makes something else stand out: his eyes. They are a light brown, almost amber. And they're afraid. I wouldn't need to see the frozen, deer-in-the-headlights look on his face to know that something deep within him has been disturbed. Just like me.

And suddenly, seeing the blood still pouring from the goose egg bump on his head, and seeing the way he grips the plane, leaning away from my own terrified body like I have three heads, suddenly, this strange boy is no longer all that strange. His fear is no different than mine. His memory: just as muddled. I can identify with the small, fluttery minnow of uncertainty that poisons his gut. I can see it splashed all over his face - all over his dusty, bloody face - because he knows it. I know it.

An unspoken pact - however weak and hostile it may be - is made in this moment, when we recognize our dire similarity. Whether we like it or not, we're in this together, because nature doesn't give a shit. Life doesn't give a shit.

Me and this strange, awkward boy have to . . . have to . . . Survive? Walk until we drop dead, what? I guess that doesn't matter. We both realize - and I can see it on his face that he knows this - that we have no choice but to bear this cross.

After Wyatt breaks his gaze with me, he slowly walks over to my crumpled figure, still propped up on the hot ground after my fall. With a nearly expressionless face, he extends a hand. His eyes are soft, like the color of vanilla extract. Or brown sugar.

Dumbfounded for a second, I reach up, grunting, and shake his hand awkwardly. He just peers at me, and, with a strong grip, he pulls me up.

~

My name is Terra Lombardi, and I am a shooting star falling from the heavens.

<u>December 18, 2007 - Terra</u>

I'm not really sure about what approach I should take about telling this story, so I suppose I'll just start off simple. As terribly simple as I can.

~

I was nine. I wasn't yet old enough to work the desk/secretary job that I currently hold, but I still helped out around the lodge as much as I could. It was also pretty late at night, maybe nine or ten p.m., and the hallway lights had been turned low for the sleeping patrons. Nothing seemed unusually eerie about all of the locked doors and humming silence. I did this almost every night, and everyone was in their rooms by this hour.

But apparently, not everyone.

I was coming back from delivering fresh sheets to each unoccupied room. I remember I had just dropped off sheets to room 117 and was heading back for another basketful from Mom in the basement laundry room. Everything seemed normal; it always does right before these kinds of things happen. The vending machines buzzed and glowed colorfully at the end of the hall, right next to the exit sign going down to the basement. The basket I held was full of used sheets, and I carried it in my little nine-year-old arms.

I walked down the hall and turned right, down to the basement. I slid my all-access card through the slot with one hand and pushed the door open. The steps were concrete and usually cold, although the air down in the basement was very temperate. The laundry room was just to the left when I came down the stairs, and the fluorescent lights cast unflattering shadows on my mother's face.

"This is the last round. I'll be up after I turn off all of the lights," my mother said, placing a stack of crisp white sheets into the basket.

My mother's voice always reminded me of a mug of hot, herbal tea: deep, warm, and sweet, with a kick of natural power. Her lips curled up in a smile at me as I 'oomph'ed when she put the towels in the basket. Her eyes always melted when she smiled, and they were soft, a light brown, nearly hazel. And they were the color of vanilla extract, or brown sugar.

~

I lugged the last batch of towels up the stairs and the door shut behind me with a loud clack. The vending machines still rattled, trying to keep their contents cool, but I looked up at another noise, far down the hall.

A man was standing there. He looked about forty and had a slight potbelly, but was muscular in a way that some old guys are. Beefy, almost. He was pulling out a diet Coke out of the glowing vending machine. Peculiar, but nothing out of the ordinary. Yet still, something fluttered inside of little nine-year-old me. But also that innate sense inside of me that knew something was wrong, knew something was happening outside of my five senses.

~

He raped me. I didn't know that's what he was doing at the time, but that's what he did. He charmed me, even offered me the Coke he just bought, but I knew better. I knew something was wrong, but I was only four foot three and sixty pounds, and unable to fight against a five foot eleven, two hundred pound man. The only way to fight was with my voice, but after a short while, even that was silenced by a gag around my mouth. He kept me tied in his room overnight, which is unparalleled as the worst night of my life.

When he was sleeping, I snuck out and immediately told my parents, bare and beaten and trembling, even though he made me promise that it would be "our secret". What else could I have done? I didn't know what to do. I had to explain it quite thoroughly to them, since I didn't really know the word for it. So, yeah.

My parents called the police, but the man had escaped our hotel, leaving behind most of his stuff. When the police asked for the name and records given to them when he set up his reservation, they discovered he had given them false information. And paid with cash. My description of him matched a registered sex offender with pedophile charges hanging over his head, so the officials recognized his faulty information almost immediately. The police did their job, and the chase was on. For a few years, my rapist, and apparently 7 other children's rapists, popped up here and there all over the US, and even escaping into Mexico a few times.

~

By that point, it was almost the morning. The sun hadn't yet hauled itself over the ledge of night.

But while my parents were busy setting up STD testing appointments and quieting the public outcry, they shoved me back into the house.

I remember showering. The water cold, scaling up and down my body like his calloused hands. I remember showering with my clothes on. I remember not knowing why I needed to shower.

I remember being alone.

~

I felt worthless. Cut open and filleted from the most sacred part of me. I felt like an object, used and thrown away when the job was done. Like being taken advantage of was somehow my fault. I felt incomplete. Like him violating me stole a deep, special part of me that could never be replaced.

I felt like shit.

And, at times, I still do.

To this day, I feel incomplete. Broken. A wine stain on the white sheets that I had taken down to my mother. I never could pull myself out of the hole I had been thrown in.

And I could only just dig myself deeper.

~

I don't do the laundry anymore.

CHAPTER TWO: The Coalition of Juxtaposing Forces
Day 1 - Wyatt; August 5th, 2015

My eyes jar open. Flinching with a throbbing pain, I am blinded by white sunlight on hot metal.

Heat. The world askew, I push up on anything I can get my hands on. My viewpoint shifts, revealing more and more of the monotonous desert. Dizziness like cool mist floods my head.

Pushing air in and out, the belly of a metal beast creaks around me.

Trapped. The word bounces around in my chest. By the stale air, I can tell that I'm contained here.

Reaching forward, I feel the scorching leather, the pinch of shattered glass. A cloud of blinding pain congeals around my head.

Lilly. Her name floats up through my consciousness. I cling to it as I come to. Grasping onto the seat in front of me, I feel the thick keratin of hair rubbing beneath my fingers.

I pull back, electric. My pale fingers ebb and flow in my vision. Fuck, my head hurts so bad.

The sun beats down through the busted open sunroof. I reach up, steadying myself - everything trembles. But the edge splits open my palm.

Fuming, I wipe the blood on my pants.

How the hell do I get out of here?

The door. No shit, Sherlock.

I turn around, exacerbated by an unforgiving pulse of my head injury, and grab the handle. Locked, or jammed. Or both.

I sweep the glass off of the divider between the seat next to me, from the sunroof. While I'm at it, I think, why the hell is *that* glass broken?

I turn and kick at the door. Power, and then pain, vibrates through my legs, screaming into my head. The metal groans, and I nearly smile with joy. Aw, hell yeah. I'm getting out of this shithole.

With one final blow, the door blasts off, barely hanging on to its hinges, and crashes to the desert floor.

Just as a human scream shatters the silence.

Blackness punching holes in my vision, I push myself up. Lower myself onto the ground.

Walk around the nose of the plane, sniveling and smashed into the copper sand.

Lay my hand down with a hollow thunk. It burns.

And see the girl there, bloody and dirty and very much alive, staring up at me.

I slowly walk forward and take her hand. She bizarrely shakes it, and I fume and pull her up.

And the world slips away, like the blasted sand beneath my feet.

~

I open my eyes. Not exactly the stuff of daydreams.

And her eyes bore down at me. I flinch, thrashing and kicking at the sand beneath me. Confusion like high tide drowns me. Her small, silver necklace dangles in front of my eyes, maddeningly out of focus.

Grunting I push myself up. The girl's hands hover around me, one barely touching my face.

"What happened?" My voice comes out like tires on gravel.

"Our plane crashed," she says. Eyes wide, torn open in horror. I don't say anything, so she continues. "You came around the front of the plane, and, you stared at me for a minute, helped me up, and then you passed out."

Dragging my fingers on the hot metal, I stand. "Great." She immediately pulls away, countering my movements as we stand.

Anxiety boils in my chest. I lean back and breathe, the movements of my chest the only sign of life on this barren stretch. "Where are we?"

The girl licks her lips, pulls her cardigan closer around her. Refuses to meet my eyes for long. "Arizona."

I resist the urge to glare at her. "Where in Arizona?"

She turns away from me and says with a new texture to her voice. "I - I don't know."

I swallow, my neck contorting in pain. I hope a good gust of wind doesn't come. It might just knock her over. But peering around her curvaceous body I see, I see why. A man - the pilot - lays prostrate, torn apart, flesh like tissue paper on Christmas.

I rip my eyes away. A golf ball forms in my throat. For moments that drag to an eternity, I grasp the hull of the plane, my fingers digging into the malleable metal. My breaths echo off of every bare surface. Loneliness like pounding waves drowns me.

Someone's dead. And we don't know where we are.

I push myself up. I walk out into the sand. The girl watches me, her arms crossed over her chest, trembling as if it's freezing out here, which, of course, it's not. My mind races to dark places. Peering into the abysmal distance, a shout tears from my chest. "Hey!"

We're alone.

My voice bursts forth into the dry air, hitting our ears then disappearing into the vast expanse of desert. I hear it echo. A bitterness, of cold and ravishing loneliness, hits me like a smack to the chest.

The wind carries my voice into the great unknown. "Hey! Is anyone out there?" I stumble forward like a zombie. Someone. There's gotta be someone nearby.

I turn. To the left, to the right, sending my voice out like fireworks into a vacuum, pain shooting through me. Screaming. The desert swirls around me, the blues and the oranges and the greens and the browns blurring together in a perverse painting.

Lost. The word comes to me. Hits me. Smacks me in the face, grinds me into the ground. This can't be fucking happening.

The world settles around me. I am the epicenter of an earthquake that reaches to the ends of the earth, what little of it there is.

"How do you not know where we are?" I ask, rushing over.

"I . . . I just don't!" she says, peeling back. "We . . . we were flying a routine course, and I guess we got off-"

"C'mon! There's got to be something!" Vibrating with frustration, I look up into the endless flat sky. "Help! We're lost! Hey! Someone?!"

"Stop it!" the girl's voice suddenly explodes behind me. She breathes hard, wiping the grime from her forehead. "There's no one. Not yet."

Fuming, I turn to her. Words dance on my lips, awful ones. But inertia swallows, consumes me. Heaving, I stumble to the plane, and turn around, pressing my back up against the plane, the only thing remotely familiar, buried in the dirt, and rest.

~

The girl goes back into the plane to look for supplies. Why she would do that, when there's the stench of death hanging around, I'll never know. My head throbs, screams at me with pain. It pushes me down, compressing my spine into the dirt.

"Water." She hands me a can, a triangular hole in the top so I can drink.

"Thanks." I suck it down in nearly one gulp. She sits across from me, legs crossed, favoring one over the other. Gasping for breath with a dripping chin, I ask: "What's your name?"

"Terra," she says, playing with a silver charm around her neck.

"Wyatt." I scoff. "Sorry we had to meet under such unfortunate circumstances." I shake her hand, thinking back to the seconds before I passed out.

"Yeah." Unsure. I guess she doesn't find me funny.

"What do we do now?" It takes what little energy I have left to keep my voice level. I want to scream again, to hear my voice conquering the world

She squints up at me, through wavy brown hair and wispy bangs. "We wait for rescue to come."

"Right."

Eternities pass. I nearly fall asleep against the smoking plane. It was just so hot and my head hurt so bad . . .

But I can feel myself losing it. My mind tumbling down, down, down. Back into that ferocious rabbit hole.

So I take out my wallet. Something to ground me.

Check the money pocket - maybe twenty bucks. The coins jangle around aimlessly, and I slide out my cards - a few unused gift cards, my school ID, my driver's license. Not much else.

I turn it to the side and an accordion of photos flick out, but none of them are recent or provide new information. But then my eye catches on her face and I remember. For some reason, this moment is imprinted into my memory like the flash of film - taking a selfie with my little sister, Lilly.

Why this stands out, I don't know, but all I do know is that I've got to find my phone. Slipping my drawstring bag off, I pour the contents into the sand. My phone drops out, and I scramble through the items to get it. I brush off the little red rocks and press the home button - 87%, but no service. It's not surprising - I barely had cell service at that lodge place anyway.

At that lodge place.

My fingers trembling, I go to my photo album and scroll through the dated entries - August 3rd - two days before today. Scrolling through, my eyes scan rapidly, trying to find something of value. My eyes catch on Lilly's face and see the photo we took on August 5th - today, as evidenced by the home screen. I click on the photo and, like looking into a mirror, I see myself looking just as I do today - complete with the yellow and blue striped shirt. The grounded plane surrounds us, still in the hanger, as evidenced by the window. I push back against the darkness to find the memories surrounding this photo, but come up with nothing but the fact that 'hey, we were in an airplane and took a selfie'.

But Lilly wasn't on the plane, was she?

My question answers itself, for once: No, because Terra's here, and Lilly's body is nowhere to be found. Then why didn't Lilly come?

Turning on my heel, I walk back toward the plane, trying to think of the last thing that I remember - someone driving, my harmonica music drifting through closed quarters.

My blood boiling, I get into my side of the plane, with Terra still rummaging around back there, and shut my eyes. The magnified heat from the plane bakes my body from the inside out.

And then something comes over me. Like a trance, like I know what I'm doing. I flick upwards on my phone to the camera, see my reflection and smile, my lips cracking. Click.

Then, time grabs me by the shirt collars and drags me back. It comes in flashes: the jolting turbulence. My mother turning around, her silver necklace shining in the high sun. Saying something to me.

Sounds come back, but in incoherent fragments. Voices like static wafts up through my memory - deep and textured.

Static. But what if that voice really was static?

Pulling my eyes open, I shoot forward into the open space between the front seats. I bump into Terra, who doesn't acknowledge me. God, it smells bad in here.

Fumbling with the dormant controls, I search for a spiral phone cord and a mic. And hanging down, there it is. Frantically, I pull the device out and back, pressing button after button, but hearing nothing but irrevocable silence.

Terra comes up next to me - I can feel her presence on the back of my neck. "Oh my God, is that a radio?"

I swallow the seeming lump in my throat. "I guess so."

Terra reaches for it, and our hands fumble together awkwardly before I just drop the microphone and she catches it.

"I know how to work this," she says, immediately enraptured by her work.

"Do you, now?" I ask, not really caring, just wanting to fill the empty space I feel seeping into my gut.

"Yes," she insists, leaning forward and flicking a switch on the control panel of the plane. Nothing.

Chills creep up and down my arms like icy spiders, and suddenly, I feel a rush of terror boiling at the back of my throat.

Electric emotion flowing through me, I scramble out of the plane and land on all fours on the hard, unrelenting dirt.

I get maybe five grueling steps before I vomit, hot and revolting like this entire fucking desert. My head rocks inside of my skull like a fishing bobber as it all comes out. I drop to my knees, feeling like a gutted fish. Concentrated sobs shoot their way out of me as I stumble away, far away from all of this.

Planting my feet to find some stability, I reach up and run my fingers through my hair, spreading more, wet blood from my head into my scalp.

I couldn't stand being in there, in that malevolent cabin of the god-forsaken plane. It reeked of death, and I couldn't fucking stand it. Something funky is in there.

Catching my breath, I turn to see Terra kneeling in the doorway of the plane.

Swallowing hard, I walk back over. "Sorry. It's just, uh, my head, you know."

She looks at me, her piercing eyes unreadable. "Yeah."

I stumble over, back to the plane. "Continue with the radio," I say, leaning on the frame of my door.

Terra continues flipping switches and pressing buttons, and even hitting the dashboard one too many times before she gets out a spare battery and hooks it up to a few plugs. A red light blinks on. She flips the same switch she has been for the past ten minutes, and finally, static comes out over the small, circular speaker on the control panel, but the sound chokes the cabin.

"Ha ha!" I punch the metal in glee. Nausea ripples through me.

"Not yet. Static is better than silence, but it doesn't mean we have a signal."

I scrunch my face up, holding in a strike of emotion. "Just try."

"I am," Terra hisses. Normally emotionless and distant, she releases it all in a pulse for a second.

Sighing, she turns dials, and the static wavers, but she gets nothing. Nothing. Monotonous and abysmal static that fills every corner of the desert.

Suddenly, Terra slams the microphone down and pushes past me and hops out. The microphone hangs off of its silly cord, flapping against the plastic median. I pick it up, soaking in the static as it flies out into the desert. I hold the meshed wire close to my lips and press the button.

"Hello?" I say, hoping that someone's listening.

Of course, no one is. I slam it down, swearing. Leaning against the seats, I push my own way out, but Terra holds up her hand, nearly pushing me back. Stuck in the cabin of the plane, I crane my neck out to see what she's looking at. But I am blinded by her and the cabin.

"Wyatt," Terra says. I don't think she's looking at the desert anymore. Her eyes widen, flooding with terror.

"What?!" I shout again.

"Shush!" she hisses, dragging her feet as she moves backward. I climb out behind her, to face her.

She bends down slowly, but surely, and grabs a black handle sticking out of a pile of supplies. As she takes it out, the sun catches on a battered, machete-like blade. "Wyatt," she whispers. What the hell is going on? "Catch."

She then does the unthinkable. She tosses me the knife. It floats in mid-air for a second before I wrap my hands around it. "What?!" I exclaim.

Without breaking her gaze, Terra nearly shouts "shush!" She bends down and scoops up the survival supplies in her arms.

And runs for her life.

Suddenly, a throaty growl crescendos next to me, making the hairs on the back of my neck stand to attention like soldiers. And around the cabin of the plane comes a gangly coyote, teeth bared and saliva dripping.

Digging its claws into the sand, the overgrown mutt jerks forward. Its skinny, warm body slams into me, pushing me back onto the seats. Thankfully, the knife hasn't moved since Terra gave it to me, so it lays directly in front of me, and the coyote dives straight into it.

Panic wraps its bony knuckles around my heart as I struggle to push the animal off me. When I do, there is a muted sssshrrk as the blood-coated blade comes out of the dead coyote. I gape in horror. My lungs become heavy with liquid fear as the bloodied coyote and its enraged mates circle closer into the small doorway that remains my only escape.

But I can't shut down. I can't.

Cut off one head, two more will take its place. Two coyotes block the entrance, hissing and barking and rearing.

The sunroof.

Laughing spitefully, I plant my feet and jump up. The sudden motion triggers the mangy dogs. I grasp at the metal roof, shards of glass poking into my belly.

One of the coyotes rakes its claws down my calf. Pain runs up my leg like flames. I kick blindly at the animal, red-hot fear crawling inside of me.

Flinging my legs for purchase, I pull myself up, trembling. Still hearing the coyotes snuffling and barking, I scamper down the roof, onto the nose of the plane, and tumble into the hard earth. Pulsating, I drag myself up and run. Run to where Terra is, headed toward a tree.

Sprinting after Terra, I hear the pack of coyotes snort and growl as they claw at the metal of the plane. My legs pump at a lightening pace while I try to ignore the thumping pain coming from four, long claw marks down my leg.

Slamming to a stop, my knees give. I crumple to the ground, overcome with pain and unadulterated anxiety. I look towards the plane to find that the coyotes were not chasing us, but are more interested in something inside the plane.

They scuttle around the plane for a while, sticking their snouts in, yelping when they step on broken glass. A few rake their claws down the metal, creating ear-rattling noises. But mostly, they just sniff around, howling and barking sometimes.

One of the coyotes, who looks like the default leader, gets up on his hind legs and crawls into shotgun. He gets up on his hind legs and seems to wrestle with something in the cockpit. Then the coyote pulls something stiff and red out of the front seat. I try and think back who was in that seat, but I can't pull anything up from my stream of consciousness. Besides, it makes my head hurt, too.

The coyote seems to be chewing on the thing, that now lays at a 45 degree angle out of the plane. The other coyotes take an interest to this odd appendage, and I squint against the blazing sun, trying to distinguish the figure.

I hear Terra take a sharp inhale of breath that comes out as a scream, so sudden it must be painful. Realization flashes across her face. I look back to the plane, and another group of coyotes circle around the front of the plane and begin exploring the pilot's side, just like they did with shotgun.

Terra starts to move forward, keeping her eyes locked on the plane. I slowly get up, ready to catch her if she runs. The words "My father," escape from her mouth, just barely reaching my ears. She whips around to face me, her face panic-stricken. "The coyotes . . . they're . . . they've got my father."

Suddenly, she takes off running. I stand up, grunting, and chase after her. It takes a while, but I eventually catch up with her and grab her by the arms. She immediately jerks away, but I grab her again and force her to look at me. Tears pour down her cheeks, but her face screams of anger.

"Let go of me! Do you know what they're doing to him?" She continues to struggle violently, sobs racking her body.

I feel the churning in my gut, but I don't believe it. I stare right in her eyes, as if staring into deep vats that contain her soul. "Stop it! You can't go over there!"

"Let me go, you son of a bitch!" she shrieks, thrashing like a fish out of water.

That's when it hits me. I remember who was in the front seat, and every ounce of humanity, energy, life I had saps out of me: Mom. And the pilot, her dad. And the coyotes, drawn to the festering flesh, have come to feast on an early dinner.

I thrust Terra away from me. "Go, get yourself killed! It's not like I care!" Suddenly weak-kneed, I fall to the ground once more. I have the overwhelming urge to rush over and take the machete to each and every one of the coyotes. And then turn the blade on myself.

But I don't. I just watch the coyotes devour my mother like the coward that I am.

Terra pauses, coming back over to the tree. Falling back at the horror and the sheer lack of control I have, I stumble back over to the base of the old tree and collapse, each sob marching to the beat of my pounding head.

~

My eyes swell. Slowly but surely, the heat of the day simmers off into the cool of the night. The darkness is all-encompassing, and as the sun flickers out of sight, the terrible place in the hollow of my stomach clenches. Oh, hell. I really don't want to sleep here. It gives me that strange feeling in my bones.

The only light comes from the clear night sky, with the stark moon and the chorus of stars. They cast hollow and harsh shadows across the desert, but the darkness is still ever-present. I press my back up against the tree, feeling for tactile safety. Exhaustion pulls at my eyelids, but the silent terror of the night keeps my goose-fleshed skin alert.

When the gnawing in my stomach refuses to let my mind shut off, I feel pressure against my leg. I pull out my wallet - the nice leather one that my mom spent fifty dollars on when I was twelve. It's comfortably worn but built like an ox. It carries a sense of belonging and home with it, and I breathe in the lonely scent as I flip open the wallet. I open the clear vinyl, accordion-type photo holder. I swallow hard when my eye catches on Lilly's school picture, tightly nestled into a slot right next to another photo of me and Lilly at Swirly's Ice Cream Parlor, with two straws sticking out of my nose and chocolate ice cream all over Lilly's mouth like a mustache.

Next to those are scribbled Bible verses on scraps of paper. I tear the pieces of paper out of my wallet and stuff them deep within my pocket. Why do I still have those in there? The empty words are useless to me now.

However, I carefully pull out the picture of Lilly and I at the ice cream place, holding it only by the corners, as if it is an ancient document and it could dissolve with the wind. It probably could, since that moment might as well be universes away right now. I stare into the picture - into my wild eyes and into Lilly's cheeky grin - and try to remember that moment. What I saw. Heard. Smelled. Touched. Felt.

And I feel it. Somewhere, deep within the chaos that has been rumbling around me, I can hear the cars whizzing by, feel the cold ice cream melting out of the cone and down onto my fingers, see Lilly's teeth nearly shine against the chocolate covering her face.

"Who's that?"

Terra's lonely voice jerks me out of my reverie. She is tying her hair back with a hair tie and opens a first-aid kit.

I swallow hard. The aura left from my daydream leaves a warm feeling inside me. "My younger sister, Lilly," I pause, but I can still feel Terra hanging on to every word. I know that's not enough, so I start back up again, laughing spitefully, almost out of the irony of it all. "The only thing worth fighting for in my shitty life."

Terra licks her lips, possibly chewing on my heavy words. She eventually sits back, turning to her side of the tree, biting on her lower lip again.

The silver chain on her neck, glinting in the sun suddenly rises up to the front of my mind again. I glance up at the stars again for a second, gathering my thoughts into a knot.

This time, it's me who turns around, to find Terra sopping up her own blood. With her eyes closed in pain, she pulls her head back, upwards to the sky. The pale starlight casts a faint glow on her sunburnt cheeks.

"Hey. What's on your necklace?" That sounded a lot cooler in my head.

Terra opens her eyes and looks up. She puts her hand down on the sand to support herself as she reaches under her collar and takes out a necklace with a silver charm. I still can't see it well though, until she holds the charm in her palm and I see that it's a silver cross with some engraving I can't read, with a small silver ribbon-like metal decoration twisting around it. In the balance hangs a single ruby that reflects the thin moonlight.

As I reach out to touch the metal, she pulls back, clamping her hand around the bone-chillingly cold metal. Not only is Terra's necklace and the metal on my wallet already cold, I feel a chill run down my spine and remember how freezing it gets on these open desert nights.

"What does it say?" I ask, hoping my husky voice doesn't get swept away with the runaway wind.

Terra looks at the ground, squeezing her fist together. "It says 'More Precious Than Rubies'. My, uh, grandma gave it to me."

Now the words engraved on the post of the cross come into focus. That explains the ruby.

"That's nice. Looks . . . expensive."

"Yeah, thanks." Terra tucks the necklace back into her shirt. I wish she'd leave it out so I could see it. But she hesitates and looks like she's going to say more. The moonlight has turned her normally auburn hair into a ruddy red. "She gave it to me just before she died. That's really the only reason I wear it. Sentimental reasons, you know?"

I squint, some dust blowing into my eyes, but I don't look away. Because there it is. I see it. A flash of something. A flash of a raw person beneath . . . boundaries and walls and shyness. But the second I see it, it's gone, and Terra's paper-thin walls have gone back up, holding me at arm's length again, telling me loud and clear that she's not interested at all. But, I swear it. It's there. I saw it.

But in the moment that I was lost in the mystery of this strange girl, she has turned back over to her side of the tree, and says sadly, "Nevermind. I've said too much. Goodnight, Wyatt. Sleep well." She sets the first aid kit by my knees.

And she leaves me hanging. Her back is facing me now, and the only sound is the slight rustling of her settling in on her backpack.

"I'll try."

I sigh and settle back into my own lonely spot on the adjacent side of the tree. The wind cuts right through my jacket draped around my bare arms. I probably should bandage my gashes, but oh well.

I listen to the cacophony of owl hoots, coyote howls, bugs creaking, and animals scuffling, trying to quell the buzzing fear. But I don't think I ever really fall asleep.

~

My name is Wyatt Hartman, and I am a meteor crashing from the skies.

July 14, 2008 - Wyatt

The day was cool, or, at least, cool for a mid-July day. The sun was bright, piercing through the one all-glass wall in our apartment. The hum of the Los Angeles traffic seemed to buzz right below my bare feet, even though it was ten stories down. When you live in LA, it's kind of something you get used to.

I turned my eyes away from the window and onto the hardwood floor, where Lilly continued to play with her Barbies. She loved those things. I'm not so sure why; they all look the same, with blonde hair extensions and two-inch waists and massive breasts. But I played Ken with her anyways. She always loved it when I did that. Maybe because, most of the time, she had no one else to play with. Her little face always lit up when I grudgingly agreed to play with her for the umpteenth time. I was always Ken (or some variation of the male specimen of Barbie), who goes out and rides my old monster trucks and fixes the hand-crank elevator. Barbie, complete with a funky haircut administered by Lilly herself, always came out and gave Ken a cup of coffee and a big smack on the lips, no matter how many times I insisted that we were brother and sister. But then she always looked up at me and pouted: "But *Ken and Barbie* aren't brother and sister!" And I would always roll my eyes and give Barbie a plastic kiss as well.

But that time, Lilly didn't ask me to play with her. She just sat there, Barbie and Ken limp in her hands. I remember going over to her and asking: "Aren't you going to ask if I will play Ken?"

She shook her head, her thin blonde hair drooping in her face. She pouted her rosebud lips and said: "No. Barbie and Ken are mad at each other right now. Really mad."

I sighed, knowing exactly what this was about. I kneeled down on the thin rug that Lilly always used for her Barbies and looked her straight in the eye. She shied away from my firm gaze.

"And why are they mad at each other?" I said with the most gentle voice I could muster.

"Because Barbie thinks Ken is drinking too much coffee," Lilly said, still as fuming mad as a six-year-old girl could be. But then her expression softened, and she leaned in to whisper in my ear. "She says he's 'addicted' to it." She didn't need to use her fingers to insert quotations. Her voice did that just as well.

But after I got past Lilly's impressive social skills, it hit me. I'm going to refrain from saying "like a ton of bricks" even though that's how it felt. But I understood it. Mom was Barbie, Dad was Ken. Interchange coffee with alcohol, and you're set. Lilly understood far beyond her years the effect this had on our family.

There was a part of me that wished she didn't understand, but another, darker part of me thought this whole experience might keep her away from the evil in this world. Because I know that I'm never even going *near* a place that might contain drugs, alcohol, anything. I don't think I could bring myself that low to do so. But my six-year-old sister could comprehend and fathom more than we ever imagined.

Lilly slumped her Barbies to the floor, and the second her little brown eyes fell, my father stormed in the door, bringing a crop of darkness with him. I put my hand over Lilly's nose when the rancid smell of him hit my nose, of unwashed hair and motor oil and liquor.

Not a second later, my father noticed me and his first reaction was to rip at me with his eyes, thrusting his bag on the floor. I wish I had enough sense to cover Lilly's eyes, but, instead I took both hands and flipped my own father off, anger immediately jolting through me. But he didn't give me the time of day - he was gone before it probably registered in his head what I had done. My parent's bedroom door slammed behind him before I could blink.

I put my hands over my face, the sudden burst of adrenaline seeping out of me. The hardwood floor felt cold beneath my bare feet. Lilly looked back at me, her brown eyes remained dry, but terror and pain was splashed all across her little face. Sometimes, she didn't need tears to be sad.

I scooted back against the glass wall, releasing a tense puff of air as the back of my head hit the cold glass. Lilly dropped her dolls at her sides and threw her body into mine. She curled up in my lap, my legs criss-crossed around her, pressing her head against my chest. I wrapped my arms around her, stroking her thin hair lightly. She still didn't cry.

For a moment, the apartment was silent. We knew Mom was in her bedroom and not at work on a Saturday morning. I braced myself for what was to come. I knew it wouldn't last long - it never usually does - but I didn't know what would happen in that short period of time.

At first, muffled voices came traveling out of their bedroom. I couldn't tell if they were mad yet. I also had no idea what they were saying at first, but I kept holding Lilly in that same spot. I held her tighter as the voices rose.

It drove me insane. I couldn't make out more than two or three words per sentence, if they were actually speaking in sentences. Other times, there were just screams. Long strings of screamy syllables. The screams were the worst, by far. They were piercing, but not the terror-laced ones that made your blood boil - I'd rather hear those any day. These were stronger, had more voltage behind them. They didn't evoke fear, like the screams of terror would. These evoked pain, confusion and a sour mix of an anger and hate of your own, because how could someone hate someone that they married, that they had kids with, that they have to live with?

It all seemed like a bitter lie. There were rare times when my father wasn't stressed and drunk or high, and it actually seemed like he could function, but then the next day something would happen at work and he'd come home, the month's paycheck already spent, a cigarette in his cracked lips, and he'd come home and hit Mom. Actually hit her, on the face, with his huge, disgusting palm.

The anger tasted acidic in the back of my throat. They're screaming now, Mom's screams high-pitched and like an arrow, his foul and forceful, like a club. I can feel them resound in every cell of my body. It doesn't even matter what they're screaming about, all that matters is that their voices cut to the core, leaving a throbbing, empty feeling where my stomach should be.

I hate them. I do, I truly do. If I could leave, I would. But I can't, because that would mean leaving Lilly here, alone. That would be a more heinous crime. The hate is bitter, and it consumes me, drowning me, until I find it hard to connect with anyone. Lilly remains the one unsoiled gem within me.

We hold each other, begging for the storm to stop.

~

A slam jolted me out of my trackless train of thought. The shouting fell silent. There was a small cry that erupted, muffled. Keeping my eyes trained on the door, I stood up and

48

pushed Lilly aside gently. The cry was obviously Mom's, but it didn't sound like she was hurt. It sounded more like a whine, a beg, an expulsion of sound from deep within her throat. But I couldn't tell if she said anything. My heart began to thump against my chest. Lilly reached out and touched my leg. I flinched, and brushed her hand away.

The whole apartment was still silent - even the air seemed to have settled. I found myself waiting for something, hanging on to every sound that came from their room, like twisted reality TV.

My hand hovered over the doorknob when the white wood pulled back, revealing a terrifyingly familiar and infuriated man. It all really felt too fast to be happening this way. There was a split second where his face changed from furious to insane. He grabbed the front of my shirt and dragged me out of the doorway. I could feel the rage in his grip, leaching right into my helpless shell of a body.

Reality came slamming back when my father smacked me up against the wall, his forearm up against my neck. His breath was hot and sticky. I could taste it. When Lilly came up beside me, whimpering "Stop!" I screamed at her to go away, to go into her room. But he absent-mindedly put his foot up against Lilly's chest and pushed her away. Pushing was an understatement.

But I writhed and clawed at my father's iron grip, pressing my nine year old body up against the wall, unrelenting. His anger has only fed the fire kindled within me. Outraged, I tried to push my father's body away with my palms, but that only led him to punch me in the jaw. The pain flaring in my face, I held my jaw with a trembling hand.

"What the fuck do you think you're doing? This ain't none of your fucking business!"

Like a siphon, the air was pushed out of my lungs as he slammed me into the wall again, sending me crashing to the floor. I scrambled to find a footing.

"You worthless piece of shit! What have you been telling your mother?" Dad hissed down at me. I could see every little needle-thin vein in his eyes.

Shameful tears pricking my eyes like needles, I could see my chest heaving up and down in my peripheral vision. "Wh-what are you talking about?" *Strong, Wyatt. Be strong.*

He gritted his teeth together. "You've been feeding her lies about me. It's your sorry ass that's fucking up our marriage!"

He's talking about how I always tell Mom how awful he is, how terribly he treats us. Uncontrollable rage. It stopped being in me and started becoming me. My voice, starting out thin and growing to a scream. "They're not lies. They're all true and you know it!" Every word felt good on my lips, acidic and satisfying like hate, thick and sweet like revenge.

Again, my father leaned down and grabbed me by the shirt, jerking me to my feet and sending pain through every single cell in my body. I heard Lilly whimper, and I took a small glance at her, watching all of this unfold. But not before my father clawed his fingers into my chin to whip my head around and face him.

"You're a fucking awful piece of shit I'm ashamed to call my son." Each word stings, bites. He'd inflict less pain by just hitting me. Please, just hit me again. Physical wounds would heal, emotional wounds would not. "You good-for-nothing whiny little bitch." He broke my gaze for a second, and when he did, my eyes burned with tears. "Lilly doesn't give a shit about you, you know. She'll grow up to be better than you'll ever be."

He pushed me backward onto the glass wall. A bang slapped me in the ears, but no shatter followed. For a second, I thought he might break the window and throw me out himself. I couldn't inhale for one, terrifying second before the grip on my shirt released. I slumped to the floor.

I still struggled to catch my breath, and all of the nerves inside of me seemed to bunch up in a tiny, hollow place in my stomach.

With an accusing finger, my father looked at me and Lilly, crumpled on the floor. Every one of his syllables was accented with rage like steel. "Go die in a hole, both of you. I wish I never fucked your mother, she wasn't worth any of it anyways."

Taking his burning foot, he kicked me square in the gut, right under the ribs, sending me writhing on the ground like a dissected worm.

The apartment door slamming shut behind him sent nearly every ounce of terror in me flying outward and falling to the ground, like a firework.

Immediately, Lilly rushed over to me, utterly silent. Tears streamed down her face and leaped off of her chin, but she did nothing to wipe them away. Again, she threw herself into me, her wet face leaving little dark patches on my shirt.

"I'm sorry," I said. Lilly pulled away, taking her little stubby fingers and wiping the blood inching from my nose to my lips.

Eventually, my mother emerged. Still in her bathrobe, her hair wild, she rushed over, spewing sound into our now silent apartment.

Falling to her knees, she wrapped both of us in her arms. I pushed her away, my entire body aching with pain.

"Don't touch me."

"Wyatt," she reached out, her ashen eyes and highlighted hair desperately clinging to normalcy.

My lips ripping into a sneer, I stepped back. "Don't."

Pushing away, storming out the front door and into the deserted hallway, I looked down at my hands, covered in my own blood, face already bruising up, and slid to the floor.

~

He left a couple months after I turned twelve. I was the one who walked Lilly home from school everyday. I was the one who made sure she got her homework done every night. I was the one who told her everything there is to know about boys and how dumb we are. I was the one who was there for her, when no one else was. When my mother was too busy with work and Dad left, the burden of a family was left on me. Whether I took on that burden or it was handed to me, I still felt the responsibility to protect and care for Lilly and even my mother at times.

It grew. My anger, my hate. Like a leech, I always knew it was there. Anything I did, I did to try and get rid of it.

But I couldn't.

And continuously, perpetually, I felt like shit.

And, at times, I still do.

To this day, I feel incomplete. Broken. A blood stain soaked into the carpet of my apartment. I never could pull myself out of the hole I had been thrown in.

And I could only just dig myself deeper.

~

A few days later, Lilly stopped playing with Barbies. I hate to admit that I missed being Ken.

CHAPTER THREE: All These Roads Lead Nowhere
DAY 2 - Terra; August 6th, 2015

There are a few sounds that pry the pillow of sleep off of my face - first, it's the god-awful scream of a hawk, circling overhead. Second, it's the slight, wet sound of something that I could never in my life identify unless I saw it first.

As I drift into consciousness, I writhe around, clawing and thrashing. An odd thought travels up through my mind as I find myself slowly moving around in a dead-end effort to get comfortable: Why is my bed so hard? Groans escape from my scratchy throat as my fingers run over the palpable sand.

Sand. My eyes jar open.

I thrash around, pulling myself up in the process, kicking at the sand with vigor, like it's a poisonous snake hissing at my toes. A scream punches out of me, shooting forward into the vast expanse of desert.

We're alone.

A hand grabs my wrist. A new, familiar breed of terror capsizes through me, and I fling myself away. My eyes travel up to the strange person beside me. Wyatt. He slowly releases his hand.

"Whoa, calm down," is all that he says, squeezing his eyebrows together.

Hearing another, slightly familiar human voice drags me into the present, kicking and screaming. I realize that the gurgly, wet sound I heard was Wyatt chugging his Gatorade because he continues to swig the red stuff back nonchalantly.

"Want some?" he says.

I swallow hard, my neck straining. "No. Thanks."

I vaguely hear him say, "suit yourself", for my attention manifests somewhere else. Pain boils in my gut - hunger. I slip off my backpack and search for the familiar crinkle of the wrapper. I take out the slightly stale granola bar. I slide off the wrapper and lay my eyes on the sticky granola and chocolate.

Swallowing hard, I open my teeth to take a bite. Already, my stomach cramps. I focus on taking small bites and chewing them thoroughly, trying to trick myself into thinking that I'm eating more than I actually am.

My tongue pricked with the sweet and crunchy granola in my mouth, I look over to the plane. It still sits, defeated, nose buried in the ground like a pitiful ostrich with its wings cut off.

I turn away, awful images flooding my head. Those coyotes must have done unspeakable things to their dead bodies. Devoured their flesh, mutilated their faces, ground their blood into the sand, all in a selfish, animalistic binge. All of it, gone. No proper burial, no respect. Bile burns hot in my throat.

If a frog is placed in boiling water, it will jump out, but if you put it in cold water and slowly turn up the heat, it will remain there until it dies. While this isn't entirely true, I can feel encroaching sadness falling over me, like snow. Softly and steadily, the kind that seems fun and harmless until you can't open your front door and the attic collapses.

I tuck my knees up tight and beg it to go away. Even when I hit the end of my granola bar, it's still there.

I crumple the wrapper between my trembling fingers and grind it into the sand. Maybe someone will find it and wonder how it got there.

This whole thing feels like a child's amputated finger. Abruptly ending something while it's still growing. Not killing it, not exterminating it, just ending it. Like ending a book right before the climax.

And I hate it.

I take out my water bottle, squinting against the already pounding sun. Wyatt gives me an odd look when I start to lick the cool condensation off the sides. Fumbling because I'm so thirsty, I madly twist the cap off and put the bottle up to my lips. I have about three-fourths left, but I tilt the bottle back anyways.

My mouth fills with lukewarm water, thick and refreshing, but stops just before my throat. Something within me screams to release my throat and chug the whole bottle down, but I can't make myself waste clean water on an impulse to satisfy myself just in this second.

Because, no doubt, an hour later I will be thinking the same thing that I am now.

I lean my head forward and pull the bottle away from my lips and hold the water in my mouth. I screw on the cap and gulp down the water.

It feels like life running down my throat, injecting it back into my cells. My body cries out for more, and I could drink the whole thing right here, right now.

Running my tongue over my now wet mouth, I stuff the bottle back into the bag, so the temptation is out of sight, out of mind.

Heaving, I wipe my lips and sit back. Stress boils like a simmering pot in my gut, and my thoughts the spoon, coaxing the bubbles to spill over.

"We should probably search the plane for supplies, and then take into account what we have," Wyatt says, towering over me.

His voice cuts deep into me, reaching far past my outer layers and striking my core. "Right," I say.

I don't take his hand when he offers to help me up. He just brushes me off, and with brisk steps, he walks ahead.

However, hearing his suggestion becomes a command, pushing away all thoughts for a while. I now have a job, an objective, a mission to complete. Something to throw myself head-first into and let the world fade away. My mind is already powering, full speed ahead, looking for things to ensure our survival.

Because we're all alone.

Aside from that, a warm, numb feeling floods my core as I remember what else resides in that plane. It hangs over me, my cross to bear, until we reach the plane, no longer smoking like a dying dragon.

But as we are walking back, I notice something that wasn't there before. An . . . odor. Distinctive, actually. Anyone could be able to distinguish it from any other foul smell - rotting flesh.

But not just any rotting flesh - human flesh. Caustic and like stabbing the gag reflex, I recognize it immediately. God, the late summer heat must be baking the flesh off.

We stop. I shut my eyes until the image disappears, for an acidic, sour taste has begun to fill my mouth, and my stomach begins to roll.

I can sense that Wyatt is having this same sensation because he freezes beside me. I look over and find his jaw clenched, and his eyes as focused as lasers. "Let's go." His voice has no inflection of emotion, although every ounce of his body shows that he smells it too, that it has the same effect on him.

I swallow hard and follow him to the plane.

And, suddenly, I see my father. Lying at a crude angle out of the airplane smeared in blood. The surfaces hard and soft alike seem to be soaking the blood up, accepting the slamming reality of death. And this crude reality also buries its fist into me, but, like stabbing pillows, it never reaches far enough inside me to produce a reaction. I just glance, take in the information, swallow hard, and keep walking around the tail of the plane to Wyatt's passenger side. But what I do know, is that my father's disassembled figure, crude and festering and bright red, will never leave my mind for as long as I live.

~

My hand slams down on the side of the plane, gasping for breath. Pain constricts around my chest, burns up to my face. The hot metal boils against my hands. The more I fight it, the more it grows.

My stomach lurches like a spring. No. No. This can't be happening. It feeds on my energy. I *will* keep that granola bar down.

I turn my eyes to Wyatt. He gapes at something behind the cabin door, opened to conceal whatever it is from me.

Wyatt furrows his caramel-tinted brows and disappears behind the door. My heart throbs to know what he's so focused on, but I don't know how much more I can handle. Heaving, I stare up at the white hot sun. Something to wash clean my tarnished mind.

"Holy shit," he hisses, quiet and strained, first. Not a second later, he reappears in my field of vision, from where I was standing behind the door. He has transformed entirely, his brown-sugar eyes wide with fear, his entire torso reeling back from whatever is in the passenger seat. His mouth is slightly ajar, his lips peeled back in horror. He scampers back, but in a much more careful manner than I must have done it when seeing my father.

Something tugs at me, that I should probably go over to him and do something, but when he finally breaks his gaze with the passenger seat, he marvels down at his hands, caustic as if they're covered in blood. The fear on his face solidifies into hot rage.

I watch, stunned, as Wyatt falls to his knees, burying his face in his hands. With every breath, his entire body heaves, until I realize he's sobbing.

I feel like I know what I'm going to find, even before I see it. I turn around the corner and find a middle-aged woman hanging out of the passenger seat, just as my father was, who I presume is Wyatt's mother.

Blood, crusty and brown, stains the desert ground around her cockeyed body. The coyotes have devoured his mother up just as much as they did my father, her pink flesh gnawed away until white bone shines glossy in the sunlight.

Unfortunately, the coyotes weren't kind enough to finish off their bodies, so the remnants of the disfiguration by the crash remains. Her chest has been peeled open by boiling red burns, patched across her face as well.

Her legs are half clothed with flesh and appear off-balanced as they are crushed under the plane's dashboard. A gnarled red clump of flesh remains of what must be her blown off ear, and her head sits at an awkward angle. Her eyes are shut, but that doesn't mean I can't see her eyes. One of the eyelids was burned away, revealing a glossy, Jello-like pink eyeball, just resting in the socket.

I twist away, even more disturbed by this image of a half-stranger. My hands tremble uncontrollably at my sides. I wring them together furiously.

But then, something changes. Something jerks violently within my glass case of a heart, and in a sudden instant, I can feel again. Disgust evaporates into pain and then evaporates into empathy. I look down at Wyatt's writhing figure, and it strikes that soft place inside of me. How different did I really look, seeing my father's cold eyes, seeing his hard face, seeing the life sucked out of him? How different did I really feel?

Before I realize it, soft and sweet tears are pouring down my face. *Finallyfinallyfinally.* It's like a slap to the face. I know what Wyatt is going through, and it reveals something damaged and beautiful inside me - making sense of this crazy world. I know the swallowing guilt he feels, at not being able to be there to say his last words. I share the guilt he feels at being the survivor - why did she die and I lived? I relate to the anger he feels at fate, karma, God, whatever the hell you want to call it, the anger at the powers that be that didn't spare our parents but spared our sorry little lives.

It weighs on me like the world itself, like a pack all of a sudden strapped around my shoulders, not rough, not uncomfortable, but soft and fabricked and weighing a thousand tons, like the souls of every human on earth. Like an anchor, tied around my heart, for the purpose of stability but only forcing me under the crashing waves.

I move over to where Wyatt has crumbled to the ground. I rest a hand on his shoulder and lean in toward his face, flushed red.

"Was that her? Your mother?" I say. My voice remains level.

"Yes," he hisses back. His hands have now moved up to his ears, as if blocking out a high-pitched, ear-grating sound.

With each tear that falls from my eyes, I feel better, as if, little by little, my pain is being released through each saltwater tear. "It . . . it's going to be okay. I know what you're going through." I bite my lip, hard, before my voice becomes hiccupy and riddled with sobs.

I don't have time to take a breath after I've ended my sentence before Wyatt snaps up, fuming mad. His eyebrows knotted together, his eyes wide and boring straight at me. I reel back in surprise and wait for his reaction because I honestly cannot predict what he's going to do next. He looks like he's about to physically explode until horrible words come spewing out of his mouth.

"What the hell are you talking about? It is not going to be okay! You have no idea what I'm going through!" Wyatt exclaims.

I draw back at his words. What does he think I'm talking about? More like, what does he think *he's* talking about! I swim through a turbulent sea of words I could respond to that with, but eventually come up with: "My father's dead, too. Don't say that I don't feel the same way!" I shoot back, the fear and anger obsessive. Where? Where is this all coming from? My face burns with a strange, irrational heat. Emotions rape and pillage my soul.

I only seem to have thrown coals on his fire, eating my assuming and prideful words.

"You don't know how I feel!" he spits out every word like it's going to disintegrate his mouth if he doesn't say it. "You don't know me at all." But the last one comes out pitiful, angry, and quiet. Dismissive.

I'm taken terribly aback by his words that ring true. He probably doesn't want to talk to me, not while he's going through this. It was my fault for intervening, when it wasn't my place to say anything. Guilt swallows me once again. I turn my eyes toward the ground, to the plane, to the sky behind him, anywhere but Wyatt, and back away. I'm such a bumbling fuck-up.

I push the air out painfully. "You're right. I don't know you. I don't know what you're feeling, I don't know what you're thinking. I'm sorry." I really am. I realize what I have done was wrong and out of line, but then something awful spews out anyways. "I'm sorry I tried to help." My words bite into his psyche, and I can tell. Damn it, Terra.

I pick my things up, leaving the contents of the compartment back in the plane on the dusty ground, and walk back over to the tree, where I can have some peace and quiet. The harder my angry feet stomp on the ground, the more sobs tear down my cheeks. I still feel that thing, those aching contractions of my heart. They don't seem to be sharp or directly painful, but more like a dull ache, a discomfort, an emptiness, that becomes more and more prominent with each pump of my blood.

Tears pour down my face, and I don't really bother to wipe them away. An overwhelming feeling of dread passes over me like a storm cloud, except that once it blows in it doesn't blow on out. It stays there locking in place, just to downpour right on me. My chest racks with sobs, heaving and caving in, but I don't let a sound escape from my mouth.

A single word grinds into my head, is branded on my dirt-covered face, written into my blood. The single word that holds so much power over me is despair.

~

Wyatt eventually wanders over. His face appears emotionless, even though his eyes are still red. I don't dare look up.

"Help me bury them," he says, standing over me, the hot sun beating down.

And, for the first time in the 16 hours I've known Wyatt, we don't disagree.

The sun claws at our flesh as we trudge back over to the plane. Once we get over there, Wyatt turns to me and hands me his machete. "I'll bring her over while you dig."

I nod. I count my steps as I stride away from the plane. The thick sunlight warps the air around the fraying edges of the horizon. Stopping a good fifty feet away from the plane, I take the tip of the machete and outline a rectangle. The packed earth cracks like peeling skin as I dig the knife in, and finally when I think I have a good enough space, I plant my feet and lay down.

Immediately, I feel the infectious heat seeping in through my clothes.   It reaches up and curls around my ribcage, threatening to suck me under like quicksand. I am a corpse trapped in an ecosystem of life.

Like the skittering of spiders, I fling myself off of the unholy ground, screams threatening to rocket out of me like vomit. Falling back onto my knees, I curl up and press my forehead against my thighs. I need water.

Pulling myself off the ground, I open up my pack and twist open my water bottle. Trembling, I put the water to my lips.

Before I know it, it's all gone, sloshing around in my chasmic stomach, being absorbed by my insect shell of a body.

I have to do this.

Picking the machete back up, I walk back over to the grave. Deep-seated rage bubbles within me as I slam the blade into the ground, over and over, turning over the damn sand. Taking armfuls of sand, I throw them out, the sand sticking to my sweaty skin like fire ants. I tear roots from the ground, toss rocks at trees, until I have dug myself into a grave.

I am a corpse trapped in an ecosystem of life.

Heaving, I pack together the walls, forming the rectangle. I don't want to do this.

Wyatt stands over me, pain scarring his face. He extends a hand and this time, I let him pull me out. He has his mother over his shoulder.

His eyes glazing over, he leans over and puts her onto the ground, flipping her wooden, swollen legs down onto the ground. A rancid smell burns inside my head, and I turn away and cough as Wyatt's mother's body lays there, exposed and crusty.

"C'mon," he says forcefully, his voice cutting through the thick death. I warily turn back and see that his shirt is pinned up over his nose and mouth, resting on the bridge. Swallowing down tickling vomit, I pull up my own.

Struggling against rigor mortis, I wince as Wyatt crosses her arms over her raw chest, the bones cracking and the muscles ripping. As the body rocks back and forth, I see the raw stump of an ear, like ground beef, pressed on this strange woman's face. I can even see the golden hoops melted into the side of her face and a necklace, taut around her swollen neck.

Wyatt grabs her shoulders, and I follow suit with her legs. They feel rubbery and oddly malleable. Like balloons.

As if in unison, we sidestep over and hover her body over the grave, and slowly lower this woman into her final resting place. And step back to admire our perverse work, and to take in what a number that the world has done on us.

And suddenly, Wyatt's voice gives piercing light to the abysmal darkness. "Alicia Mary Hill. Mom. April 1975 to . . . August 5th, 2015." He stops, for an eternity. "I wish I could say something . . . that could amount to who you were -"

When Wyatt's voice cuts off so harshly that I flinch, I look over to him. I can nearly see the hurricane of emotions that whirl around him, fighting for claim of his tongue.

And I watch in awe as he breaks down, kicking at the loose sand, pushing the fragments over to their pungent death, sprinkling it over his own mother's corpse.

His Adam's apple bobs up and down, like a drowning child through the layers of sobs. "I'm sorry," is all that he can say.

Do I know the context? Do I know what this means to him - to his mother? Do I know why he says this? No, but all I do know is that I feel the pain, visceral and real, of what it means to me. The words, full of regret and buzzing anger.

"I'm sorry," I say, filling the grave with sand.

"Shut up," he chokes, throwing handfuls in.

~

Hours pass. We fill the grave, and Wyatt works on fashioning a cross with two sticks and twine. My throat becomes raw; sticky like a vacuum. Wyatt offered to do this part for me, but I said no. He was my father, and I have to do this.

I have to do this.

Steadying myself against the piercingly hot metal of the plane door, I feel my stomach thrash inside of me.

Dad. His flesh torn to shreds, left to the mercy of the elements. A deep unfairness, burning hot and white, rises up within me like a pole, pushing my throat out of me. And the suppleness of his face, the familiarity that strikes painfully close notes, reminds me of home.

Moments flash before me, of our family, of Mom, of Nick. How my father was always reading a good book with his thick fingers and strong arms. Of my mother's laugh, rich and layered like coffee with cream. Of the always-closeness of Nick, that could be found like a gem in his kind actions.

And it hits me - that my father is not only gone but so is my family. I can feel it crumbling apart in the deep strings of my soul.

Sobs lurching in my chest, I turn away and vomit, thick and mucousy. The stomach acid eats away at the tissue of my mouth, and tears burn at my eyes. I collapse against the plane, coughing rampantly, screams rocketing out.

It's not fucking fair.

My chest still vibrating with sobs and vomit, I spring up and tear the seat belt off of my father and pull him out of the seat. But his fleshy legs are still attached. I am thrust forward, and his slick and rubbery wrists fall out of mine.

"Come on, damn it!" I scream, grabbing on again and pulling, thrashing, kicking at the god-forsaken sand that fills this god-forsaken desert.

And suddenly, I rip my father's legs off at the knees, popping and ripping and tearing off like stringy asparagus. Thick, congealed blood oozes out of the now four meaty sockets.

Dumbstruck with horror, my blood corpse and I shoot back, onto the hard sand. My body writhes, and sobs tear at my body. Tears sting at my eyes and cheeks. I grovel on the ground, slammed over and over with the waves of tragedy.

My body convulsing, I pull myself up and keep dragging and walking and never looking back.

Soaked in sweat, I take my father's body over to the grave Wyatt has dug, and lay him down. Turning away as Wyatt labors over the baking sand, I grasp onto some scraggly bushes and fall to my knees.

What has happened? Questions swirl like madness around my head, pulled under by the tide of my emotions.

"Are you ready?" Wyatt asks.

I push my clumpy bangs out of my face. "Yeah."

Making the lonely trek over, I pick up my father by the shoulders. Even with Wyatt's help, the 200 pound, six foot two corpse of my father is still a heavy burden, physically and mentally. Never in my infinitesimal little life did I think that it would happen this way.

We lower him in, and I step back, suddenly feeling the world zoom in and out with alarming realism. My head throbs, and I believe that I might pass out. But the image of my father, torn and still, anchors me in this raging sea.

Words flow out. "Michael Emmett Lombardi. Uh, October something, 1966, to August 5th, 2015." And then they cut off, like a kink in a hose. I can feel Wyatt's steady presence beside me.

All I can think of is home. Home with warmth and safety and life. And how this has all come crashing down. This is Jericho at its fucking finest. The walls of life are tumbling down, caving in, threatening to suffocate me. This has changed everything, and I hate it. Oh my good God, I hate it.

Stone faced with trembling hands, sobs crackle through my body and tears leak out of my eyes, soothing the burning of rage on my cheeks.

In one soft, swift motion, Wyatt puts a hand on me and pulls me into his unfamiliar embrace. For a full second of eternity, I panic. It boils over and grips my neck, and I'm viciously afraid that it's happening again. What is he doing to me? But then, the overwhelming kindness of his actions translates to me, and I realize, that this pain has connected us.

And we mourn together, two souls throbbing in the heat of the unforgiving sun.

~

I take the last handful of dirt and sprinkle it over my father's grave, while Wyatt fashions a crude cross, carving my father's name in. With the butt of the machete, he hammers the cross in, marking the grave. Two crosses, made of brittle sticks and frayed twine, stand tall in the melting sun, the day croaking into afternoon, piercing the thick air, refusing to succumb. Forever shouting I was here into the neverending void we find ourselves in.

Eventually, we stumble back over to our tree with the supplies. The plane broils in the heat, warping the air around it. We collapse, sucked dry by the world.

The sun, the earth, the stars, move around us in a cacophony of life. But we are death. Our eyes black, our cheeks sunken in, our limbs like lumber. My mind is blank, as smooth as sand after waves beat the life out of it.

I have nothing left.

The day rots into the stinking afternoon. I flinch when Wyatt pushes himself up.

"We ... we should go."

"Go where?"

"Away from here," he says. He looks over at me, to meet my eyes. They are glossed over, but, pushing past that, I find a depth in them that I grasp onto. "But we should gather more supplies first." He stands.

Something pinpricks in me, that this is a bad idea. I don't entirely know what he means. "We can't leave. What if they send helicopters or a search party?"

"Twenty-four hours," he says. Not harshly, but matter-of-factly. As resolute as a concrete wall. "It's one p.m., so it's been twenty-four hours. If people were coming for us, they would have come by now."

Immediately, the voice in my head shouts that he's right. "Well, where would we go?"

"To civilization."

The normality of this conversation brings me to the surface of myself. I suck on the inside of my cheek. Doesn't he know that I don't know where we are? "Well, we flew west, because that's where the tours always go-"

"Tours?" he asks, scratching the stubble on his chin.

"Uh, yeah. That's what my family does."

"So then, do you know the way back?"

"No. I . . . I have no idea where we are. We could be five miles from Phoenix or five hundred. We could be five miles from the Californian border - which is the closest civilization other than Phoenix - or five hundred. We'll never know." Suddenly, exhaustion hits me in the chest, drowning me with pummelling waves of dread.

"What's our best bet?"

Anxiety rolls in my gut. Why? Why is he putting so much faith in me, this strange, haughty boy? I look him up and down once more. Sandy blond curls, freckles, brown eyes. The hard face and the sparkling eyes and the puffed chest like a city-walker.

"You're the nature guru here. I'm waiting . . ." He kicks at the dirt, cringing when a hard-shelled insect scuttles away.

No wonder.

"West," I say, my stomach immediately flooding with doubt. "Then, at no matter what latitude we hit it at, we'll still make it to the Colorado River, and then to civilization."

He nods his head. "Sounds good."

Yet again, Wyatt offers me his hand. After hesitating for a moment, I take it.

~

We begin gathering supplies from the plane. The smell is considerably less, but the stains of blood and the heaviness in the air buzzes around like a swarm of flies. Maybe there is literally a swarm of flies around here.

Wyatt finds a large rock and begins banging on the side of the plane, in an effort to reach the cargo hold in the tail of the plane. I climb in through Wyatt's side and brush some glass off of his seat. I find the sloped area right in the back of the seats, just before the back windshield juts up, covered in gray, tight carpet.

Each motion becomes more and more natural. I lift the hatch. Inside the compartment is a horde of survival supplies. There are some empty spaces where I took out the machete and first-aid kit. I focus the energy I find buzzing inside of me into a laser pointer.

I breathe, and my hot air fills the stuffy cabin. Focus, Terra.

I put my hand in the space between the seats and lift up the hatch - this is where I found the first aid kit to bandage myself up. I know most of my father's planes like the back of my hand. I can find all of the nooks and crannies in a second, along with that are a few of my father's personal items he always keeps in here in case of something like this.

I squeeze my eyes shut. I remember all of the times I would poke fun at his adamancy at having these supplies in every plane, saying to him that something like that would never happen, and him always saying back in a playfully dismissive tone, "You never know," meaning he was right and the conversation was over. Now, it hits me that he was right. You never know when something like this will happen.

I force myself to open my eyes, blocking the ballooning pain, and pull out the first thing I can get my hands on.

Turning ninety degrees and laying my back against the cabin door, I lay all of the supplies out on the seats. A survival kit. Bright orange and plastic, I unhook the clips and see what's inside. Two wound up bungee cords with hooks, a hardy compass, and a small metal whistle.

Putting the two items back, I pull out a small baking pan, maybe the size of my hand. It's made of iron, meaning it can be a skillet, but the sides are high enough for it to function as a pan. I also find a bag of cotton balls and a box of waterproof matches. There's also some Saran wrap and a spool of wire.

I take out a huge, plastic flashlight and flick the switch a few times. It works, thank goodness. Next to that are two neatly folded ponchos.

But then my eye catches on a slim, leather-bound book with pages like golden angel hair. Thumbing through it, I realize that it's a Bible. Since when does my father ever keep a Bible near him within a five-mile radius? Next to the Bible is a thin, leather-bound journal with crisp, blank pages. A black ink pen lies clipped to it. I open up the front cover to find a name written on the inside cover in smooth cursive - Gideons International - and a date - 8/5/11. Four years from yesterday. That's when we got this plane, when we packed it.

I stick my head out of the cargo door and see Wyatt still focused on the cargo hold. "Did you bring this?" I shout, clutching the Bible.

He stops, lowering the machete. His eyebrows writhe up into a confused expression. "No," he says, squinting at the sun. "What is it?"

I shrug, trying to physically shake off the creeping, vile nostalgia inside of me. "A Bible," I say, tossing the book out of the cabin. I tuck myself back into the cabin, curled on the bloody, debris-ridden leather, bitter remembrance boiling in my gut.

But I watch from afar as Wyatt picks up the Bible, with a mirrored expression on his face, stricken with my realization and confusion. He thumbs through the pages as well.

He then looks up at me, and I jump, taken aback by his brown eyes, hardened and indifferent. "Maybe we can use it as kindling." Then he stops and walks back to his cargo hold, and I'm left, frozen, listening to the banging against the hollow metal.

But I find myself, saying just above a whisper, "Yeah, maybe."

~

As Wyatt drops the supplies and sits down on the ground in the shade of the tree, I begin to take notice of something. His impulsiveness - just as unruly as his hair. His quick wit, his grimly satirical look on life. Maybe he's one of those types who likes not knowing what's going to happen. The pieces seem to fit together, for even now he seems on the edge, jittery, apprehensive at sitting down and talking about what we're going to do and not actually doing it.

I smirk at this and push my mind to other tasks. "Get out all of the things that you had with you when you got on the plane. Like, your bag and stuff."

Wyatt removes his drawstring bag and takes a few items out of his pockets, setting them in front of us. I then scoop all of the materials we have until they are sitting in the space between us, all in a small heap.

I sigh softly. "Where to start," I say, under my breath.

My brain begins working like cogs and gears in a clock, rapid and well-oiled, reaching for an ultimate goal. "Do you have anything to write on?" I ask Wyatt.

He furrows his brow, then takes his iPhone out of his pocket.

"You're kidding me, right?" I say, looking at the life-proof case around it.

He squints at a few things on the screen, then stands up, holding the phone up at arm's length. After a few more moments, he grimaces and says, "No service."

I snort a little, reminded of the time when our satellite dish broke after a thunderstorm, when we had no TV, no internet, and no cell or phone service for over a week. It was bizarre, but it didn't affect me much. "We barely have any cell service at my house and the lodge. If there's a bad storm, we lose all connection with the outside world. You'll get used to it."

Wyatt sneers at me and sits back down, narrowing his light brown eyes. I assume he opens the Notes app. "Okay, what do you want me to write down."

I snap back into business mode. I scoot back on the gritty sand and hold up the first item - the box of saltine crackers. But as the cubic shape registers in my head, I suddenly find myself gazing at the out of focus figure behind the box, running his fingers through his dark blond curls that aren't restricted by the sloppy bandage he put around his head wound anymore. And, maybe without his gruff demeanor and grime covering his face, he'd be kind of cute.

"Saltine crackers?" He asks, almost sneering.

I nod a few times and lower the box of crackers. Wyatt shoots me a peculiar look.

"Yeah, sorry. Saltine crackers, write that down."

I give my head another good shake and move onto something else. I mentally scold myself as I lug the sleeping bag up.

I blink a few times and force the words out: "One sleeping bag."

~

Everything is all packed, all our useful - and even unuseful - supplies has been stuffed into our bags. Our most notable find was 16 cans of fresh water.

I take his hand. With a strong grip, he pulls me up once again.

And we stand, facing the endless, lonely, deadly, and dangerous stretch of west.

One step in front of the other. I kick at the bowling ball of anxiety in my stomach, forcing it down. I don't want to leave. I don't want to leave my dad, the stagnant plane, everything I know.

Turning around on an electric impulse, I stand, facing the scope of the plane and the two crude crosses rising from the dirt. I bite my lip hard.

It doesn't bleed, but, oh God, I want it to. Clinging to what I know, even if it sucks, I refuse to move.

I can't.

My heavy eyes travel to the right cross - my father's grave. And, by the mystery of the universe, I know that he would be okay with this. With me leaving. He would want me to go, to chase the moon and the sun and the stars and find my way back.

So, like a massive, old turbine, I turn around. Wyatt stares back at me, shoulders hunched, forehead wrinkled with the ash of life.

And I say: "Let's go."

~

At first, walking isn't so bad. The sun is high and mighty, and the colors make for a beautiful display to travel towards. But still, the sun scorches hot here. Sweat leaks into the cuts on my arms and face.

Then, it becomes excruciating. My back aches, pain pinching through with every step I take. The sand swirls around my feet, in a mesmerizing array as each step loses more and more meaning. We seem to travel nowhere.

Why does it have to be so hot out here? I'm usually used to this kind of weather, but we're in the rotten, late summer heat and monsoon season, and at home I would have the leisure of a cold drink and a change of clothes. Not now. Maybe not ever.

I wipe the prospect of *not ever* from my mind and swallow hard. But I look and see that Wyatt is a few yards ahead of me. I keep walking.

Making sure to keep up with the monotone pace of Wyatt ahead of me, I pull off my backpack and take my phone out of the pocket where it resides.

86% battery life. Not bad. I turn up the screen brightness only so I can actually see the screen in the blaring sun. I hold up my phone higher, confirming the myth displayed by Wyatt that raising your phone up about a foot will not improve its cell service.

~

Much later in the afternoon, after I am drenched in sweat and breathing hard, we stop at a cluster of rocks to drink. Since I'm pretty sure neither one of us slept very well last night, we decide on taking naps in the sweltering afternoon so we'll have the energy to walk in the cool of night.

He lets me rest first, but the heat suffocates me, so I let my eyes drift open. My eyes set on Wyatt, sitting on the rocks, legs spread and planted firmly on the ground, with his arms slung around them.

I observe Wyatt in his wholeness and ponder on him for a while until I can nail what I'm really thinking. Wyatt is, at best, intriguing. His whole demeanor emanates a jovial nature on the surface, but there's a much darker, maybe even more steady nature to him that I can't quite place. A natural leader, I suppose.

But he also has a mask, I can tell . . . not a literal one, of course, but a mask of something that protects other people from seeing the real him. Not that the real Wyatt is bad, but that he's just . . . protecting himself. Keeping on a constant face so that no one suspects anything, so that he can continue functioning no matter how he feel or what happens.

I snort to myself as I peel the dry skin off of my bottom lip. Boy, can I relate to that.

Pricked with guilt, I turn over.

~

When I open my eyes, the sun hangs much lower in the sky, the red and oranges of the sunset just now distinguishing themselves from the bright yellow of the sun. I slept, but I don't feel refreshed in the slightest. I sit up, rubbing my dry and burning eyes. Wyatt hasn't moved.

My lips and mouth have been glued together with dried saliva, and I peel them apart before I drench my mouth in water. It feels fantastic going down, but the water swishes around down there, in my stomach, lonely in a rubber-band chasm. I open my backpack and search down at the bottom for something I just remembered I had in there. I pull out a cup of unopened, warm applesauce.

I see Wyatt catch the cup with his eyes, and immediately, I know I'm going to have to share it with him. I peel back the foil and make a sort of spoon with it by cupping one end and twisting the other, but Wyatt, however, just takes a grubby finger to the pale slush, scoops out a bite, and licks his finger satisfyingly.

He smacks his lips. "Delicious." I nearly smile and dig in myself. The soft, mushy texture soothes my mouth and throat, and the carbohydrates are like a shot of adrenaline to my bloodstream. I savor every bite, holding it in my mouth as long as I can, and then letting the stuff slide down and crash into my stomach.

In no time, the applesauce is gone, and we're left, jamming our tongues in the plastic container to lick up the last bits of the moisture. We sit back, sighing in content but ever so unsatisfied. Applesauce has never tasted so damn good in my life.

Wyatt looks out at the horizon, his face stricken with concentration. He pulls out his phone and squints at the screen. "Dude. It's been a whole day since we woke up," he says, a grave expression creeping up on his face.

I swallow hard. Has it been that long? A pounding sensation wells up in my head, as if my thoughts are becoming so overcrowded in my mind that my skull is becoming a balloon, taut and stretched to its breaking point. A flicker of pain boils inside of me, and my knees slowly come up to my chin, my arms wrapping around me like shields, as if I can snuff my fear out by compressing it. How long will this last?

I look up, if only for a second, to see Wyatt, jaw clenched but eyes soft, mirroring the tidal wave that I am drowning in on this dry, barren sea.

CHAPTER FOUR: The Ghosts That Haunt Us
DAYS 2 & 3 - Wyatt; August 6th and 7th, 2015

The moment eventually passes, and Terra and I trade places on the rock. She lets me sleep until sundown. I sleep long and hard, but I don't feel much different.

The desert takes on a different form at night. The sun has long exited, but the reddish afterglow stains the sky like a bad aftertaste. The shadows seem longer, the plants like black paper cut-outs.

I sigh, pulling myself out of a sleep that feels more like a drug-induced stupor - and I would know. Slinging my backpack over my shoulder, I nod to Terra. "Let's go." She nods, swallowing hard.

We start walking, and soon, I find that it's much easier walking in the cool air of the night. The darkness, however oppressing, is the lesser of the two evils over the boiling sun. Still, I have to watch my feet, for everything from venomous snakes to beady-eyed rodents to scuttling bugs occasionally rush over the tops of my shoes.

The indigo of the sky deepens into black, and the noises in the underbrush swell in my ears. Once I get past the sounds and the fact that it makes my head throb, I choose to observe and enjoy the orchestra. A hollow, yearning howl pierces the air, sending a ripple up my spine. Damn coyotes.

Even though I'm hungry, thirsty, blood soaked, and caked in dust that turns into mud on my sweaty skin, the desert is, in an eerie, perverse way, beautiful. I'm just in no mood to admire it.

I look up and keep planting one foot in front of the other. It becomes mind-numbingly boring, and a couple times I trip, wanting to fall and just let the desert sand envelop me and never get back up. But I always keep walking.

Slowly but surely, mountainous figures begin to line the horizon, stretching as far as the eye can see, hard and gray in the thin light. We'll have to go over those at some point. But they look a good half day's walk, so we'll get there by sunup.

Eventually, something changes in my field of vision. Since the only light comes from the scooped out moon and stars, I can't tell what it is, even when my vision is still iffy from my head wound. It appears to be a cluster of something, closer than the mountains jutting up far on the horizon, but from this distance, it could be another pile of rocks, as useless as the rest of this desert.

But as the images creep closer - or more correctly, *we* creep closer - I see that they are too boxy, too uniform, too tall, to be rocks. Then what could they be?

As we get closer, I find myself squinting hard at these bizarre silhouettes, now appearing much different than the rocks behind them.

About 100 feet away, it suddenly hits me - they're buildings. Buildings - built by actual people. Before I know what I'm doing, I sprint towards the boxy figures. My legs pump beneath me as something hot and sweet - hope - surges in my chest. It's like a huge hand, pushing me forward, refusing to let me stop.

"You know what those are, Terra?" I shout behind me.

She's just catching up. "What?"

"They're buildings! We're saved!" I scream to the heavens. Maybe this isn't all so bad.

But as I speed closer and the details of these buildings become more evident, I see rotting wood, shattered windows, and the distinctive reddish hue of rust. I tumble to a stop as the words finally register into my head - it's a ghost town.

Terra skids on the dirt as well, nearly running right into me. "What?!" she exclaims, reorienting herself after the dust has cleared. The recognition blares across her face, and she hunches on her knees.

Suddenly, all of the hope inside of me has been sucked dry and replaced with a caustic anger. Frustration buzzes through my body, and I have the lurching impulse to tear every one of these stupid buildings down with my bare hands.

"You've got to be fucking kidding me!" The words tear from my throat, the anger racking my body. My heart pounds against my bones, wanting to escape my chest and jerk on the dusty ground like a fish out of water.

Once my breathing slows, I turn to Terra, whose brow is knotted, mostly at the disappointment in front of us. I simmer down.

Ramshackled buildings rise out of the desert soil, the tallest being only about three stories tall, even with its bell tower. We realize that it looks like a lame, double-sided strip mall as Terra and I circle around the back of the buildings into the main drag.

The whole place looks gutted out, like a sepia-toned shell. Blackness swallows up the windows and the busted open doorways. Loose pieces of wood sway in the nipping night wind.

"Pathetic," I hear Terra mutter.

"You can say that again," I say as we begin walking down the lonely strip. The whole place gives off an empty, lonely feel. Not necessarily eerie or creepy, as you might think. The way that the wind rattles the buildings like skeletons, the abyss provided by the deep windows, and the way that the land seems to travel on into the distance even when this measly town ends, all makes it just look sad. Lonely.

I sigh, walking over to what appears to be a general store and ease myself down onto the porch. It groans at me, and the moment that I release my weight onto it, the wood snaps.

It leaves a Wyatt-sized hole, my rear end buried and my chest, arms and legs sticking out awkwardly. Grimacing, I look up at Terra, standing on the dirt, poised in the moonlight, smiling tight-lipped, her eyes bright.

I sneer, and this just makes her snicker more. Pushing up with my arms, I lift myself out and stand, brushing the wood chips off my behind and legs.

"Let's find somewhere else to sit," I say, deadpan. This sends Terra audibly laughing this time. As I walk away, I find myself smiling, even though she can't see me.

I lean on another porch. The wood still creaks, but nothing happens, so I sit.

"Well, this looks like a nice place to settle in for the night," I say.

"Please tell me you're joking," Terra says, rubbing her hands up and down over her goose-fleshed arms.

"No," I say. "At least this gives us real shelter."

Terra doesn't reply - why would she? There's nothing more to say - and she stares out at the ground, nervously twirling at the ends of her hair with her finger.

After some more adamant listening to the wind, Terra asks: "Are you hungry?"

What kind of a question is that? "Hell yes."

"Can I have your Swiss army knife?"

"Sure," I reply, taking it out of my pocket and handing it to her.

Solemnly, Terra gets up and walks out of the ghost town, taking her backpack. Intrigued, I follow, not too closely.

Terra walks over to a the shrubby plants that spring up a ways away from the first building. She begins . . . searching. Holding a flashlight between her teeth, she moves smoothly from plant to plant, picking and paring away with the knife and cupping them into her shirt.

I remain hidden around the corner of the building and continue watching her shape moving in the dark. For the first time, I realize how excruciatingly dark it is. It smothers the desert like a thick blanket, letting the animals and plant life scuffle under it. If it weren't for the moonlight, I wouldn't be able to see more than about ten feet in front of me. I find it stifling, as if I only have the few inches directly in front of me to move around and breathe.

I relax against the post of the building as Terra turns around and starts walking back over, my legs suddenly turning to jelly because she saw I was watching her. Turning on my heel, I sit back down on the creaky steps, soreness rushing through my scratched calf.

The moonlight is soft on her face as she looks down at me. Silently, she hands me a bundle of leaves and these greenish, raisin things. I glance at her, doubtful, but she just purses her lips at me.

But I see the food, and my mind registers it as a salad of raisins and lettuce, and my stomach growls, scraping at my insides. I toss a few of the raisins in my mouth. Odd flavor, but surprisingly sweet. Now for these leaves. I take one in my hand and hold it up to the light. Pressing it up to my nose, I can't smell anything discernible.

"What are these?" I ask, keeping the sting out of my voice.

"Amaranth leaves," Terra says, eating her own. "They're good, I promise."

So I take a bite. Crisp, yet thin. Slightly glossy and textured, like eating the pages of a crumpled magazine. The flavor, however is unlike anything I can place. Spinach-esque.

Terra's still eating when I have finished. I guess she's trying to savor the food, tricking her stomach that she is eating more. But her dark eyes pierce the darkness, the gears behind her eyes turning.

Her feminine figure is burned into my mind, and now, I look down to see her cascading hair, the pale light of the moon making it shine redder than autumn leaves. The condition of her hair shows that she's not too concerned about her appearance. But, yet again, why would she be? I rub my own hand on my oily, grimy forehead. I don't blame her for that part.

But something Terra can't change so quickly is her body. I can see the seamless curves over her waist, hips, and thighs. Nor are her breasts too gigantic or too small. The perfect size to admire.

Shaking my lustful thoughts away, the only way I can find to describe her is perfectly soft in the right places, despite her harsh demeanor.

I pick at a hangnail. Now that I think about it, that's kinda weird. If I would have seen her on the street, Lilly would have pointed her out to me, asking if I thought she was pretty. Would I have said yes? Probably. Lilly always daydreamed about me getting married, having kids and a life of my own, because she secretly dreamed about it as well, wanted it for herself. I always told her no, I probably wouldn't do any of those things. Because I thought I'd be dead long before any of that could happen.

God, now I'm thinking about my sister. I miss her.

~

After we finish eating, I don't feel full, but at least the hunger is at bay for a while. Heavy silence falls over us as we drown under the noises of the night. The ghost town groans in unison like a large, old man, attempting to pull himself out of bed. The deep, blue-gray wood blends in with the blackness of the sky.

Every once in awhile, the moonlight glinting off of a broken shard of glass catches my eye. And every time, panic jolts through me, the hackles on the back of my neck raise, and my grip on my machete tightens. But every time, I realize it's nothing.

There are times when I forget Terra's presence beside me, and sometimes even her slight movements startle me. Swallowing hard, I put myself in check. Why am I so on edge?

A gust of wind drags through the ghost town, sending some loose boards rattling, glass tinkling. This time, true fear crawls up my back, and it won't go away. No matter how hard I push my focus onto something else, the big, hairy spider of fear's fangs drip, eager to sink into my neck.

When I can't think of anything to talk about, I abruptly stand. I feel Terra flinch beside me. "It's cold. I'm going to make a fire."

Grabbing my bag, I storm off into an open area. I shove rocks away and kneel down and form a small fire pit with stones.

"Um," Terra says, above me. "Do you need help?"

"Yes, actually," I say, surprised that she cares enough to think to help. "Can you scavenge around for some branches or dry stuff for kindling?"

She looks at me for a moment, nods and licks her lips. Terra leaves, becoming a silhouette in the shadow of the desert again. I pull my cigarette lighter out and flick the switch. A translucent, orange and blue flame pops up. Letting go, I stuff that back in my pocket to conserve the fluid. This lighter's pretty new, though, so we should be good.

Good for how long? How long are we going to be out here? How long will we need it?

Jeez. Not again.

~

Digging a small ditch in the firepit, I sit back and wait for Terra to bring over the firewood.

She comes back, arms full. I'm actually quite surprised, considering I haven't seen many trees around here. Well, what do I know?

Terra kneels down on the ground, tucking a strand of her hair behind her ear. "I found lots of this dry kindling," she says, setting this thick, dill-weed looking plant at my feet. "There was a dead tree, so I snapped branches off of that."

I find a smile creeping up my face. "That's great. Thanks."

She curtly nods. I furrow my brow as I put branches on the bottom, and fill that up with the kindling stuff that will catch on fire easily.

Terra sits directly across from me, watching the dark coals. She takes out her ponytail and fastens it on the crown of her head, tucking her bangs in with it as well. Honestly, I'm not sure what to make of this girl. Helpful at times, but also hard-nosed, stubborn, and . . . arrogant. But all in the subtlest way possible.

Many times, the kindling catches aflame . . . but burns right out, without catching anything else on fire. Frustration burns within me, and I wish that I could replace my damn cigarette lighter with the anger boiling inside. But honestly, exhaustion lays heavy. I'm just done.

After another failed attempt, I throw the cigarette lighter down to the ground and swear under my breath. I was a Boy Scout, I should know how to do this. But we all know I didn't get much help from my old man.

"What?" Terra asks, snapping to attention. "Can you not get it started?"

"What does it look like?" I snap, then immediately sit back.

Terra just half-scowls at me and shrugs it off. She sighs heavily and comes over next to me. Fiddling with the fire, she stuffs the bottom with the dry, weedy plant.

"Part of what makes a good fire," she says calmly, looking up at me. "Is the three components of the fire. Tinder, kindling, and bulk."

A scowl pushes its way onto my face.

Terra works on loosely packing the 'tinder', and then stacking some of the smaller branches on top. After a few times, she does catch the kindling a flame, and then, as those burn, she works up on stacking some larger branches. Then she stops . . . and begins building a tepee-like contraption around the fire. Terra gives the fire a few more blows, and then sits back on her knees. "Voila!"

Narrowing my eyes, I sit back. "Why didn't you tell me that you knew how to do this?"

Terra shrugs, wrapping her cardigan around her. "I guess I just wanted to watch you try." A hint of teasing shows in her voice.

Smirking, I sit back and let myself relax. Restlessness stirs within me, but soreness is much more powerful. I outstretch my leg, feeling the scrapes rub against the bandages. I lay my head back on a rock. Even though it is hard and angular, it feels great to let my neck relax.

"You want me to take the first shift?" I pull my eyes open and see Terra crouched by the fire. The golden light carves out the features on her face. Her chin rests on her knees, tucked up close to her chest.

"No," I say, shaking off exhaustion as best as I can. I push up from a slouching position and force my eyes open.

"You sure?" Terra says, brow furrowed. Concerned.

"Yes," I say, forcing my body to move, my heart to pump, and my eyes to blink.

But Terra just sits. She sits, upright, and stares at the fire, her eyes twitching as she follows the dancing flames, performing for this sad, little crowd. I sigh and sit back.

~

As the moon just tips past midnight and begins its morning descent, Terra eventually lays down and rests her head on her hands. Curling up into the fetal position, I watch as she falls into a rigid sleep.

Seconds pass. Minutes. Even sitting still, it becomes a tremendous effort just to let my eyes sag, and then pull them back up again. As the minutes turn into an hour, the desert remains deathly quiet as even the most nocturnal of animals become weary.

Checking on Terra one last time, I stand, each muscle screaming at me with regret. I take just my pocket knife with me and walk over to the ghost town, looming and ominous, but less eerie. More like a presence in the room. Like an elephant.

I walk up to the first building. Medium-sized, nothing special. I do, however, see a faded, yellow sign, etched with fancy lettering, saying 'Sweet Shoppe'. How absolutely adorable.

The building has no door anyways, so I just waltz in. Moonlight streams in through a grimy window, reflecting off of the particles of dust in the air. Small, round tables and chair stand erect, their cushions long worn away.

A wooden counter sits lonely, deserted. I fill in the blanks with children, sitting at the counter, sucking on bright red lollipops, colorful, not-peeling wallpaper.

Mothers in lavish skirts guiding their children, fathers with their beers and cowboy boots chatting in the corner.

A smiling man at the counter, handing out starlight mints to the wiry-haired, skinny child who comes in every day for a treat.

And music floating in from somewhere. Music, sweet music. Light. Sound. Sight. Swallowing and all-consuming. So easy to get lost in ...

But, like all things, the colors fade, the music stops, and the people die. And all that's left is their remnants, sweet, yet bitter, leaving an impression of lovely but an aftertaste of black licorice. And again, the moonlight registers to my right, still coming in through the window. The creaky floor. The bare tables and chairs. The dark, seedy counter.

I turn on my heel and walk out.

I make it to the next building, and deem that it's nothing but a bank with a lack of money, of course. The next one, however, is obviously a saloon. Stereotypical, sure, but definitely real. It bears the same nostalgic weight that all of the other places had. There's nothing useful, just like the other places. I explore, nonetheless, trying to keep the mounting depression I feel at bay.

A resounding crack sounds under my foot, and before I can move, the rotting wood gives out, and I go down. I brace my hands on the floor, but only one leg went down. My groin is crushed in the folds of wood, and my other leg sits, hyperextended and folded.

Obscenities shoot out of my mouth. I kick blindly at the darkness below me, but I feel nothing. There must be a basement.

Grunting, I push up with my arms to get enough leverage. I finally get my foot under me and push up.

But the force I used to rocket myself up, must have been too much because I go stumbling forward, right into a square table and some chairs. In a hard, angry mess, I tumble to the ground, staring up at the musty ceiling.

Pinned under an old bar table, something seeps up from within me. Ravishing and powerful, writhing like a snake held by its head. It squeezes every ounce of inhibition from me, and claws at the inside of my throat, yearning to get out.

"Fucking shit!" I scream, but the last word is cut off by a harsh sob that tears from my throat. I spring up and push the table off of me, sending it crashing into the wall to my left.

I take off running, but get tangled in the legs of a chair. I hit the ground again, this time, face-first.

"Stop it!" I shout, the words tearing out of my throat. "Just stop it!" With every ounce of exhausted energy in me, I shout these words to the four lonely walls. Sobbing, I drag myself to the opposite wall and feel the hot, angry tears screaming down my face.

Why? Why am I upset? Why am I sobbing? But the anger, the sorrow, the grief is much too real, much too relevant, to ignore any longer. It's right here. It's swallowing, drowning, and all-consuming. It's just me and the unrelenting fact that this is real.

That I am here. That my mother is dead. Dead. She's fucking dead.

No matter how angry I was at her. No matter how much I defied her and hated her and rejected every vile thing she did, she was my mother. No matter how much she forgot about me, how much she neglected me and didn't care, *I* did.

I hate myself for it, too. I hated myself for caring. I hated myself for being so attached to my own mother, even though she never did anything for us. Even though she never did anything a mother was supposed to do. I mean, what else was I supposed to do? Just let everything fall apart?

Despite the vile hate, it all boils down to the fact that burns me alive. That I cared.

But it was all me. I had to hold down the sides of our little tent, flapping in the winds of the storm while my mother did nothing.

And I have to let it go. Or else, I'm afraid it might kill me.

The pain is violent and coursing, sucking up the function of every cell in my being. The desert responds with its own lonely ballad. And it hurts.

But . . . the sobs are releasing. They are satisfying. And finally, I feel the warm glow of peace inside of me.

~

Slowly, I pick myself up off the floor. Sighing, I feel bad for the mess I made, even though no one is here to care. I straighten up the pub, setting the chairs back up, and sneezing because I aroused dust. But when I lift up the square table, however, I find that the corner landed right on the head of an unfortunate jackrabbit. The furry head is completely bashed in, leaving the large, trademark ears intact. the glossy blood and guts stick to the corner of the wood and metal. I grimace, but I am somewhat thankful. This will be food for the next day or so.

Hacking off the head with my machete, I pick up the sufficiently large rabbit by the tail. Terra will be pleasantly surprised.

The peculiar girl is sitting up, rubbing her tired eyes when I come sauntering back over. I toss the beheaded animal at Terra's feet. "Dinner."

December 6, 2010 - Terra

Air jerks in and out of my chest like the mechanical motions of a machine. My chest is being pulled apart and then slammed back together, over and over, as each toxic breath enters my system. Out of the corner of my eye, I see the hot breath curling out of my mouth like gnarling fingers of an old woman as she tries to push her way out of my system. However, each time I inhale, I suck her back into the depths of my soul. These agonizing breaths ring in my ears, drowning out my gripping thoughts.

With each contraction of my leg muscles, the screeching pain spreads, undulating in a perverse rhythm. The panic is like a huge hand, pushing me forward, refusing to let my pumping legs stop. My rapid motion only fuels the fear inside of me, burning like a fire. Every once in awhile, my legs will fail me, and my stomach will lurch forward, threatening to burst out my chest. The hand of panic, however, keeps pushing my crumpled body along, taking no care for the gashes it opens on my face and the way that it crushes my skull. Somehow, every time I fall, I manage to pull myself up again and, then, seeing what's behind me, I panic again and run along with the impending hand.

My hair, whipping around my head like writhing snakes, pokes me in the face and purposefully obstructs my view. The fuzzy blackness ahead blinds me, and like smoke, it coils around my eyes. I break my neck from trying to be free, my arms occupied by trying to pump me forward. But once I whip my head around to look at what's chasing me, the black smoke releases its grip on my eyes, and I can see clearly again. But when I turn back around, panic-filled at what I saw behind me, the choking blackness is ready to blind me again.

It's none of these present things that truly terrify me, though. It's what I'm running from. Elusive, haunting, and yet omnipresent.

This cycle of tripping, looking back and being shoved along and drawn forward is seemingly the only life I know. When I'm drowning in this, it is all consuming, swallowing, drowning . . .

It's not until my legs tangle up like spaghetti for the final time. I am thrust forward, and I skid on the dusty ground, the hand looming over me, grinding me into the ground with shame. Beaten, bloody, and bruised, I refuse to get up. I refuse to run, for my fear of the future is much greater than my fear of the past.

The hand, however, stops - pauses. I roll my head to look up at it. Wrinkly, yet with taut skin that is a flaky gray. Plump, but with rippling muscles that serve no other purpose than to inflict suffering upon me. I can see each and every angular bone, like a poorly assembled swing set. Suddenly, it dives down and coils itself around me and jerks me around, until the smoke is to my back and I am facing the monster in all of its pathetic glory.

And I am struck with a new breed of terror, because the horribly disfigured monster who was terrorizing me, chasing me, swallowing me whole, is him. My rapist.

~

Still feeling that terrifying grip on my forearm, I jolted awake. Sweat drenched my body like a thick, wet film. Red dawn streamed in through my curtains, and I gripped the sheets.

It's not real, Terra, it's not real.

Nearly hyperventilating, I stared up at my ceiling and forced myself to breathe - slowly and surely.

I jumped again when Nick poked his head in my room. "You okay? I heard you scream," he said.

"Yeah, sorry," I said, sitting up and kicking my feet over the side of my bed. Although I had woken up only minutes ago, I felt as awake as I ever could have been.

I pressed my lips together. "Where's Mom and Dad?"

"Where do you think? Working their asses off. It's the weekend, you know," Nick said, leaning his awkward teenage body against the doorframe.

I swallowed hard, a longing reaching out within me. "Yeah."

H pulled out his phone, clicked some buttons. "You still going out with Grandma today?"

"Yeah."

"Well, if you need anything, I'll be around," he said, glancing down.

"Thanks," I said, earnestly.

Nick slowly clicked the door shut behind him.

Sighing and rattled to my core, I picked up my phone and called Harper. It rang for a while before she finally picked up.

"Hey." Her voice was deep and rough.

"Hi. You don't sound too great."

"I'm not. Dad lost his job again." Aside, she commented. "Damn, that man can't keep a job for more than a year."

"I know. Sorry." I swallowed.

"Don't apologize," she mused.

"Well, it's my day off. Do you want to hang out before I go to my grandma's house?" I said, feeling already more at peace and wandering into the kitchen.

"Heck yeah. Anything to get away from my family right now."

I scoffed. We hung up.

I ate breakfast in silence since Sundays were busy days for the lodge and I graciously got the day off.

Twenty minutes later, Harper was at the door, her glossy black hair tousled violently by the wind and her bike helmet.

Groveling, I hugged her anyway and welcomed her in. She flopped down at the breakfast table.

"I can't wait until your grandma gets here. She's always so chill," Harper said, rubbing her fingers against her temples. "So why did you call me today in the first place?"

I stopped, the cereal in my mouth turning to dust. "I just, I had a dream and I thought you could help me."

"Well, sorry for being so selfish," Harper said, snorting and helping herself.

I didn't say anything. She could be that way.

"No, really. Talk to me, Terra," she said, peeling her orange.

"It was just another nightmare–"

I halted when I saw that look that Harper always gave me when we discussed this issue. In reality, only she and my family knew. While it can be an overbearing burden, like a floodlamp I constantly had to hide from people, talking about it with Harper helped. A little.

"Yeah," I confirmed her suspicions, and she drew back.

Empathetically, she squeezed my hand. "That doesn't make or break you, Terra, you know that, right?"

"I know. You tell me that almost every time we talk about this," I said, trying to lighten the matter.

Harper got up to butter her toast. "I guess we all need to be reminded these things every once in awhile."

"Like how you think your dad doesn't care about you guys because he is so bad at being responsible."

She threw a handful of orange peel at me, and I ducked. I guess that was a little too soon.

But I was thankful regardless. At least I could talk to her about these things.

~

Grandma arrived at 10 am sharp, knocking on the small front door. After forcing Harper to change into something a bit less disheveled, I ran to the door.

"Hey!" I said, a smile immediately plastering itself on my face.

Grandma Abigail smiled and scooped me up in her arms, despite me being nearly as tall as her at age twelve.

I let her in and she asked, "How have you been?"

"Okay."

"That's not a very strong reaction," she said, smiling.

"Well, at least it's an honest one," I said.

Grandma squeezed my shoulders and smiled, but said nothing. Harper came out of my room, looking much better.

"Oh yeah, can Harper come?"

~

The ride to the botanical gardens was short and sweet - Grandma let us listen to our music, and even pretended to like it. But otherwise, we arrived at the Phoenix Botanical Gardens with ease.

It was on the west side of town, far away from the noise and pollution from the city and closer to our suburban outskirt. It was mostly an independent organization, with sculptures and small little benches and gazebos, and a man-made stream flowed through the garden like veins. It had to, since five acres of desert are barred off for this garden. Partially, it was informational and educational, and while I loved learning about the world around us, I loved it because the place was teeming with beauty: majestic and winding and, although inanimate, just as alive and breathing as you or me.

We paid and got in, getting a small paper bracelet. Speeding through the greenhouse, we breathed in the fresh air. Waterfalls danced over rocks, and small weeds sprang up, fat with water and fruit. Dense, soft bushes with dainty yellow flowers provided for a small path leading through the garden. Tall, hard trunked trees bursting with desert fruits weaved through the blue, dappled sky above us. Thick Savannah grasses waved in the wind, and small animals, lizards, bugs and rodents alike scampered through the garden. Cacti of all varieties sprung up like regal kings. This whole place was like taking the Sonoran desert and compacting it down, removing all of the sparse places and accentuating the great parts. This place never ceased to amaze me.

The garden captivated me, pulling me out of my shitty life and transporting me to another, unscathed and exquisite, yet different than being in a fancy, rich place. This place was alive and resilient - my footprints in the sand would be gone in hours.

And it was here, with the two people that I loved most, that I could truly lose each fragment of myself completely in the beauty, so that I could find them all again.

~

Later, we sat, swinging in a bench, kicking our feet and thinking. At least, I was thinking.

I found myself standing and picking a flower and bringing it up to my nose. Harper remained on the bench, relaxing while Grandma rose.

Grandma Abigail (Abby, as we called her sometimes) was a small woman with curly, faintly blonde hair and soft, blue eyes, but the woman herself defied her small, feminine features. She was feisty and more alive than any other adult I had met. Tenacious and dreamy, Abigail was ready and up for anything my childlike mind could propose - when I was with her, the world was at our fingertips. She kept me dreaming and I kept her young.

Sundays were our day. Sometimes, like today, Harper would tag along, mostly because her grandparents were either dead or didn't care. At least not like mine did.

Grandma and I wandered off down the path lined with either stones or savannah grasses, waving under our feet.

Suddenly, Grandma broke away from our walk and to a plant along the side - a thick brush, like something that, once it died, would become a tumbleweed. Rustling with her hands for a moment, I craned over and tried to look.

She turned back around and opened up her calloused hands to reveal a vibrant cicada, sending out its shrill call. Large, bulbous eyes that looked like they might pop and delicate wings weaved with silver that barely looked like they could carry its fat body. Crawling on its segmented legs, it spread its wings and flew off, landing on a tree.

"The cicada," she said, then paused. "Do you hear that? That 'hhhm-ahmm' noise?"

Suddenly, I heard it and the chorus of insect noises swelled around me.

"That's a cicada. Hundreds of them just in this garden probably," she said, and then leaned down onto the ground to pick up something. "Just waiting to be devoured by little guys like this one." And my Grandma came up and was holding a tarantula the size of my palm.

My core rattling with horror, I stepped back ever so slightly.

"See, they're not so bad. As long as you keep it moving and don't threaten it, it won't hurt you," she said, letting the spider crawl across the back of her hand, the other hand coming up just in time to keep the spider from falling off. The thing was dark and textured, the coarse hairs flattened against its squishy body, moving with ease and nonchalance across her hand.

"Would you like to hold it?" she asked.

"Not particularly," I said, the disgust evident in my voice.

"I'll be right here. We can do it slowly, if you'd like," she said, her expert hands moving carefully and swiftly to let the thing crawl over the back of my hand. With each step of its padded and tickly feet, a chill ran up my arm. But the thing took no care to the hand it was walking on. It only moved with the supple shape of my hand and back onto Grandma's.

"That wasn't so bad, was it?" she said, smirking at me.

"No, I guess not," I admitted, smirking and still rattled with nerves regardless.

Putting the spider down and letting it slowly meander away, Grandma came up beside me, wrapping her arm around me and squeezing my shoulder.

"Like always, there's a lesson to be learned here," Grandma said, her voice wise and aged like fine wine.

"Like always," I smiled.

"Take chances, Terra. Make mistakes, because nothing is so terribly messed up that it can't be fixed."

Nothing is so terribly messed up that it can't be fixed.

These words rang true in my mind, and their tendrils reached far beneath the realization surface and grasped my heart.

How? How could something of this nature be true? I wanted to believe it so hard, and so much. I needed it.

Suddenly, I stopped. Grandma Abigail also paused, looking at me, and she came over close to me, looking me straight in the eye, and said what I hadn't heard in years.

"I love you, Terra."

CHAPTER FIVE: Dissection
DAY 3 - Terra; August 7th, 2015

I turn the skewer over the fire to cook the other side of the jackrabbit. Fat drips off, arousing the flames. My jaw pops as I yawn.

I look over to Wyatt. He sits there, his knees up to his chest, as if a flaming firework might explode out of him any moment. Shaking slightly. His eyes bore deep into the fire, as if he desires to control it.

"Say something," he says, his voice tearing out from his strained vocal chords.

"What?" I ask.

"Terra, say something. Please." It bursts from him in a way I haven't seen before. An insane desperation teeters on his lips.

My eyes widen. I'm bad at this stuff. What does he want me to say?

"One time I stole a barrette from my friend."

"Seriously? That's all you've got?" he shoots back. It bites, and the primal flesh inside of me wants to tear away from him.

"Well, you asked me to say something, and I did."

"Then continue," he says, lacking everything that makes him human.

A numbness rises within me, starting at the back of my head and spreading over my body. I travel to a simpler place, a simpler time.

"I had this one friend. She wasn't like a best friend or anything. One of those friends you have for a season, you know?"

He nods in assent, still dead-focused on the fire before him.

"Well, so I slept over at her house, and we were playing with each other's hair that night, and she had this barrette that was shaped like a piece of candy with pink and blue rhinestones on it, and, being the nine year old I was, I fell in love with it. So when we were undoing our hair to go to bed, I took it out and put it in a place where I would remember it."

I smile just a little, gazing out deep into the desert. The valor inside of me kicks at the numbness.

"So, the next morning, when we were packing up to leave, when my friend wasn't in her room, I just took the barrette. I just took it and stuffed it deep inside my bag."

I find myself laughing. "And, heck, I maybe used that barrette twice outside of that instance. Then I lost it because I was - and still am - terribly scatterbrained."

I dig my toe into the sand and smirk. Each and every second plays out in my mind like muscle memory. I am drowning, losing myself in the past, and hell, it feels good. "But for the longest time, the guilt ate away at me. That was the one single 'illegal' thing I had consciously done at the time. I was just like 'holy crap I actually stole something from someone'. Of course, it wasn't actually a big deal, and I don't think the my friend ever actually noticed."

I hear a breathy laugh from Wyatt. He pulls me, head-first, out of the past, and into the cold, slamming reality. But his muscles have relaxed and the light has returned to his eyes.

"Did that help?" Suddenly, a chill runs up and down my arms. I feel exposed, open, raw to the biting wind, like a dissected frog open for Wyatt's inspection.

"Yeah."

There's a good, long nothing for a while.

I turn the rabbit and decide that it's done. I hand Wyatt a leg, and he sits back on a boulder. I never noticed that before. My eyes follow a zig-zag pattern of rocks that increase in size, up until the rocks turn into small mountains . . . and then actual mountains. The only reason I can tell is because the stars abruptly stop, forming the silhouette of these mountains, as black as the sky.

I stare down at the browned meat. Wyatt has already dug into his. Food helps blood sugar, blood sugar helps mood.

"You looking forward to climbing that?" Wyatt asks, chowing through his rabbit leg. My stomach screams at me to eat, but I just can't bring myself to it. So hungry, I'm not anymore.

"No," I say, looking down.

"Yeah, I mean, think of all of the animals that could be in there," Wyatt says, swinging his almost-bare rabbit leg in the air. "Cougars, foxes, coyotes, huge, carnivorous birds . . ."

"Snakes," I cut in, finally taking a bite of my meat. Still sizzling, grease drips down my chin, and the rabbit is tough but succulent.

"You don't like snakes?" Wyatt asks.

"Oh, God no. Who does?" I say, shuddering. I push the irrational fear from me as I stare out at the barren desert, the brush wavering in the cool, night wind. The small, shrubby plants look like thick, short hairs, held in ugly clumps, maybe even by a pink and blue rhinestoned barrette.

Every once in awhile, I'll see the smooth top of a rock, but my mind wanders to all of the things under the rocks. Scorpions breeding, lizards in the crevices, and a snake's hole under the shaded, damp shadow.

"Wyatt, it's your turn to talk about something," I say, whipping back around to face him so hard I think I might snap my neck.

"Oh, uh, okay," he says, visibly thinking. "Have you ever played 'Never Have I Ever'?"

"Who hasn't?" I say, still trying to distract myself. I run my fingers through my bangs, which had previously fallen in my face.

"Alright, I'll ask first. Never have I ever flown in a plane previous to this," Wyatt says, holding up his rabbit leg triumphantly, his face glowing in the firelight. The heavy mood around us dampers.

"Sucks for this to have been your first experience." He nods. I take a big, proud bite of my rabbit leg, savoring every bite. Okay, I guess I did need food. "I flew up to Montana to visit family, and other vacations out east. And besides, my family owns this business. Okay, never have I ever liked coffee."

Wyatt peers at me, eyes sparkling and mouth ajar. "What? I'd kill for a cup of warm, rich coffee right now."

"Eh, I like tea."

Wyatt gnaws on his rabbit meat. "Pretentious ass."

I smirk, letting the good feelings bubble to the surface. "Correct."

Wyatt adjusts himself, sitting up. "Alright." A devilish smile crawls to his face. "Never have I ever had sex." And then takes a little nibble. "I, uh, made it to second base once."

The question pulls me up short. Do I count The Worst Night of My Life as sex? Would I call what I had with Adam, my childhood friend, as second base?

I can feel my knees clenching together, the blood rushing to my cheeks. Sighing, I take a small piece of meat. Trying so viciously hard to laugh it off, I say, "second base as well."

Smirking at me, he says, "Your turn. Ask something."

I snap out of it. "Oh, uh . . . never have I ever . . . been arrested."

Wyatt purses his lips and me and guiltily raises the leg to his mouth, and bites.

My jaw drops. "Seriously?" I scoot in closer, enthralled.

"Yep," he says, shaking his head. "I . . . get into a lot of fights." He scratches his blond curls and looks down. Redness pushes through his sandy freckles. He's embarrassed.

Laughter finally breaks through my oppressing emotions. Finally. Laughter bubbles inside of me like sugary fizz, and once it gets started, I can't get it to stop. I laugh and laugh and laugh, falling back onto the desert sand and dropping my half-eaten rabbit leg into the sand. Tears sting at my eyes, but they aren't acidic with grief - they're toxic with glee. Wyatt eventually stops being mad and joins in with me, our howling laughter reaching out past the arms of the Milky Way in the sky.

Everything seems so far away. The crash, centuries ago. My father's death, a lifetime away. I am just here, present, in the moment, laughing around a makeshift fire with a person I've known a total of four days. Each piece of my soul is laughing at the fact that Wyatt Hartman, at some point in his life, was actually arrested by actual policeman and put in actual jail. And that, I must admit, is pretty damn hilarious for some reason.

~

When I awaken, the heat from the fire still pulsates warmth onto my frozen face. I push myself up on my hands and shove the hair out of my eyes. The sun shines down with white, warm light, not yet scorching as it evaporates the cold night. Everything that appeared ominous is normal and if not cheery in the daylight. Non-threatening and overwhelmingly normal.

I look past the smoldering coals to Wyatt, peaceful and sound asleep. Whoops, I guess we fell asleep at some point after picking that rabbit clean.

Packing up my stuff and kicking at the coals, I wait until Wyatt awakens. Slowly, he sits up and rubs his eyes. "Good morning, Sparkles."

I stop. Sparkles. Why is he calling me 'Sparkles'? "What?"

Wyatt looks up at me. "I said, 'Good morning, Sparkles'."

I shake my head, a pulsing growing like a tumor in my brain. "But why did you call me 'Sparkles'?"

He visibly hesitates, scratching his head. "Uh, I don't know. It just kind of came out ... "

I lick my lips and stare into the ground. I sift through meaningless puzzle pieces until one stands out. Distinctly, Wyatt's voice wafts through my memory.

"You and your friend Sparkles here," he said, gesturing to me as the alleged 'Sparkles'. "Need to calm your tits. Remember that we're paying you guys."

I took a deep breath. I've had to deal with some nasty customers before, but none quite like Wyatt Hartman.

~

We walk the short mile or so to the base of the rocks. Wyatt stands, staring up, and up, and up. I eye him, waiting for his reaction

He sighs and looks over at me. I immediately advert my eyes and stare at the slabs of rock, carved away by the bully of the elements: water.

The rocks themselves are a rich sandy-orange color, with deep, purple shadows in the early morning light. Ragged stairs climb up the sandstone walls, making a monochrome rainbow, laying horizontal on the rocky ground. Monumental pillars of stone jut up into the sky, pensive and assured.

I reach over and press my hand to the rock wall, closest to me. Each little bump and crease rest under the pads of my fingers. The stone is gritty, like poorly smoothed concrete, and when I pull my hand away, some dust and sand remains on my fingers.

"Well, there's no time like the present," Wyatt says, and reaches up and grabs onto a ledge above him.

"Be careful," the words bursting out of my mouth before I have time to think. Putting my hand up to my lips, I bite my tongue, and I realize that I only said that because fear dawns on me like the scorching sun climbing up the sky.

"I will," Wyatt says. He hoists himself up on the first rock, steadying himself.

I stare at the slabs of sedimentary rock, which appear to be just jagged stripes of dark and light running across this vertical wall. Sighing, I rest my hand on a ledge above my head. I find a sturdy place for my feet, and look up. Climbing precariously, Wyatt glances down at me and winks. I muster a smile back.

Swallowing hard, I force myself to climb steadily upward, taking it step by step, to the top of the first crest.

~

Walking is mind-numbing, to say the least. At least then my mind had the reins while my body trudged onward. I am able to entertain myself with my stream of consciousness, however dark and deep it reached.

But here, placing one hand or foot above the other, finding purchase, and pushing against gravity takes every ounce of willpower I have. I have no room to let my mind wander because a broken rock or a slippery hand means a snapped neck, forty feet below.

The only thing I am able to focus on is the mechanical motions of climbing - moving my right hand off, and up to another outcropping, moving the opposite foot up to a ledge, moving my left hand up, followed by my right foot. And repeat. And repeat and repeat and repeat until I finally reach the top, where Wyatt pulls me up.

The outcropping where we stand is a mere two feet wide, and even then, boulders and anomalies litter the path. I lean back onto the next rock wall, feeling my breath tickle the back of my raw throat.

"Water?" Wyatt says, holding out a freshly opened water can. Sweat shines on his face and forms a small T shape on his chest and back.

"Definitely," I say, and Wyatt hands me the can. Absently, I chug half of it, barely tasting the liquid life restoring my body. I shove the can back at Wyatt so I don't suck the thing dry, heaving with exhaustion. My muscles clench and ache. I'm definitely going to be sore.

Uncomfortable sweat pools in the creases of my underarm, inner elbow, and back of my knees. The dripping sweat tickles the canyon between my breasts, and the curve of my back like small, childlike fingers wavering over my skin. The heat makes my muscles twitch.

Laying my head back on the rocks, I stare up at the pale blue sky, like a sheer, periwinkle curtain. The only hole is where the sun pushes out.

The world blurs before me as I space out. I half-heartedly focus on a black, wavering spot high up in the sky. Probably a lost little fly come to scavenge. The black spot moves mostly in a straight line, coming from the left, and inching across the sky.

I shake my head to remove the blur from my vision. The blackish object is a lot further away than I had originally thought, and it has a small tail for its plump body . . . and something spins on top of the bulbous object.

That's when I see the metal runners glinting in the sunlight. As the realization moves like molasses through my brain, my jaw turns to mush, and I blindly reach over and grab for Wyatt.

He comes over, confusion marring his face, but I can't take my eyes off of the flying machine in the sky.

"What?" he asks, with just a hint of urgency.

For some reason, all of my anticipation is caught in an angry knot in my throat. Excitement and thick anticipation all push and shove for a way out, but my lips and tongue flap uselessly.

"Is that . . . a helicopter?" Wyatt says, eyes widening in awe. "Hey!" he shouts. "Hey! Hey! Down here!" Wyatt yells, waving his arms and jumping up and down.

Wyatt continues shouting as the helicopter flies across the sky and as my breathing quickens. I can't say anything. The emotions are so gripping, so real, so strong, I can't breathe, I can't think, I can't move.

Suddenly, the tendons and ligaments in my throat rip apart, and sound tears out of my mouth. "Hey!" I shout, shaking.

"Hey!! We're down here!" Screaming, I can feel my throat and airways vibrate painfully. I jump up and down frantically, no longer caring whether I'll fall and break my neck.

But even through our ear shattering screams and comical flailing, the helicopter continues to inch across the sky, stretching the hundreds of thousands of miles between us. I can feel a deep part of my soul tearing, seething, yearning for hope in the shape of a helicopter to come soaring back.

As the helicopter continues to rip out of sight, my cries for help morph into whimpers of despair. "No . . . no . . . " I am barely aware of the words spilling out of my mouth. Sinking to my knees, my insides writhe and clench up in anguish. Hot tears squeeze out of my eyes. Caustic frustration hijacks my entire body, wrapping like fingers around my neck. "Please . . . please . . . come . . . back . . . " I squeak out, but then, as hope flies out of the sky, all of the boiling anger is sucked out of my body, and I am left with the stark pain of hopelessness and abandonment.

Sobs rack my body in waves, and from afar, Wyatt's coarse swearing hits my ears. And we sit, alone, as the mechanical whipping sound of the helicopter disappears into oblivion.

Hopelessness suffocates me like a sadistic mother, holding a pillow over a child's head while tucking them in. I sob and gasp for air, drowning in my own emotions. Wyatt's despair emanating off of him is palpable, as he lashes out at anything around him.

It's not fucking fair.

Suddenly, I feel fingers digging into the flesh of my arms. I peel my eyes open and squint at Wyatt, facing me. A gentle, but stern look is etched onto his face.

"We have to keep going," he commands.

"No," I whimper. "I can't. We should follow the-"

"Yes, you can," he grunts, shoving his arms under mine and yanking my body upwards.

I moan, feeling the angst rush through me. Once I am standing up straight, Wyatt suddenly wraps his arms around me and pulls me into his embrace. Even though I push and fight, he remains steadfast.

Eventually, I open myself up and fall into his embrace. The crying comes, but softer this time. That was a helicopter. With actual people who could have actually saved us. But just as fast as it came, it vanished like a puff of smoke.

Wyatt begins to sniff as well. He must have just realized that all hope is lost, too.

~

Eventually, the mountains cease, and we are met with another ravine. No, not a ravine, a canyon. By the gritty, dusty surface, it reminds me of a lopsided ceramic bowl that has yet to be glazed.

And in this stark, crater lays a smooth pool of water, pale blue and reflecting the sky, concealed by lush plants and tall, wide trees, bursting with green, like a drop of rain forest.

"No. Way," Wyatt says in awe, the wind rustling his curls. My mouth gapes open, too stunned to speak. I've only seen one of these before, in a state park. But here it is: an anomaly in the thick rock and warm, ground water boils up, blooming like a flower into an oasis.

"Well, what are we waiting for?" I say, and Wyatt bounds ahead of me as we precariously slide down the rock incline and run across the bottom of the ravine.

Before we're even near the grove of plants, we begin tearing our clothes off. The shoes are the first to go. I unwrap my jacket and let it flow in the wind. Lastly, Wyatt's shirt comes off, and he waves it like a surrender flag.

I can see the cool water coming closer, glimmering like a mirror, a slice of heaven in a stretch of hell. We push through the lush growth and break into the blue pool.

A gleeful "woo hoo!" erupts out of Wyatt's mouth as he ricochets off of a rock and into the deep waters. I push past the plants and lean over, sticking my face full in the crystalline water and suck back gulps. It's unnervingly warm, like everything in this baked-potato of a place, but it's nourishing to the cracks in my lips and the sunburn on my skin.

"C'mon! The water's warm, the air is fine! Get in, Terra!" Wyatt says, throwing his hands up in the air.

Gulping, I lift my head up, wiping my mouth. I drop to my knees in exhaustion. Damn, that water feels good. But still, I glance at Wyatt. "That's not very smart, Wyatt."

"So?" He says, smirking.

"We should fill up our cans and see if we can gather food here, and wash our clothes . . ."

"We can do that later," he insists.

"Fine," I say, and get on my bottom, and ease my feet into the water. Again, the water is pure, boiling hot, and feels mildly of sweat, but it's water nonetheless.

I lean back onto the sand, and my head plops onto a rock. Grunting, I look back up at Wyatt, who I find staring at me. I look away quickly, but his brown sugar eyes are still there, floating in my mind.

"Come on," Wyatt says. "Get in. Not only will it cool us off, but we'll get a wash as well."

He's right. Playing right into my weakness, I dip myself in. The water soothes the sunburns my searing skin.

"Don't you think we should hurry? It's getting dark. And cold," I say, pulling myself out of the warm water. A gust of chilly night air comes, striking my body like a baseball bat, and I quickly sink back in.

Wyatt dunks his head under the water and runs his fingers through his curls. They drape around his face, already coiling as the water drips down his face and onto his chest . . . He looks at me, a smirk plastered on his lips. "Nah," he shrugs. "We might as well take advantage of this 'oasis' thing while we have the chance." Wyatt then smirks, pointing a finger at me. "Because, as you know, you only live once."

A groan bubbles inside of me, but a smile crawls over my lips. I roll my eyes and say "You live every day. You die once." But something else pulses inside of me. Something that boils with awkwardness and pinches with something I can't identify.

Wyatt rolls his eyes and snorts. "That's not the point." He scoops up a handful of the clear water and tosses it at me. I reel back, squealing with laughter. My outer layer simmers with playfulness, but something about this, I'm not sure of.

Oh, hell. I push the heel of my hand forward across the top of the water, spraying some water at Wyatt. He cringes but comes back around a second later.

"Oh, it's on!" he says, pushing off of the rocks to get up and attack me. He cups his hands and flings them forward. The cool droplets soak my frame. I back out of the water, my cargo pants clinging to my legs. I squeal and kick my legs in the water. An arc of water flies into Wyatt, but he grabs my ankles.

Laughing gleefully, I scoot on my butt across the sand as Wyatt pushes his dripping figure out of the water. He takes one last launch at me with the water in the spring, but I'm too far out.

"Not fair!" he calls out, still grinning.

"Is too!" I cry, and a guilty feeling as sweet as syrup fills me. I haven't acted like this in a long time, but it sure does feel astonishingly good. I feel it pulsing through me like light. Damn it, maybe I do like it.

Wyatt's smile turns from adrenaline-fueled glee to tight-lipped and cocky. Uh-oh.

He's fully out of the water now, shirtless and dripping and utterly powerful with bubbling energy. "Oh, I see how it is," he says, charging toward my damp figure.

I squeal and make it to my feet before Wyatt grabs me by the torso and picks all five-foot-eight of me and carries me over to the spring. Damn, I didn't know he was that strong. I scream as he tosses me into the spring like a rag doll. I plunge into the deepest depths of the spring, and the dark blue water encompasses me. I am just about to come up when I realize that Wyatt never let go of me. He just jumped right into the water with me.

And so there we stay, suspended under the water, half naked, in an oasis in remote Arizona where only our screams answer us back and the only souls to hear us are the stars, just poking their heads out from behind the setting sun. His eyes are a striking soft brown as they appear only inches from my own icy blue eyes, probably muddled by the water. He laughs slightly, and silvery bubbles escape from his mouth and nose and float up to the Saran-wrap like surface of the water.

Wyatt eventually pulls me up, and we gasp for air. A weird, hard feeling pokes my gut. I feel odd, like a flower blooming overnight. I wade over to the rocks and grab on, panting. This pool must be at least twenty feet deep. My legs kick at nothing. And the water is sweet and warm, and increasingly so. Or maybe that's just me.

Wyatt swims over to another rock and pulls himself up. He laughs a little, running his hands through his hair and eyeing me. "You really need to get out more often."

"Hey," I protest. "It's not like we're in the middle of the desert or anything. Cut me some slack." I pull myself out of the water and wring the bottom of my cargo pants. No need to clean those anymore. No need to clean anything anymore, really.

"You're so funny," Wyatt says, completely, deadpan, drying himself off with his shirt and then putting it back on. I try my hardest not to look.

"Don't look," I say, turning around. I crane my neck around to check and see if Wyatt has his back turned. He does, so I pull off my wet tank shirt.

"Why not?" he says a second later.

I yank the soaking shirt back down around me. "Excuse me?" I say, horrified. I turn around to check, but Wyatt hasn't moved. I still see the back of his cocky head.

"I'm joking. I won't look," he says, giving his head a good shake. Water droplets shower down.

I press my lips together and pull off my tank shirt once more. Even out here, I'm self-conscious that someone will see me naked. It's not until I'm done wringing my shirt out over the spring that I realize that I kind of wanted Wyatt to look.

And then again, I didn't.

I slip off my pants and wring those out, section by section. I feel a sense of guilty euphoria, like it was so wrong, swimming with him, even when there was nothing sexuall about it. But nothing happened . . . and I wouldn't let anything happen, right? But I wanted something to happen. Sure, I can say that I want to keep my virginity when there's not a half-naked, soaking wet teenage boy who wants to swim with me. And when there's not a soul around to nitpick my actions.

However, my mind wanders to how infinite I felt, in that split second under the water, Wyatt's arms wrapped around me. I clench my jaw shut as I twist my pant leg with a painful fervency, and the water comes spilling out. I can hear my father saying to me something he would always say when I would talk to my parents about boys and my feelings: "I'm so sorry that you like boys. We suck, don't we?" And I would always cringe and blush and get a little frustrated, but still feel those butterflies in the hollow of my stomach.

Tears well up in my eyes, as I remember that I'll never hear that husky voice again. That when I do find a steady boyfriend, he won't be there to remind me of that. And when I get married, he won't be there to walk me down the aisle . . . . Anger and bitter pain expand into a hard knot in my chest, crowding out my lungs. I close my eyes and two hot tears fall out I breathe in through my nose, and out through my mouth until the lump slowly unravels.

My knuckles have turned white against the muted greenish fabric of my cargo pants. I release my mostly dry pants. I sigh and put them back on, button them up and put all my stuff back in the pockets. "Okay, I'm done," I say to Wyatt.

He turns around. "Finally," he says, smiling crookedly. "What took you so long?"

Peeling my lips back into an utterly fake smile - he can tell - I lug my backpack over my shoulder. I peek over some rocks and see that only three-fourths of the sun still hangs in the limbo of the sky.

The orange afterglow is slowly being taken over by its deep blue-black counterpart. I look back up at Wyatt and wring out my knotted ponytail. The blue-black bruise on his head wound mixes in with the darkness creeping over the rocks like smoke. He is in the process of trying to squeeze his damp feet into his dry socks. A line of blood trickles down his temple amidst the water. His head wound has opened up again, but he hasn't noticed.

I take off my backpack and lick my lips. Already, I feel thirsty, even though I was just basking in water. It seems as if my conflicting feelings and thoughts have come to a head. I go over to Wyatt and stand by him.

"Your head wound has opened up again," I say, genuinely concerned.

"It's alright," he says. "It needs some air anyways."

"You sure?" I ask, raising my eyebrows.

"I'm sure," he says earnestly, dismissing me and doing something else.

I stand up and put my backpack on. The hard feeling returns, but as cold and as limitless as the sea. I just don't understand. A deep longing stretches out in me, for my father. God, I wish he was here. But he's not. He's six feet under by the carcass of his own plane.

And like the clear ringing of a bell, my psyche recoils back, back into the deep recesses of my soul where it can stay, protected and safe.

I am going to be kind to Wyatt. I'll going to be cordial to him. I'll travel with him until we make it back. But I am not going to get connected to him. I am not going to feel any feelings for him. I'm not going to flirt with him, or even talk to him too much. I'll tolerate him, I'll live with him, but I will not like him. That's not what this is about. This is about surviving and an ultimate goal. I tighten my ponytail stoically, feeling somehow justified in my unrighteous self-protection.

CHAPTER SIX: The Impossibility of the Unknown
DAY 3 - Wyatt; August 7th, 2015

Terra dips an empty can into the warm spring water. I watch as the silver air bubbles up while I rub my dirty shirt against a wet rock. I work on cleaning the clothes as best I can with no soap, and Terra collects water and food.

The sun hangs plump like an orange in the purple sky, and air grows cool as it weaves in between the underbrush. I sit back and watch the sun sink beneath the high horizon.

After finishing the clothes, I pick at the food Terra is gathering. She frowns at me, but waves me off regardless.

Terra sighs and sits down next to me, gathering up the food in a piece of cloth and tying it. "I'll keep first watch."

"Nah," I say. "We seem safe here. I'll watch first, only for a few hours. Then you, and then we can both sleep until the morning."

Terra looks at me, a solemn expression carved on her face. "Okay," is all she says.

Terra spends many a minute getting situated, but finally, she curls up next to the rocks, on her back, and stares up at the stars. It takes her about an hour to drift off to sleep, but she eventually does.

I breathe a sigh of relief, my warm breath hitting the cool air. The plants flop in the cool night air, swirling around in this crater like a tornado. I see the sides of the rocks, climbing up the sky into mountains all around us.

I lean my head back onto a rock, seeing the stars twinkle at me, almost accusingly. They are free, however I am trapped. Trapped inside myself. Trapped in this desert, yet free to be lost wherever I please. My fingers fiddle with a few dull leaves.

As the stars brighten in the sky, my breathing slows and becomes heavy, like I am coated in lead, and my respiratory system is an old, creaky machine.

Seconds . . . minutes . . . hours pass. My wandering thoughts are loud, fighting against the lulling desert sounds. Over these long days, these sounds fill my ears, as if I am listening to old friends chat about their lives.

I find myself pulling my eyelids open every few minutes, but finally, the stars disappear for good.

~

The plane engine rumbles, coughing up dark black smoke. The glass is cold against my finger, and the clouds tumble around my vision.

I look to my left and see Terra there, her face like a Greek bust. I reach over and touch her, but, again, it's electric and cold, like the glass. I still hear the plane engine, the smoke traveling into my ears and strangling my thoughts into oblivion.

The pilot's seat is empty, the wheel shuddering back and forth with the turbulence of the wind. The engines scream, but the plane cabin is silent. I find myself floating up out of my seat, and touching the smooth, grooved leather of the equipment.

Bright, white light streams in through all of the windows. Bright, but not blinding. My eyes do not squint against this odd, soft light. I feel the leather between my tingling fingers, and take a deep breath.

Suddenly, something warm and wet drips down my forehead, onto the side of my nose, and dribbles over my lips. I look away from the windshield for an instant to feel the hot blood dripping out of my head, but when I look back, the scorching ground appears beneath me in the windshield.

My body coursing with panic, I immediately pull up on the yoke, but nothing happens. I pound on buttons, rip off nobs, brake levers, but not a damn thing happens.

The ground leeches closer and closer. I can feel gravity gaining a grip on me as the plane falls and falls and falls. The ground and the nose of the plane collide like crashing cymbals.

~

And that's when I wake up.

Electricity jolts through my body. All at once, I become aware of my surroundings again. The rocks under my palms, the spiky, cool air around me, and the screaming silence of the desert. Cool air sucks painfully into my lungs, and reality swallows me. I sit up and look out into the dry desert, alone and dark.

Terra stirs next to me, and slowly sits up. I forgot she was there, yet I am still haunted by her marbled appearance in the dream.

"Sorry," I mumble, unfriendly anger seeping into my voice.

"No, it's fine," Terra says, rubbing her eyes. "It's not like I was really sleeping anyways."

I shrug, my feelings exposed like a carcass left to rot in the heat. After a moment, I turn back over away from Terra.

I hear her move over towards me. "What happened?" she says, her voice temperate. Unreadable and disconnected, as usual.

"Nothing," I hiss, curling up.

Terra audibly sighs. "Fine then. Suit yourself."

"Yeah, maybe I will," I shoot back. I'm not sure why I'm being so defensive. I guess it just comes naturally.

"I had a dream," I blurt. Terra looks at me, intrigued and wanting me to continue. "It was about the crash."

"Mmm," Terra says, nodding. "Yeah." She pauses for a moment, before opening up. "Did you remember anything important? Like where exactly we crashed? Or why?"

I shake my head. The owls hoot in response.

But I eventually speak. "Why do you think that is?"

"Trauma, maybe," she says. I reach up and gingerly touch my head, still wet with blood.

"I'll get that," she says, reaching out.

I cringe, turning away. "Don't touch my face."

Terra draws back, like she always does. "Why do you hate me?" Her voice is sharp and caustic, like a rusty nail. But then she looks down, away, shaking her head.

"I . . . I don't hate you," I say, rubbing my temple.

Terra sits back, sighing, furrowing her brow. "Then why do you act like it?" she says, her voice softening. "You know, I'd like to not die out here, and you're making that kind of hard for us." She laughs spitefully.

I shrug, trying to avoid her convicting gaze. "Because I don't want to be here. Because this sucks." I pause, thinking of whether I want the words to come out. "Because I finally got what I wanted - which was to get away from my life, from my family, from my mother, and it worked."

"And I hate it." My voice chokes up, like strained ropes, so I stop, and bat the tears away from my eyes.

Endless empathy collects in Terra's eyes, but in no way is it condescending. The truth is finally coming out, and it burns me like acid.

"I . . . I wanted to get away too," Terra says, matter-of-fact. "I had no idea what I was doing with my life, where I was going. I still don't. But, then this happened."

"So, you think this is a good thing?" I say, sniffing, and finding myself hanging on to every word.

Terra sighs, deep and strung out, like a fishing line chasing its prey. "I never said that. I wish things were different, but, maybe this is all for a reason."

"Bullshit," I say.

"Think about it: when we get back, we could be on TV." Terra sits up and holds up her bag, eyeing my head wound. I reach up to touch it, but Terra grabs my hand.

"It'll get infected," she snaps.

I sigh as Terra dips her hands into the spring water and pours it over my head. The cool water is nice as it runs down my face. I can tell that we're running low on bandages, because Terra takes an old one and cleans it in the water and lets it dry, then wraps it around my head, tying a knot in the gauze - much less clean this time. But I can't complain.

It's a lot more awkward when Terra has to take off my pants to clean and bandage the scratches on my leg.

After finishing me up, she starts on herself, sitting over by the rocks and scraping off dried blood from a cut on her arm.

Again, she's silent. Feeling the pressure against my goose egg lump, I fold my arms and rest my chin on them. I want to talk - mostly because if I don't, I'll either go insane, or fall asleep, and based on the dream I just had, I'd rather not.

When Terra finishes, she comes up next to me. "I'll keep watch. I'll wake you up early so we can walk when it's not to hot."

"That sounds great to me," I say, yawning and leaning back. I lay on my side and dig small holes for my arm and hip so I don't wake up with bruises. Terra lets me use her jacket for a pillow.

Exhaustion overwhelms me, but sleep doesn't come. Even through closed eyes, I can feel Terra watching me.

"How'd you break your nose?" Terra asks.

My eyelashes feel like lead, but I pull them open anyways. "What are you talking about?"

"Your nose," she says, pointing to the bony bridge. "It looks like you broke it at one point."

"Oh yeah," I say, the guilt and the flashing reminder eating me alive. "I . . . get into a lot of fights."

"Sure, okay. You say that a lot." She pauses. Again, I can see the gears working deep within her head. I know it because a small, spiteful smile pokes at her lips and her eyes go dark, go deep.

"But that doesn't explain why you're so closed off. That doesn't explain *why* you get into fights like you say you do. That doesn't explain why you're so angry." The words flow out of Terra's mouth like flames on a branch. She's calling me out on my bullshit, and we both can feel it between us. "It's just annoying how I'm trying to help you not die and you just push me away."

"Sorry".

She groans. "You know, you act like you have it so bad." Terra's hands clench in pulses. I can see her receding into herself, letting the vicious layers have their moment. "You know, I'm here with you too. I didn't have such a great childhood, either, but you look at me like I'm nowhere near as complex and deep as you are."

She's not wrong. But like hell I'd let her know that, though. "Where in the world would you get that idea?" But it comes out a lot more sarcastic than intended.

Her jaw set, she says, "You don't take me very seriously. You don't want my help, which, is kind of stupid."

Boiling with an angry kind of confusion, I say again, "Sorry."

Terra laughs, exasperated. She's wrong; it's because caring is all too easy. It's not caring that's hard. My breath presses against my chest like hands against glass. "This is almost ironic. You got angry at me when I assumed how you felt about your mother, and you've been doing that exact thing this whole time."

I react, finally. "Okay, this is different-" My voice rises to match hers.

But she pulls back, quiet and reserved but like there's a hurricane under her skin. "How is it, really? Don't you dare think you can possibly know the extent of my own pain."

Feeling a bit castrated, I reach out and say, "I didn't say-"

But just before I touch her, Terra visibly curls back. Suddenly, her voice takes a one-eighty and tears out into the void. "Don't touch me!" she screams, putting her hands up to block something.

"I . . . I wasn't going to hurt you!" I say, but as soon as I do, Terra unfurls herself, running and crashing through the trees into the shrubs of the oasis.

Shaken, because I know this is something beyond my own arrogance, I find her curled up, balanced on the balls of her feet, hands up around her head, like the walls of Jericho are going to trap her in a cave of misery.

That weird, little voice inside of me tells me to do something. To talk to her.

"Hey." Shame burns inside of me. "I'm sorry."

Terra nods. I take this as an acceptance of my first genuine apology. "Do you really wanna know about me? You really wanna know the 'why'?"

Her hands claw at her matted hair. "Keep talking."

"My father . . . he was an alcoholic. Almost a fully functioning one, but my mother had to support us while my father was wasting his life away. But, as we grew and as our situation became worse, he began . . . " I pause, looking up at Terra. I can't do this. But, by the grace of some god, I say it for the first time. I say it and I say it and I let it go. Because hell, he's gone, and there's no one to scorn me for my words, to pity me. Fear slithers its slimy fingers off of my heart, my throat.

"He began to abuse us. It started out as just mental, but it grew to be physical. So, about the broken nose thing - I've broken it three times, once when I was . . . abused, and two other times in a fight. But that's not important. What is important was that my father eventually left us, and the abuse stopped. But . . . I took after my father's ways of being an asshole. So yeah, that's why I'm so -" I choke up, knowing I might drown with the weight of it all.

But my voice cuts off when I realize that Terra has unfurled herself and is staring right at me. Terra touches my freckled face, her soft hand running down to my neck. Slowly, she leans forward and wraps her arms around my neck, burying her face in my hair.

Something soft explodes inside of me. She's the first person outside of my family that I've told. Who knows what every scar on my face means. I slowly hug her back, but something stops me. I push her away and say, "No, no. Please don't feel bad for me."

Terra sits back, silent. "Do you see this here?" she says, pushing back her hair and pulling up her eyebrow to reveal a long, deep scar on the protruding, fleshy part of her brow bone.

I nod.

"That's from where I was hit, over and over and over again. That scar is a constant reminder of the time, and the shame that still lingers every day of my life." Eternities grow to infinities as she gazes at me. "So, uh, thanks for pulling me out of it. It, uh, wasn't your fault, me reacting this way." Something pulsates in me. Words come to my mind, and I think I know.

But I push through. I force my lips into a smile. "I don't know why you're thanking me - I didn't do a damn thing worth thanking."

Terra's mouth twitches, shattering the black veil over her. "Yes, you did. And I forgive you; there are a lot of things worse than hubris."

"Hubris? What the hell is hubris?"

"It's Ancient Greek for 'you're an arrogant asshole'." She takes my hand as I pull her up.

I smirk. "Sounds about right."

~

We walk back over to our campsite. Sit under the stars.

Tiredness rests in my bones, but neither of us can sleep. We didn't make a fire, so the cold just works its way into our bones.

We stare at the stars, the glinting moonlight on the oasis spring. Mindlessly eat.

Somehow my voice gives identity to what I'm truly thinking. "Why do you think we're here?"

For a long while, my questions just bounces around in the desert. She sniffs. "Depends on who you ask."

"I mean, why do you think this all happened? Like, why did the plane crash, why did our parents die? Why do we have to go through this?"

"I don't know," Terra says, looking down. "All I do know is that my grandma always quoted some verse to me whenever I ask why bad things happen. 'We rejoice in our sufferings, knowing that suffering produces endurance, and endurance produces character, and character produces hope,'," she says, getting that faraway look again. "I, uh, never understood what that meant. I was little and I just kind of nodded and sucked on the caramel candies she always carried in her gigantic purse." She smiles, her face fading away again.

I snicker, but it hurts in more places than one. "I like that one too, I guess. Everything happens for a reason. People'll always tell you that . . ." Images of my father's fist, the end of his belt buckle, flash through my mind. My mother's frazzled hair, and the next night, her drunk, dead eyes. Cream foundation over black and blue next to blush in a makeup bag. Many different images, bleeding into one movie that plays in my mind. Did all those things happen for a reason?

Terra's voice cuts through my rabbit trail. She sighs. "I wish I could believe that was true all the time."

She slowly puts her stuff back in her backpack and scoots on her bottom to sit on a rock. She ends up sitting next to me, our bodies about a foot away. With a clenched jaw, she stares at the spot where she was just sitting, and her hands are still planted firmly on the stone. Stress ripples through her arms as she pushes herself back into a sitting position. I can tell that she's nervous.

I can feel the electric tension in that one-foot space. Every hair on the arm closest to her stands poised, and a jittery feeling runs up and down my body, like a magnetic pulse.

I want her to touch me. I want to touch her. I want to run my fingers along every soft curve, along every hard edge, around every corner and bend until every little crevice of her is known to me . . . but, I stay back. I don't touch her, I don't even make my intentions known. I let her come to me.

Without looking at me, Terra slowly moves over, closer and closer, inch by inch, until our arms are pressed together, our legs are touching. And with shaky breath - I can hear - she leans her head down onto my shoulder. I slowly pull my arm out from between us and wrap it around her, pulling her even closer. She feels warm - pleasantly so. Her cheek is nice and fleshy against my shoulder. A few strands of her stray hair tickle my ear.

The night wind is cold as the blows in between the trees and lush oasis life, and we snuggle up closer. "Why are you doing this?"

Terra pauses before answering. "Shh. Just listen."

So I do. I listen to the aching pain: the beautiful music, and the melody it plays.

~

Like always, sleep eventually visits me and takes me off to a place where there's no pain. My eyes crack open just after dawn.

I yawn and take a stretch, but my bones still ache. Terra's not there in my arms when I awake.

"Morning," Terra says, leaning casually against the rocks, cutting stalks of aloe vera with my pocket knife.

I breathe, rubbing my eyes. "Good morning."

Terra adjusts herself against the tree she's sitting against, and bites into a plum, juice dripping from her chin.

"Dude! Where did you get that?"

"There are these plum trees everywhere. Go get yourself one," she says, motioning to the foliage behind me.

I spring up, and frantically search through the leaves, and take armfuls of these delicious looking plums back to our little clearing. I set them down, take one and dig in viciously. The sour-sweet juice dribbles down my chin, and I chew the flesh with the thick skin.

I walk back into the rocky clearing, the clear blue water almost white against the shine of the sun. "You know, I wonder what would happen if we just stayed here," Terra says. She seems better than last night, as am I.

I swallow my huge bite of plum. "Well, we'd probably survive fine for a while, but then one of us would get an infection, or get sick, and then they would die. And the other person would be left alone to survive by themselves, and probably throw themselves off of a cliff because they probably went freaking crazy." I smirk, moving my hands with my words to animate the gruesome scene. "Then, a hundred years later they'll find our perfectly preserved bodies and we'll finally get the fame we so deserved."

Terra snickers, crossing her legs in front of her. "Well, that took an interesting turn for the dark. But yeah, that might happen. That wasn't what I was asking, however," she says, taking another bite of these delicious fruits.

Already, the sun scorches hot, shriveling up the crisp green leaves and blowing sand into our eyes.

I sigh and sling my bag over my shoulder. "We should probably get going."

"Probably," she groans, standing up. We begin packing the food into our bags. "Part of me kinda wants to stay here."

I draw back, slightly, still holding an armful of plums. "Why on earth would you want to stay here?"

"Well," she says, pausing and looking up at me. "I've always liked nature, and it's gorgeous out here." Terra pauses, her brow folded in stress. "We've got water, food. I'd rather stay here where it's predictable than go out into the endless desert."

She's got a point. I sit back and smirk, hoisting my pack over my shoulder. "But . . . what about home?"

Terra swallows, a darkness settling on her demeanor. "Yeah, but that's assuming that we somehow get out of here alive in the first place."

"Touche."

March 31, 2011 - Wyatt

Chatter filled my ears, and occasionally, I could pick out a phrase or a word. But otherwise, it was just a blur as I strode down the sidewalk, the heavy school backpack clawing at my shoulders. Sun streamed in through the dappled, green leaves, still fresh and smooth from their buds. A sheen of clammy sweat covered my face from the wind chill as I turned to look at the elementary school kids streaming out of the building. Lilly came rushing up to me, nearly swinging me around with her tiny body. Her flowered skirt twirled around her and she fell back, her hair tousled from the day.

While her face was glowing, I could see a flicker of hurt in her eyes.

"What's wrong, Lilly?" I said as we walked down the sidewalk.

"Nothin'," she said, shrugging slightly.

Her childlike voice was always tinted with some kind of emotion inflicted, so I didn't believe her flat tone.

"What stupid boy pulled your hair today?" I said, distracting myself from the toils of my own school day.

"No, the boys left me alone for once. It was the girls. They teased me because I didn't want to play ball with the boys," she said, the twinge of trivial hurt flashing in her voice.

"Well, where were your other friends?" I asked, reaching up to brush my fingers on the tree as we step off of school grounds.

"They wanted to play kickball so they could talk to their boyfriends . . . ," she said, looking up at me as I took her hand and we dashed across the street.

"What!" I exclaimed, smiling at the absurdity of it. "These second-graders have boyfriends already?!"

"No no no, silly," she said. "They just like hanging out with them because they liiiike them. Like, they like-like them."

"Oh wow," I said, smirking. "I guess things are getting serious."

Lilly pursed her lips and backhanded me on the leg. "It's not funny, Wyatt!"

"Oh, I'm sorry," I said, biting my lip. But right before we walked into the ice cream shop, I knelt down to face her. Her pink lips pouted and she pushed her wispy hair out of her eyes with defiance.

"Now, you listen to me, Lilly Hartman. Don't let anyone make you do something that you don't want to do. And I am very proud of you that, despite the ridicule, you still did what was in your heart."

She smiled, then stopped and cocked her head at me. "What does ridicule mean?"

I threw my head back in laughter and smiled at her. "Oh, I love you, Lilly."

At Swirly's Ice Cream Parlor, we got two chocolate ice cream cones. I always give Lilly the one with the prettiest swirl. That time, they looked pretty even, so she kept the one the cashier had given her. I shoved a few crumpled dollar bills at the cashier, complete with writing on them and rips and shreds.

This cashier was new, a teenage girl with straight, blue hair that nearly covered one eye and a silver ring on her lip and eyebrow. She popped some bubblegum in my face and said "This is nearly half gone. Doesn't count."

"Nuh uh!" I said. "It's obviously more than half; it works!" I had been in quarrles like these many a time.

"You can't fool me. Now give me the money!" she said, leaning forward. Her hair looked like a fluid curtain, coming to swallow me whole.

"One, two, three, four dollars and thirty eight cents." I counted the change back to her and slammed them in the girl's stubby fingers, ending in black nail polish. "Can we go now?" I snapped. Lilly cowered behind me.

She stared at me for a moment, chomping on the rubbery, pink gum and said, "Get outta here before my boss sees this bullshit."

I grabbed Lilly and we scurried out like trash pulled by the wind.

"Was that really fake money, Wyatt?" Lilly said as we sat on the curb, watching the cars go by.

I sighed and pulled out half of a dollar bill. "Just pinching pennies, quite literally."

Lilly looked at me, her round face squinting in the sun as she took a sloppy lick of her cone.

I looked back, hoping she couldn't see the burning shame inside of me threatening to heat up my face.

"Wanna play slug bug?" I asked.

"Ooooh! Sure!" she exclaimed.

We didn't actually end up punching each other over Volkswagen beetles but counting the colors of cars. Whoever has the highest total won. I won with 7 blue and 3 black.

After finishing our ice cream cones, we stood up, barely missing a car whizzing by.

"Are we going home, Wyatt?" Lilly asked. "Because I got homework to do."

I swallowed hard, thinking of the desolated apartment. Thinking of Mom who doesn't come home until midnight each night. "No," I murmured. "We're going to Aunt Angie and Uncle Judd's house."

Lilly smiled, but sadness glowed in her eyes. "Mkay, let's go."

One of the reasons Lilly and I always go to Swirly's is because it's so close to our aunt and uncle's house - but their house is so far from our apartment, so they usually give us a ride home.

The air was still warm when we arrived at their house, but it had that nippiness that only spring air has - where the air feels soupy but the wind sends your hairs standing on end.

I rang the doorbell, and from inside the house, Aunt Angie shouted, "It's open!"

We came in and flopped our stuff down onto their plush carpet, exhausted from the day. It was already past 4 pm. Angie, already hard at work on making dinner, put down her bowl and hugged us. Angeline is a hard, ornery woman, who is constantly making food - evident by her pleasantly plump figure. Dare I say never a dull moment with Aunt Angie, even if we have nothing in common.

Lilly quickly hopped up and helped Angie with the food, and I leaned over and hugged her. "Judd's out in the garage, like he always is."

I started to head out, but Angie again called out behind me. "Dinner's in an hour!"

"Like always!" I shouted back. I closed the door behind me, and the scent of gasoline, oil, sweat, and metal filled my nose.

Displeasing to most, but home to me. Already, I saw my mother's brother, Uncle Judd, leaning over a rusty red car, clunking away. Flannel shirt and ripped denims made for an odd pair against Judd's salt-and-pepper hair. While he's a bit of an odd-ball, a certain genuine streak and wisdom runs unaltered in his veins, under his leathery skin.

He looked up at me and smiled, and already, I could let go - I could finally breathe.

"Hey, my man!" When my uncle tried to be cool, it was always cringeworthy. He embraced me in a side hug - which is good enough for me - and I leaned over the dead engine. "How was school? How many chicks did you pick up this time?"

I snorted. "None, Uncle Judd. Whatcha working on this time?" I asked, leaning over the engine.

"A friend brought this in the other day. Said he wanted to get it up and runnin' again, but didn't wanna take it to a shop - just wanted me to see if I - we - could work our magic before he paid big bucks for it," Uncle Judd nudged me. I smiled, knowing we could fix it.

While we worked on the car and alternated talking about mechanics stuff, Uncle Judd asked me, "How's your ma handling the whole thing?"

"She's . . . " I paused, contemplating to lie, but I was afraid my pause had already given me away. "Well, life is never-changing, right?"

"Don't screw with me, Wyatt," he said, smirking at me, but with a sharp seriousness.

"I mean, it's been about 6 months since he left," I said.

"Still no official divorce?" Judd said, putting down his greasy tool.

"No, ah . . ." My voice trailed off. I still haven't told him. We haven't said much to anyone about the split, much less why.

"Your ma still won't tell me why it happened," Judd inquired. Dammit.

"He, uh, broke my nose. That was the end of it for mom, I guess."

"I'm so sorry, Wyatt-"

"Don't be," I snapped, pouring in the windshield washer fluid.

I heard Uncle Judd sigh. With a smack, I screwed the lid back on and put the jug on the concrete floor.

We continued working on the car, in mostly silence, until Uncle Judd and his mysterious ways spoke again. "You know, Wyatt, we're always here for you if you want to talk, or need anything-"

"Yeah, I know," I interrupted, still hard at work on fixing that damned car.

"No, I didn't finish. You need to listen to me," Uncle Judd and his muscled arms whipped my gangly, twelve-year-old self around to face him.

"Wyatt. Honestly, if you ever need anything, you come to us," he said, his eyes piercing deep into my soul, clipping past every wire, knocking down every wall I had ever put up.

"Yeah, I know," I said, more earnest and slowly this time, turning my eyes downcast.

Suddenly, that large, teddy-bear-with-teeth of a man pulled my curly head into his arms and held me there. He just held me there until I finally wrapped my grease-stricken arms around him and . . . then something happened.

I melted. Twelve-year-old Wyatt Hartman had had enough of this shit.

Finally, I felt like I had a home - a safe refuge far away from all of the gunk. Angie was the mother I should have had, and Judd was the father I never had.

Which, at the moment, was all I ever needed.

Uncle Judd sucked in a breath, pulled me away from him. Giving me a reassuring pat on the shoulder. "Now let's fix this car like real men."

CHAPTER SEVEN: Falling Skies
DAY 4 - Terra; August 8th, 2015

We leave the oasis, which I'm still not too pleased about, and scale back up the crater, back into the textured rocks. The mountains stretch to the heavens, climbing up like indifferent towers of Babel.

We walk for hours. We don't even talk much, because that would take energy.

Eventually, we come upon a bridge - an actual, man made bridge - crossing the ravine. Two rickety poles, stuck into the rock with nails, and a rope with wood plank bridge. The ropes are gray and look gnawed away at, but they continue to hang on with their gnarled grasps. The wood is dry and rattles together like bone. The whole bridge looks like it would tear with one nasty gust of wind and travel across the ravine and shatter into dust.

I swallow hard, looking over at Wyatt, also inspecting the bridge. We have to at least try.

"Do you want me to go first?" I say, tentatively touching the the wooden post in the rock.

"No. I don't want you to fall. And if these ropes can hold me, they can hold you," he says, looking dangerously far down into the canyon.

I press my lips together. "Just . . . . let me carry your supplies over."

Wyatt reluctantly slides his backpack off, but keeps the items in his pockets. Swallowing hard, I step back. Every cell in my body screams to hold Wyatt back. But he steps forward, and my brows unconsciously knit together.

"Wait!" The word tears itself from my throat before I even know what passed through my mind. Wyatt whips around, terror etched in his eyes, but his eyebrows curled in annoyance.

I breathe hard, and drop to my knees and fumble with the damn zipper on my backpack. I pull out the 20 foot bungee cord. "We should, uh, tie you to something, in case you fall."

"Okay," he stammers. "That sounds good." I can see it - he's afraid. It's a look I've only seen once before - right when I saw him after the crash. Because his death is just a broken plank or a snapped rope away.

Wyatt returns to solid ground, and I begin tying a knot on the bridge post, since that seems sturdy. If not, I'll always keep my hands on the cord. I tie a Blake's Hitch knot around the robust pole, sucking up three feet of the cord. Wyatt stands still while I make a seat-like contraption with the opposite end of the cord. I knew the Blake's Hitch knot, but I'm very much making the rest of this up as I go.

Starting at his stomach, I go up and around his thighs and in between his legs. I then make a few loops around his bottom so he can use a scaling maneuver if need be. Then I use the last few feet to secure his upper body - up and around his shoulders, crossing over his chest and back. I triple-knot the end and tuck it under where the ropes of his thighs meet on the side of his hip.

I stand back, admiring my work. "Okay, you're good to go," I say, trying to come off as cheerful and optimistic, but it comes off of my tongue awkward and satirical. I twist a clump of hair between my fingers as I say: "Uh, sorry. Just, go."

Wyatt flashes me a dazzling smile just before he steps onto the bridge. I drop to my knees and grasp onto the bungee chord with both hands, anticipating it to suddenly stretch, meaning he's fallen, and that the bridge is nothing but dust.

I stop, pushing that image from my mind. Focusing my anxiety on holding onto the cord, I watch in anticipation as Wyatt steps forward, the wood bending and creaking under his weight.

He takes a step. I watch every movement he makes as my stomach twists itself in knots. He takes another step. The creaking grows and rings hollow in my ears. Another. Wyatt holds the ropes tight, but the cord in my hands stretches. And another.

Suddenly, there's a crack, and Wyatt screams. A flinch jerks my body so hard that I almost let go of the cord. A plank goes out from under Wyatt's front foot, and he falls forward in a sudden flash of motion.

"Wyatt!" I scream, preparing to stand.

"I'm okay . . . I'm okay," he insists, glancing back at me. His voice shakes like the trembling wooden boards. But, as if carved with a cruel knife, terror is unmistakable on his face. He grips the ropes at his sides with a certain passion.

I let the fear subside, and it eventually does, just like taking a boiling pot off of a burner. He's okay. Tactfully, he braces his foot that's not hanging out of a hole in the bridge and pulls his leg straight up, leaning on the ropes. He flashes me a wavering smile as he continues on.

His smile is still impressioned into my mind like a head indentation in a pillow when life plunges into slow motion.

The rope connecting the floor part of the bridge snaps, and the floor swings out from under him as smoothly as a door opening. But Wyatt holds onto the railing ropes, dangling as if from a noose, kicking his feet for purchase on the remaining floor rope, which promptly breaks.

"Wyatt!" My scream tears from my throat before I can even register what has happened. The cord burns my hands, but I don't let go. I can't let go.

"D-don't let go!" I shout, unable to find any other cohesive words. Fear manhandles my insides like a baby's rattle.

Soft creaks erupt as one of the railing ropes slowly breaks, thread by thread, and Wyatt swings with a terrifying momentum to the other rope. A painful grunt escapes his mouth as he reaches to grab on to the other rope. My lungs have turned to lead, my breath like water in my chest. Gravity will win.

"Thank you so much! I never would have thought of that!" he shouts back, unable to turn and face me. His words are sharp and sting with a fervor, but I don't take offence to them. I couldn't possibly.

And that's when the last rope breaks.

The ropes tumble down like loose threads on a shirt, and clack against the wooden bridge, hanging down off the cliff below my feet, rattling in the wind like perverse wind chimes. But, Wyatt however, being connected to the cord around his body, falls at a curve down to the jagged rocks, pivoting at the exact spot where I'm holding the cord. The cord screams with fire on my hands, but I pull and pull and pull until the velocity ends with a deafening crack against the cliff. Now the cord gently swings between my hands.

Screams pour out of me as smoothly as liquid. I nearly throw myself over the cliff to see the end of the rope. Wyatt dangles, unconscious, the momentum of falling still slapping his lifeless body against the ravine wall like a flimsy piece of paper.

Frantic, I grasp the cord and brace my feet against the posts. My entire body - from my arms to my back and my thighs scream in protest. Sweating, I yank the cord up as Wyatt's body slowly scales the cliff, parts of his limp body periodically hitting the rocks. Every pull sends waves of pain through me, but I don't stop. I can't.

Trembling with adrenaline, I pull him up onto the rocks where I stand, grunting. Hot tears scald my cheeks as the blood pouring from his head strikes my eyes.

I turn away, on my knees. Pain wraps its fat fingers around my heart and begins to squeeze. Sobs jerk through me like electric shocks, stifled by my teeth digging into my bottom lip.

I push back against the sobs. I put it under so much pressure that it becomes inert. I turn back to Wyatt's body and carefully scoot it back to a diagonal place where I can sit him up. I feel his soft neck for his jugular vein. It pumps steadily beneath my fingers.

I untie the cord from the pole, and then work on untying the cord from his body. With mechanical and gentle movements, I remove it and throw it aside. I open my bag and take out the first aid kit, which we are using much more than I would have hoped. I open a can of water and pour it over his head, cleaning out his old head wound. He seems relatively uninjured. My guess is the momentum rushed blood to his head, making him pass out.

Then I work on his new cuts and scrapes from the fall. They're all superficial and not bleeding that badly, but he'll definitely have some nasty bruises.

After that, I focus on cleaning the mild rope burns I have on the palms of my hands.

After that, I sit back and wait, listening to the hollow clanks of the broken rope bridge clattering in the wind.

The silence sucks every ounce of energy out of me. My eyes throb.

I find myself brushing my fingers over the smooth rock, scrambling for the bungee cords. I wind them around my palms. Pull them tight. Unwind them, and then do it all over again.

Turning my knuckles white, I look over at Wyatt. Unconscious and helpless.

Just like I was.

Slowly, I move closer to him. The harsh sunlight makes the scars on his face stand out. I run my thumb across his brow bone, and across mine.

"D-don't let go!"

Let go.

Control slips from my fingers like the bungee cords that held Wyatt to me.

I think about it every day. It binds me to the past like shackles bolted to a wall. It has unwillingly molded me into the selfish, unfeeling monster I am today.

And I can't. I can't possibly hold onto it any longer. It rots me from the inside out. And if I don't let go, it's going kill me one way or another.

My chest rattling, every visceral detail of my rape tears across my mind, every second before, during and after. It's my fault if he dies; I sent Wyatt across the suicide bridge. I didn't think about it for a second.

I look down at him, the photograph of his sister flashing through my mind. I want to open myself up to him, but I can't. I almost literally, physically can't. And I hate myself for it.

But I open myself up, like the waves crashing against the shore, like a flower opening up to the sun.

I was forced open to my rapist, whose name I still don't know, representing everything malicious and awful and evil, and I believed it. I believed that this is what it was all like.

I opened myself up to Adam, my childhood friend who I thought completed me, and he left me, sniveling in the dirt.

I encased myself in a shell, a core as strong as steel, thinking that would help.

But it didn't. All it did was let me fester in my own wounds.

Lurching forward, I sob. Gripping onto my pain because it's safe. Because it's familiar. Because I'm so fucking afraid of what would happen if I let go and threw myself off of the ledge of life.

And, like the ebb and flow of the sun and the moon in their eternal dance, I blossom like a flower, thrusting away the glossy green leaves of the past.

~

Wyatt awakens slowly, with slight shifts in movement on the outer edges of his body and low sounds coming from his throat. And then, suddenly, he's wide awake, thrashing and screaming.

Breaking out of my stupor, I whip around, bracing his body against the rock with my legs and taking his face in my hands, crushing his cheeks just a little as he comes to, still consumed with adrenaline and fear.

"Wyatt. Hey, Wyatt," I repeat, familiarizing him with his name. "You're okay, you're okay," I begin to repeat softly after the recognition of myself and himself pass across his face, but the terror still seizes his body and leaks out of his eyes. Hot, rapid breath passes over his mouth. His chest rises and falls, as if he can't breathe.

"You're okay, you're okay," I whisper as Wyatt comes to. Disoriented and scared, Wyatt's arms slowly come up around me.

Eventually, we let go, and eventually, Wyatt can stand. Regret pumping through my veins, we trek on into the evening, leaving behind the pathetic bridge, waiting for this damn ravine to condense down so we can cross it.

But as the evening drags on, the orange sunlight has a narcotic effect on me. The air is clear and the sun seeps into my skin like warm milk. If I had a nice, soft bed, this would be perfect to nap in.

Wyatt and I stop to eat once the sun has just kissed the horizon. When I open my bag and take out a can of water, I find it empty. I check my water bottle - also empty. It's only been a day, and we've already sucked down all of the water from the oasis. And I'd really rather not open any more of the 7 water cans we have left. I swallow hard and decide not to tell Wyatt about our water predicament. We devour some more of those plums and assorted plants I found at the oasis, but we have nothing to wash it down with. Guilt burns inside of me, but I refuse to let up. We have to preserve the water.

We walk some more. I notice that the ravine has decreased, and will continue to decrease further down. The rocks become larger, and the canyon shallower and wider.

My mind wanders like the lost children we are, and I begin pondering the question Wyatt asked me this morning. "What about home?"

The names come to me like rapid fire. Harper. Nick. Mom. For an instant, I think of Dad, but the second thought reminds me that he's gone. It runs through me like painful lightning That still lays on me, unsettled. But I sigh and admit that Wyatt's right. Other than the beauty and serenity, what else is here for me? Depending on what Wyatt chose to do, I'd be out here alone. I'd never get to marry, have kids, never have a career, never have any other human contact. My life would be nothing but this. Besides, what about modern conveniences? Those are great . . .

I could use a nice, cold shower. And some coffee. And a hug.

~

At twilight, the ravine becomes small enough to cross. It's only about five feet deep but pretty wide, so we climb across.

Rocks. Even more rocks. They appear much more menacing in the darkness, each edge like a blade that could cut my head off if I fell on it the wrong way.

Tonight, we have less than half a moon, so Wyatt takes out the flashlight and we climb together. Tiredness pulls at my limbs, and I take my life one rock at a time. Wyatt keeps reaching for his empty water bottle and sucking down any last drops.

I wipe cold sweat off of my forehead, and the evening becomes increasingly chilly. Soon enough, I can see my milky breath in the navy background. Finally, I give in.

"Hey, can we stop for the night? I'm tired and it's cold," I push out when we're over the last cliff.

Wyatt's eyes immediately melt. "Oh, yeah, sure! We can start looking for a safe place now."

With our flashlight, we find a spacious, deep cave. Here, the rocks are smooth and layered. Carved by the supple hands of water.

The LED lights wash out the rich pigmentation of the rocks, but as we enter the cave, something else comes into focus. Exquisite, faded cave paintings line the walls. People dancing, horses galloping, mountain lions and cougars and coyotes and words . . . words neither of us can read, obviously. But the archaic and simplistic beauty . . . is utterly overwhelming.

I smile, my dry lips cracking. "Look!"

Wyatt pulls up next to me, our arms nearly touching. The hairs on my skin stand on end from the cold. "Wow." He runs his grimy fingers over the rock. The paintings smear just a little, and ruddy dust comes away on his fingers. "I wonder if anyone knows about this."

I walk further into the cave, dripping water echoing further down, breathing. Being. "Probably not. Or else they'd probably have it sectioned off or cut out the rock from the mountain."

Wyatt laughs, throaty and husky. "Well, I'm glad they didn't."

I stand where the cave ends, and look out. Look at my ancestor's creations. "Me too."

We settle in. The incessant dripping in the cave drives us mildly insane. I can just imagine the cool drips soaking my tongue . . .

Wyatt shines his flashlight into the darkness, the white beam striking out far.

I close my eyes, ignoring the sticky feeling in my mouth and try to sleep since I requested this pit-stop.

Suddenly, Wyatt's voice pulls me out of half-sleep. "Hey! Look here!" I force my limbs to move, and I stand, wobbling ever so slightly.

"What?" I say, not freaking out because Wyatt's voice sounds excited. Abandoning our cave and supplies, Wyatt leads me over a plateau, where the walls dip down to the canyon at almost a ninety-degree angle.

Once I'm over that, my eyes come to rest on a small, angular structure made of wood, standing tall and dark in the weak moonlight. "Is that a . . . house?"

"Evidently," Wyatt says. I can see the slope of the roof, the broken glass windows, the chimney, the front door. Now, all of the modern architecture feels foreign, like an itch I can't and don't want to scratch. Wyatt bluntly shines the light directly onto the house, and fear runs through me for a hair-raising second. But the house is beaten down and broken - nothing to be afraid of.

"Do you think we should go inside?" Wyatt asks me.

"Yeah," I nod. "There might be something useful in there."

A sign stands, bent and rusted from years of weather. Wyatt takes his shirt and wipes off the dust. In faded lettering, it reads Native American Historic Site and Museum. A thin layer of red spray paint covers the metal sign.

"I guess we know why they didn't cut those rocks out," Wyatt muses. I hold the sign in my hands. He moves forward, into the house.

"I'm one-fourth Native American, you know," I say, smiling a little. I think of my mom, and her thick, voluminous hair and hazel eyes.

"Cool. I'm uh, one-sixteenth Japanese," he shouts from inside the musty house.

Smirking a little, I lean on the doorpost. "That's something white people say just to sound ethnic."

He just rolls his eyes.

"Nah, I'm kidding. I could tell by your eyes." I'm glad he didn't die in the plane crash, in our incident with the bridge.

Wyatt nearly snorts. "That's racist."

~

Wyatt then searches the perimeter of the house, while I venture inside. When I step in, little critters scatter to the shadows. I cough and wave off cobwebs. It seems to be a one room house, complete with an overturned speaker's stand, a small table and chairs, glass cases, and a fireplace. I search inside the cabinets - nothing. There's absolutely nothing of use. Not even artifacts. Defeated, I walk out of the house empty-handed.

"There's nothing in there," I shout, trying to find Wyatt with my voice. I hear him grunting and work my way to the back of the house. Wyatt is viciously pumping something up and down, and I recognize it to be a water pump - the ones connected to wells in the ground. The paint is peeling, and more chips fall to the sand with each of Wyatt's pumps, but the only thing that comes out is the rubbing, creaky sound of metal against metal. I rub my eyes, forgetting all about sleep and focusing every ounce of energy, willing water to flow out.

After a few more aggressive pumps, the thing sputters, gargling and choking. Glee erupts on our faces and Wyatt immediately pumps harder, and eventually, black sludge vomits out. But Wyatt keeps pumping, and soon enough, the black gunk turns to milky, cool water. And somehow, I feel a little better about keeping the number of water cans from Wyatt.

We both lunge for the substance, and, like lunatics, shove each other back and forth for mouthfuls of the water that could taste like shit for all we care. But we suck it down like small children who want lemonade on a hot summer day.

Sitting back, we swallow our last gulps satisfyingly. I feel pregnant with a water balloon, but it sits inside of me, humming with satisfaction.

I wish we could stay here forever. Sometimes, I don't care about anything else in the world but right here, where I am. This feeling - right here, of having a full stomach of cool water - I wouldn't trade for anything.

Then, an idea pops into my head. I spring up and run back to the cave, ignoring the pounding in my head. I search frantically in my bag and pull out the empty silver water cans.

I look at Wyatt, holding the cans, hoping that he gets my mental message. We proceed to fill the cans with the glorious water and carry them back.

And finally, sleep comes in the warm cocoon of the cave we have found, finding solace in the darkness.

CHAPTER EIGHT: The Purge
DAY 5 - Wyatt; August 9th, 2015

As I become starkly aware of my surroundings, it's like I have just blinked. But I know I haven't because the moon has dipped low into the sky - approximately 4 or 5 am. The first light of day peeks out from the mountains, slowly pushing away the darkness. My stomach grumbles, and creaks. A pang runs through me, and I try and sit up, but I feel bloated and odd. Nausea arises within me.

And I can feel it bubbling up, like a red, inflamed white-head pimple that is begging to be popped. I can feel it burning the lining of my throat, and vomit comes up like swallowing hot soup . . . except, it's going the wrong way. It slops on the rocks and splatters to the side of me as I retch. The thick, snot-like vomit flows down the rock and drips down to other rocks like a fountain. My throat burns and my mouth is overcome with bitterness. I lean back onto the rocks, counting my heartbeats that I can feel in my head, wiping my mouth. The taste wallows, making me want to retch even more.

Sucking in air and praying not to vomit again, I try and spit the revolting taste from my mouth.

I sit back. Look across from me. Terra sits, stirring uncomfortably in her sleep.

Trying not to clench the sore muscles in my abdomen, I take out some water, eyeing the open water cans. I grab one, sniffing the pump water. Taste it.

Immediately, my throat constricts, and the awful taste floods my mouth again. Shit.

I dump the nasty stuff in the can down the ravine. I sip the water from a fresh water can, leaving the rest for Terra when she awakes.

Setting the can far away, I lean back and close my eyes.

Breathing hard through my mouth, I hear Terra stirring across from me. The light shines off of the clammy sweat on her face.

The moment she opens her eyes, they dilate in terror. Her body undulating like someone is giving her the Heimlich maneuver, she vomits as well.

"Join the club," I say, my throat raw like a rug burn.

She chuckles, then coughs, holding her gut. "What do you think it was?"

"What do *you* think?" I sneer, gesturing to the hand well pump.

"Dammit. That sucks," she says, reaching over to the collection of water cans we have, filled to the brim with that demon-water.

She proceeds to dump the rest of them into the ravine, but, still shaky from exhaustion, one of them slips out of her hands, and she reaches forward to catch it. Terra, never very coordinated, slides over the edge. I am unable to cry out because it's all over in just a split second. The fall, then the sickening crack of her body on the rocks that sends a spear through me like a kebab.

I lean over and vomit endlessly, my stomach and heart lurching.

Grasping onto the edge, the rock tearing my fingers to shreds, I scream for Terra.

Blood like oil pools onto the sandy rock. Trembling, I scale the rocks down, calling her name. But each motion digs the knife deeper into my turbulent stomach.

I cradle her in my arms, pressing my hands against the spurting wound. Her skull feels like puzzle pieces beneath my fingers.

Sobs wrestle in my throat. What have I done?

The wind hisses at me, rearing like a snake. But syllables catch on something that sounds like ... *Wyatt.*

Pressing my lips to Terra's quickly cooling forehead, I lay her down softly, keeping my eyes trained.

The wind screams through the canyon. Screaming my name.

The small trickle of a stream lies ten feet below, surrounded by spearing rocks.

Inching along the sides, I grasp on for dear life. The wind, ever so tempting, runs its fingers through my ratty curls, dragging me along.

Wyatt.

And just around the corner, stands a figure, far below, hair traveling with the wind.

Lilly.

Bruises explode on her face. Blood pours from her busted lip.

I scream for her. I scream and I scream and I scream for Lilly, my Lilly. But she doesn't move. Only the terror stricken in her eyes tells me to move, tells me to live.

I jump down from the ledge, into the murky, pungent stream. My sister flinches at the splash of cold water.

I reach out. I reach out to touch her, but she flinches away, her statuesque figure suddenly jumping to life.

"Don't touch me!" she screams. They rocket forward, bouncing off of the narrow walls, creating a cacophony of horror.

Suddenly, I can speak. "Lilly, no! It's just me! Wyatt!"

"Stop it!" she cowers as if she is afraid of the mere sound of my voice. "Please stop hurting me!"

I hold my hands up, but oh God does it take all of the willpower I have not to throw myself on top of her and stop whatever is happening.

Lilly's voice rises to a piercing shrill. Heart throbbing and skin pulsating, I throw myself protectively around Lilly, to shield her, to knock her out of this.

And as we tumble to the ground, my sister's head smacks against a rock with a crack that shatters my bones, explodes my heart.

And blood like oil pools onto the slick rock.

Trembling with horror, I recoil back.

No.

My mind screams. I . . . hurt her. I killed her.

It's all my fault it's all my fault it's all my fault.

In my own selfish preservation, in my own want, need to keep her with me, I hurt her.

Fear coils its way up my body, and I know, I know that's what I'm most afraid of.

I've tried so hard to protect Lilly from everything, taking the brunt of our shitty life.

And, now, cradling her in my arms, it rips through me like a hole in a sheet.

I wish she was here, I wish I could talk to her. But she's not. And it spirals out of my control, like sand flowing through my fingers.

What if she turns out just as fucked up as I am? And what if I can't stop it?

Pulling my hand back, I feel her warm blood on my fingertips. I can't stop it. I never could. I try and I try and I strive so hard for something so unattainable, when really . . . really I should be helping myself.

Now that Lilly's gone, surely, I should be able to do that. I curl her body up to mine, pressing her head into my chest, hoping that if I believe hard enough, she'll be okay without me.

And that someday, I'll be okay myself.

~

I awake to the sound of Terra dry heaving over the side of the ravine.

Heart pounding, I push myself awake. "Be careful!"

She coughs, deep and throaty. "I'm trying to vomit here."

My stomach rumbling, I scoot over to her. "Don't lean over so much!"

She looks at me, peers at me. "I'm okay, Wyatt. Since when are you so concerned anyway?"

I take my hand off of her shoulder. "Since we drank psychedelic water."

She snorts. "Tell me about it." She reaches for the cans and our water bottles and begins pouring them over the edge.

"Wait!" I exclaim.

"What?" she insists.

I reel back. My vision, dream, whatever, boils to the front of my mind. I debate on spilling what I just saw to Terra, but the words come out anyway. "I saw you die." My abdomen clenches. Something still doesn't feel right.

Terra stops, reeling back. "What?"

I bite my lip. "Well, I dunno. I just hallucinated you falling over the edge of the cavern, and then . . . and then my sister showed up."

"Lilly?"

I nod. "Yeah, she was like calling my name. Then she freaked out, telling me I was hurting her. But, I wasn't doing anything. And, then," A ball forms in my throat. Damn it. "Then, as I was trying to protect her, I killed her. Her head smashed into a rock."

"And then I realized I was a selfish bastard." I smile at her, self-deprecating.

Terra snickers at this last comment, then proceeds to cough.

I can see Terra processing this on her face, the gears turning, the neurons firing. "Oh."

"'Oh,'" I say, laughing a little. "That's all you have to say to your hallucinogenic death?" I react almost automatically. I want to touch her, to make sure she's really there.

"Yes, at the moment." I smile.

Terra smirks, sitting back after pouring out the poison water. We bathe in the cool night air, which is odd - unlike most nights, where the air is cool but thin. Tonight, it is thick and cold, like that disgusting feeling when you feel the sliminess of cold soup from yesterday in the fridge.

We spend the rest of the night retching uselessly. Eventually, I think, Terra falls asleep. Or maybe she's just as good at pretending as I am.

Regardless, I turn over and face the ravine, so even if Terra is awake, she can't see me.

That moment plays over and over in my head, like a skipping record. It was so bizarre, I almost couldn't wrap my mind around it.

But then again, is any of this something the old Wyatt could wrap his mind around?

I reach in my back pocket and take out my wallet. I keep it there for nostalgia's sake. It's always been there, and it always will be.

When I see the photos of me and Lilly, my throat constricts. If she were here, she'd know exactly what to say, how to pinpoint my exact feeling. She'd curl up with me and would make me feel somewhere that I belonged.

She and Terra are so similar, yet so different. Reserved, full of life. I find myself laughing a little at this comment. I just hope that I never get the chance to hurt either one of them.

Behind all of the useless money, I find a more candid photo. One at Swirly's, not long ago, where I accidentally bumped her ice cream right into the gravel. The horror, and, admittedly laughter, marks my face. But childlike anger flushes her face.

We fought like cats and dogs, but damn it, our highs were astronomical compared to our lows. We loved each other, flaws and all.

Loved. I scold myself. Damn it, Wyatt, already talking in past tense. Digging your own damn grave.

If only she were here. My heart aches for familiarity, but the pulsations of my cries don't reach even outside our little cave.

Crushing my face in my hands, I sob.

I might not ever see her again, so I must forgive, I must let go. For my own sake.

I snap out of it when I see a groggy Terra dragging herself over to me.

"No, just, go back to sleep, I'm fine," I say, angrily batting at my cheeks.

She doesn't say anything, and forces her way into my arms, like that first night in the oasis. She doesn't say anything as I continue to mourn, feeling a bit castrated. She just lets her warmth soak into me.

~

For the rest of the darkness, we try to sleep. Eventually, the sun is too high up for us to keep our eyes closed, so we pack up and leave, grimacing when we pass the water pump.

Dew condenses on plant leaves and collects under rocks as the white hot sun rises higher into the air.

We start walking and leave the cave behind just as the sun paints the sky red.

But soon enough, problems plague us. My mouth tastes like acid and chalk, and even though my stomach has settled a bit, my body aches from lack of sleep. We both know it - we should drink. Our water can supply is dwindling at best - so I don't say anything.

The sky turns from the color of a corn poppy to a deep orange, and then finally to that yellow-white, scalding light that is all too familiar, and time goes on. My entire mouth hurts.

My stomach grumbles again, and I am afraid that I'll vomit again, so I stop walking and waver on my feet for a moment - nothing.

Just then, Terra, not watching where she is going, walks straight into my back, and we tumble to the ground. Except it's not romantic or funny - it's just painful as our knobby, exposed bones hit the hard-packed earth. My head explodes in an array of fireworks as the world wobbles beneath me, ebbing and flowing like the sea.

Suddenly, Terra pulls herself off of me and coughs, dry and rattling, like the eerie chatter of a rattlesnake. I push myself up and grind my feet against the sand. "Let's go."

"Wyatt, wait!" she says, her voice just as scratchy as mine.

"No, we have to go," I murmur, licking my cracked and peeling lips that sting like lemon juice.

My heart thumps in my ears, making them burn red-hot. I can feel it under my fingernails, in the callouses and blisters on my feet. Mirages of non-existent water cut through the endless landscape, and the chatter of the bugs swells to almost a scream.

And then I'm on the ground again, and black, wavering polka-dots swell until they have filled my whole realm of vision. I have to get back to her, because I can't seem to let it go.

~

I awake to someone slapping my face. The moment I open my eyes, Terra pours some water down my throat, and I sputter for a moment, catching my bearings, but then suck down the water regardless. A pounding in my head swells, like my head has swollen to the size of a party balloon.

After getting my satisfying fill, I push the can away. "What happened?" I say, but it comes out incoherent.

Terra sniffs. "You passed out."

"Oh, sorry," I say absently.

"No, no, it's not your fault," she says. That's when I finally look up and take in my surroundings. Tears have cut trails like roads in the dirt on her face, and we are nestled in the shade of a short, shrubby tree. Thankfully, Terra then takes the rest of the can and drinks, the water dribbling down and streaking her face.

Grunting, I try and push myself up, but Terra forcefully pushes me back down onto the ground, staring up at the gnarled branches above.

"We need to rest," she orders.

During this, we mostly just sleep and drink another water can against our better judgement.

Late in the afternoon, while Terra is sleeping, I take out my harmonica. I haven't played it in a few days, mostly because I haven't had time. I dust some of the sand off of it and squint into the horizon. Terra lays at my feet, curled up around her backpack.

While I'm feeling a little better, my head still throbs deep within. Again, I'm tempted to open another water can. But instead, I distract myself by pressing my lips against the harmonica and blowing.

Sand and gunk vomits out, but I keep blowing and making ear-shattering noises until the clear hum shouts into the void.

Sighing, I make aimless noises, rubbing my lips raw, trying to think of a tune.

Then, my aunt's favorite song comes into my head, and I pause, going over the tune in my head. Licking my lips, I begin to play 'Folsom Prison Blues' by Johnny Cash.

"*I hear the train a comin'. It's rolling round the bend . .* " When I've gotten through the first verse, Terra rolls over, still half asleep, and begins singing along. "*Well, I know I had it coming, I know I can't be free. But those people keep a movin', and that's what tortures me . .* "

Her voice is airy, but carries a deep soulful tune that is pleasing to the ears. I never knew she could sing. I mean, it's not perfect, but it will more than do.

"*Well if they freed me from this prison,*

if that railroad train was mine,
Bet I'd move it on a little farther down the line.
Far from Folsom Prison, that's where I long to stay,
And I'd let that lonesome whistle blow my blues away . ."

August 17, 2012 - Terra

"Happy Birthday!" the gleaming crowd of people most dear to me shouted. The light of the camera flashed into my eyes as I blew out the candles, signaling my unofficial entrance into high school.

"Ah, welcome to being fourteen, Terra," Harper said to me, smirking and lightly socking me on the arm.

"Oh, and I guess you would know," I mused. Harper had only been fourteen for a week.

"Happy Birthday, you loser," Harper smiles, her sleek bangs brushing her thin, expressive brows.

"Yeah, happy birthday to me," I say, sneering and cutting myself a piece of cake.

~

The festivities died down, and by that, I mean that pretty much all of my other extended family and friends had left. My brother, and parents were all doing other things. The party was over. All that remained was Grandma Abby and Harper. The latter, however, was working on her fourth piece of cake.

I sat down on the couch, across from Grandma, who was sipping water from a plastic party cup.

"Your friends are quite nice," she said, smiling coyly at me.

"Heck yeah, I am!" Harper shouted from the kitchen.

I laughed, rolling my eyes. "Ignore her."

Grandma smiled. "Gladly. Happy Birthday, Terra."

I smiled genuinely, for nearly the first time since this party began. "Thank you."

With skillful and determined hands, Grandma reached deep into the pocket of her canvas pants, the knees frayed and open. She pulled out a small velvet package, slightly larger than an engagement ring box. "For entering into almost-adulthood."

The heat rushing to my face, I took the box and opened its soft lid. A silver cross met my eyes, delicate and barely an inch tall. Two silver ribbons weaved around the cross, and in the crosshairs laid a sparkling red ruby, like the heart of the cross.

"Read the back," she says, her voice husky and close as she turns the cross around on its silver chain. Engraved on the back of the post is 'more precious than rubies'. And as the light catches the precious metal around the ribbons and I see on one side is 'Proverbs', and the other is '3:15'.

A smile breaking onto my face, I held the delicate metal in my fingers, Grandma took the box from my hands, removed the necklace and clasped it around my neck.

I would never take that necklace off for 2 years.

~

After the clasp closed, I turned around and threw myself into Grandma's arms. Although she was smaller than me, her arms always made me feel small young again. And in those moments, I could reflect on how far I had come.

I froze, however, when I felt the deep cough rising up within her chest. But she didn't break the hug quite yet. The cough was allowed to rise and come out, the horrible noise racketing through my bones.

I pulled away, slowly but forcefully as horrible sounds rocketed out of my grandmother's frail chest. She never smoked much, but her family did all her life, and now she was paying the ultimate toll. Bad genes, too. Cancer infested my grandmother's lungs, tearing away at the fragile tissue like paper in a shredder.

She had already had surgery and rounds of chemo, and her lung capacity was half of what it should be at her age.

I hadn't heard her cough like this in months. Was it coming back?

"Grandma . . . ," I started, my voice breaking in anguish.

But still, she was coughing and wheezing, the red panic crawling up her neck and onto her face.

The woman I once knew was curled over, chest rattling like the vibrations of a drum. It wasn't until the whites of her eyes shone and burned holes into my mind that I screamed.

August 29, 2012

My parents were always pretty overprotective of me; Nick too. While I could still consume media and do what I pleased within reason, they tried to protect me from the realities of the world. Drugs, violence. Death. Like all parents, they ultimately failed.

But, like how they couldn't protect me then, they couldn't protect me now.

~

My eyes opened. I sucked in air, hard. Through the thick sleep and nighttime darkness, I could see my mother's face above me, worn and crinkled with time and toil. Her chilly hands were hard and trembling, her mere grip instilling fear into me the moment I awoke.

"Terra. Get up," my mother said, her words clipped and breathy.

"What...?" I mumbled, pushing myself up, and seeing my shadow-enclosed room.

"Get up!" my mother nearly shouted. "It's Grandma!"

Immediately, my blood ran cold. I knew this day would have come soon enough. But I didn't think it would have come so soon, or in the middle of the night.

I dragged myself out of bed, but panic swallowed the house. I could already feel it simmering inside of me. Numb, I ripped open my door. Nick ran past me, still in his white tee shirt and flannel pants.

The four of us were in the car, the rumbling of the car against the gravel only accentuating the nervousness jumping like electrified frogs inside of me.

I looked over at Nick, his wavy, dark brown hair tousled violently from sleep - or from a lack of brushing, who knows. But his bright, blue eyes spoke of a fear neither of us could express.

As I watched the Phoenix city lights flash by, I felt my breathing - how it filled each sac of my lung, how it tickled the back of my throat like rejuvenating water, the normal rising and falling of my chest. And I realized how I take this automatic, mechanical process entirely for granted.

A haze collapsed onto me, restricting my breathing like a noose around my chest. A tremor seeped into my veins. I reached up and pressed my fingers up to the cold window, realizing that my clammy hands shook with anticipation.

I tried to breathe through the suffocating blur and the electric fear, but I was still swallowed by the drug within that dulled every sense, slowed down every reaction, and threatened to drag me into a soft insanity.

Because I knew. I could feel it in every fiber of my being. I knew what was coming. For years, that monster in the corner of the room had sat dormant, asleep. And then, in that very moment, its eyes shot open and the hackles on the back of its neck stood straight up like arrows.

To this day, I remember every excruciating detail. I remember the piercing scent of death and antiseptic soap and starchy white. I remember each second, minute, hour that passed by as we waited while the doctors tried to save her life. I remember the increasing dread creeping up on me that I still feel, crawling out of the pits of my soul every once in awhile. And I remember the doctors coming to get us, to tell us that these were her final moments, that nothing more could be done.

I remember taking the death march up to her hospital room - one I had visited many times before, knowing that someday, it would come to this. But I kept plugging along, step by step, through the neck-deep fear, as real and as tangible as you or me.

I remember having to push with all of my strength just to push her door open. I remember the blur of the tiles beneath my still-bare feet. And something I will never forget was my grandmother's emaciated body, skin like shed snakeskin and veins like water hoses. I will never forget her swollen rib cage, jerking drastically beneath the thin sheets. I will never forget how her eyes pierced into my soul for one last time, and I saw everything we had ever had flash before my eyes.

And then the death rattle began, screaming out from deep within her throat. The muscles and connective tissue in her neck ripped and tore as my grandma gasped for breath, and suddenly, every wisp of oxygen from my lungs was sucked out.

And . . . then . . . I couldn't breathe back in. I couldn't.

As my grandmother, my most treasured human, my maternal figure when my own mother was too selfish, too emotional, too busy, began to tremble and pick at the sheets, all I could hear was the horrifying, gargling, sucking sound emanating from this new being before me. Death gripped every corner of the room.

Suddenly, someone wrapped their arms around my waist and picked me up like a sack of fucking potatoes. Every pain, every fear I had been holding in came lashing out.

"No!" I screamed. "You can't take me away from her! You can't do this!" I screamed and screamed and screamed, but that didn't stop my father from dragging me out of the room, a sobbing mess.

But as I held on to the doorpost with trembling hands and kicking at nothing, I experienced my beloved grandmother take her last breath, and all of the life that was left was stolen from her as the machines went silent.

And that was the moment everything became real - sharp and caustic and incredibly painful. Everything came crashing down all at once. I would, to this day, trade the pain I felt in the moments after my grandmother's death for any form of physical pain.

And as the door to her room slammed shut in front of me, I couldn't breathe.

Awful, painful sounds exploded from my chest. I couldn't breathe.

My mother crumpled to the floor with me, wrapping her ensnaring arms around me.

Skin burning, I threw her away.

I slammed into the cold, hard floor and sobbed until my insides hurt and my eyes swelled shut. Every wall was coming down. This was Jericho at its fucking finest.

~

I would do a lot of crying after that. I didn't make it to school for about a week and a half after that. Still, my mother had to forcibly drag me in, and even when I would make up a sick story so I could leave early, my mother refused to come and get me.

I never had the guts to go to the funeral.

But eventually, the crying ceased. The pain didn't end, however. Instead of being a pang that ravished my entire body, it transformed into a constant, low vibration of grief that followed me around throughout the day and haunted me in the deep hours of night.

Sure, Harper knew all about this, and she was there for me. And still, I appreciate that, but there was only so much she could do. There was still a void, still a scar even she couldn't reach.

But the people who should have known about all of this were my parents, but they knew none. My mother was too busy caught up in her own grief, and my father trying to console her and take care of everyone else, holding the tent down in the torrential downpour, I ended up being shoved under the rug, forced to take care of myself, fourteen and barely knowing even myself.

Betrayal and white-hot anger build up within me and at the receiving end of the spear were my parents. Why didn't they care? Why didn't they see? Why didn't they do anything about it?

I guess that's why I became even more closed off than I was before, because the people who were supposed to be there for me through this were too busy with themselves and their problems to see me, cracking and crumbling with grief in plain sight.

But eventually, I would get doused with a cool water, putting out the flames of rejection and betrayal, drowning out the perpetual grief, and overflowing the void left by my parting grandmother. But, I guess that's a story for another day.

CHAPTER NINE: Two Birds, One Stone
DAY 5 & 6 - Terra; August 9th and 10th, 2015

Our mood improves as I sing and Wyatt plays, and, in the late afternoon, we finally get going. The sweat that beads up immediately evaporates off of our cracked and dry skin. My stomach rumbles, but the feeling has become so constant that I just assume that I'm hungry, so I sip some water. We don't have any food.

We find a safe place in the rocks and set our stuff down there. Wyatt, exhausted, leans back onto the rock, hands above his head. I readjust my makeshift sweat band around my hairline.

"Let's stop," he says nonchalantly.

"Gladly," I say. My stomach rumbles again, but this time feels different, harsher and deeper, as if it's far inside of me past any physical thing. Anxiety.

Sighing with the weight of the world, I flop down in our little crevice: a sturdy ledge with secure rocks above. Every inch of my body screaming in pain, I drop my bag off of my shoulders.

Breathing hard, I let my eyelids slide closed . . .

~

And then Wyatt is shaking me awake.

Electric panic convulsing through me, I gasp awake and grab onto his arm.

"I got some food, and, uh, I guess I'll keep watch," he says, holding out a handful of berries he found.

I rub my eyes until a grayscale kaleidoscope appears in my eyes. "Did you seriously wake me up just to say that?"

"Uh, yeah."

Controlling my rapid breathing, I say, "I'm not hungry. And thanks for letting me sleep."

And then I'm out again.

~

I can't breathe. Tight beings, like cords, rip around my chest. I am hyper aware of every sensation. The sand in my toes. The scorching wind whipping across my bare body. The way that my joints crack as I stumble against the elements.

Naked and exposed and worn to a nub, I am yanked apart by an unseen force. Drawn and quartered.

As if the sun were an overhead light, it flicks on, as effortless as a light switch. And then I can see.

The sun. Its stark whiteness burns at my eyes. This is all that I can see. This is all that I am.

Like many times, though, I wish I couldn't see, for my bare body is covered with scars like skid marks from the relentless world around me. The vile desert comes into focus, every cactus, every rock, every lizard, every stabbing wave of heat.

My head screams at me. My eyes are the vehicles to my demise, as my brain overflows with visceral emotion.

I fall on my knees, then on my face, throwing myself at will to the world to be swallowed up by the darkness.

But then I feel something. A lizard crawls onto my mangled hand, resting it's rough feet there, cocking its head at me like it can hear my every thought.

My dry skin tearing, I reach up to touch the lizard, to become his friend.

But just as I do, the lizard breaks apart into fragments of ash and is whisked away by the rushing wind.

Panicking, I kick my way onto my back. Trembling ferociously, I claw and grab at the sand, but even the ground itself shrinks under my grasp and turns into soft, useless ash, markers of everything soiled and what once was.

Suddenly, I'm running. Running as the ground disintegrates under my feet, into the void that I know as life, grabbing onto rocks and cacti that blow away and flicker like fire.

But I am overcome. Everything I touch, everything I know, reduced to ash, to nothing but a byproduct of chaos.

And I fall, the brilliantly rusty desert sand spilling off of the edge and dispersing into the void.

Nothing. There's nothing. Nothing that ever mattered or that I care about. Just an emptiness where I am alone with my thoughts.

My thoughts spew out of my mouth involuntarily, as unforgiving and as relentless as chains. And they fall around me, coiling themselves around my lungs and tearing every fiber of my being.

This is it.

The chains grate against my skin, tearing me open like the crumpling of tissue paper. The pressure inside of me builds and builds, itching under the bones that encapsulate my throbbing lungs.

It swells like the climax of an orchestra until I feel that I am about to explode, my body shattering in all directions in this directionless void.

There is nothing, and I am nothing.

I am jerked back up to the ashen desert. A flat stretch of gray now, like the sun is a candle snuffed out by time and wear.

And bracing myself against the shifting ground, I cough.

Hot, painful blood comes up and stains the desert with my sorrows. Every cell in my body protests, but they work together to thrust me out of myself.

I cough until I have nothing left. No more blood seeps through my veins, and it all lies, slippery, in between my fingers on this god-forsaken desert floor. No more fight is left in my soul.

And, with desperation, I fall onto the ground, and it sucks me into oblivion.

~

Gasping in painfully, I wake up, thrashing. My body hits against the rock, the dream still flowing hot and vibrant through my veins.

And then I'm falling again.

Like a snapping rubber band, I react and claw onto the rocks swirling around me, but never do I gain purchase.

Tearing at my skin through my clothes, I tumble down the rock incline as my extremities are scraped raw.

I can't do this anymore.

So I go limp. I give up struggling in this chaotic whirlwind and let myself unravel as I fall.

And finally, I come to a skidding stop at the bottom.

Tears streaking down my face, I let the dust settle around me before pushing myself up.

And the immediate darkness closes in.

I am struck by how far I have fallen. I can see part of Wyatt's leg dangling off of the edge of where I was, about fifty feet up. Thankfully, the angle upward is shallow, so it shouldn't be hard to climb back up, right?

Feeling the thick blood seeping out of my arm, I look down to see a good portion of my elbow and outer forearm skinned to the flesh, the blood pushing out of the skin in pockets. Wincing at the pain that rushes through me like static, I brush my hand over the wound. I'd rather not see the rest of me.

The world zooms in and out around me, and the darkness encroaches, but instead of shuddering in fright, I press my palms against the sides of my forehead and groan.

"You've got to be kidding me," I say, but my voice doesn't get a foot in front of me before it's carried away by the wind, racing through the ravine like a roadrunner.

But, like the survivor that I am, I begin looking for a way to start climbing.

The wind scales across the rocks and ripples across my skin. My entire body clenches at the icy feeling of it. I grip against the rocks until the wave is over, pressing my body against the rocks so I don't balloon out like a parachute in the flimsy wind.

And, like all things, it passes.

The night drags on and the darkness only seems to deepen. And the cold digs deeper into my bones until it runs electric around my ribcage, and I begin to cough. Dust and sand rakes at the insides of my lungs.

Shattering coughs that boil wet in my throat. I react involuntarily by going limp and losing my footing. My chest explodes from the inside out, like the relentless hammering of pickaxes.

Scrambling for purchase, I shut my eyes and wait for the worst.

But all that meets my eyes is a fleeting image of Harper, shrouded in birthday streamers on the last good day. Smirking and turning away from me and walking into the dusk.

And then she's gone.

I open my eyes, my lungs fluttering like tissue paper in a storm as I breathe hard. In and out. In and out.

When the moment passes, I continue climbing. My mind wanders to deep places as the wind scales the rocks. The dream - what the hell did it mean? I can still feel the tightness in my chest from the dream, and Wyatt's steady warmth next to me.

Does any of this have a reason, a meaning? As the events and moments swirl around me, I can feel myself slipping, losing my tight, controlling grasp on reality. Reason - ha! Does reason even matter? Grumbling to myself, I hike up my pants and keep climbing.

But being oh so lost in myself, my eyes don't look before reaching, and I trust where my fingers hold.

And I slip and fall. Again.

The chaos is swallowing and all-consuming, but I can function. I know this because I catch myself. I skitter down the rocks, my hands tearing like tissue, and finally, I hit a ledge and crumple to the ground, stagnant.

Mushed in a puddle of my own worthlessness, I breathe. Letting my ribcage expand and enclose in the capsule that is my body.

Toxic thoughts turn to flashes before my eyes of the worst. I push up on my bloody elbows to see what is around me. Nothing but the bruised darkness and the thin light of the moon striking the washed-out, purple rocks. A perfectly normal sight, right?

Leaning my back against the rock wall, I press my hands to my forehead, pressing on the sore bumps like holes that puncture my skull.

But as soon as the pain shoots through my head, a light goes off, shining in my head, leaking out of the fissures of my eyes.

And I am met with the same, fleeting image of none other than my grandmother. She stands far off, deep across the chasm, in a silk nightgown that shines blue in the moonlight. Crinkling around the edges like used tissue paper that used to cocoon a present, she smiles back at me, piercing deep into my soul, drawing me forward, deeper into the realm of the past.

But I snap back, peeling my hands off of my forehead and willing my eyes to open.

Whispers of forgotten words trail off with the wind. The lost smile dance with the moon.

And forever, I am alone.

"She's dead, Terra."

My muscles convulse. I whip around, to where the sound came from, but the wind whirls it around and around - the sound has no seeming origin.

"You know it. She's dead, just like you." Hissing and spitting, so close I can grasp the sound with my fingers. And I turn to face the spitting image of myself, shining Wyatt's knife on the tail of her shirt.

Laughing, she lets the curved tip of the knife spin between her teeth, letting her lips and tongue graze the surface. But the silvery tip comes back out shining with blood.

A lump like a tennis ball grows in my lungs - swelling and ready to pop.

Crawling animalistically toward myself, I spit, "stop it."

She just smirks, peeling back her rosebud lips, easily manipulated into just the right shape at any moment.

"You're not here," I hiss, reaching for my knife - or, in this case, Wyatt's.

Smirking again. "Of course I am." She says, admiring the knife even more. "Because what you don't realize . . . is that *I am you.*"

And then she jumps at me.

Screaming and fighting, my skin presses on my own skin. Eyes red hot, she stares down at me. Drawing out every sickeningly sweet syllable, she says, her hot breath soaking my face, "You don't have the balls to do anything, much less let it go . . . . "

The cold blade of the knife presses against my neck, sending goose-flesh rippling over my pale skin.

My demented doppelganger begins to laugh, like the sputterings of an engine in the deep of winter. Her face peels and morphs as blood as black as the night seeps through her reflective teeth and drips down her face, and onto me. It's cold, like the drips of condensation on a cold drink.

The cancer in my lungs that's killing me throbs with every heave of my chest. Grabbing onto my (her) shirt with my fists, I struggle beneath my own self-hatred. Self-guilt Self-doubt. Self, self, self.

As I'm staring down the barrel of my own gun, that's in my own hands, the mirror image in front of me melts. The vile rage peels off of her face like candle wax, and her eyes flood with terror as coughs as deep as ocean trenches rocket out of her, spewing warm, moist blood in my face. Reeling back, I launch the bitch off of me.

And she goes tumbling down the rock wall, just like I did moments before.

As I stare down at my own reflection being dropped like rain into the desert chasm, she says something, screaming just loud enough for the words to tickle my ears.

"Abigail ..."

I catch it at the last second before it falls into the chasm along with my doppelganger where I'll never see it again. Grandma Abby.

As my stomach lurches for longing in my gut, the pressure dissipates in my chest, and I am left with nothing but raw sorrow and relief.

Falling back against the rocks, hugging my knees like there's no tomorrow, the emotions finally come. And I let myself cry. Let myself feel the pain, and how it ravages my heart.

~

Having been sapped of every ounce of sentiment, I push myself up. I look down, past the chocolate brown hair that the wind blows in front of my face, and see Wyatt's unscathed knife in my hand.

Tentatively, I reach up and pull back my hair away from my face, feeling the weight and texture of it. The length. I stop when I get to the rough split ends that wave and curl in every direction.

And then I finger my bangs. Twisted and curled and flipped up, but smooth and healthy.

I swallow, remembering that this was the haircut that I got a week before my fourteenth birthday.

And I haven't cut my hair since.

Before she died.

Splitting my hair down the middle, I part it at the nape of my neck and bring the two equal halves around to the front. I admire the way that it shines auburn, even in the washed out moonlight. Feeling where it brushes my lower back, I gather the hair together and take the knife up to my hair.

I have to do this.

And I saw. I saw the fibers off of my hair over the chasm, and down the strands fall. Gone forever, left to blow in the wind and decay into nothingness.

And a weight that I never knew was there falls off of my shoulders as easily as snipping off my hair was. As if the cage trapping my heart was unclipped, and the world was able to fall back into its rhythm again.

I look down at my choppy hair around my collarbones and feel anew - washed clean. And I begin climbing again.

I'll fix the choppy edges later.

CHAPTER TEN: Foolish Bickering
DAY 7 - Wyatt; August 11th, 2015

Something rustles me out of my light sleep. I turn over, but the hard rock beneath me inhibits my ability to fall right back into sleep. Becoming aware of my body once again, I push up with my arms and pull open my eyes. Terra, who now has considerably shorter hair, sits against the rocks fiddling with an empty water can, making an incredible racket with something rattling inside of the can. An intense breed of focus is stricken on her face as she holds the can inches from her face, her arms resting on her bunched up legs.

"Would you stop that?" I say, my voice glitching like a broken record. Already, the heat is blistering.

Terra's intense gaze doesn't change, it only directs its laser-like focus to me. Something is obviously wrong, but, like many times, I never know what's going on inside her head.

"Sorry," she says.

"What are you doing?"

Terra puts the can down, looks at me real serious. "I have something to tell you."

"Yeah?" A boil of anxiety forms in my stomach.

"We have four water cans left," she says.

My jaw tenses. I shut my eyes because death is about 60 ounces of water away. Every symptom of dehydration rises to a scream.

"Why did you wait until now to tell me?" Anxiety itches on my skin.

"I don't know, I just remembered now! I'm sorry-"

I take the can from her hands. "Well, what are we going to do about it?"

"I . . . I don't know! That's why I was going to ask you and maybe we could have had a discussion about this."

I sigh, rubbing my temples. "Well, it's a little late for discussion," I snap back.

Terra swallows and glares at me, cocking her head. Her silence is enough.

"I don't have any ideas. Please tell me you've got something," I say, shoving the thing back in my backpack.

"I don't know! We walk ourselves out of this desert, that's how," Terra says, rolling her eyes.

"Be serious, damn it," I sneer. I search, scrape, at the bottom of my pack for any water, any other unopened cans.

"Sorry."

"No, you're not," I grimace. "I'm just . . . really pissed you didn't tell me."

She doesn't respond. Our bodies are still frail from the bad water a few nights ago. We have yet to find another water source. Terra runs her fingers over the smooth metal of a full can, around and around. She mutters it, barely, but I hear it.

"Maybe if you didn't chug so much we'd have some more water."

I shut my eyes against the blinding sun, already baking our skin. "What?"

"I'm not the one who acts like he's got it all together and thinks he knows what's best, even when that involves consuming mass amounts of water," she licks her lips, avoiding my vile gaze. "Don't always come crawling to me for answers when you act the way you do." Her voice calms down.

It rises in my chest like vomit. "You arrogant asshole," I say.

Terra snorts. "Yeah, maybe." She pauses, exasperated. "We should have just stayed at the oasis, with all of that wonderful fresh water." The words sound innocent, but they cut deep.

I stare at her. Breaking my gaze, I press my palms to my temples. "Well, shit, it's too late to go back! But what you're not understanding is that it's *water*. And we're in *the desert*. And that you should have told me, for God's sake."

"Okay, well it's a little late for that," Terra mocks.

I shove things, stupid, stupid things that I'm probably going to die with on my back, into my bag. "Shut up. You're just blaming me because you're frustrated."

"That's not at all the point. You don't know a damn thing."

"Then what is? What is the point of you overreacting like this? I was just trying to help because I was thirsty - because we're in the desert." I yank on the fucking zipper to close my bag.

Terra suddenly bursts forth, speaking with harsh words and spitting syllables. "No, you overreacted because of your poor, awful life." Terra throws her hands forward and hitting me square in the chest, shoving me backward and I hit the rock wall. "'Oh, poor me.' Poor Wyatt with his broken family. Poor Wyatt and his sympathetic drug abuse. Poor Wyatt and your heroic heart. Poor Wyatt and his bastard sister." She moves forward, cornering me, hands still pressed on my chest.

And that's when I wrestle my elbow up and ram it across her face. The moment these words tear from her lips, regret floods her face as the hair whips around her raw cheek. My entire being burns with shame as I look down in disbelief. How did she know? She must have found out before the crash.

But she's right. Lilly is a bastard child, in the legitimate sense of the word. Born out of an affair to my married mother and another man, who is not my biological father. But she is just as much as my sister as any other blood relative. And I take this as a personal attack.

The gravity of what she's said registers on her face. "I - I'm sorry."

"No, you're not," I hiss.

"Yeah, but you hit me," Terra says, still in awe of her tingling cheek.

"Yeah, but you shoved me."

Terra's jaw clenches, but then her features soften into vile sarcasm. "Hopefully we work this out before we die of dehydration." Then, with stricken eyes, she turns away and goes to sit out on the rocks, facing the gray overcast sky, just as rocky and rolling as the landscape.

I sigh and sit back on my knees. Already, I run our exchange over and over in my head. Cutting phrases and clever insults flood my mind, awful, hateful things I could and should have said to Terra about her range of flaws. For a hot minute, I think of saying these things, but then I take that fucking water can and throw it across the cave. It bursts open, and water darkens the rocks as it dribbles out.

Shit shit shit. Frantically, I suck on the open hole of the can and cup the still spilling water in my hands.

But by that point, I've lost half the can anyways. After drinking a mouthful and restraining myself, I look out at Terra's figure, still sitting in the distilled light. She was still wrong. She had most of the control of the water cans; she must have known. She should have told me so we could do something about this sooner. I wish I could explain this to her and I wish she would listen. I wish I could take all of my anger back. I wish we could make it right.

But I shouldn't have hit her, either.

In a half-assed effort, I take the rest of the can and walk over. I stand above her and clear my throat.

"You want the rest?"

She looks me up and down, and while I can still feel her animosity, her eyes are clear. "Thanks."

I slowly back away as she drinks the rest of it. Watching with apathy, I watch as she fiddles with the can in her hands, then violently smashes it against the ground, crumpling the can, and tosses it over the cliff, grunting with catharsis.

I breathe out, rubbing the elbow that made contact with Terra's jaw. Hot, awful tears prick at my eyes, because I'm not on the path to becoming my father. I already am.

Slowly, rain starts to fall outside, glossing over the dry sand. I watch for a moment, as the textured sky continues to spew rain.

I stand, still somewhat angry. "Let's go," I say. "We can't stay here, in this cave."

"Why not?" says Terra, gritting her teeth defiantly.

"Because if it floods, we'll be stuck in here like rats," I say, throwing my bag over my shoulder.

Terra raises an eyebrow at me. "Well, yeah, that makes sense, but you don't have to be so rude about it."

My chest lurches forward, and I want to say something cutting, but I don't. I hold my tongue and duck out of the cave. Already, most of the rocks are stained with a darkened, polka-dotted pattern.

As we walk, the rain only falls harder, in blinding, gray sheets. Every once in awhile, I'll look back and see Terra behind me, spotty like a hologram with bad reception. The rain is cleansing, somehow, as the warm water washes away the sweat the moment it beads up on my face.

Suddenly, lightning strikes the sky, contorted like arthritic fingers. Its large and long and seems to light up the sky for a full second, and I take in what's around me before the afternoon plunges back into darkness.

Moments later, thunder makes the rocks tremble.

"Whoa!" Terra exclaims from behind me, the awe sparkling in her voice. I hesitate, then keep walking, barreling through the rain. "C'mon, " she shouts through the rain. "Look at all this water! We should be appreciating it, not barreling through it!" she snips. It seems that she's already gotten over our little ordeal.

When I don't answer, Terra speaks again. "Can we at least collect this water?"

I sigh and turn around. "Hopefully it won't make us vomit and hallucinate our siblings."

I can tell, she wants to smile, but all I get is a glare.

We sit on some rocks and watch as the raindrops ping off of the cans, and some making it in. And we sit here, watching water pool at our feet and stream away, carrying stones and plants with it. The rain doesn't relent, and the desert seems to not be soaking much of this water up - at first, when it started raining, the desert soaked the water up as a whole, being rejuvenating by the light rain. But then the downpour started, and the plants droop, berated and downtrodden by its once savior.

"I'm sorry. For everything," I say.

She looks up at me, with an unmistakable genuineness that so, purely *Terra*. "Me too."

I smile at her. She smiles back. I'll take that as forgiveness any day.

This rain is like being constantly drenched by a bucket of water poured over my head. I rest my elbows on my thighs, and press my hands to my forehead, pushing my hair out of my eyes and letting it rest on my hands, dripping in a halo around my face. The water still leaks between my fingers and down my cheeks. I am constantly wiping the dirt and sweat off of my face, but it seems just to be rubbing the gunk around.

I look up, and see Terra looking up at the dark clouds, arms outstretched, water dripping off of her like sweat from an angel. Her arms are outstretched, and her mouth is open, overflowing with the warm rain. After gulping down the water, she shakes out her hair and wipes her eyes with the pads of her fingers. She smiles at me, and for the first time, I can truly see the happiness radiating out of her, evaporating the sad rain and pushing away the darkness.

"Why are you smiling?" I smirk and shout through the rain.

"Because I'm trying to enjoy it!" Terra says, shaking her mane of hair, sending droplets flying into the drenching rain. She leaps over towards me and grabs me by the hands. Groaning, I move along with her as she pulls me up and yanks me around, twirling in the mud and rain. Her laughter bubbles like soda overflowing a glass, bubbling onto me, and we turn the dark drizzle into shimmering diamonds. We prance with our mouths wide open, our bodies drinking in the rain instead of wallowing in it.

And I am swept away in the majesty of this moment, I pull Terra closer, because why not? And suddenly, her back gives out and she lets me dip her down like a glass ballerina. The rain has changed from a bucketful of downpour to the shower setting on a hose.

And as the clear water falls in crystalline rivulets down our faces, the world zooms into one fine point - Terra's face, right here. Just us. And the hum around us swells, and the rain turns into a roar that fills my ears.

And then my heart drops to my stomach and turns to an ice cube as both of our heads snap to the left, breaking our gaze like a snapping branch on a thigh. Flowing down the mountains and across the plains is a morphing, bubbling, and hissing flood. Hundreds of thousands of gallons of water scream toward us.

Tearing ourselves apart, we grab our bags and run. We run away, our shoes slipping on the wet, gravel-like sand, sopping plants grabbing our ankles as the water boils closer and closer.

High ground. The one, single phrase pops into my head, the one ingrained thought whenever there's a flood. Get to high ground.

"Get up!" I scream to Terra, the rain like the assault of darts. I grab her arm, but she slips away. Thinking that this isn't clear enough, I shout out again. "Terra, get to high ground, on the rocks!"

But I can't see her. All I know is that she's running beside me, but I peel away and up. The flood is rushing like an inhuman monster throughout this low ground. I begin scaling the slick rocks, trying to somehow to make it to high ground. But truly, we're stuck in a little bowl. These rocky areas are just the cereal, drowning in a flood of milk. There's nowhere to hide. Because as I make it to the top of this rock structure, the wind and rain beat down harder. I clasp onto the rocks and straddle them as I look behind me. And finally, the water overcomes where I just was, rushing like one slick being, filling every crevice with its evil.

"Terra!" I scream, but it seems that the sound doesn't make it past my lips. I can only really see anything when the frequent flash of lightning electrifies the murky water beneath, ferociously lapping up higher on my rocks like a dog barking up a tree at a cat - but my tree is being chopped down.

"Terra!" I shout into the oblivion, hanging on with every ounce of strength I have until it hurts like hell. I scan the shiny water. "Terra, where are you?!?"

And through the pounding rain, I see a counter-movement in the water. Far below, on a stone, I see Terra gripping onto a rock, gasping for breath.

Immediately, I launch myself into the valley, scooping deep into the water. The water sucks to me like tiny, soft leeches, and bubbles swirl around me. I open my eyes, but I am still met with blackness. The water feels warm and gritty on my skin and eyes, and I kick, still not hitting the bottom, even with my bag dragging me down. I break the surface, water pulling me along, yanking at my limbs. The rain crashes down, and the sound of the thunder pierces my ears like cotton balls. I ferociously kick and swim over to Terra, and I feel her hand reaching out for me, so I fumble and grab for it. She pulls me up onto her rock.

"Why did you do that, you idiot!" she screams at me, her entire being weighted down by the water.

I heave and hack, grabbing onto the other side of the rock. The waves slam me into the side of the rock. I still have no grasp of how far down the actual ground is.

"Well, sorry, I was just trying to help!" I shout back, shaking my head.

"I could have made it over. Now we're both stuck here - "

Just then, a wave crests over my head, slamming my head down onto the rock, sending warm blood dribbling out of my throbbing nose. But Terra got the wave right to the face. Coughing, she pulls herself back up.

"Damn it," she shouts, throat gargling, clawing at the slick sandstone.

I grab onto her arm none the less. And her eyes meet mine, and the fear inside of her runs through me like a jolt.

The water flows past us, clawing at us, taunting at us to come with it like the chaos in a high school hallway, and then when we don't comply, grabbing us by the neck and putting a bag over our heads and dragging us off regardless. Waves lap up around me, getting more powerful by the moment, hitting me square on the back and dragging me to the side, with the current. But I refuse, holding on with aching muscles as we go blind from the water again.

And we stay here for a while, willing to wait out the storm. But Terra's slick skin keeps slipping from my locked fingers, so now instead of her mid-forearm, I am ripping off her hand at the wrist. And the waves eat away at my strength, the cool rain sapping away my body heat. I am exhausted, but I take life each moment at a time. One wave after another, one blink, one breath, one drop at a time, even though I know I'm slipping. Destruction is inevitable.

And it comes in the form of a wave, lit by a crack of lightning through the sky, like being on the inside of a dark vase, and it finally cracking open and seeing the light of day for the first time.

We tumble through the water, blindly, bubbles and water and plants and water and hell. Pure chaos and hell. But it all ends abruptly when my back slams into a rock, and I am able to suck air into my lungs. My hand is still interlocked with Terra's, and I writhe around to see her, hanging on as the white water rushes past, grabbing and tearing at her like a thousand angry human hands. I hold on to the rock and try to pull Terra up against the current . . but I can't . . . I just can't.

"I'm so sorry, Terra," I shout, my throat like rubber.

"Wyatt, I hope you can forgive me," Terra says back, spitting water out of her mouth and coughing once to her side.

And then she lets go.

My entire body screams. It just screams. But after we lost touch, I couldn't see her any longer, for the water swallowed her up like a hungry beast, and going back to its normal flow like nothing happened.

My bitter tears mix with the cloudy blood on the rock from my nose, and I sob. What have I done?

And I hang on and weather the storm, alone.

April 16th, 2012 - Wyatt

Mom forgot. Again. But I didn't care. I don't much like school. Sure, my friends are there, but that's all that I really enjoy. But here we were. 8:01 am, all ready and dressed and clean, and Mom hadn't come home until 1 am.. And the minutes were still ticking by and she still hadn't come out - or even made any noise, until it was half past eight.

During this half hour period, Lilly would often get worried and fidget, wanting to go in there and wake Mom, telling her that we'd all be late. But I suppose you could say that I was playing a cruel, if well-deserved, joke. I was going to wait, in the tiny entry hall of our apartment, until my mother awoke. And she always did. And she would shout, but then blame herself, then curse and rush and curse some more until we would be carted off to school.

I was right. I usually am, but Mom stumbled out of her bedroom at 9 am sharp, hungover and messy, took one look at the time and at her two children, all poised and ready at the door, and swore so viciously that a sailor would be offended. I covered Lilly's ears, but not before she heard the first half of the obscene alphabet.

Mom was ready in 15 minutes. I swear, she literally grabbed us by the collars and dragged us into the elevator. That was probably the first time she had taken a breath since she saw the clock.

Looking into the polished metal of the elevator, my mother straightened her collar. She didn't say anything, so neither did we.

It didn't occur to her until we had just pulled up to my middle school. This was evidenced by what she said when we made it to the front drive. She handed me an excuse note and paused before she unlocked the doors so I could get out.

Mom swallowed and tucked a piece of her dishwater-blonde, curly hair behind her head. "Why didn't you wake me up?"

Dry anger burned in my throat. I wanted to smack her, tell her that this was all her fault, that she should try and take some responsibility around here, but I didn't. And there is a part of me that regrets not saying those things that she deserved to hear because maybe it would have mended something.

I got out of the car and swung my backpack around onto my back. I ducked under to look at my Mom in the car. Words finally bubbled up and out. "It's not my job to wake you up."

Mom looked like she was going to say something, but I didn't care. I just slammed the door and walked inside the building.

The secretary lady looked quite suspicious when I handed her my note, but she let me sign in and go to class.

I was angry, and my friends could tell, but they knew that I got this way sometimes. They'd talk and they'd comfort and they'd smile, but there was only so much they could do.

The only real interesting thing that happened that day was during gym. It was a beautiful, mid-spring day, and the air was so thick you could almost see the clumps of pollen drifting with the wind. The gym floor was getting rewaxed, so we had a free day in gym. I was playing basketball with some acquaintances on the blacktop, since my friends weren't in this gym hour. They were nice and good basketball mates, but no one who would stick their necks out for me. Like today.

"Hey, Tony! I'm open!" I shouted, dodging around another kid whose name I forgot. Tony chested the ball to me, and I caught it just in time to do a jump shot into the basket. I loved days like this, when I could just get lost in the sport. No matter what happened before or after, I could always do something I loved and everything else would fade away, at least for a while.

The three on three game ended its second round, and I ran my fingers through my hair and high-fived Drake, the other player on our three-man team. My curls always drooped in my face when I got sweaty. Girls said it was cute, but I always thought it was annoying.

Just before we were about to start game three, a blunt object nailed me right in the side of the head. A football dropped to the ground, bouncing awkwardly on the blacktop. I picked up the football and looked to my right, from where the football came, and the playing field stretched out. A pack of four boys sauntered over, but they weren't the football player guys. These were the bad boys who were popular for the mere reason that they were bad.

From afar, I could identify Alex, Colin, Jacob and someone else. I immediately knew it was them. Who else could it have been? And why would they have been walking over here anyways?

"What the hell was that?" I shouted once they were closer.

"Just give the ball back, sissy," Alex snorted.

Six words and they already crossed a line. But before I could respond with some equally snide comment, Drake snapped: "Screw off, Alex."

I stepped closer to Alex, but he didn't move. "What's your problem with me?" I said, my voice going up a decibel. This wasn't the first time Alex and his gang had been assholes to me. I was just hoping this time it would be the last.

"My problem with you is that you think you can just say whatever you want and hang out with whoever you want and do whatever you want. That was for your asshole comment yesterday, dickhead," Alex said, trying to raise his voice louder than mine. He was talking about how I called him out and said he didn't deserve to be in honors classes because all he does is bitch. Which was in response to him commenting on me not pulling my weight in a stupid group project.

"Take your stupid ball back," I shout, tossing the damn thing over my shoulder. I see out of the corner of my eye that we've caught the attention of the surrounding boys, and even a few girls.

I'm just about to tell Alex and his crew to fuck off when Alex shouts, as loud as he can: "And besides, we all know about your sister, the retard."

I stopped. A crowd clustered around us like we were an open wound and they were the blood. Everyone's eyes were on me, peeling away at my skin, seeing what I'd do. I know exactly what he's talking about. My sister, God love her, didn't have a lot of friends. She was dyslexic, and when she was younger would have breakdowns at school that gave her an odd reputation. Everyone associated me with her, and that was usually the source of my torment. And that was usually the reason why I got in so many fights.

But Alex had a point: I was also a dick.

Air puffed in and out of my nose, and I could feel my fair skin growing hot. I spun on my heel and got up real close to Alex, so he could feel my hot, angry breath on his skin. "What did you say?" I made sure to spit out every consonant, right into Alex's arrogant little eyes.

"You heard me," Alex said, narrowing his eyes. He reached up to grab my shirt and thrust me away from him. Quite gutsy, knowing that I had two inches and ten pounds on him.

Fuming mad, I stomped forward and grabbed Alex's own gym shirt and socked him straight across the face. It felt good, impossibly good. And also incredibly bad, because rage burned at my soul. I could hear the crowd take a collective inhale, like this was some freaking WWE broadcast.

Alex slowly turned around when he was on the ground to look up and face me. His little henchmen tried to help him up, but he waved them off. He just looked me in the eye and said: "You little shit." I parted my feet and prepared to fight.

Thinking that he was going to punch me, I was unprepared when Alex charged for me and knocked both of us to the ground. We fell so hard the wind was knocked out of me, but I refused to let that falter me. In Alex's own breathless state, I thrust him to the left, so I could be on top of him and beat him to a pulp. It worked well, for I threw punch after punch at Alex, feeling every ounce of anger flood out of me as my knuckles came in contact with his revolting skin. I wished these people would just go away. There's nothing to see here. But I refused to stop until this conflict was resolved. Because I refused to let Alex win.

The gym teacher obviously heard the commotion, but I didn't care. All that mattered was that Alex was getting what he fucking asked for.

A pair of arms latched under my own and pulled me up. I kicked and I screamed, but the gym teacher pulled me away. But Alex pounced. All three of us slammed onto the ground. A ripple of pain went through my cheekbone when Alex's fist smashed into my face. The gym teacher managed to pull Alex off of me.

His voice screamed into the distance when he shouted: "Stop it, both of you!"

I wasn't finished. I was starting to get mad at the gym teacher for getting in my way. Charging forward, I prepared to hit again. The gym teacher put both of his forearms up, and both Alex and I, blinded by anger, knocked into him.

The gym teacher, normally a chill guy, grabbed my shirt by the fistfuls and got up real close. "Back. Off," he said and wrapped his meaty hand around my arm. I could have struggled and got away, but it wasn't worth it. Alex was being dragged in with me anyways. Blood poured from both nostrils, and the side of his lip had been split open. His right eye was already swelling. A twinge of guilt ran through me. It didn't last, though, for he still looked as mad as high hell. And besides, I wouldn't have punched him if he would have just left me alone. I didn't resist as the gym teacher pulled us into the building.

He took us to the principal's office and threw us down onto the bench outside. "Park your butts here and don't move," he said and went inside.

I gripped the armrest hard, until my knuckles turned white. I could already feel them bruising from beating the snot out of Alex. His eyes were on me, drilling vicious holes into my face. I turned my head to look at him, but he just narrowed his eyes.

I crossed my arms, slouched low in the chair, and rubbed a sore spot on my cheek. Alex only got a few punches in, but those would surely create a bruise. I felt the inside of my cheek with my tongue. Blood filled my mouth, and I poked at the ragged flesh in the soft spot where my teeth met.

We were in there for about an hour, as students came in and out, and our parents were most likely called. I'd been in plenty of fights before, that's usually how these things go. But then, I thought about Mom. She'd definitely be pissed that I had gotten in another school fight, and nag me about it. But how much did it matter, anyway? A day or two would pass, and she wouldn't care much anymore.

The anger that seared between my eyes had subsided, and I could breathe normally again, but I was still mad. I still hated Alex. I still hated my life. I still hated school. Nothing changed, except for another kid knew that I shouldn't be messed with.

Tony and the other guys I was playing basketball with went in, and they eventually came out. Then went in Alex's friends. Now all we had to do was wait until our parents arrived so we could receive the latest death sentence.

My mom eventually came, flustered and stressed out like an old rubber band. She scowled at me, and I stared back at her. She was in there for a while, then the principal opened the door and summoned me in.

I made sure to slouch as far down as I could in that soft, slightly stained chair. The principal was a young man, with salt and pepper hair. He walked with a casual, no-nonsense demeanor that was just strict enough to unnerve you, but he had a casual, warm smile that reassured you that he wasn't actually going to whoop your ass.

"So glad to have you, Ms. Hill. And Wyatt." He shook my mother's hand. He just nodded at me. Maybe Mr. Shane knew that it wasn't really my fault. Maybe he wasn't going to blame this all on me. He knew I never fought without being provoked.

My mother's smile appeared plastic, for I knew she was really pissed. Maybe she'd be pissed at me for a whole 3 days this time.

Mr. Shane sat back in his swivel chair and sighed, looking at me. I tried not to wince when his chair squealed loudly. "Now, Wyatt. Why don't you tell me what happened out there." I kept my eyebrows knotted, but parted my lips. I told him about how my friends and I were just minding our own business when Alex threw a ball at me. He got mad, and I got mad, blah blah, he said this, I punched him, stuff happened, you know the story. But Mr. Shane just stroked his stubble when I finished.

"I know, Wyatt. That's essentially the same story everyone else has told me. But what I really want to know is, why? Why do you feel the need to do this?" He said matter-of-factly, almost kindly.

I genuinely thought about this for a moment, but the only answer I could come up with was subpar. "Because . . . I have to defend myself."

"Against who, Wyatt?" Mr. Shane said. I caught a hint of 'psychologist' in his voice.

"Against everyone," I said. Where the hell is this going?

"Why? Why do you feel like you have to fight when anyone comes against you?"

Shut the hell up, Mr. Shane. You don't know a damn thing. But I didn't have an answer. Or, at least, one that would have pleased him.

Mr. Shane sighed, deeply, sadly. "Wyatt, you're a good kid." I sat back in my chair and relaxed, not realizing I was so uptight. "You've got straight A's, always have. You have lots of friends, you're outgoing, you're involved with the school and, based on your records, you hardly ever have classroom misconduct. But . . . then there's this." Mr. Shane rubbed his temples with his hand. "You can't keep getting in fist fights like this, Wyatt. I just don't understand - "

"You don't have to understand," I said, and walked out.

~

The issue was resolved, as it always is. Alex and I were both sentenced to a week of detention and no after school activities for the rest of the year. I was right; Mom stayed mad for 3 days this time. But I still felt bad. Nothing changed. No matter how many assholes I beat up, I was still stuck, in the mundane, endless cycle of my shitty life. And I hated it. But, of no surprise to anyone, I hate a lot of things.

I always took to violence. It just seemed natural. Then again, my hatred seemed natural as well.

This cycle kept going. I kept hanging out with terrible people, kept beating assholes' faces in. Kept up the facade for Lilly. Because I had to.

But eventually, I would get doused with a refreshing stream, putting out the flames of hurt and spite, drowning out the perpetual grief, and overflowing the void left by my abandoning father. But, I guess that's a story for another day.

CHAPTER ELEVEN: Stabbed with Irony
DAY 8 - Terra; August 12th, 2015

I jerk awake, like the snapping of a twig. But as soon as I am conscious, the awareness of my lungs comes slamming in like a tidal wave. My lungs constrict from the inside out, like the snapping of elastic cords.

Suddenly, I lurch forward, and water sputters out of my mouth, burning like acid as I roll onto my side. Water, saliva, and something sharply metallic dribbles out of my lips as I can do nothing else but expel all of the water out. Pain blossoms in my chest, and I heave in and out between coughs to get the last painful drops out of my lungs. Bracing my hands on the ground, my whole body undulates as I violently cough, but even when I relax, I still feel pain deep within my chest.

With disgruntled motions, I roll back over and lay flat on my back, just where I was. The bright sun stings my eyes, but I focus on taking deep, full breaths into my abdomen, not my chest. However, a sharper pain remains in my right side. I begin to chest-breathe, because that doesn't feel quite as painful, even though it makes me cough more.

After I'm sure I won't begin to cough out my lungs again, I slowly sit up, but painfully grunt when I recognize an unnatural tightness in my right side, a squeezing and pinching of my flesh. Glancing down, I draw back in horror at the cactus spines jutting out of my side. There are at least four large spines, along with a few smaller ones in the general vicinity. I must have hit a cactus when the flash flood carried me away.

It all comes slamming back - the argument, the rain, the dancing, the flood, me letting go, the water, all around. Then black. And now pain. Just cactus spines embedded into a pool of dark red blood encircling my side, resembling spilled wine.

I gingerly touch the spines, sticking awkwardly out, moving stiffly with my body. I repress a sigh, knowing I'm going to have to pull these out at some point.

Grunting, I ease my backpack off of my back, wondering how it stayed on my back. But my mind immediately drifts from it, for that doesn't really matter. Instead of focusing on the drilling pain blossoming in my side, I focus on trying to get these fuckers out.

Two are sporadically stuck on the flat, outside part of my arm, so I pull those two out first. Shooting pain races through my arm. I internally groan. If the two-inch long one stuck in my arm hurt that bad, how much more will all of these larger ones hurt?

I grit my teeth and work on pulling out another spine from the fleshy part just below my ribs, around my waist area. That one hurt just the same as the one in my arm, so I suspect it didn't puncture much of anything. However, blood dribbles out, seeping into the band of my pants.

And then . . . the last two spines, long, thick and sharper than a needle, jut out of places that cannot be mistaken for anywhere but my ribs. I decide to take out the longest one first since that might leave less pain for the finale. I reach over with my left hand and grab the spine firmly and pull directly out . . . but it slides out of my flesh a lot easier than I expected.

Pain ravishes across my side. Tears prick at my eyes, and I have to bite my lip to keep from screaming.

I look down to see only about an inch of the cactus spine was embedded in my flesh. Great. That means the other one is surely further in.

I swallow hard and grasp the last one. Pain jabs in my side the moment I touch it. Shit.

But I begin pulling. An awful squishing noise erupts as I pull the damn thing out. Blood pours down my side as I feel a sucking sensation. . . . and suddenly it's out, blood gushing out of my side. I lurch forward, only slightly aware of the drilling in my side. Sputtering for air, I cough violently. Blood and saliva dribble from my lips, clumping in the dry sand beneath my double vision.

Claws of pain scrape and gouge at my side. I find myself on the ground, my cheek grinding my own blood and saliva into the sand, shaking and groaning in agony. Soft, shallow sobs escape my throat, tears cutting gashes in my face. I'm going to die.

I push myself up on my wobbly arms and collapse onto a boulder beside me, my bloody, punctured side baking in the hot sun. Even after the water and rain has washed away, the air still remains unnaturally humid and pungent, like the sharp taste that wallows in my mouth.

I reach down and begin to slowly pull off my tank shirt, now a good third of it blood-soaked. When the torn fabric brushes over the puncture wounds, I wince, causing another round of coughing. Less blood regurgitates this time.

I finish yanking my shirt off and give a shallow sigh of relief. I've found out that stomach breathing hurts too much and makes me cough, so I resort to uncomfortable chest breathing. Lifting my arm, I crane my neck around to see deep red puncture wounds, still dribbling thick blood and ground up flesh. The smell of my own metallic blood and festering flesh sends me reeling. I look away and gag as the gruesome images flood my brain. I swallow hard and suck it up.

Straining, I reach into my bag and pull out one of my four remaining water cans. Since I can't find the pocket knife - correction, I just don't want to look for it - I bash a small rock against the top until a jagged hole appears.

Looking away, I pour the lukewarm water over my side at an angle, but as I breathe, a horrid gurgling sensation rises in my chest, and I have to drop the water can to keel over and cough again. These coughs, however, are deep and rattling. Not because of a tickle in my throat, or even an irritation in my bronchial tubes, but they are something deeper, something more serious. This realization sends a cold terror running through me, turning to milky ice in my gut.

I force the rest of the water over my flesh, rubbing in soft, circular motions to get the rest of the dried blood off and clean the wound. The bloody water soaks into my pants, but I don't care. The water is colder than my baking skin, which I appreciate. The pain makes my hands tremble.

Heaving, I lay back down on the rock, wounds up. The blood still runs down my side, tickling my skin like damp fingertips. I reach over and grab my jacket and press it against my side, wincing, squinting in the harsh sunlight. But I don't remove the rough fabric. I have to get the bleeding to stop. It feels as if my whole side is exposed, not just this small part, my body spitting like a leaky pipe.

Eventually, I peel my jacket off and gently feel the skin around my puncture wounds. Blood only trickles out, no longer gushing. I decide that's good enough, and slowly maneuver up into an upright position, on my knees. I take out the first aid kit, and pull out some clean gauze - actually, it's soaking wet - with my grubby hands I ring it out as much as possible. I press lots of gauze onto my wounds and quickly tape up my side. I pull my bloody shirt back over my head, the blood now rust colored.

And breathe.

Sipping at the rest of the water can, I down two painkillers.

My tank shirt now hangs a bit loose on my frame. like a small mannequin with a large shirt on. I put my tattered cardigan back on, and sling my sopping backpack over my back, a spike of pain striking my side.

And I look out, and something cold creeps into every like vein of my body. The light is blinding, and the wind wraps around me like a blanket, swaddling me like a small child. For once, seeing the stillness around me, I am struck with the true realization that I am alone out here. A vast and encompassing loneliness rubs its hands up my arms and gently draping itself over me. At first, I welcome this soft sensation, but once I realize the toxicity of the grip, it's too late. The feeling has coiled around me like a boa constrictor. I can't breathe, and it's not because of my punctured ribcage.

I am alone. Truly, utterly, alone. I am encompassed with a childlike fear. And suddenly, I am jolted back to a simpler time, a simpler place. A place where fridges were stocked with food and shelves stocked with items. A place where I am a small child and lost in the supermarket, where the fluorescent lights are impending, and the adults all speak in loud voices. And where I am small, and everything is large. Where I am an insignificant speck of wandering dust in a rotund world.

Where every fiber of my being yearns for someone, anyone, even my worst enemy for some solitary company.

The sun dangles low like a shiny Christmas ornament in the sky, so I find a bare swatch of land that seems safe. But I don't seem to care. I just need to lie down. The painkillers barely take the edge off of my pain.

I start a fire with ease since I have the lighter, and watch as the glow of the fire seems to make the sky darker. The sparks crackle and hiss, making for a nice chatter to fill my ears. I listen while the fire tells me his life story, along with a fable about his family. The flames are animated while he talks, writhing and flickering and dancing to the beat of his own drum. Still, the fire seems disconnected from me. I bet he can tell I'm not listening because I periodically nod my head and say shallow things in response, but I stare right past the translucent blue fire and to the empty space across from me. I can nearly see Wyatt there, laughing, throwing around some casual words. I can see his eyes sparkling with joy or burning with passion. I see him shining his pocket knife on his shirt.

Air leaks out of my mouth, whining like a sad balloon. Reaching in my pocket, I take out Wyatt's pocket knife. Relief floods my stomach. I shine the blade on the tail of my ratty shirt. Words, engraved on the metal, glistening in the firelight. Wyatt Hartman, Eagle Scout.

Hmm. I never knew that about him. It explains some things, though. Yet, it also doesn't explain some other ones, though. I hope he's not hurt.

I sigh, feeling the pain jab through my chest. Absently, I shove the knife back in my pocket. The fire keeps chattering, but I have no use for its light-hearted clamor. I lean my head back on the boulder supporting me, and my body rolls half-heartedly to face the darkening desert. Apathy and exhaustion wash over me, and I am trapped inside my body - a soul in a glass jar. And as my vision disappears into the purple darkness, an illuminating, human figure walks toward me.

CHAPTER TWELVE: Leaking Frustration
DAY 8 - Wyatt; August 12th, 2015

My consciousness is dragged from a deep sleep, and I become aware of my body, lying limp over a rock. I lift myself up with a grunt, already baked sore by the sun.

Rubbing my eyes, sand makes me tear up. I look around, but such a small action sends bones cracking. The bare stretch of desert has changed, but I haven't moved much. Cacti are overturned, cracked at the base. The cool water wades up above my ankles, cloudy and red, littered with roots and plants. The dark water has pooled in the lowest spot, where I reside, still and already buzzing with mosquitoes. Small, shrubby plants are only noticeable by their small branches that poke the surface of the water.

A certain tightness worms its way into my lungs, and I reel over and cough, spewing water out.

After heaving, I stand up. My muscles ache and burn, and it's a tremendous struggle to lift my sorry ass from the ground. But I check myself. No new wounds, no life-threatening ailments - despite being a little banged up and tired, I'm fine.

I check my bag - sopping wet, but everything remains intact. I sigh and swing the pack over my shoulder. I am alone.

Where to next?

My tongue rubs like damp sand paper up against the roof of my mouth, and I search inside my bag for any water cans. One. I fumble in my bag and pull it out, bash the top against a sharp rock. Silky water spews out, and I furiously lick at the water on the rocks. I suck back every single ounce of the water and sit back, feeling the swollenness of my stomach.

A moment later, my thirst returns. I slosh my boots in the oddly warm water that I can still feel in my socks. Intrusive thoughts flash in my mind's eye. I drop everything and cup my hands around the leftover flood water. Warm, like hot tea. But I cup the stuff in my hands. Cloudy, and gritty at the bottom and riddled with insect parts and plant segments. Pigmented a deep terra-cotta and tan from the sand, I sniff the water. It smells fine, if a bit salty, but it's so cluttered, that I throw the handful back into the water. Better not.

I sit on the rock I awoke on, the water rippling around my shoes. I watch, hungry and defeated as the ripples splay out, touching rocks and enveloping plants that jut up. My eye follows the stream of water around the rocks, leaking down the curve of the land. The water ripples, reminiscent of the monster it once was.

But it's moving. Still leaking and moving and morphing. Away from me, towards something else . . . The water is leaking to the lowest point . . . . a flash goes through my mind - of the water flowing past, the waves, and Terra. Terra being swept away. Maybe she's that way. Maybe I'll find her if I follow the way the water took her. So I start sloshing through the mud in the direction of the current.

I keep going to lower and lower ground. Eventually, I find a rock to rest on and stare out at the desert stretch. No animals in sight. The plants are droopy and sopping in water - and besides, I'm not yet apt enough to identify the plants we have been eating, or make decisions about new ones.

I swallow hard, my gooey throat sticking to itself, and keep walking.

As I am treading along, and the water diminishes for some reason, I kick something hard and metal. It wavers in the water and eventually floats up. It's a . . . water can. Obviously one of the ones that we had because it's got that grimy shine and those ridges. One of us must have lost it in the chaos.

One of us. Us. However, there is no 'us' anymore. Terra is . . . gone. She's absent at the moment. I realize that it's entirely bullshit, but it pacifies me for a while. Hell, she might be dead. But I refuse to miss her.

I walk until evening. I finally conclude why the water is disappearing so fast - it's evaporating in the heat. Nearly right before my eyes.

Exhausted from the day, I climb to higher ground. I find a butte in the mountains to rest in, overgrown with brush.

I set my sopping wet stuff down against the rock wall and sigh. The mud caked on my body chills me to the bone. I search for my lighter - nothing. Dammit, I must have left it with Terra. Not even a drenched match.

The desert is beautiful - coming alive after the rain - unfortunately, I am unable to appreciate it because of the encroaching loneliness. Instead, I put my mind to something more productive - making a fire.

Before this, a flame has always been provided for us - either with a match or my lighter. But now, I have resorted to a pile of tumbleweed brambles and a few sticks. I strike two rocks against each other, but all that happens is that the rocks scratch against each other, leaving white streaks.

Shaking with anger, I throw those pieces of shit over the edge and watch as the clink against the other rocks and fall. Now all that's left is a friction fire.

Trying to remember what I learned in Boy Scouts, I reassemble the little pile of tinder and pull back. It's all very damp, and a wet spot stains the dusty ground. It's not like I was making any sparks anyways.

I throw the pile of junk over the edge for good measure as well. It's no use, everything's too wet to start a fire.

I wrap myself up in the jacket and sleeping bag - I do have that - as the night plunges into ice.

CHAPTER THIRTEEN: Visions of Life and Death

DAY 10 - Terra; August 14th, 2015

My nerves slowly awaken. One by one, they start sending signals to my brain. I feel my toes in my socks. My legs rubbing against my pants. My belt pressing up against my hips. The creases of my armpits already pooling with sweat. The pads of my fingers rubbing up against the hard rubber of the pocket knife's hilt.

Small, poking sensations run across my leg, and it's this that makes me open my eyes. I see its large and flat body, like the flattened pennies you get from those machines in museums. I see the curving tail, erect with a shining stinger. I see the angular legs and claws, moving with casual precision. An Arizona bark scorpion crawls up my leg.

"Holy SHIT!" I scream. With lightning for blood, I kick my legs frantically and push away from the rock I was sleeping on. I bat at my legs and torso, searching for the nasty creature.

I stop once I realize I am on the still warm coals from my fire. My breathing works like painful, creaking motions of a machine as I heave hard, clenching the pocket knife. I frantically search the area and find the camouflaged beast scuttling away under a rock as if nothing happened.

"Son of a . . . " But I stop, the words burning my dry throat like fire. I can feel someone . . . someone's eyes on me.

Horrified, I turn and look at the boulder to my right. I glance up and down her modest figure and see that her dark black hair is matted tight, her face smeared with dirt, and clothes worn at the knees and torn at the edges. Harper sits, casually fiddling with her nails, but with a stare like sweet acid.

" . . . bitch," I finish, still curled up and defensive of the scorpion.

Harper smiles back, and her genuineness surprises me. "Well, hello to you too."

~

"Wha . . . you're not here! You can't be here!" I exclaim, pacing right over what once was my nice little home.

Harper snorts. "Well, why not?"

My eyebrows clench, hard. "Because . . . because of the plane crash, and my father, and Wyatt . . . how are you here?"

Harper rolls her eyes. "Maybe you should stop asking how, and start asking why."

I draw back. "Why, then? Why are you here?"

Harper sighs, and looks at me, square on. My soul quivers in my boots. "Because you need me to be."

~

Harper and I talk about everything under the scorching sun. I tell her all about Wyatt, and our ups and downs. I tell her my fears, my hopes, my dreams, even though she already knows all of them.

Harper walks over the rocks with ease, whereas I am too distracted by our hefty conversation to be bothered by walking aimlessly. Every moment is to be enjoyed.

Eventually, Harper sits, looking me in the eye, her hazel eyes melting before me. I pull up short, unsure of what she's doing and why we've stopped moving. "Terra," she addresses. The soft, genuine quality in her voice shines like a rainbow. "You know you might not ever see me again."

My entire demeanor drops. I can already feel my shell hardening. "Stop."

But Harper remains unphased, her soft voice cutting like harsh words. "Terra, please listen."

"No," I hiss, letting all of the frustration out in one single word that rips through my being.

Harper visibly draws back, and I heave. This is probably all bullshit.

But Harper lunges at me anyways, waving around the Swiss army knife like a madman. How the hell did she get that from me?

I hit the ground with startling force, more than she's ever exerted on me before. The cool blade presses up against my neck, smooth and unrelenting. I breathe carefully.

"You will listen to me. Now stop whining and hear me out, dammit!" she says, every piece about her emanating rage and force, but her eyes pierce with convincing fire.

She swallows hard and peels herself off of me. With a skillful flip, she hands the knife back to me. "Be careful, Terra."

I nod and take the knife.

"Now, I've got to show you something."

Not waiting for a response from me, she grabs my wrist and runs off, dragging my disheveled figure behind her.

We climb and scale the rocks for hours until the yellow light of the afternoon just dips into deep orange, and, of course, she talks my ear off.

Suddenly, she stops, and hoists herself onto a ledge, and offers to pull me up. I less-than-politely decline and drag myself up, although she looks at me with friendly disdain.

She leads me under a seemingly regular rock. But after crouching under, I feel along the wall as the ceiling rises. A flicker of panic ignites in me. Where am I going? Why am I following Harper? These thoughts tickle in the back of my mind, however, don't stop me. I keep walking on in blind faith.

I literally run into Harper, as she has stopped in the middle of this large cavern. I can tell because even our heaving fills the room with breathy acoustics. I cry out after bumping into her, and the noise seems to expand forever, eternally reflecting off of the angular walls.

"Fascinating, huh?" she says, but the sound floods from every direction, buzzing as if I am surrounded by ten thousand Harpers all shouting at me in a maddening scream.

"Yeah," I manage to choke out through the splendor of the place, and also my rising panic at this Harper being.

Suddenly, there's a resounding click, and light floods the cavern, mimicking the chaotic echoing of the sounds. Harper's face lights up from below, her features distorted by the awkward angle of the light. She's holding a nice, shiny flashlight, but then she pulls it away from her face, sending the light scattering like ants after their hill has been destroyed by a child's shoe. The way that the light bends and refracts is unlike anything I've ever seen. The light - it's something surreal, just off of the norm to be noticed but not enough to be alarming.

Water drips off of the cave walls, and something stinks of rotten eggs. I splash in this standing water. If I could get this out of here, I could purify it and drink -

"Terra?"

"Yeah," I say, snapping myself out of my primal thirst reverie.

"I have something to show you."

Her tone of voice worries me.

Harper leads me to the far cave wall, where the orange glow of day is just a pinpoint. I press my hands against the smooth, slimy rock, and then Harper points the flashlight directly up toward the ceiling. Again, with the psychedelic light effect - something unnatural, yet completely plausible.

Suddenly, even more light explodes out of the flashlight, brilliant, hazy colors seeping into the cracks of the wall. A galaxy.

My jaw becomes involuntarily slack, and I wave my hand over the beam of the flashlight, but the cavern stays lit. Harper smiles.

"What is this?"

"It's us," she says, the stars sparkling in her eyes. Out of nowhere, the spiraling galaxy rushes toward us and zooms in on earth, luscious and warm and teeming with greens and blues in a neon universe.

"That's the earth," I say.

Harper smiles, and the image zooms in even further, to show the dusty, cracking surface of the Sonoran desert.

"This - is us." she says, and an image appears of me - not with Harper, but in the desert, in broad daylight, stoking last night's dying fire. "Or you, more specifically."

"This is me," she says, moving the image just a little to the right, and I see Harper, fully clean and dressed for society, not in the dusty rags I see her in now.

"But, you're here with me now?" I ask, still not understanding this insanity.

Harper gives me a smile full of so much sweetness and sadness, I am taken aback. "I'm always with you, Terra. The physical is just that - one dimensional."

I swallow hard and keep listening.

"And this is Wyatt," she says, and my ears perk up, almost violently.

"You know where he is? Where is he?" these questions stream out of my mouth like white-water rapids - not making much sense.

"Where he needs to be," Harper says, disregarding my ramblings.

I open my mouth, gasping for words, but Harper continues.

I see him above, clear and warped by the ragged cave walls. I walk across the planetarium-like cavern and touch just the beginnings of this ethereal light, my fingers brushing across his face - but nothing changes - not even a mere shadow at my interference.

"This time - it's for him. Him and no one else." Harper pauses and walks over to me. The light remains unchanging. Her hands rest on my shoulders, and she looks at me directly. My ego is shrunken down to a raisin - I feel about an inch tall. "And this time - it's for you. Just you. All of this is happening for a reason."

And then Harper reaches forward to embrace me in a hug - and that's when she falls into me, her entire body dissipating.

Before I can fully realize that she's gone, the light goes out. I slip on some damn rocks and slide down and out of the cave. At the last terrifying second, I clasp onto an outcropping rock. My body slaps against the cliff like a flag fluttering in the wind, and I let go.

In case you were worried, I survive this. But not before tumbling down the mountain in a haphazard human ball with my head tucked under and my knees up to my chin.

Eventually, after what seems like an eternity of bumps and scrapes, I skid to a stop in the sand. My knees, elbows, and outsides of my hands bleed and pulse a bright red, and I can feel my back scraped raw from under my shirt. My puncture wounds scream at me, and my breath has turned wheezy.

Despite my better judgment, I open a can of water and douse my shallow scrapes with it, and down the rest in a few gulps. The time seemingly hasn't changed, although it feels as if an eternity has passed since I followed my best friend up that incline.

I pat my cuts dry and let them bleed and eventually scab over. But then, someone presses their hand on my back. I flinch violently and my scrapes rub up against the gritty rocks again.

Breathy words escape out of my mouth - "Oh my God!" but then I realize who it is as they circle around and come to face me. Dad.

Not unlike the first time I saw him, I scramble back, trembling with terror. But unlike the last time, his skin appears unbroken and leathery, his eyes alive.

"No no no! It's okay, Terra. It's okay. I'm here," he says, outstretching a hand.

That salt and pepper hair, that gravely, comforting voice - it's all too startlingly familiar, like a sensory overload.

"No!" I scream, feeling the anxiety and chaos buzzing inside of me. "Go away!" My throat burns with something other than the screams, and as I continue to let the sound rip into the void, a lump the size of an apple gets caught in my throat.

And the screams morph into sobs, each tear burning terrible cuts into my face, my father leans down and scoops me up like I am a mere doll and forces me to stand.

And as the emotions swell inside of me like wave after wave of choking on salt water, my father forces me into his arms, even though I resist with kicks and screams.

Eventually, I melt into him, as if he's really there. Words spew out of my mouth like sputtering from a hose. "You're dead. You're really . . . truly dead." These words cut out of me from a deep, dark place, but they are irrevocably true. And I have to stop denying it.

Pain. There's nothing but it. Lashing out like twisted strobe lights. Ravishing and all consuming.

"I will always be with you," my father says.

My father. My dear, dear father. Daddy. Strong and soft. Loud and quiet. Disciplining love. Forceful love. Love. In every definition you could imagine. So wrong and so right, a lifetime of both pain and love flashes through me all at once.

"Even if you let me go, I will always be with you." His words, husky and rich, seep far into my soul, and I know, I could never let go in a million years.

With violent sobs that snap from my chest, I release the rubber-band grip I have on my father's soft, supple yet strong body. My throat ripples with cries and my vision has long been washed away with soft tears.

Slowly, I back away, my body crumpling with the buzzing fear, the crippling sorrow, and when my touch finally leaves my father's robust hands, he walks away into the distance. But I don't go after him. Because I can't. Because the further he walks away, the more he washes away with the wind and the dust.

I fall to my knees, weeping with a grief that is fresh and raw, less angry and more sorrowful, staring far into the distance until my vision disappears in the line of the horizon.

And I scream. I scream with the howl of the wind and the hum of the sun and the singing of the moon, and they all cry out in sorrow with my estranged soul.

~

The fire burns bright, as the day turns into deep scarlet evening. I poke at it with a stick, my eyes swollen and nose blocked. The flutter of emotion still lingers deep within my psyche, but it's not clawing at my throat and demanding attention anymore. I can deal, even though I don't want to.

I lean my head back and watch the ashes flutter up like ugly butterflies, and float down like pathetic shreds. But past that is the endless, dimensionless sky, teeming with stars and the hazy galaxies, and I allow myself to escape, to soar up high above everything and let it all go. Let myself go.

My father's words echo in my mind, and burning tears threaten to spill out of my eyes again. I blink violently, and they roll out over the sides of my face.

"What's wrong, honey?"

"Dammit, why do you people keep appearing everywh-" I stop. After looking up and wiping the saltwater from my eyes, I see my mother there, sitting across from me, her familiar wrinkles and wisps of hair drilling into my mind. These looks, I have seen time and time again.

But now it's different.

I swallow the lump from my throat, forcing the tender emotions down, and letting the anger boil over.

"Why did you make me come?"

"What?" my mother says, her tea-colored eyes softening.

"I said, why did you make me come? Why did you force me to come on that stupid fucking plane ride? None of this would have happened if you had just let me do what I wanted!" Now, all of it has gone away. Every ounce of cracking inhibitions being thrown outward. I rise up onto my feet, crouching defensively, ready to pounce.

"Terra, you know why."

"No!" I scream, for what seems like the thousandth time today. "No, I don't know why! Nobody will tell me *why*!" I stand up, backing off, and pacing back and forth.

"I . . . I can't tell you."

"Yes, you can, dammit! Nobody's stopping you! You know why? Because you're. Not. Here. You're not here!"

My mother sighs, looking at me with that classic 'mother' look. "You're right. I'm not. I'm at home, fretting my ass off for you. But you still have to listen to me, because, I am your mother, Terra."

"No! I don't have to listen to you!" I scream, covering my ears and squeezing every muscle in my body. "You're not here - this is all in my fucking head!"

"Stop trying to rationalize it!" my mother says, shouting at me with tears in her eyes. I fall back, startled at my mother's passionate urgency. There's something about her cool demeanor peeling away, and revealing this white-hot, raw woman before me.

I'm rationalizing it. I realize now. This whole time - I've been denying it. Been pushing it away, stuffing it so deep down inside that even my subconscious refused to recognize it.

"I'm still angry at you," I say, hissing with bare urgency.

"I know," my mother says, her voice kind and real, in contrast to mine.

"I'm still angry at both of you." My mother looks at me, motioning for me to continue. "For . . . for leaving me. For abandoning me when it happened. For abandoning me when she died. For being so wrapped up in your own shit to care about your own children at all. So wrapped up you let all of us down, fucked both me and Nick over. And I couldn't believe it. I refused to!" I say, my eyes flitting around, setting the scenery around me aflame. "And . . . I hate you because of it. And none of this makes sense. Life has never made sense - which makes me more angry and frustrated at all of this. I . . . I don't understand!"

Just then, my mother bursts out laughing, throwing her body back, her face glowing, filling me with rage. I glare at her, disgusted. "What the hell?"

She smiles, her body still pulsing with laughter. Clearing her throat, she says, "Sorry, continue."

"No, I don't have any more," I say dismissively. I fall back and sit down on the rock, defeated and actually quite pissed off. But all of the passion has seemingly seeped out of me like a leech. I was so afraid of saying it. Because saying it made it real, and oh hell, I didn't want it to be real.

Not that this will do any good, but I say it anyways for good measure. "I'm still mad at you. You neglected me in the darkest of times." And a burden flutters off of my shoulders.

My mother stands there, her frame soft and athletic. "I know."

I can't cry. My insides boil with emotions, and my eyes burn, ready for tears, but they never come. I am empty - dead to emotion - a cracked and empty shell of a fragile egg.

But my mother still comes and sits down next to me, even as I sit, sullen, staring at the fire, willing myself to cry, willing myself to cathartically release.

But I can't. I have nothing left.

Mom wraps an arm around me, and slowly, even though I long surpassed her size, I rest my head on her shoulder and curl up like a small child into her embrace. Oh, how I wish I was small and life was simple. But it's not. And it will never be that way again.

~

"How come Grandma hasn't come and visited me yet?" I ask, deep in the dark of night, partially wishing she would.

"Maybe because you've already let go," Mom says, hearing the soft, primal vibrations soak into my body.

All of my muscles relax, and I finally feel something odd - something unfamiliar. Peace.

"I love you, Mom," I say. I know it, but it's still just as hard to force out of my mouth.

She presses her lips to my forehead and pulls away, and I feel the familiar rush of the panicky fear that came so tangible when I had to let go of my father.

"No no no no no no no. Don't go. Stop it!" I babble as Mom lets go of me and floats into the fire.

She says one last thing, which will stick in my mind no matter how much it is ravaged by time: "Don't ever forget that I'll always love you."

And then she breaks off into ashy gray pieces like the shards of broken pottery and floats up into the endless night sky.

And again, I fall, humbled to my knees, and sob, the emotions clawing at my face and soul.

God, I hope I see my mom again.

CHAPTER FOURTEEN: Visions of Death and Life
DAY 10 - Wyatt; August 14th, 2015

I awake, suddenly, and kick at the tangled jacket at my feet. Nightmares not gripping enough to wake me haunt me as I come to. Thirst leeches away every ounce of attention I have. I still have some food left, so I take that out and snarf anything edible down. My stomach eats itself; I'm still so fucking hungry.

I look down, over the incline and see some water in the low ground. Mucky and waving water still floats, although I can see the end of it as it trickles away.

I sigh, shimmying down the incline, but at the bottom, the momentum builds and I curl up as I tumble to the ground. "Shit."

On the fall, I scratched up my elbows. Blood seeps through the sunburnt, torn skin. Groaning, I wipe them on my pants and start wading in the water.

It hits me that I have nowhere to go. The thought of leaving Terra - not knowing where she is - and just carrying on with my journey west without her, is absurd and out of the question. But I have no idea where she is. She washed off - and then violent, stark images of the storm comes flooding back, and my head rams against my skull. I fall back against a boulder, and I remember what I was doing. Following the flow of the water to find Terra. I start walking.

Sloshing through the now muddy ground, watching the water whirl through the ground is hypnotizing. The bubbles that float up are not a silvery color like they are in the pool - these ones are darker and like bulbous gray things that catch the white light.

And that's when I topple over and fall into the mucky water.

Immediately, hands take me by the shirt and pull me up. After the dizziness wears off, a familiar face comes into focus.

My sister, Lilly.

This must be a hallucination, brought on by trauma and lack of water. I shake my head - nothing. I even reach out and touch her - as real as I am. Horror grips my bones, but I can't do anything. The logic center of my brain refuses to let me react. But then one thought forms, a dire one that restricts my breathing. The last time I saw Lilly, I killed her.

"Am I dead?" I say, the words tasting bitter.

Lilly smiles and shrugs. Her joyous indifference strikes an odd nerve in me. I reach forward and grab her as she turns away.

"Hey! Answer me!" I say, frustrated at this apparition of my sister.

Lilly shrugs again. "Why does it matter so much?" Her innocence pierces me down to the core.

"Because it does!" I shout, then breathe. "I just want to know." At this point, my intrigue for the subject as a whole has simmered away. "Because . . . because I thought I killed you. I thought I hurt you."

Lilly sighs, and plops down on a rock, kicking her little feet in the water, sending fireworks of water raining down. "I dunno, but that's not why I'm here."

I narrow my eyes, but then I draw back. I must be crazy. But I say it anyway. "Then why are you here?"

"Because, Wyatt, you need to confront some things."

"What the hell is that supposed to mean?"

She doesn't answer. Suddenly, Lilly springs up and charges into me and gives me a hug, wrapping her child-like arms around me and burying her face into my hollow stomach.

Every memory of loving Lilly, of every time she came to me for comfort, comes slamming back. Like a perverse slideshow, I think of every moment we shared together, the good, the bad and the ugly, and a longing explodes out of me. My heart crushes like a soda can.

But the moment I touch her, she's gone, just as she had appeared.

Doubling over at the emptiness clawing inside me, sobs catch in my throat. What the hell is happening?

However, I stand, tall and shaken up like a rag doll in the backseat of a van, doubting that that encounter ever happened at all. Maybe, just maybe, if I concentrate, I can still feel her, next to me.

I walk, following the current downhill, but unfortunately, as I go further downhill, the water turns from a surging river in the middle of the land to a damp trickle, and then, nothing at all at around midday.

I stop for lunch, but I have nothing. Absolutely nothing. I sigh, frustration rising up in me like a boiling pot of grease. And that boiling hot grease could fry up some juicy, golden brown chicken . . .

I look up. There are quite a few more clouds in the sky than there have been lately, other than the storm. Nothing to be concerned about yet.

But I scour the limp, waterlogged plants. I see a few that I recognize, but some look so similar that I drive myself paranoid thinking that I'll eat poison instead of roots.

Eventually, I resort to hunting. I haven't seen any lick of an animal around since the storm, especially not now, but I take my knife and hunt anyways.

Nothing. Not a single freaking animal. Anywhere. The entire world just seems to be entirely devoid. Just a sucking hole of nothingness.

But as I am hunting, thunder starts to rumble through the loose pebbles, and rain drips onto the already saturated ground. God, I hope it doesn't flood again.

As I am scanning the quickly darkening horizon, lightning ignites the sky, and I see a furry little hare shivering and huddling under a plant. I flick open the blade and sneak up to the hare. It sees me and freezes, poised to run. In an instant, I shoot the blade forward, and that's when the innocent little rabbit morphs into my father with a knife in his chest.

I literally fall back, scraping the skin off of my hands, and slamming my tailbone hard into the wet ground, the world shaking and spinning before my eyes. Holy shit, what is happening?

Then, of course, the knife disappears, and the pool of blood is gone, and my father is just standing there in the desert, stone-faced and vile. Every angle, I know. Every strand of hair, I see. Every awful mannerism, every movement, I experience with an astounding clarity that it sheds every inch of doubt I had.

But for the moment, all logic is pushed away, and all I can feel, all I can see, is the mix of emotions inside me. Anger that is white-hot and sears my face. Anger that runs through my veins like caffeine on heroin, and makes my extremities tremble with rage. Anger that swells my heart and makes it thump for its sole purpose. To kill.

Nothing would be like this if it wasn't for him. Breathing hard, I charge forward, but my father - jeez, I hate even associating with him - is like a damn statue. But when I ram into him, he falls to the ground, struggling, gripping me by the shirt.

I am stronger, fueled by rage and pure hatred. I am finally stronger than my nightmares.

Once I get this son of a bitch to the ground, I straddle him around his torso, so his little stupid legs are stuck out behind me.

I pause, for just a moment, to soak in the beauty of this moment - for once, I am not the one on the ground, my safety, my wellbeing, my life being threatened.

And then I reel back and punch my father in the fucking face. And I punch him again, and again and again. With each impact, anger dissipates through me, but it is quickly replaced with more painful memories until I am a relentless tornado of anger, punching and clawing and kicking and screaming.

Suddenly, I am thrust back, and I hit the ground with alarming force. When I look up again, rain pouring down my face like tears, my father is still fucking standing there, blood gushing from all the holes in his face, limping and crooked like a robot that was thrown into the wash.

I charge again, punching and kicking, the anger gripping a hold of me just as I am gripping my father.

And that's when the flashes start.

Each time I make contact with his skin, for just a split second, I am transported back in time, to a much different place, where my father is spitting caustic words at me, where *he* is throwing the punches. Bloody memories. With each violent painful motion, I am infused with something much deeper, much more refined - much more true.

The anger was just a cover up. It was just a blanket smuggling the true, underlying emotions I feel. Hurt. Betrayal. Fear.

With every hit, my angry growls turn to cries of pain. Energy saps from my body, and I heave. Slowly, I stop beating my father, and once the veil has been torn and the light can touch me, sobs well up in me and rack my body. Painful and as hot as the tears on my face.

I can't. I can't I can't I can't do this anymore. Live like this anymore. The anger isn't doing me any good. I'm beating a dead horse.

Still kneeling over my father's bloody body, I sob. I cry and cry and cry and feel no shame, because this is all there is now. I bury my face in my bloody hands and weep, the sobs racking my body like waves.

My father is still underneath me, but he is gone. He is, and he always will be. I have to accept the fact that he left me, that he hurt me deeper than anyone else has.

But what I really have to do is forgive him. I have to forgive what he has done, even if he goes to his grave never showing any ounce of remorse.

Because if I don't, it's going to eat me alive. It already has. I put my forehead in between my knees, seeing the swirling colors of the desert sand below. The last dying shreds of anger contort within me.

As the rain simmers my aching heart, I realize that the anger isn't who I am, the sobs tearing at my body, at my soul.

It has no power over me anymore.

~

Eventually, the rain stops, and I find that I am lying flat on the ground, curled in the fetal position. My eyes are swollen and my cheeks raw. I rub my fingers in the mucky sand. Unfortunately, the sun doesn't come out after the rain - the clouds just keep floating by.

However, rain has collected under rocks and on leaves, so I drink that, and already I feel better. Still, I have no food.

Sighing, I keep following the trickle of water as the fresh rain joins with it.

~

Late in the day, after the water appears to boil around my ankles, I find myself dragging my feet, then dragging my knees, the sand clouding around my pants.

Eventually, I take to crawling on my hands and knees, but the water has evaporated in the heat. Even the sand is burning, each particle digging into my hands and feet like searing needles.

I fall to my face, sticky sand cupping my cheek. I can see my eyelashes as my eyes float shut, and a light burns from behind my eyes.

~

I awake. That's it. My eyes just . . . open.

I become aware of everything as signals travel down my nerves. The first thing I see is my machete in my hand - thank goodness.

I push myself up, feeling much better after that unexpected cat nap. I sit up and dig patterns into the sand with the tip of my knife.

I just sit for a long while and let the desert aesthetics swallow me. The sound is like milk, the sights branding into my mind. The hot air swirls around me and I breathe it in, feeling good for once in a long while. However, something is lacking. I can feel it deep inside of my gut, gnawing and chewing and heaving like a dragon.

Food. I need food.

I scramble up ravenously and grab a hold of my machete. Food.

I search along the ground for holes, for footprints and nuzzles along the rocks. I find a hole, just a bit smaller than my fist, and jam my hand in there, half expecting to be mutilated by a snake. But there's nothing but packed dirt.

But a few yards away, a large hare with erect ears pops out of another hole from under a sagebrush. I dash forward, knife poised and ready. Chasing after the erratic moves of the rabbit, and its panicked leaps, I feel like I might lose it.

But then I dive forward, grasping the animal in my fingers, tearing at its fur. The rodent squirms in my hands, kicking and pumping, but I claw into its lean, hard flesh as I pin it down by the neck with my forearm. I take my knife and come down hard, blood pouring out. The animal struggles for a moment, and then it bleeds out, clumping the fur and the eyes going still.

Life: 0, Wyatt: 1

~

What seems like hours later, I am turning the spigot with the hare on it over a small fire with wet wood, that seems to be producing nothing but smoke. My eyes and face are incredibly swollen, and my nose throbs red. Sniffing, I turn the stupid thing for the hundredth time.

My mind swirls, but I stop it. I cannot try and understand, for the struggle to understand, to comprehend such immense things, caused me strife. It still does. Emotions seem to be my driver, and I have seemingly abandoned the driver's seat long ago.

Why is this happening? Why did I have to be born into such a shitty family? Why am I feeling this way? I don't want to be this way.

The pain courses through me, but I let it run its course. I sniff back some snot, and rub my eyes. This was the life I was given, and to that, I say, 'I'll always survive.'

~

The hare is the most delectable piece of meat I have ever eaten in my entire life. I pair this off with some half-rotten looking fruit I found on a bush. The protein is rejuvenating, the carbs are energizing, and, truthfully, I feel much better.

Maybe it's the substance, but emotionally, a weight has been shaved off my shoulders. It's not entirely gone - I'm not sure it will ever go away, but it has been significantly reduced to the point where it is not all consuming, to where I am okay, taking steps to be alright. This will do.

CHAPTER FIFTEEN: Electrifying Love
DAY 11 - Terra; August 15th, 2015

My eyes split open, but they strain with swollen catharsis. I push up with my arms, everything hurting with a pain screaming up and down my body - this is unlike any aching pain or soreness I have ever felt before.

Groaning, I pull myself up and grip the rock for support. Intentionally sulking, I stare at the long-dead fire.

I sigh. Nothing. I feel nothing. I experience nothing. I am nothing.

Clouds hang over the sky in dull, gray ripples. Instead of seeming angry, they just seem apathetic, indifferent to little old me or what they are about to unleash onto the poor, poor desert.

After I chug down a whole can of water - two left - raindrops begin to patter down, slowly, leaving gray drops of watercolor on the desert landscape. Reluctantly, I pack up all of my stuff and get a move on. North.

I'm not too terribly worried about the storm - I've survived everything thus far.

I keep walking.

Suddenly, my side pangs with a sharp pain. I nearly keel over and cough up my insides, but I grab onto a rock and lift up my shirt to reveal my carelessly arranged bandages soaked with blood over my meaty and mechanical ribs.

"Damn."

Stripping down in the bone-cutting rain, I rip the bandage off of my side. I huddle underneath a deep outcropping of rocks. My bra is chafing the tender areas around my wound, so I unhook that as well. Staring out at the deserted desert with dry and swollen eyes, irony runs through me. I remember, not long ago, when I would be ashamed and self-conscious to be half naked in broad daylight, even if there was no one around, but now, the only shred of clothing on the upper half of my body is the long band of pant leg I have wrapped around my head to keep the hair and sweat out of my face.

I try and rub the oil off of my face to stop the stinging in my eyes, but this only rubs the grime around in different patterns than it was in before. I set my stuff down and shove it deep into the crevice, away from the rain. I peel away my pink, flaky skin to see leather tan beneath.

The rain continues at its measly, annoyingly slow pace. I step out into the drizzle and let the rain wash over my red-hot puncture wounds. I nearly forgot about those, but now, the pain is fresh and stinging again.

Testing myself, I breathe in deeply. The further in I breathe, the more the pain in my lungs increases, centering around the wounds on my right side. But once I get to a certain point - which is not the full capacity of my lungs, I sputter and cough, keeling over, like I have just inhaled maple syrup.

"Damn."

After soaking myself until I'm pale and shivering. I let myself dry inside of the slightly damp - yet warm - cave. This place is barely big enough for me to sit in, and when I outstretch my legs, they easily hit the other side of the nook.

Tucking my knees up to my chin, I let myself dry off and the blood scab a bit before I start bandaging myself up again.

Thankfully, the rain doesn't increase. I'm not too worried about it flooding, since it's been raining for an hour, and puddles have barely started forming.

But suddenly, lightning rips through the sky, hitting the ground like a punch to the face, and I jump, accidentally scraping my wounds on the hard rock.

"Shit."

Breathing hard and calculated, I press the other side of the already used bandage to my wound. But instead of just taping it down, I wrap a few strands of the stretchy gauze around my chest. Feeling satisfied that it is better concealed, I reassemble the upper half of my clothing.

Through the light rain, the clouds are still visible, lit up by the hot, morning sun.

The water falling from the sky, however, isn't a big problem. What is a problem, is the lightning. Every two minutes, a bolt tears through the gray sky, and leaving jolting thunder pounding through the landscape.

Each time, I curl deeper into the crevice, and for the first time today, I feel something. I feel scared - a deep, tickling anxiety that claws at my organs, willing to be free.

Even though it really is not pleasant, I watch the lightning overcome the sky regardless, as it intricately weaves across the sky like white-hot cracks. Sometimes, more than one bolt will strike at once, giving the illusion of twisted dancers on the most lonely stage in the world - the desert. It's a spectacular light show, nonetheless.

I begin to doze off as the slight pitter-patter of the rain and the clamor of the storm provides for the entertainment of my mind as I relax for the first time in a while.

Just as I wade into the pool of sleep, a truly terrifying jolt of thunder drags me out.

But then, the thunder doesn't stop. I sit up and nearly hit my head on the ceiling. I press my hand to the rock wall and feel the head buzzing with electricity. And rumbling with something else, something closer and more tangible.

"Shit."

I grab my stuff and bolt out from the cave, coming out pumping my legs with painful contractions. And that's when the avalanche comes crashing down over the rocky incline and fills in the space where I just was moments ago.

Panic. I turn back to see an ashy cloud and still rumbling rocks swelling towards me.

"Shit."

The hesitation has lost me time and length. I run faster than I thought possible, my right lung throbbing with pain and exhaustion.

I weave through rocks and plants, playing a game of twisted hopscotch as the rain pierces my exposed skin with needles. Live electricity swirls around me, bursting rocks open and incinerating plants.

Suddenly, and this all happens at once, my hair stands on end, the necklace around my neck floats above my skin, burning white-hot. And the sensation of a million tiny ants floods my skin.

"Fuck fuck fuck fuck."

Immediately, I stop running and crouch down, with only the balls of my feet touching the ground. Lightning slams into a nearby tree, sending it up in flames despite the rain. My eyes wide with horror, I run in the absolute opposite direction of the tree, wondering when this will ever end . . .

Of course, it eventually does. I take shelter under a different rock outcropping, my entire being buzzing, making sure I won't be buried in an avalanche or burnt to a crisp. I put my hand down to my side. It's wet with something other than water.

But to this, I have nothing to say.

It only strikes me now of how lonely, how alone I am. Also, how trivial and ineffective. As teenagers, the world revolves around me - I see this in full light now. Things change and form, and exist, or don't exist, because of me. The advancement of the ego is all I care about. But here, alone, at the hand of mindless nature, virtually expendable, I realize that I am an ant in an anthill, waiting to be stepped on. Quite a humbling and depressing thought, really.

Too little, too late, maybe.

~

The sun comes back out around lunchtime, and as do the animals. I kill a Gambel's quail by luring it in with the last of my food. Making a fire, however, is a challenge, with the wet wood and soaked ground. The only upside is that everything seems much more alive. The plants perk up, full of water, and animals scurry around, salvaging for their own food. A cactus wren performs for us.

After finally getting a fire started with wood found under rocks and in caves, I precariously use Wyatt's Swiss army knife to cut off an arm of a swollen Saguaro cactus. The arm plops to the ground with a rubbery thud. I stick my head under the cut off appendage as clear water drips down. It has an earthy, vegetable taste that reminds me of bitter green beans, but I lap it up regardless. After peeling the outside, I suck on the cactus flesh while the bird cooks.

It's nearly two in the afternoon before I get a move on again since the moisture, protein, and carbs have put the life back into me.

Going perpendicular to the sun, I continue walking north, since I most likely drifted south. All hope of seeing Wyatt again has slipped out from between my scabbed knuckles. All that's left is the dry hope of surviving. Finding the next meal. Dodging obstacles. Dragging myself up every morning and forcing myself to go to bed each night and not ingesting poisonous berries or throwing myself off a cliff because there's nothing to live for.

~

Walking. The contractions of my leg muscles become methodical and ache with a dull pain that keeps me moving.

Sweat. Sharply salted moisture that I lick from the insides of my elbows just to keep my tongue from shriveling up into a magenta raisin.

Sun. Burning my skin, yet also baking it to a perfect golden brown. Thick and textured, it cannot decide whether its leathery brown and tan, or baby pink and burnt.

Mirage. The orb of white needles that is the sun. The warping of the horizon like wet wood. The tricks of the eye that all too often look like familiar figures.

~

Late in the afternoon, I debate on settling down for the night, but something keeps me going. Maybe the possible factor that I can squeeze in a few more miles into the cool of the night.

But I keep walking.

I keep glancing over to the sun, swollen and orange in the sky, casting deep shadows. A small walking figure and its shadow stretches across the horizon, nearly reaching me. I wonder if it's another visitor, like my brother or my grandfather, since the figure looks a bit masculine. But, I guess, If I'm supposed to meet him, he'll come to me.

But still, I stop, staring, squinting at this form walking towards me. It limps and drags its feet in the same downtrodden manner such as my own.

But again, I pause, not believing my eyes, squaring my body straight at this figure, feeling ripped open and exposed by the sun.

My jaw pops open. Suddenly, this figure starts coming at me faster, with pumping arms and a spring in its step.

And then suddenly, I start running as well, my heart buzzing in my chest and elation building exponentially to a shrill cry of joy that rises in my body.

And then his face comes into full view and I can't stop, waiting for the moment when I can touch him again and hear his laugh, see his smile.

It's Wyatt.

~

We hug immensely, and as our bodies collide, he swoops me up in a hug and I wrap my legs around him like a small child.

He's here. He's really here. I can now feel the supple movements of his muscled body and the warmth and life he emanates.

Tears, but warm, sweet ones, fill my eyes as he pulls back and sets me down. Sobs of pure joy burst out of me, but I can't take my eyes off of him. First, he laughs, then tears well up in his eyes, and he begins to cry as well.

But then, he grabs my face with his hands and kisses me.

For a split moment, I explode with surprise and panic, but then it all fades away and I am left with an expression of love and passion so sweet that I can't help but feel it all right then and there. Intensely innocent, the kiss awakens me and leaves me wanting more and still satisfies me to no end.

When we finally pull back, we pull in close, nestling my body in close to his. He rests his head on the top of mine.

"I never thought I'd see you again," he chokes out.

I wish I could reply, but I can't. The reunited joy and elation is too overwhelming for any words to express, but Wyatt knows that my tears show all the words that could not be said.

July 4, 2014 - Terra

Breathing. Such a simple task that had become clenching and mechanical. Painful.

I was alone. There was no one else.

~

My parents fought like dogs, with snarling teeth and biting words. Each scream, each word painted in their own flaws. What had I done? Why were they doing this?

My entire life was like my big, looming secret. No one could know. No one needed to know.

The longer I kept it safe, curled up in myself, rotting my soul, the more it ate me alive like a parasite - a parasite I let in. A parasite I was okay with.

I leaned back against my door, emotions lashing out of me like fireworks. I couldn't bear to see it, so the hate and the pain worked its way into my mind via every slam of the door, every harsh footstep. But like a trainwreck, I couldn't look away. I couldn't tear myself away from everything I knew. Everything I was.

It felt like I was dying. Like every safe place, every hope had been sucked out of me.

I jumped when the front door clicked open and slammed shut.

Nick was home.

I sprung up, stifling my hiccuping sobs. He would be there. He could empathize. He could make it stop.

Then, I saw him, in the darkness of our house, the moonlight streaming through windows, chiseling harsh features on his face.

I didn't even get to say a word before he stormed past me and into his room.

"Wait!" I cried out, banging my hands on his door.

"Go away!" he shouted back.

The ball of glowing, buzzing anger in me fell to the ground and kicked his door, each muscle movement releasing no pain, just adding fuel to my fire. Stupid, stupid Nick. Stupid, stupid me.

Heaving, Nick had finally had enough.

"Stop it!" he screamed down at me. But I saw. Despite his drunken rage, and past his misdirected fury at me, I could see it in his eyes. I could see that he felt how I felt. He understood.

But never. He'd never let me in. Trapped in a web of his own world of school and girls and friends and alcohol, Nick shut me out.

And I shut everyone else out. Spider web threads are surprisingly strong, and the only reason us humans walk right through them is because they're thinner than a strand of hair. When they build up and congeal and form solid walls around a poor insect, they are indestructible.

Like how I thought I was. A shell of a person.

People are fragile, animalistic to the core. I guess, if you knock them around, they'll think they did something to deserve it.

~

He came over right after I called. Adam and his family were our closest neighbors, so he was just down the street. Half a mile, give or take.

I opened the door, his jet black hair sticking out wildly. His boxer shorts were creased; it was late. My heart leaped, and I immediately hugged him. Really, the only reason we were friends is because we kind of grew up together, always being adventurous, outdoor kids - since he was the only kid around.

But as we had grown older, our relationship had deepened to some extent. We spend less time joking around in groups, and more intimate time, alone. Where it was going, I didn't know. But I had let it happen, because, in the moment, it had felt okay.

Boy, was I wrong.

"Hey, what's up?" he whispered into my ear.

"Parents. Nick." That's usually all I had to say.

We exited the hug and stepped out into the refreshing night air, toward his house. Running in the night air, my cares slipped away like ribbons into the sky.

Adam's house was also dark - it seemed like no one was home at this late hour. Tomorrow was Saturday, so we were good.

Flopping on his couch together, he said. "Talk to me, Terra."

I sighed. "Nick . . . he's drunk again. Probably out partying with his friends, and realized how bad he effed up."

"Yeah, and . . . ?" he asked.

"And, my parents. I just don't get it," I said. Looking away, I heard the air conditioning go on and hum through his empty house - which was much larger than mine.

Adam put two fingers to my chin and directed me back. Again, I felt those same emotions being stirred up inside of me. "Keep talking."

Adam was the only person who made me feel safe. Harper, - I mean, she was my best friend - but we were more equals, as in partners in crime - like iron sharpening iron. Adam and I - we felt like a cooperative unit, completed only when we came together.

So I told him. It's not like he didn't already know, but I recounted every painful step by how Mom got mad at Dad because he was being insensitive about her feelings. How the past was all that mattered. How Dad's parents were glad when Grandma died, because they never approved of my parents' marriage in the first place. How slowly but surely, they became less and less tolerant of me after being raped. I was annoying, a burden. And everything I had wanted to say so badly, to scream to the world, just came out.

And he told me exactly what I wanted to hear. That I was beautiful. That I mattered. That everything was going to be okay. So many lies that nothing else mattered in life but me and him. Lies that he would always be there for me.

And after I was deep in his embrace, arms wrapped protectively around me, I looked up to see his face inches from mine.

And I leaned forward and kissed him. That was my first kiss, by the way.

Did I know what I was doing? Hell no, but it felt so natural and fulfilling that I just had to have more and more and more and more.

As we literally tumbled onto the ground, his hands ran up and down my body, my hands grasping at his hair. But while my body surged with fluttery feelings, something deep inside knew this was wrong, as burning and as powerful as a molten core of steel.

I tried to ignore it. I really did, because that empty place inside of me was full, at the moment.

But something about giving myself away, giving himself to me, just seemed invasive and wrong. I didn't want this. Not now. Gooseflesh ripped up and down my skin. I remember being torn open in what was my most sacred place.

And I can't let that happen again.

So, that's what I did. I pulled away from his lips and steadied myself on the suddenly shifting ground. Adam was on top of me.

"I can't do this," I said in a breathy whisper.

"What?" he exclaimed, peering at me in the dark.

"No," I whispered, whipping my hair back and forth, as if someone was going to jump out of the shadows. "I can't."

"My dad has condoms in his sock drawer if you're worried abou-"

"No!" I shouted. In a frenzy, I pulled myself off of him and scrambled out the door.

"Terra, wait!" he said, grabbing my arm with alarming force.

Paralyzed with terror, I ripped my arm away, smacking him in the process. Panic so visceral vibrated in my chest. "I'm so sorry, Adam, but this isn't what I want. It's not you, it's . . . "

"No, fine," he snapped, his eyes soulless. "I get it. Just, leave."

And just like that, he slammed the door in my face leaving me in the swirling darkness and the cold of the street. We didn't speak much after that.

His family moved away two years later. Somewhere up north and cold. Colder than here, at least.

~

That night, however, my family had abandoned me and I had broken things off with the only other tie I had. But then, I remembered - there was always Harper.

Unable to reenter my house for a few different reasons, I called her on my cell phone. Anxiety boiled in my gut like tar as the phone rang.

"Hey, Terra. What's up?" she said.

Swallowing hard, I forced myself to reply. "Uh, could you come by my house. Things are . . kind of rough right now. I can't go back inside my house-"

"Did you lock yourself out of something?" she asked.

"Uh, sure." I had to pause, because my voice was threatening to show my overwhelming emotion. "I just . . . " I cleared my throat, and again, and then again, but still, I couldn't speak.

So I hit end. And threw my phone on the ground.

Less than twenty minutes later, Harper was there, having ridden her bike the three miles.

And there I was, crumpled on the ground, in the dead of night - who knew how late it was then?

Harper hopped off her bike and let it fall into the sand and the dirt road. "Hey, she said. "What's up?" she repeated, the inflection in her voice much more kind and empathetic.

But I couldn't speak. My tears had run dry - there was nothing left.

Her eyes stopped. She stopped, reaching deep inside of her mind. Swallowing hard, Harper dug for something in her pocket.

"Take this," she said, pressing a slip of paper into my hands.

I wished she would leave - but at the same time, I wanted her to wrap my arms around me and tell me everything was going to be okay.

But the love in her eyes spoke volumes. While I was unaware of what she gave me, I knew it was important.

And then, with a tough kindness in her eyes, she left.

And again, I was alone.

The night was cool, and the air thin, and as Harper rode away, I ran through the night. I wished I could get over myself. I wished I could escape. But I couldn't - I was stuck here. In a grave that we had all dug, with my name written on it.

I climbed and climbed, tearing my tissue paper skin on bark. Sitting from my spot in an acacia tree, I stare up past the sparse, clumped branches and see myself. Out of place, unable to save myself. On the outside looking in, out of control.

Trembling, I take out what Harper gave me - the small piece of paper.

It was a handwritten letter. Already, tears welled up in my eyes.

Dear Terra,

I love you. I just wanted to get that out of the way. I love you with all of my heart, Terra Lombardi. You've helped me through thick and thin and shaped me to be the person I am.

Now, enough being sentimental. You may never read this. If you are, it's probably because I felt the need to share this with you and you were in a low place in your life.

Because I know it will help.

I averted my eyes because I could no longer see through the tears as thick as blood.

As I continued reading, the heartfelt text was woven with verses of brokenness. Salvation. Redemption. And then, I could see. There was nothing more sound and sure than the truth of the matter.

By grace, through faith, was the only way that I was going to make it. I wasn't strong enough to live this life, despite that it was given to me. But what was also given to me was strength. My own blood, other's blood, could never save me. It was only the blood of the spotless lamb.

~

I wish I could have known this now. I wish I knew that my life wouldn't be perfect from this point forward. I wish I could tell all of you that this was a turning point, a complete 180. It was merely a step in the right direction, followed by two steps back.

And I wish I could tell my past self that everything would work out. That there was never a point in my life when there wasn't hope. Because I never put a gun to my skull and pulled the trigger, because I didn't jump out of that acacia tree that night.

For a while, I kept up with the faith. Went to church with Harper, prayed with her, made some new friends, and life was okay for a while.

But then Harper's dad lost his job, and she started hating God - which cut my rides to church, and those seasonal friends drifted away. Our family came alongside hers, and we helped, but yet again, that animosity - that disconnect - was always there, not only between my family but between Harper and me.

I wish I could have stopped myself from receding. I wish I could stop myself from falling back. I wish I could have taken myself by the collars of the shirt and shaken myself to see the passivity of what I was becoming.

I wish I could have shown myself that things would change. That I wouldn't always be stuck in this meaningless cycle of life. That there was so much more out there for me.

Because if there wasn't, then what is the force that keeps our hearts beating?

CHAPTER SIXTEEN: Empathetic Temptation

DAY 12 - Wyatt; August 16th, 2015

I awaken first, and hear the sizzling and sweet, thick scent of smoke still rising from the ashes. Terra is still curled up next to me, her hand lying protectively over my abdomen. Cautiously, I take her hand off of me and position her so she doesn't fall over when I move. But then I feel something. Something fabric and hard bound around her chest. I continue to feel until I realize - it's a bandage - what the hell did she do?

Suddenly, I realize that she's awakening, giggling and smiling in her sleep and saying deliriously: "Stop it, Wyatt. That tiiiickles."

I pull my hands back, with her shirt ridden up to the start of her ribs when I see the thick bandage.

Sitting back on my knees, I ask. "Way to go, slick. What the hell did you do?"

"Whaddya mean whaddid I do?" she mumbles, rubbing her eyes.

"Oh, wake up you dim-wit," I say, rolling my eyes.

Terra rolls over to face me and her eyes flutter open. She smirks. "Yeah, well the first day after the flood, I, uh, kinda had a run in with a cactus. My lung - I think it's punctured."

"Oh my God," I say, half disgusted by the thought of all of that blood.

"I'm fine," Terra says, sitting up and coughing up a deep rattling in her chest. She grips the rocks until her knuckles are white, brushing me off.

"That doesn't sound fine," I say, grimacing.

"It is though," she says, wiping her mouth and taking a drink. "I was unconscious when I was stabbed, so I guess that makes everything okay. I'm guessing that part of my lungs just - collapsed? I dunno, but the bleeding stopped and it's all clotted."

"Alrighty then," I say, acting a lot less concerned than I actually am.

"I'm fine, Wyatt. I've been okay for, how long? Days?" she says

"Not long enough," I murmur, throwing my bag over my back.

Now, Terra looks over at me with a startling deepness to her cool eyes. "I . . . I'm just glad you're back," she says, reaching up on her tiptoes to kiss my cheek.

"I never left."

We get a move on, kicking at the fire to put it out. We turn on our phones to check for any cell service, but then mine shuts off and dies. Terra, however, has a full 20% left.

Walking over the rocks really becomes a mind-numbing activity, but since it takes great amounts of concentration, the parts not focused on climbing are allowed to wander - and distract.

After a while, I look back at Terra. She seems alright if a little lonely. "You know, you don't have to walk behind me. I was only doing that so I could protect you. And besides, you didn't seem like you wanted to be anywhere near me."

Terra laughs, just a little. "Well, sorry if I made you feel that way." Fixing her hair, she comes up and walks next to me. Her presence beside me is comforting, almost.

We walk, silently, for a while again, just with the sound of the sand and rocks crunching beneath our feet. The wind is deafening, blowing to the northeast, cutting over the rocks and making odd jet-streams around us. The terrain gets hilly. We don't talk much for a while.

~

But in the mid-afternoon, we have to stop for a drink, but we have no food. It's 2 pm, and it's the hottest part of the day, so we search in the rocky areas for a small cave.

Eventually, we find one, deep and so low that I have to crawl on my hands and knees to get in.

Seeing mostly with my hands, I use the reflection of the harsh light from outside to help me illuminate the cave.

We crawl in the cave, thankful for the relief of the shade. Terra rubs at the red, peeling skin on her arms.

Even in the dark cave, the heat crawls its way in. We both nap, I think.

I wake up when I'm literally about to die of thirst. Every limb feels heavy, and from my stomach to my lips I feel the yearning for water.

Terra swallows hard. "I'll go gather dinner."

~

After dinner, in the deep of night, Terra almost immediately curls into my embrace. She's becoming much more comfortable with me, and I can't say that I don't like it. From our place in the rocks, the moon shines brightly, casting skeletal shadows on the desert. For a while, we sit, soaking up the desert sound, sharing body heat.

I feel Terra shift as she begins to speak, like it might burst out of her without her consent. "Sometimes, I think about the future . . . and can't see anything. Like, it's all fuzz. My life . . . could go a million different ways, and that's what scares me the most, I think."

"Thinking is . . . good. Can't say I do it much, though," I say. Dammit, I can't help but joke around a bit. Her hair is just so soft against my face and we're just so comfy and warm.

She jabs her fingers into my side, reeling back in laughter.

"Okay, okay!" I say. "Serious time."

"'Serious time'," she sneers.

"Okay," I muse. "So, I totally get what you're saying. Back when I was little, maybe eight or nine, I never thought I'd make it this far, much less grow up to have a job or family. I thought, one day, my father might come home and actually kill me." Always gotta make it about yourself, Wyatt.

"I'm . . . so sorry." She pauses, chewing on her words before saying them like she always does. "For the longest time, all I thought there was going to be, all that I thought existed, was pain. And then my grandmother died. And . . . I realized I was right."

I pull her closer, as if our fragile human bodies could ward off the evil of the world. "I'm so sorry."

"Don't be," Terra says, leaning in to me.

And then I kiss her.

The moment her soft lips touch mine, I feel my body surge with power, like an old machine awakening. Against my better judgment, I lurch forward, kissing her harder and parting my lips.

Everything shatters away. Any hope, any candle of the future is snuffed out. The past is just a memory. All that is, all that might ever be, is just us, here, right now.

Her hands fumble up to my chest, and she tugs at my shirt, rubbing her hands luxuriously over my neck and chest. My fingers work my way up her curvy legs to rest at the smallest part of her waist.

We're kissing, so hard. Sweat races from my pores. Moving like we know what the hell we're doing.

Soon enough, it's skin on skin. My hands on her breasts, her hands running up and down my back like warm water.

Through all of this, my mind is racing, through the uneasiness I feel. What if Lilly was here? Lilly's not here, you might not ever see her again.

What if my mom was here? My father? Hell, they'd probably congratulate me on finally becoming a man.

Suddenly, I suck in a breath. I can't do this.

I pull away from Terra's sensual grasp, and this breaks the haze around her. Trembling and naked from the torso up, she breathes like a leaf in the fall.

Her lip quivers in the cold. The blood rushes - and it has to rush quite a long way - up to my face.

"We can't do this," I say. It comes out much huskier than intended. I rub my mouth. "Not now."

"I . . . I know," Terra replies, almost immediately. Her face is almost contorted in pain. She won't meet my eyes.

"I'm sorry," I say, grabbing my pants.

"Me too," she says.

Redressing, we are silent, but lay next to each other again.

I couldn't do it.

Not because I didn't want to. But because I shouldn't.

What turned me off what made the hackles of shame stick up, was the fact that I was becoming like them. Like my parents.

Selfish and terrible and wasted like bitter wine spilled on grimy streets. I can't be that.

Now, I don't know why Terra chose to stop, but she must have had her reasons. But what I do know is that someday,

someday I'll know when it's right. I'll know when it's not me and my tarnished silver and chipped wood. It'll be us. Whole and made one.

CHAPTER SEVENTEEN: New Friends
DAY 13 - Terra; August 17th, 2015

Breathing hard, I awaken to a sharp pain in my side. Feeling the burning skin beneath the fabric, I tear my shirt off. Check my wounds. Pulling back my breast, I crane down to see my side - still shiny and wet with blood. Now, they're tender and pink, the skin swollen like rings. Shit.

Swallowing the lump in my throat, I yank my shirt back down.

"You okay?" Wyatt asks from behind me, and I start, my cheeks flooding with heat.

"Yeah, I was just, feeling a little warm," I say, fumbling aimlessly with supplies.

We finish up the rest of the coyote meat from last night and try and get a move on, but it feels as it there's a bowling ball in my stomach, so we rest for a while.

I feel the thirst pulling at my mouth, and reach into my backpack. And then it hits me as I pull the dented, rusty thing out from the bottom of the bag.

"Wyatt?" I say.

"Yeah," he says, gnawing on a coyote bone, trying to get the last of the meat off.

"This is our last water can."

He nearly spits. "What?"

"Yeah. There's no more full ones," I say, suddenly feeling every crevasse of the dry wasteland that is my tongue.

He gapes at me with a horrified face, then it drops, and stress pokes at his brow. He sighs. "Well, in all honesty, I'm just surprised that they lasted us this long."

Suddenly, I stop. "How long? How long has it been?"

"Uh, twelve, maybe thirteen days. Why?" he says, shrugging.

"Wait," I say. "We crashed on the fifth, right?"

"Yep."

Before continuing, I recount each minuscule step in my head, remembering each trauma, and am convinced that we have been out here exactly thirteen days.

"I know it, we've been out here for thirteen days. Do you know what that means?"

"Uh, it means that we have been in this living hell for over two weeks?" he says cynically.

"No, silly," I say, punching him on the arm. "That means it's August seventeenth, the day I was born."

"It's your birthday?" he exclaims.

"Well, yeah. That's kinda what I just said."

"Haha! Well, that's great! Happy birthday!" he says, smiling gleefully. I peer at him. "I mean, uh, sorry. That sucks." His voice drops.

I swallow hard - believe me, I was trying to be optimistic - I just refused to let it show when the realization hit me.

"Yeah, I know," I say.

Then, Wyatt bites his lip, and bright inspiration explodes on his face.

"What?!?" I ask.

"Hold on," he says, rushing to his bag to get something.

"Wyatt!" I say, getting up.

"No no no no no!" he shouts, whipping around and holding out his arms.

"Alright, alright," I say, rolling my eyes ever so slightly, playing into his joke.

I lean back onto the rocks and sigh. He's got something up his sleeve, I know it.

"I was waiting for the right time to give this to you, and now is the perfect time!" he says echoing and haphazardly searching in his bag for something. "I, uh, made it when we were separated."

He comes out, smiling coyly, and holding something behind his back. "Close your eyes," he says.

I laugh slightly and play along, covering my eyes. A moment later, he says, "Okay, open."

Laying in his hands is a necklace with the chain made of twine and the long, robust leaves from the yucca plant. The charm is a marbled rock, most likely turquoise, chipped into the shape of a heart - except the end, where the image comes to a point, is sharp like an arrowhead. Wire keeps the necklace together and forms the clasp.

He smiles, noticing my gaping face. "The heart charm doubles as an arrowhead."

"Well, yeah. I assumed that," I say, smiling. He directs me to twirl and lift my hair as he ties the necklace around my neck. The metal wire is cool against my skin, and I hold the charm in between my fingers.

"Thank you, though," I fumble, forgetting that I should probably have said that earlier.

"My pleasure," he says, brushing away my hair.

After he finishes, his hands come away, and my hair falls back down around my shoulders, feeling matted and greasy from root to tip. Impulses run through me like zaps of electricity, but all I end up doing is leaning back into his embrace. He wraps his arms around me, nuzzling his face into my hair, and then we just stand there. We hug because we have to because otherwise, the heat might swallow us right up.

"I want to go home. I don't want to be here on my birthday."

Wyatt speaks into my neck. "I know. I hope I can suffice."

I smirk, turning to face him. "Yeah, this'll do."

He leans in close and smiles, and says in a husky voice, "We're wasting time. We need to find water." But not before he winks. I smile. The bastard knows how to play the game.

The moment ends, but the longing emptiness inside me remains. We pull away and I take my backpack. "Should we walk or find food and water?"

The moment is over, evidenced by Wyatt's stoic voice. "Water. We have none left, and that's more important at the moment," he says, reaching up to feel his cracked lips.

Swallowing hard, I stop, mostly because my Adam's apple stops clear in my throat, like swallowing honey or molasses, and for a moment, I choke. After my throat unsticks itself, I sputter a bit, my lungs shuddering with my coughs. My lips are split and textured like his. Who I wouldn't kill for some lip balm.

I breathe, sighing in relief that Wyatt didn't see my endeavor. He's already combing the shrubby plants for food. Taking a strip from my outer jacket - which is barely recognizable at this point - I begin lifting up rocks and soaking up dew condensed on the rocks and pooled in crevices.

Twenty minutes later, the cloth is barely damp. After having not much luck under smaller stones, I try and overturn larger rocks. A task that wouldn't have challenged me while my body was at its finest now sends my veins straining and sweat seeping out of my pores. Once it has flipped over and is sitting on its side, a nearly liquidus body seeps out of the rock itself and the place where it was, only visible because of the harsh angle of the sun and the fluid motion with which it spreads.

A scream wells in my throat, but then I just realize that I have disturbed a nest of honeypot ants (myrmecocystus, to be exact), evidenced by the slower moving rotund abdomens of the storage ants, and the deep molasses color of the worker ants.

And I cry with glee. We have found our lunch! Grabbing our dented pot, I begin scooping ants up of all shapes and sizes, hoping to get the fat, nutrient filled ones. But almost immediately, some climb out, so I grab the cracked glass lid and coax them in until I have a hive of crawling and shifting ants in a pot.

Running like a madman, I hold the lid on tightly as I show Wyatt what I have found. He wrinkles his nose, and a few freckles on his face disappear.

"If we cook 'em, they'll be great!" I say, holding a squirming, fat ant between my fingers.

"I'll believe that when I see it," he says, continuing his failing search.

"Then soak up water under rocks and be useful," I say teasingly, still ecstatic over the ants.

"Yes, ma'am," he mutters, smirking.

But I don't take much care. I've had these ants one other time, on a school field trip, but they were covered in hard candy like brittle.

I get the flames of the fire back up. Standing, I hold the pot over the fire as the ants heat up and die, some even popping like popcorn.

Once I'm pretty sure I've burnt some of it and every ant is dead, I take the steaming pot off. I don't dare open it to lose that precious water vapor, and instead let it cool keeping all of the water vapor intact.

Wyatt comes back with a wet cloth, like one that's been soaked in water and wrung out, so that it's wet but not dripping. That will have to do.

While the ants cool, we suck on the ends of the cloth until it's dry and we just begin to dry our tongues on the cloth. Cupping some leaves, I finally open the top of the ants. But I stop, because drips of precious water nearly fall off of the glass lid and are about to crash onto the parched earth.

I flip it inside facing the sky and let the water pool. We then lap it up, and soak up the rest with the cloth and try to squeeze any remaining bits out.

Eventually, we dig in. Slightly bitter and tasting of dust, they have a sweet tang. The meal is soupy and textured and crunchy all at the same time, but we stomach it down, needing the calories. I see Wyatt wincing at the odd texture, but I don't see him gagging at the taste. However, I must admit that it does feel like these ants are still alive, crawling and creeping like they were along the rock, except on my tongue and seeping down to my stomach.

He licks the spoon with the fervency of an experienced chef. "Mmm," he says, smacking his lips. "Nectar from the agave plant. The crunch . . . is quite firm, blends well with the sauce . . . "

Wyatt mimics a food connoisseur as he narrows his eyes. "I taste wonderful notes of sweetness, contrasted nicely with the aromas of dirt and animal shit." Dropping the act, he smirks at me, stomaching the food down.

I laugh, breathy. "Why, thank you for those colorful compliments, Critic Hartman. I hope you thoroughly enjoy our birthday meal."

He smiles at me, and, for the first time in a while, it doesn't seem provocative or sarcastic. It feels like he's actually enjoying himself.

After that unsettling and slightly traumatizing meal, we finally get going. While it took the edge off of the thirst, it comes back stronger in the screaming heat, like I am an endless river, yearning for water. I find myself reaching in my bag to take out a water can, but then, over and over again, it hits me that we have no more water cans left.

It's late morning when we start walking, the sun only getting hotter with each passing second.

We've been out here, alone, for thirteen days, and, boy, has it felt like a lifetime.

~

In the mid-afternoon, we see something in the distance. Flat-topped, hut-like things. Tendrils of smoke peel up in various places out of the huts, and there is one large one in the center of this humble huddle.

Maricopa Native Americans, most likely. They live around the Gila River, which should be around here. I've heard about them, but never seen them, mostly because, other than my father's plane trips, I never go further west than my home. And they're not exactly social butterflies themselves, either.

Interestingly, Wyatt and I both see this collection of homes, but unlike before, we don't go sprinting towards it. We just acknowledge the fact that it's there, and keep traveling towards it. Something inside my chest jerks forward, but my beaten demeanor keeps it from exploding out. We'll get there sooner or later.

We eventually set our stuff down as the afternoon melts into evening. I make a fire, but since we have nothing to eat, we just stare at the flames. Wyatt sits there, nodding off. I let him as one of the logs flops down into the ashes, spraying out embers.

I stare up at the moon, and at its shining light. My eyes run over the gritty texture. The man on the moon smiles back at me, peeking out through the navy blue velvet of the night. The moon is blindingly bright, as it dims all of the stars and bears down with a thin light, like a flashlight. The brightness of the moon reminds me that the sun is bearing down somewhere, on someone not quite so lonely as me.

With this thought in mind, I fall asleep, still sitting up.

~

Confusion envelops me the second I peel open my eyes. A bobbing motion grips my body. I open my eyes to see four figures carrying me by the arms and legs. Panic bubbles inside of me, teeming and threatening to burst out in cracks of lightning.

But I stay still as they drag me off into the darkness.

Light shines from behind me - I can only see the afterglow in the sky. Evidently, I have moved around too much, because one of them whispers to another about something, and one of them reaches down . . .

That's when I begin squirming and screaming, but there seems to be something tied tightly around my mouth - a cloth gag. And I am suddenly jerked back to a time when I was tied and dragged and raped and left for nothing.

That's when a harsh pain shoots through my head and I fall unconscious.

~

I drift awake to careful hands dabbing at something wet on the side of my head. Fire crackles in my ears, and I smell the comforting odor of smoke. A middle-aged woman with long, braided, black hair wipes something pungent and gooey on my head, rubbing the stuff into my hair. She turns away and says something in a language I don't understand. Maybe my head is just all jumbled up . . .

But I can feel it, the lack of weight. I crane my neck down and see my bare neck. Both the necklace Wyatt gave me today and the silver one from my Grandma is gone.

Blossoming panic from the inside out, vibrant anger ravages through me. "Where are my necklaces?" I hiss, still pulling myself out of unconsciousness.

"Just calm down - we can explain," the woman says, and I am startled by her command of English. I take such a sharp intake of breath, it hurts the sore spots in my ribs.

"Where are my necklaces?!?" I exclaim, tearing my flesh against the ropes that bind me.

"They're right here," the woman says back with astounding force - she's just as pissed as I am.

"Give them back," I spit.

"Not until you tell us why you're here," she says, holding my possessions in her leathery hands.

I swallow, fuming, partially angry that I have nothing cutting to say. I look around, gaining my bearings. I realize that I'm tied with my hands behind my back, around a stake that's holding up the thatched roof.

Just as this uncannily motherly woman wraps a piece of cloth around my head wound, a commotion erupts outside. Grunts, and shouts. I can feel the air rustle outside from inside this hut.

I perk up. Wyatt.

I turn to the woman stoking the fire. "Hey, thanks for the bandage and all, but can you let me go now?"

The woman looks back at me. "Unfortunately, that's not for me to decide."

Just as I open my mouth to say something, the woman rushes out of the tent. I try and get a glimpse of what's going on in the heat of night, but all I get is flashes of limbs, clothes, and smoke.

"Dammit," I hiss, looking down. Realizing the awkward position I'm in, I pull my legs out from under me. It's like a breath of fresh air when the tendons and ligaments are released. My feet aren't tied, thank goodness, but my bag is gone, as is everything in my pockets.

I feel the rope constricting my hands. They are tied at the wrist, looping over my thumbs, and crossed over each other. I fumble in the thorny twine for a knot, but as I'm scooting up back against the post, I feel it. They wrapped my hands up, and then tied them around the pole, so the knot is stabbing into my back, so there was no chance of me being able to untie it. They obviously aren't newcomers to this kind of thing.

Just then, the woman comes back in. I go limp.

She kneels back down in front of me, an odd expression tainting her face. "We've got your friend. The boy. They won't hurt him. And we won't hurt you, but we just want to know who you two are."

God, I hope Wyatt doesn't make up some elaborate story because then we're both screwed. I sigh and decide to tell the truth, because if all else fails, don't lie.

"My name is Terra. His is Wyatt. We are the only survivors of a four-person plane crash. We're just trying to find civilization. We don't want to hurt you, we just want to be on our wa-"

"Yeah, yeah. That's all I really needed to know. Thanks, Terra. I hope your friend can extend to us the same honesty, though. He was a little harder to drag in here."

"Not surprising," I smirk.

"Unfortunately, I can't untie you until I get the word from the Chief. If Wyatt's as cooperative as you, then that shouldn't be long."

"Now can I have my necklaces?" I say, still harboring a decent amount of animosity.

The woman sighs and looks around the hut for a while. And then she places them in my lap. Son of a bitch.

The woman leaves again, and I am left with the crackling fire and the lonely smoke wafting up to the stars.

~

"Wake up!" the woman pulls me out of unconsciousness again. I guess I fell asleep.

"Oh, sorry," I say, reaching up and rubbing my eyes. I look down at my raw wrists. "Thanks for untying me, by the way." And immediately, I put my necklaces back on, breathing a sigh of relief.

The woman smiles. "No problem. Your friend, Wyatt, eventually did tell the truth, so you two are free to go."

Standing up, I see that this woman is quite short. "If this isn't too imposing, could I ask a favor?"

~

The Native Americans are fantastic hosts. It takes less than five minutes for the whole tribe to come out. The women gather the food, which they humbly admit isn't feast worthy, while the men make a drum circle around the bonfire. Hell, I only asked if we could fill up on our way out.

My sleepiness is immediately brushed away at the liveliness of the party in front of me. Their fruit, grains, and meat rejuvenates my brittle bones. Their cool water soothes my aching muscles, and their dancing and singing infuses life back into me.

I swear, Wyatt and I spend the first twenty whole minutes just eating and drinking. They even have alcohol that they let us drink, even though we only take a sip each.

Once we think that we could fall over because of our full bellies, the woman who had me tied to a pole thirty minutes ago is inviting us into their dancing circle.

With hoots and hollers, we jump in with the young and old, and we dance and clap and jump and shout until our sides hurt, but somehow, all of the wonderful food stays in our stomachs where it belongs.

I have two left feet, so the women graciously teach me how to dance, following a simple four-step motion around the fire, while Wyatt is given a drum and pounds on the taut leather like his life depends on it.

Eventually, the drum circle and the dancing dies down, and the Native Americans swirl around us, men on one side, women on the other. Embarrassed, Wyatt catches my eye as we go to our respective genders.

"This one's the couple dance," a young girl, about seven or eight, whispers to me.

"Fun," I say, really meaning it. Sweet adrenaline runs high. "How do you do it?"

"Well, first it's the married couples. They do their thing, then the singles step out in a line, and when the third bass drum beats, a boy will approach you. If he doesn't, then step back. If he does, then take his hands in yours. Then bounce on your right foot twice, then go to the left, and bounce twice. One bounce on the right, then left, then back to twice on the right, like this," She demonstrates for me, then watches in embarrassment as I try to do it.

"After that, you do that exact same thing, but he will pull you in like this-" The girl takes my hands and tucks one out, like a chicken wing, and extends one out. "You'll do this in a half-circle motion, until the bass drum beats again three times. Then he will let go of one hand, spin you in, spin you out, and then you will grab onto the hands of another." She pauses, and her tone changes drastically. "The white boy will probably want to dance with you," the girl says, a sly smile tingling on her rosy lips.

I sigh, and laugh, turning away. I now regret not staying in dance lessons when I was six. If I hadn't quit, maybe I wouldn't be as coordinated as a baby elephant on a unicycle.

Then, it pops into my head. "What's your name?"

"Chitsa," she replies, smiling proudly with gaps in her teeth.

The music swells, and, on the third drum beat, the assumingly married couples start their own dance. I see the woman who fixed my head up, whose name I learn is Kanti.

But after ten minutes, the married men and women fall back into their lines, and Chitsa drags me forward. As the women like me settle into a line, I notice that, at 16 years of age, I am among the oldest group, of ages 12-20, excluding the widowed women who still love to dance their asses off.

The drum beats increase, and I must miscount, because the men step forward before I thought they would. And one, tall and dark, approaches me.

One-third of his head is shaved, and the rest cascades over his shoulder in a black, wavy waterfall. His eyebrows, oh God, his eyebrows. I could look at those things until my eyes bleed, and I'd still be cool with it. But he's rugged, with a chiseled face and soft lips. There's no way I could get a better dance partner.

I hear the girls behind me giggle and squeal. I see one faint out of the corner of my eye and snap my gaze back to this wonderful young man.

Suddenly, he takes my hand and we start dancing. Everything Chitsa told me comes flooding back, but it's still translated in sloppy movements on the packed dirt ground.

As we're gyrating around to the primal beat of the music, he is quite skilled. What did I expect, since every female's heart sprang out of their loins when he so graciously chose me as his dancing partner.

Eventually, I get the hang of it, but by that time, it's time to change partners.

Near the end of the first round, this extraordinarily good-looking young man says to me. "Pleasure dancing with you. I'm Ezhno." He backs away, but he doesn't let go of my hand. Instead, he presses his flawless lips against the back of my hand. Every female in the vicinity shoots me with jealousy.

But by the time I can say anything, I am twirled on out of there, but there's not a hand to greet me. Bashful, I shimmy out of the crowd and back to Chitsa, who is smiling in glee at me.

"I can't believe you danced with him!" she squeals.

"Oh, uh, yeah," I say, feeling the food tent drawing me. Now that most of my body is idle, I can feel the exhaustion taking control of my body, leeching the life from me, and lacing steel into my muscles. Inertia is no longer my friend.

"Every girl would sell her soul to the goddess Asdzaa and chop off her hair for one night with that man," Chitsa says, still googly eyed, following me over to the food tent.

"That's great," I say bluntly, pushing back the animal hide. I gulp down the water and gasp after I'm done. I still don't think I'll ever get over how freaking great that feeling is.

"So who is this Ezhno guy anyways?" I ask, through mouthfuls of food.

"Oh, he's just the Chief's prized grandson! He became a warrior at age 13 - youngest ever - but is choosing to stay unmarried to fulfill his duty."

"Oh, that's great," I say, gulping down the water. Who am I kidding? Ezhno is gorgeous.

I draw back. After the misunderstanding, the Native Americans have been beyond gracious and accepting. This all has changed so fast. I'm not unthankful, but a moment of silence has made this all come slamming down.

Chitsa and I eventually wander out of the tent, and the dancing is still in full swing. I search the heads for blond curls, which is not that hard to find in a sea of glossy black and dark brown.

Through the moving bodies, his eye catches mine. It seems like an eternity since I've seen him. His feet jumble up with the girl he's dancing with as he tries to look at me *and* focus on dancing. I look down and make my way to the edge of the crowd surrounding the singles dancing.

Soon enough. Wyatt and his dance partner have worked their way around the dance floor to me. And when the switch-off comes, he drills his eyes into mine and grabs my hands. With a euphoric swinging motion, we dance together to the beating of the drum.

"What was that all about?" he hisses at me as we absently dance together.

"What . . Ezhno?" I narrow my eyes and twirl into the second stage of the dance. "Are you jealous?"

"Yeah, maybe I am," he says, sneering. Suddenly, he pulls me in close, our feet tripping over each other. "We don't know these people."

I raise an eyebrow and miss a step. "They seem nice enough."

Silence as the dance goes on. When it comes time to change partners, we don't because I can tell Wyatt's not done.

Halfway through our second round together, he speaks again, the air around us hot and lively like boiling water. "I'm jealous because I saw the way he looked at you. And I saw the way you looked at him. And I knew that it was all over. I knew that I wasn't tall enough, wasn't nice enough, wasn't hot enough, wasn't strong enough. And I hate it."

Suddenly angry at his change of heart and surprised by his insecurity, I say, "So what? Why should you care?"

Wyatt sneers, again. "'Why should I care?' Why *shouldn't* I?" Wyatt pauses and looks away. "You know, despite what you might think in your convoluted mind of yours, there's a lot people who actually care about you. But what do you do? You manipulate them, you push them away, you act like you don't care, and what do you expect in return? A whole hell of a lot."

His words bite. I am taken aback, and as the drum beats, he lets go of me and we suddenly switch partners. Glossy black hair and feathers and beads swirl around me, and another boy takes my hand.

Conveniently, Wyatt is to my back as we continue to dance. Pangs run through me like wooden stakes, as if I am to be raked over the coals.

But he's right. I do push people away. Am I pushing him away now?

Words bubble up, but nothing of substance seems to come out of my mouth. "Wyatt!" I shout over the pounding of feet and singing. "I'm sorry if I ever made you feel that way! I really do care about you, I'm just, uh, bad at expressing it."

I hear Wyatt laugh spitefully as my partner and I twirl around, and I drift further from Wyatt. "Prove it, I dare you!"

I inwardly groan. Wyatt's angry and jealous, and for righteous reasons. We can kiss and make up later, but for now, we're both manipulating each other.

When the next transition comes, I dive for Wyatt. He reluctantly takes my hands, and we begin to dance, but this doesn't last long because the words flow from my mouth like poison.

"You want me to prove it to you? Fine then, I'll prove it to you." I reach up and cup his face in my hands. He ceases dancing and wraps his arms around my waist.

A smile plays on his lips as he twirls us around and dips me down, holding me aloft as one foot pops up. And I press my lips against his.

I am vaguely aware of cheers erupting around us, but the real kicker is how close in proximity Wyatt is to me. Not just physically, but emotionally, mentally. My veins pump sugar-sweet syrup, but my bones are electrified with passion. Maybe everything will be alright.

~

When it gets so late it's early, we sit down around the fire, still burning hot, and tell stories. For the first while, the Native Americans tell their stories. Their stories may or may not be true, but they tell them in such a captivating way it's easy to let the fictional elements slide and just be stolen by the story. Sometimes, it's a single person telling a tale of adventure and grace from the gods. Other times, it's a group effort of long-lost lovers or a fateful war. We laugh, and we cry, we cheer and we shout.

Eventually, Eznho looks to me and Wyatt. "It is customary that guests tell a story during this time." He nods to us.

I look to Wyatt, hoping that he'll get my telepathic message that I'd rather not make a speech.

He nods and stands. I stay sitting, the heat rising to my cheeks. Not from embarrassment, but because of what Wyatt is like, and what he's probably going to say.

He clears his throat and stands with bold confidence in what he's going to say, even though I know he's probably really nervous that he'll trip and fall or something.

He, again, clears his throat for effect, and I lean back on my hands so I can see him. "Well," he starts, smirking. "It was a sweltering hot, late summer day on the outskirts of Phoenix, Arizona. Life was running smoothly for everyone, except for one turbulent plane over the desert."

Wyatt begins to recount our fateful steps here with a charisma that resonates in his vibrant eyes. He talks about everything from the ghost town to the water pump incident. Everything from the flood to the long talks late into the night.

But he says all of these things with an intimacy and passion that demands the attention of every listener, painting the picture with his charades. He, of course, fills in many boring and fuzzy holes with his own enigmatic twist.

Time and life itself slips away as he spends at least an hour winding a silver web with his words and presentation of our story.

I find myself swept off my feet by every move Wyatt makes, every word he breathes. I am stunned by his words and ravished by the gleam in his eyes. Desire rises up in me - not necessarily for his body, but for his time, his essence, and his soul.

~

We all wander to bed sometime between 3 and 4 am - I only know this because I can feel it in the aches of my body. They let us use a small guest hut, and all I can remember is curling up next to Wyatt in the dark and finally allowing sleep to take over my bones.

July 4, 2014 - Wyatt

Sweat seared down my forehead. I wiped the stinging liquid from my face, obstructing my already limited vision. I squinted in the dark, but my hands did most of the seeing. I pressed and felt the substances in each bag. Some powdery like sugar, some wrinkled and tough like tissue paper.

After not being able to find what I was looking for, I just grabbed a handful, jammed them down my pants, and ducked behind a stack of boxes. I tripped and sent the boxes full of nothing flying down.

"Shit shit shit," I hissed, gathering my plastic bags and stuffing them deep within my pants.

Suddenly, a light in the closet flicked on. All of the liquids in my body froze, as did I.

"What the actual fuck?" the man said. Actually, this man was more than just a man - he was my friend's dad.

Drunk and angry, this burly man stumbled through the fallen boxes in his storage closet, half-looking for the human rat who stole from his stash and half-rambling in an incoherent stupor.

As the fat, violent man moved closer and closer, I eyeballed an open spot in between his legs.

I only got one shot. If I did this too early, he would be too close to me and just grab me like the twig I was. If I went too late, well, my demise would be obvious.

I kept one eye on an open spot in between the boxes.

Just two more steps, one more step . . .

And then I burst out of the boxes and ran out of the closet.

"You motherfucking son of a -"

But I didn't stick around to hear the end of his stream of obscenities.

Making the poor decision of jumping off of the couch and crashing through the window, I knew I was safe.

Bleeding and anxious, I ran off into the night. Lilly would ask about the glass cuts later, and, of course, I would lie.

Covered in a cool sweat, I skid into the dimly lit alleyway, deep in the city bowels of LA.

I saw my friends, all leaning on the grimy walls and dressed in thin fabrics and dull colors. Their faces lit up.

"Hey, Wyatt," James said, extending a hand and pulling me into a half-hug. I addressed the rest of them. Even though these were relatively new friends since I was kicked out of my last school - most of whom were older than me - , I still felt like I had some kind of a twisted home.

"You got the stuff?" Connor said, sneering at me. Even when he wasn't high, he was still an asshole.

"Hell yeah I do," I said, reaching deep into my pants. Connor backed off, and the knot in my gut drew tighter.

We sat on the slightly graveled ground, littered with trash and oil. Everyone picked their drug of choice, but since I was the guinea pig who got the short end of the stick and broke into Logan's dad's house, I got first pick.

Now, mind you, I'd only done weed four times before this, which I had found enjoyable but not strong enough for me. The last round, I had tried ecstasy. That had been pretty fun, but I didn't take it because this week, Logan called the next dose a while back.

But then I saw a bag of something off white, tawny color. Fine and powdery, like flour and sugar.

As soon as my fingers wrapped around the bag, all four of them 'ooh'ed and 'aah'ed and reveled in my bold choice - cocaine.

With trembling hands, I gathered some in my hands, like a little line of sand. Taking a breath of smoky air, I laid a dollar bill on my thigh and rolled it up into a tight, tiny tube, and sucked the fine stuff up my nose.

I had the first impulse to sneeze and expel the stuff from my nasal cavity, but I dropped back and pressed my grimy fingers over my nose, holding it in.

And I could feel every cell of every sheet of tissue soaking up the drug, tearing through the scent receptors in my nose and eating away at the flesh of my brain.

And that was it. I was gone.

~

The world blurred around me and a warm glow screamed from my chest.

Reality slipped away - nothing mattered anymore.

Fire. Smoke. Someone tipped over the can containing the fire. Shit.

Burns. That fucking hurt - someone screamed.

Such noise. The stars scream down and rake at the back of my eyes.

Woo hoooo.

I can do fucking anything.

Warm. I'm so warm. The walls. They're so cold. They hate me.

Their words were stupid, but I talked back with insane clarity. Everything felt like nonsense, like mechanical numbers vomiting from a computer.

Every word is like a needle. Poke, poke poke.

No pain. No feelings. I am everywhere and nowhere. So much light in so much darkness. Euphoria like an anchor. Not a damn care in the world.

Electricity is my blood. I felt it here and there and everywhere.

People talked and shouted and screamed and sang. Life happens, shit happens.

But then, I felt myself slipping. Slipping from this mountain like fingers on loose gravel, and I clung on for dear life.

"No no no no no no no o o o o ."

What the fuck am I doing?

More falling. My heartbeat was an animal itself.

A clamoring beast ravaging my body.

Breathing - in and out. In and out.

~

Hours had passed. I pushed myself off of the ground.

The world blurred, rotating around a singular point in the distance - a teenage boy standing at the opening of the alleyway.

Colorful, intricate tattoos lined his arms and his hair was black and tousled. *What the hell is he doing here?* I thought But a large, screen-printed cross was strewn across his black tank shirt.

I was alone.

Somehow, I had managed to wander away from those sons of bitches. I couldn't even hear their howls in the grimy concrete.

Suddenly, this boy, who was probably only a few years older than me, lifted me up under my armpits. Grunting, words barely passed over my lips. "What are you doing?"

"Where do you live?" the boy asked, shoving me into a fabric lined, cushy seat.

My throat burned. "Mid City. Apartments on the corner of 23rd and Arizona Avenue." Chills scattered all over my body like an army of crawling ants, and cold sweat beaded off of my skin.

My thoughts ran a thousand miles an hour, overlapping themselves and repeating and repeating and repeating. I didn't hear what the boy said next.

I flinched when the engine started up. He drove me home.

And then the boy, whose name I still don't know to this day, hauled my sorry ass out of the back of his car and walked me up the stairs and into my apartment.

We stood there, shivering and clawing my fingers over my skin. All I really wanted to do was sleep, but I didn't think I could in a million years.

The boy, the silver on his nostril shining like the sun, pressed something into my hand. "Have a better night," he said.

Then left.

~

The apartment was dark and cold. There was no sound, except for the faint LA noise coming from down below.

With trembling hands, I pushed open Lilly's bedroom door.

Blue. Endless, endless blue. A blue that would drive me, a blue iris and a black pupil and blonde eyelashes that would haunt me, follow me, wherever I went.

Her eyes glowing in the dark, she stared directly at me. Already, I could feel her deep animosity. Alone, in the dark of night. I left her alone.

She knew. She knew who I was. What I had done.

And then it hit me so strong that I slammed the door shut with such force that it shook the walls of our tiny apartment.

She saw it. But I had not seen it until I saw it reflected back in her tiny, pain-stricken eyes.

~

A deep emptiness stretched out within me, had been for a while.

I was becoming my father. The more I tried to push it off, the more it leaked into my being. For every act of good I did, I counteracted it with just as many horrible things. I could not, for the life of me, save myself. My demise was inevitable.

With my back on her door, I fell to my knees, ravished with nothing but reality. A desperation like no other swept across me, and fumbling like a madman, I scoured the floor for the thing that guy pressed into my hand.

Crumpled and streaked with dirt, I squinted in the dim light to read the words.

Before long, I was sobbing at the kindness of the truth before me. And that night, I, Wyatt Hartman, came to know the truth. I came into the light, and forevermore, my life was changed. Because the simple, loving words on that laminated handout meant for the masses spoke to me - not because it was convincing but because the word of God took root in my darkened heart, in my darkened life.

~

Now, I'd love to tell you that it was all rainbows and sunshine from there, but then, I wouldn't have a story to tell, would I? Probably wouldn't have been on that stupid plane, either.

It was hard, undoubtedly, to keep up my faith. It took a week of mowing yards in run down neighborhoods to buy a Bible, and then, I had to find a ride to church. When I couldn't do that, I just read and listened to podcasts and music in my free time.

But as time went on and things grew more and more hectic, I fell away. It was a slow fade. Time I would have spent praying would be consumed with homework. Time that I could read and worship were cluttered with stress and watching Lilly.

I also had the same, shitty friends.

And like sand slipping through my fingers, in less than a year, my fire for God had burned out. I got a job and started saving up to run away with Lilly, because things weren't getting better - they never had, and they never will.

Or so I thought.

CHAPTER EIGHTEEN: Restoration
DAY 14 - Wyatt; August 18th, 2015

I awake, sore and still tired, but this is the first time in weeks that I haven't woken up yearning for water and food. Light streams in through the thin, yet sturdy walls. It's surprisingly still cool in the hut, but a glowing warmth presses against one side of my body. Terra is sleeping soundly, cocooned inside of me.

I peel myself off of her and stand up. Everything is sore but doesn't feel screamingly awful. I stretch because I find that's the only thing that helps. A fire smokes in the middle of the tent, wafting up to the hole in the top of the vaulted ceiling. Not much else inhabits the hut. I can hear obvious commotion outside, but from inside the hut, it seems like a lifetime away.

I push open the flapping, animal skin door, and jump waist-deep into a bustling morning - like 8 am in New York City. But fewer people, and, well, fewer shiny skyscrapers. Someone's already starting the fire in the middle of the huge circle of huts. Women and children fill the center, chatting and running around. A group of children kick a leather ball around. Women carry baskets on their heads, fresh water dribbling over the tops. Men gather their things to go out and hunt. They don't seem to be donning their traditional attire. If it weren't for the huts and touches of beads, tattoos and feathers, I could see them walking the streets of LA. The sky is a brilliant blue, devoid of clouds. A swirl of dust kicked up by people's feet makes another atmospheric layer.

Someone appears beside me.

"Hey," she says, smiling through the sleep. I look over and see Terra, standing next to me. "I honestly never thought we would be so lucky to find these people."

"Or be so unlucky as to crash here that we would be so desperate to find these people."

Terra nudges me. "I was trying to be optimistic for once."

"Well, it didn't work."

She sneers at me playfully.

"I'm going to go and ask the Chief what this is all about - if we can contact anyone. Can you pack up our stuff?"

"Sure," she says, and goes back inside the tent.

I make my way to the largest hut in the community. I catch many of them throwing me odd glances. Some positive, some I can't really tell.

I peek my head in the Chief's hut. "Knock knock."

"Oh hello, Wyatt!" Chief says, smiling with open arms. I take this as a gesture to hug him, so I do. Awkward. He's one of the younger Chiefs, I suspect, because he's at least forty-five. Salt and pepper hair, long and riddled with feathers and beads, and he wears what seem to be ceremonial garments. His wife is there, plugging something into a generator. The hodgepodge of new and old gives me a headache.

"So, in case you weren't already aware, we're lost - stranded. Can you contact anyone - the police, search-and-rescue, anyone, to let them know we're here and we're safe?" I say, leaning against the mud-packed walls.

The chief takes a sharp inhale of breath, and I wince on the inside. I can feel the bad news coming like a raised arm preparing to slap. "The, uh, contract we have made with the owners of the land here states that we are to have virtually no contact with the outside world, and we prefer it that way. It was part of our deal with them. And in turn, we farm and hunt on their land and sell a good part of the produce and give it to them for income. This allows us to live here, on our native land."

"So, there's no way you could just call someone?" I plead, feeling the itching mix of anxiety and frustration rising within me.

The only time we make contact with them is four times a year when we trade for technology. Any other time would violate the contract. There's a reason we treated you all so harshly when you first arrived," Chief says, striding around his hut, stirring something over a cast iron metal pot over the fire. Damn, whatever it is, it smells good.

"Well, when are you going to contact the landowners next?"

"Mid-October or November, when the harvest comes in." The Chief observes me, almost sympathetically.

I blow out air through my lips, finding myself at an impeccable loss for words. "Can you at least point us in the right direction?"

~

The Native Americans refill our water bottles and water cans. They even give us some of their limited supply of plastic water bottles. They give us food for five days, along with some more twine, batteries, matches, bandages, and cooking utensils for Terra. I think they give us some sunscreen and aloe vera, but our skin is so damaged, it wouldn't do much at this point. They even direct us a mile south to an outhouse with running water and a shower.

But the most important thing they give us is their knowledge. They show us how to navigate by the stars, using the north star, the Big Dipper, Orion, etc. They show us how to make a fish trap with just sticks in the mud. They show us a larger spectrum of edible and poisonous plants. They show us herbal remedies and shelter-building techniques. And we are eternally grateful.

Around three in the afternoon, we are ready to go. With full bellies and renewed spirits, we give our last condolences to the Maricopa Native Americans. Terra gives a long hug to Chitsa, and I give a sturdy handshake to Chief.

And we walk west, along with the setting sun.

Moments later, Terra says: "Well, that was fun."

~

That night, we sit around a fire and eat the rabbit jerky and fruit. Terra sighs, biting into a pear.

Terra's got that look on her face where it looks like her mind took a road trip. Conversation. Start a conversation. "They were nice," I say, gnawing on the salty meat. I can't stop running through my hands through my clean hair.

"Yeah," Terra says.

"You don't sound so sure," I say, the fire heating our faces. One of the logs falls, and sparks fly up. I add on another one.

"I'm not," she says, staring into the glowing flames. "I was just thinking - it would be so much safer to have stayed with them. Water, food, safety in numbers, all at our fingertips. I mean, who knows how long we'd have to wait until they traded with the people who own this land, and then we could talk to them about getting back ..."

Terra's words weasel their way into my soul. On some level, I understand what she's saying. But on another, it strikes me as completely absurd.

The electric outer layer of me hates what she's saying - despises it. "How can you say that?!?" I exclaim, leaning forward.

"Don't you ever want to, like, go on the internet again? Don't you ever want to eat french fries again?" Terra draws back, and I lean in closer, getting my point across. "Don't you ever want to see your friends and family again?"

She pauses, drags out the stars for an eternity. "Wyatt," Terra starts, a dire tone lacing through her voice. "I never said that I didn't want to see my family again - I do, I'd kill for it. But . . ." She sighs, deep and heavy, like the deepest, darkest part of the ocean. "But I've realized, and I don't think that you have. I've realized that we aren't getting back. No one. Is. Coming. To. Rescue. Us, Wyatt!" Tears, hot like acid, suddenly stream down her face. Lasers of passion shoot from her eyes right through me. "It's fucking hopeless, Wyatt." Every word comes out of her mouth like a dagger and pierces me in the heart with just as much fervor as they pass over her lips.

I run my fingers through my hair, grabbing onto the strands like they are the strings to my soul. Shame burns on my face. Images of Lilly, of my friends, of my aunt and uncle flash in the back of my mind. How could I ever stay here, in this hell hole? How could I ever let go of the hope of returning? If I let go of that, I swear, I'd lose my mind. If I let go of that, I'd have nothing.

And then it hits me - I'd have nothing. I *have* nothing. Lilly is . . . . God knows where, probably back at the resort. My mother's dead. My father's gone. My aunt and uncle - would they really be willing to take care of us? Then what? I have no freaking idea what I want to do with my life outside of surviving. All I have ever done is survive. I survived when my father was abusing us. I have been surviving ever since he left. And now, with this, I'm surviving again. Never knowing when it will end.

And even with this, I thought I had a time frame. I thought I knew that this would end at some point. Without hope, I have nothing.

Trembling with emotion, I look at Terra, a sincerity that I have never felt before running through me, grasping onto her cheek with my hand. "Terra, we can't let go. We can't let go of the hope that someday, we'll make it back. That someone will find us. Because without this hope, there's no point in anything that we're doing. There's no point to life, then, if we have nothing to hope for. So no, I won't let you stay behind, anywhere." Tears are running down my face, screaming like race cars, tearing slits in my cheeks.

Terra cups a hand over her forehead, shielding her eyes from me. Her body shakes with silent sobs. I scoot over to her and wrap her in my arms. She doesn't move, but I know that she receives my love.

Nasty sobs bubble out of her, and I push the tears out of my own eyes. "I dunno, I. . . I just want to go home," she says between hiccupy sobs.

"Me too, Terra. Me too," I say, stroking her hair, a dire loneliness gnawing at the fringes of my tattered soul.

Terra suddenly sits up, abruptly, pulling her shuddering figure away from me. Tears piercing her eyes, she stares back at me. They speak volumes, deep as a trench and flooded with emotion.

"I . . . was raped," she says. Her voice weighs a thousand pounds.

I can't think of anything to say. But suddenly, it all makes sense . . .

"I was nine. It happened on my own property."

I dare to break our gaze. My heart clenches in my chest. What kind of a sick monster would do this?

The silence pushes back at the darkness. I feel Terra sever the silver cord of eye contact as she turns her head down. I can nearly hear her mind whirring like a machine.

"I just . . . didn't want to die with it on my conscience."

"Don't talk like that," I shoot back. Stupid, stupid, stupid. Say something, comfort her, idiot. "I'm sorry."

And slowly, Terra moves closer to me and falls back into my embrace. God, I love her.

CHAPTER NINETEEN: Utter Abandonment
DAY 15 - Terra; August 19th, 2015

I push my weary eyes open, willing them to focus. Sighing hard, my body still in sleep, although wide awake, I blink my swollen eyes.

"Morning," Wyatt says like he does every morning. He pokes at the fire, otherwise motionless. Despair is carved on his face.

I cough for about a solid five minutes like I do every morning.

"You been up all this time?" I ask, leaning against a rock. I feel well rested, but that doesn't exempt me from aches and pains that inhabit every inch of my body like a blood-ridden disease.

He shakes his head.

I sigh and push my bangs out of my face. "Wanna eat?"

"I always want to eat, Terra," he says, but the darkness says something else is going on.

I lick my lips and scoot in closer. "Hey, what's going on?" I ask, slipping my hand in his free one.

"I'm just . . . angry. Frustrated."

I pull his hand out from his side, tearing the muscles. My fingers trace the veins on his arm, and his fingers go limp, relaxing. "Why?"

"Because I can't wait for this to be over. Except I know it's never going to end," he says. He turns his head to me lazily, meeting my eyes. "We're never getting out of here."

I hesitate, anxiety simmering below the surface. Slowly, I tug myself out of the molasses of sleep and lean my head on his shoulder. "You don't know that." I wish I could believe it myself.

~

Eventually, we eat. The lentils are nice and soft, and the dried fruit is sweet and vibrant, giving us the illusion of eating colorful candy. Even the jerky is savory like bacon, the flavors exploding in our mouths.

I open the small sack they gave me, where I carry most of the food. During the flood, we made the mistake of not separating the survival equipment equally. I ended up with all of the food and water, and Wyatt with all of the knives, ropes, etc.

Furrowing my brows, I pull out a hard canteen covered in animal hide. I yank off the cork, attached by a string. The smell doesn't hit me until I stick my nose in it. I know that it's alcohol by the pungent smell and the way that it leaves a slight tingling in my nose.

I pour some on my tongue and am alarmed, at first, at the searing alcohol. But when that burns away, it leaves a sweet, slightly fruity taste on the tip of my tongue, while ravishing the rest of my mouth with a strong, earthy taste. But when all of that is gone, the only remaining taste is the bitter alcohol.

My tongue juts out of my mouth, trying to rid itself of the intoxicating liquid.

"Hey, try this," I say, handing him the canteen.

Wyatt takes one look at the liquid and tips it back into his mouth.

Less than seconds later, he sputters and pulls the drink away from his lips, the golden, transparent stuff dribbling from his chin. He coughs, but it's throaty and dry like he's choking.

"God, that's nasty. Why'd you do that?" he says, his voice taut and rough.

I smile and shrug. "Just to see what you'd do."

"Ha ha, very funny," he sneers at me, then sobers up. "So why do you think the Native Americans gave this to us?"

All I can do is shrug, but mostly because if I open my lips, the only thing that will come out is my worst fear that they only gave it to us because of its dire but essential medicinal properties - antiseptic, painkiller, and narcotic. However, my mind goes to the worst places, thinking that if one of us gets terribly hurt, we'll be forced to use it.

Swallowing hard, I put the canteen away, deep within my bag.

"I dunno," I reply, half-forgetting that Wyatt even asked me that question. "We should get a move on - it's getting late."

"Yep. It's only 10 in the morning, and it's sweltering - let's rest in the afternoon."

"Sounds like a fabulous idea," I say, deadpan.

Sipping on our water bottles, we walk, following the sun as it rises high above us.

The heat is nearly tactile - the hot, inner core of my body is at least the same temperature as the boiling air around us, stagnant and beating. My spine aches.

Clothes chafe against my now exposed and protruding bones. My hair stopped having any kind of rhyme or reason weeks ago - and now it's just a matted, oily mess, even after I impulsively cut it to my shoulder.

My face burns with sweat and sunburn and grime, and not much happens until we stop for lunch. In a burst of selfish and impulsive stupidity, we eat at least three days worth of food - and then almost vomit all of it up.

As the afternoon climbs to well over one hundred degrees, we decide to stop at around 1:30.

But not before we see the horizontal cut in the land, grayish toned and burning with white and yellow stripes. An actual paved highway.

"Do you see that?" he asks, squinting at the road.

"Yeah."

"Wanna go see if we can find a ride?" he asks.

"You're hilarious."

We go out of our way to walk to the highway - neither of us has the energy to run to it. Dead in either direction, we watch as it coasts over the land.

The wind blows, a hum in our ears and the grit in our eyes.

"You know this road?" Wyatt asks, turning to me. For a flash, I'm struck by how dirty, how emaciated his face is. And it hurts because death tugs at the corner of our eyes.

I shrug. "Probably Route 95. Doesn't get much traffic."

"So, north, then?" He gestures right.

"Sure."

The sun screams down, not just on us but on everything. Besides the wind, nothing moves, nothing makes a sound. We are just the two blips moving through what is truly a desert.

The horizon warps. Wyatt trips in front of me, but my reflexes aren't fast enough to catch him as he crashes to the ground.

I stumble forward, sliding onto my knees, turning him over. Blood pours from his nose.

My throat like dry rocks, I tell him to get up, to keep moving, but he just lets the dust wash over him. I grab him by his wrists and drag him off the road.

Soaked in heat, I fall to my knees and lay down next to him. He grabs my hand, presses it to his lips. I can feel the solid warmth of his blood as it smears onto my hand.

We breathe, as the afternoon explodes into heat. We spend the day, afternoon, evening, lying in the plants and sand, just existing.

It's not until the cool blanket of evening falls that we are able to move again.

While we've wandered away from the highway to gather food, a Volkswagen beetle drives by. We don't make it to the road in time to catch it. Wyatt tells me a story of how he and his sister would always play slug bug and eat ice cream. Both make me want to cry.

We don't see any more cars. The water from the water cans is long gone, although almost all of them are still in our bags. Still no food. My eyes sting with sweat and dirt. I find some licorice plants and dig up the roots. We chew on these as we walk.

My throat, my entire body, cries for water. Some time during the night, we stop and fall asleep, curled up together next to the road, cold and silent.

August 4th, 2015 - Wyatt

The smooth metal was warm between my fingers, only made this way by my breath passing through the holes and creating sound. I got calluses, canker sores and cracked lips from rubbing this harmonica back and forth between my lips all the damn time.

The music from the harmonica was rough and somewhat rustic, filling the moving car with the sweet harmonies of blues, jazz, and some old rock. This hunk of vibrating metal was a prize Lilly won at the fair for apple bobbing, but she could never learn how to get anything decent-sounding out of it. Being the awesome sister that she is, she gave it to me, thinking I could handle it and, in turn, actually make music from it. I've had this thing for two years. Even though it was won at a fair, it's sturdy and hasn't changed a bit since I got it.

I cupped my hand around the high end of the harmonica and blew slightly. I slid my hand up and down over the high end of the harmonica, creating a smooth, jazz-like sound that seems to resonate in the car much better than a single note would.

My mother cringed beside me as the music swelled. I could feel her doing it in the driver's seat. Just her distaste for my music turned the air sour.

"Wyatt, would you stop playing that thing?" my mother snapped.

"It's a *harmonica*," I interrupted, keeping my voice cool and temperate.

"Harmonica, whatever." I watched her reflection in the glass window, waving off my attempt at quiet defiance. "Just, stop playing and please socialize with us."

I looked back at Lilly, biting her sparkly pink nail and reading a book. I looked back up at Mom, hunched in the driver's seat, looking like a lawyer thrown into a tornado, bloodshot eyes trained on the road. "Why? No one's socializing anyway." I settled back into my crouched position, away from my mother, feet on the dashboard and continued heaving into the harmonica. The clouds out the window seemed to roll by much slower than the Arizona ground beneath us.

"Wyatt, you don't realize how much time I took off work for us to go on this trip, but I was a good mother so we could spend some quality family time!" My mother slapped her hands on the steering wheel, causing us to swerve just a bit. My bony knees clacked together underneath my baggy jeans.

"One last hurrah before school starts and you barely have to see us," I muttered under my breath and stick the harmonica back in between my lips so I don't have to talk anymore. *Two years, Wyatt, you just have to get through two years.*

Mom just slumped in her chair. Again, in the window reflection. Her anger was hot and thick. It grumbled through the car.

I blew good and hard with my lips. A strained noise erupts from the harmonica and it slips from my mouth with a sputter. It hits the worn, carpeted floor with a satisfying clunk. I laugh so loud I'm chasing away the tension with every manic breath.

"Ah, shit!" I said.

"Language!" Mom snapped. It almost physically hurt.

I ran my fingers through my sandy, dirty blond head of curls. It laid right back down on my forehead like a mop. Because that's what it is. A mop. I usually crop it pretty short in the summer, just leaving the corkscrews in the front and top intact, but now that summer had begun to rot away into fall, it was back to its usual frumpy state. Not that I cared, though.

The Sonoran Desert looked barer than I thought it would. When people think of Arizona, they imagine the Grand Canyon and Phoenix and that's about it. And so far, I was not seeing any of that. What I was seeing is to a much lesser degree of grandiose - flat, reddish, rocky sand, ugly tufts of dull gray brush all clumped together, ferocious cactuses jutting up at odd angles, a nearly cloudless sky of a brilliant blue. Nothing post-card worthy in sight.

I rolled my eyes slightly and went back to humming into my harmonica. Might as well kill the silence with a knife.

~

It was like a dream come true when we finally come upon the small cluster of buildings, shining like a beacon, smooth and modernized among the mostly flat, rocky terrain. The whole thing looks a little out of place and slightly lonely, plopped in the middle of nowhere. Definitely needs an update to pull it from the nineties.

~

In our room, I flopped on one of the starchy white beds, plugging in my earphones.

"Get up!" Mom shouted, throwing my luggage on the beg.

I rolled my eyes. "What's the plan, then, Captain?"

Lilly giggled. If looks could fucking kill, my mother would be on death row for murder.

"Two days. We hold it together for two days, and I will be off your backs for the rest of the week," she said, rubbing her forehead.

Until she finds someone else to fuck. Then I'll have to remember to buy groceries for the rest of the month.

I wish I had said that out loud, but comedy is all timing, and the moment had passed.

"Tonight, we're having dinner with the owners of the lodge, you guys can swim in the pool, and then tomorrow we'll be going on a plane ride!" Her tone morphed from orderly to sickeningly positive.

"Great," I said, mimicking her tone.

"Shut up," she hissed, swiping back her hand, raising it up before me.

Fear shuddered through me as I winced. Nothing.

"Get dressed, both of you," she said.

August 4th, 2015 - Terra

He wasn't even that attractive. At least, in comparison to the many guys we've seen run their course through the lodge. He was tall, taller than me, and actually quite robust for being a teenager. He's got freckles sprinkled on his face like pepper, and his curly head of hair made his head look a lot bigger than it probably is.

He looked angry, too. Harper and I caught sight of him as soon as we walked into the lobby, my bare feet on the plush carpet. Eyes critical, he hunched over, obviously displeased to be here. Well, he can be glad that the feeling is mutual. I glanced to Harper inconspicuously.

Suddenly, I saw that my mother is gesturing to the boy, nodding her head and eyeing me, her words speaking volumes, as if to say: "be nice, Terra! Shake his hand and smile already". Gross.

However, I did so and met his eyes, and suddenly, my crocodile smile fell flat. His brown sugar eyes drilled into my soul, as if he could see right through me. But what I was truly alarmed by was that I see myself reflected back in his eyes. Resentment. I wondered if he saw it, too. I shook his glance as soon as I could bring myself to.

"I'm Terra," I said quickly.

"Wyatt," he said, his grasp on my hand remaining steady. I let go first.

My mother noticed my curt attitude and used only the subtle motions of her eyes, eyebrows, and lips to display her dissent. I rolled my eyes and back away.

Harper smiled, tight lipped, like she always does around new people. "Harper Holmes." She awkwardly shook his hand, more fervently than I'd done.

Wyatt snorted. "Harper Holmes? Seriously?" He then jammed his hands in his pockets.

"Back off," I spat.

Wyatt just rolled his eyes.

~

Unfortunately, it's a Lombardi tradition to have dinner with the new arrivals at the lodge. My mother always forced me to dress nicer than I needed to, so I had Harper help me get ready.

"Please do something with your hair, Terra," Mom said from her place in front of the mirror.

"Yes, Mother," I said and motioned to Harper. She threw my reddish-brown hair up into a messy bun on the back of my head, with my bangs and a few curls coming down.

While I dressed from my room, Harper dressed from the bathroom. "You don't have to come, you know. Nobody wants to spend time with that ass, Wyatt," I said.

"Nah, I've gotta stick by my friend, and protect her from the throes of stupid boys!" she shouted.

I laughed, pulling the sleeves of my sparkling dress over my shoulders, the fabric nicely hiding my insecurities and accentuating my figure "You sound like you're ten."

Harper poked her head out, her thick black hair spraying in all directions. "Maybe I am."

~

The dinner came sooner than expected, and Harper and I ventured out of my house and across a small parking lot in the back to the lodge.

The outdoor dining room appeared the same as it always does. Warm and homey, but elegant. The desert sun sat fat and hot on the horizon. The first person I saw was Wyatt. His hair was stiff, and gelled back, and neither him or his hair seemed to like it. Stray frizzies poked up, as if one wrong move could throw it all out of whack. And every once in awhile, he'd reach up and pat his hair awkwardly, and then his mother would smack his hand, and he'd sneer.

Warm, bright light glowed from the candlelight and shone off the shimmers in my dress as the wind blew against the thick, white tablecloth. I silently slid off my black heels and feel the gritty sandstone beneath my feet as we walked over. Harper snuck a keen glance at me and my bare feet.

Unfortunately, my seat was right in the view of the setting sun, looking like a sickly sweet orange lollipop in the sky. But thankfully, Wyatt's big head blocked the sun if I position myself correctly. That was when I realized that I was sitting right across from that son of a bitch.

Dinner hadn't really started yet, so we were just sipping water out of our glasses, the adults chatting and us just staring at each other - me across from Wyatt, Harper across from his younger sister, I assume.

Just then, Wyatt moved his head, turning to his sister, and the sun pierced my eyes. Grunting, I squinted and turned away.

Wyatt eyed me and moved back to his original position. Shadows encased my face. He moved again. I subtly moved along with him, but a smile cracked out on his face as he jerked his head around, exposing my poor eyes to the blinding evening sun.

Eventually, he stopped, and he was just sitting there, smirking all cocky. What did I ever do to him?

"What's your problem?" I said, flat faced, my scowl probably juxtaposed with my current elegant style.

"Definitely not you," he said, peeling his lips up passive disdain.

"Disgusting," Harper cut in. I sneered at Wyatt, at a loss for cocky, clever lingo myself.

"You and your friend Sparkles here," he said, gesturing to me as the alleged 'Sparkles'. "Need to calm your tits. Remember that we're paying you guys."

I took a deep breath. I've had to deal with some nasty customers before, but none quite like Wyatt Hartman.

~

The food finally came, and the rough air lightened a bit as I was distracted by eating and talking to Harper.

Harper eventually made a hesitant gesture to Wyatt. "So why did you guys choose our resort?" She was always better at conversation than I was.

"I feel like Sparkles should be asking that question. It's her parents' place," Wyatt said, between mouthfuls.

"I have a name, for your information," I snapped.

Wyatt looked up at me. "Oh, I'm quite aware."

I swallowed hard, feeling my insides turn to concrete. I ate in silence, thankful that after this, I'd probably never have to interact with him again.

Harper and Wyatt went back and forth. The adults yammered on and on. Chatter filled my ears, but a voice stood out among them all. My father. "So the plane ride will start at 11, and end at 2. The plane has a capacity of five, but usually, we only take four at a time."

"So it will be you, me Wyatt and Lilly?" Wyatt's mother said, leaning into my father. Her large breasts hung out of her v-cut shirt, and a sparkly silver ring hooked onto the side of her nose. This woman almost looked entirely different than how I had seen her at first: no nose ring, no gaudy clothing, just frazzled blonde hair and a crisp suit.

"Possibly. How old is Lilly?" my father asked, unfazed by Mrs. Hartman's promiscuity. My mother's head was spinning.

Soon enough, the whole table was silent and listening to this intense conversation.

"She's nine, almost ten," Mrs. Hartman gushed, seemingly proud of the innocent blonde haired girl.

"Alright," my father said, frowning. "We'll have to check her vitals to see if she's fit to ride the plane. Usually, no one under ten is allowed on the tour plane rides, since the risks and weather and -"

Mrs. Hartman drew back, her equally colored-in eyebrows peeling back, a mix of angry and surprised lathered on her tan body. "What? Are your plane rides unsafe? That was never in the pamphlet! We came here so the whole famil-"

"Actually, it *was* in the pamphlet. But we have hordes of other fun things Lilly can do-"

"I don't care about those," Mrs. Hartman jut in, swinging her chest around comically in an adult tantrum. "I thought we could all go on the plane ride-"

"Please calm down, Alicia. We can work this out, and it's not my fault if you didn't read the information-"

I internally groaned. This whole entire exchange infuriated me. I'd have to ask my mother to remind me why I was supposed to always be here for these endeavors, anyway.

Alicia huffed and puffed, but then sighed. "Any other news I'm not aware of?"

"If not, then my daughter, Terra, will accompany us-"

"Uh, what?!" I burst out, having not said anything for a while now, everyone's attention had been focused on the head of the table. Or the ass, depending on where your superiority complex was focused.

"Yes, she is," my mother said to my father. To me, she said, "We'll talk about this later."

My eyes widened. If looks could kill, it would mean matricide. "Mother, I am not going."

"We'll talk about this later," she hissed.

I sighed, slamming my fork down. "This isn't fair!"

"Life isn't fair," Wyatt cut in, dismissive.

"Oh, shut up," I shoot back, my emotions lashing out like lasers. "Mom," I hiss. "Do I have to go? I could be more useful here, helping around-"

"Yes, and that's the end of it."

I didn't mention how I really didn't want to spend most of the day with Wyatt and the Hartmans. Grumbling, I ate the rest of my meal in silence. Despite my better judgment, I skipped dessert, and Harper and I excused ourselves.

But not before I caught Wyatt's eye, something deep and unrecognizable piercing through his sandpaper demeanor and brown sugar eyes.

I hope Nick comes home before college starts back up again. I could really use him around here.

CHAPTER TWENTY: The Time Between Us
DAY 16-36 - Wyatt; August 20 - September 9th, 2015

Day 16 - August 20th

I pull myself out of nightmares to find that reality gives no relief. The hot sun drags us out of our sleep. We comply like whining children.

The highway is dead. The desert treats the concrete as if it's not there, and we do as well.

I force Terra to awaken, and we pack up. Start walking.

Our thirst is maddening, washing over every thought, drowning out every inkling of hope. My muscles refuse to move, each contraction treacherous and taking up every ounce of energy I have in that infinite moment.

We walk some more.

Breathing becomes difficult as the wind kicks up speed, swirling around us tauntingly. I can only imagine how much it hurts Terra. Her side is a dark crimson. She lifts up her hand as the dust and wind dances around her fingers.

Seconds drag on into minutes, which turn into hours. The subtle changes in scenery are the only thing that convinces me we're making progress. Sand flies into my mouth, the bleeding cracks in my lips.

Sweat drips into my eyes, searing the tender tissue on my eyeballs. Hot air seems to circulate and fill up any empty space between my clothing and skin. The heat crawls on my body, burrowing itself deep inside until my blood boils and my bones roast.

Terra lags behind me, each of her steps dragging out, leaving streaks in the sand like blood behind her. But I refuse. I refuse to rest - refuse to stop. I keep drilling on with an insane urgency.

My breathing becomes fast and hard. Precious water is literally just dripping from my skin and escaping out of my mouth with each breath I take.

It's not fair.

~

Sooner rather than later, my muscles give out and I collapse to the ground. Stinging pain where my clothes chafe against my burned skin.

I hear Terra rush over, but she doesn't say anything. I faintly feel her touch me, laying down next to me.

As the temperature only spikes higher and higher into a feverish shrill, we rest, lying, basking in the great heat, just as we did yesterday.

Is this the end? Could this be the way that I go? Softly, quietly. In the midst of chaotic peace.

I've been fighting my entire life. It would be damn near poetic if I died in this way. With the whole world not knowing about my fate. A decrescendo, and not a bang. Not how I wanted.

My mind soars high above my incompetent body.

I can feel the blood running through each of my veins. Back and forth, back and forth. Nothing more. Something less.

~

We should probably get going, she eventually says.

Probably, I say.

Seriously, she says.

Seriously, I mock.

Don't give up hope, she says.

Hope left when that plane hit the ground, I say.

Lilly, she says.

Don't say her name, I say.

Okay.

~

I'm hungry, she says.

Me too, I say.

Get up, Wyatt.

No.

~

What do you think our families are doing right now, I ask.

Who knows, she says.

Does it matter?

No, she replies.

~

Does any of this matter, she asks.

Probably not, I say.

I wonder if God's looking down on us, she says.

He's probably laughing.

~

We haven't used this Bible since we found it. Should we toss it? she says. To lighten the load.

Nah, give it to me, I say. I'll bear the weight.

There's a pause.

Nah, we'll keep it. Just in case.

Just in case, she says.

~

Light. There's nothing but endless, endless light.

~

The 'in case' finally comes.

When the hopelessness has grasped a hold at every aspect of us. When each and every fiber of our wills have been ripped. When death is just around the corner and the only flicker of hope are the stars above.

We start reading. Not at the beginning of course - but somewhere meaningful.

Anywhere.

The words awaken something in us. Something that could only be unlocked at this time. At this place.

The words of love give us a home. The words of hope give us life. And the words of redemption give us sparks that fly and ignite the ashes of our hearts.

And somehow, we get up and move. Because the voice within us, the fire, will not be still. This is not the end.

The light goes on forever, and it's all ours. I grab onto it like an anchor to my soul, drifting at sea.

Day 17 - August 21st

In the cool cover of night, we walk, our bodies still weary but our souls less so.

Eventually, Terra stops me, grabbing onto my forearm and stopping me.

"Do you hear that?" she whispers.

I listen. Just the wind, and a cactus wren.

"Don't you hear that? Rushing. *Woosh*," Terra says, punctuated by her wiggling fingers.

I still don't hear it, but we walk toward the noise.

Water. A surging stream of shiny water cuts through the land, and plants of all kinds spring up around this hub of wildlife.

And that's when we dunk our faces in the cold, rushing silk and drink to our heart's content.

~

The sun cascades over the horizon in an explosion of golden light. Terra is warm, sleeping next to me, but it's different from the sun already warming the earth-toned landscape.

The river boils and rushes across the rocks. Immediately drawn to it, I get up and wade into the knee deep whitewater. I relish in everything it brings.

I come up from drinking and see that Terra is now awake, rubbing her eyes.

"I hope you don't smell like wet dog when you come back over here," she shouts.

"No promises," I say, smirking.

I walk back, sopping wet, and hand Terra a water can. She drinks it up.

Gasping for breath, she sets the can down. Stares into the horizon.

I look over. "So, now what?"

"We keep walking, I guess," she says, running her fingers through her hair.

Terra sits there against the tree and wrinkles her face, neck deep in thought.

Here, it's perfect. Or as perfect as it's going to get. We have food and water at our disposal. Shelter under the tree we slept under last night. Truly, there is no logical reason to abandon this place and walk on, grasping at threads of hope that may or may not lead to a spool. We won't make the mistake of leaving behind a good thing again.

We just listen, soak in the sights and sounds of the desert.

This thought floats around my head. *We should stay here.*

A million other thoughts tell me that that's absurd. That we have so much to live for, so many people to go back to who love us, that staying here would be suicide.

But leaving would be, too.

Logically speaking, here would be the best place. We're relatively uninjured, so there's no hurry to get back. We've got food, water.

Her name bites on my tongue. I don't even need to think it. A war rages inside of me - to stay or to go?

"What do you think about staying here?"

"What do you mean, 'staying here'?" Already, she sounds defensive. Maybe 8am isn't the best time to have this conversation.

"I mean, like making our permanent residence here. As in, no longer walking. Like, uh, not trying to find civilization but trying to stay alive," I say, trailing off. My idea suddenly sounds outlandish and silly.

Terra sighs. "As much as I want to think that that's a good idea, I can't. I couldn't bring myself to just give up-"

"But we wouldn't be giving up," I say, dumping out my backpack. "You regretted leaving the Native Americans; this is the same thing. "

Terra swallows, tying and untying a knot with twine. "Why? Explain why this would be a good thing."

"Well, we've got fresh water, which is really the important thing. Food, shelter, what more could we ask for?"

"Our families. Our friends. Love, others, a life outside of this hot hell. Hope. That's what I would ask for."

"I know, but we can't have that now," I say, unsure of whether I'm angry or defeated. I flick open my lighter, shake it around.

"Don't tell me not to have hope." She's standing up now. This is not what I wanted.

"I'm not saying that. We have more hope than we could ask for! What I'm saying is that this is *smart*."

Terra's lips are a thin line. "I just want this to be over."

"Me too. But it's not." I start gathering brush, trying to distance myself from the conversation.

"The next town could be five miles thataway! We could go back to the road, follow that-"

"And risk dying of dehydration again? No thanks," I say, assembling a circle of rocks.

Terra's anger is so subversive, it could turn this desert into an arctic wasteland. "What about Lilly?" she shoots back, all of the subversion of anger and petty fear sucked out of her voice, and all that's left is raw, visceral, and fleshy truth.

"Shut up," I spit, whipping around.

"Lilly. What about her?" Terra says, yet nothing about her asserts arrogance. Just dire questions begging for dire answers.

But Terra's words pull at something in me. They grab at those loose threads in my heart that unravel every wall I've put up, everything that I'd been ignoring like a spool rolling down a hill.

I stand up to face her. "What about Lilly?" I challenge.

Suddenly, hot tears spring up in Terra's eyes - I can see them shining in the sweltering sun. "What's she going to do without you?"

Fuming, I whip away from Terra and walk in the opposite direction. Anxiety boils in my chest, humming like a bee-hive on steroids.

Making my distance from Terra and the campsite, I begin heaving. Is she right? What about Lilly, anyways? How could I live with myself if we died out here, and she never knew any of this? Would this all be in vain?

But our chances of survival - but probably not rescue - are far higher here. Forcing myself to breathe deeply, I close my eyes and verbalize a fear that never in my life have I been willing to admit.

"What do I do next?"

A nervous sweat tickles my upper lip as all I sense is silence. And I get no direction on what should be our next step. But the peace, the neverending assuredness still sits within me.

Maybe I have to make this decision on my own. Maybe I have to trust.

~

Gruelingly, I walk back over to Terra. "We're staying," I say

"But, Wyatt-"

"I need for you to trust me."

"Trust you?" she exclaims, but before she can say anything else, I cut in.

"What do you want me to say? That we should keep walking, keep wearing ourselves thin. This - right here - is our best chance."

She stares at me, unrelenting.

Tears suddenly burn at my scratchy eyes. "I thought we could do it, okay? I thought we could make it in a few days, but I guess we can't."

Kindness catches in her throat. I see it.

"We can't do this alone. But my gut says to stay here. So, that's what I'm going to do." Fuming, now all I can think of is Lilly.

Terra moves towards me, buries her face in my thin chest and wraps her bony arms around me. "Okay. I'll stay."

"One way or another," I say into her hair. "We'll get back."

~

We spend most of the day making a shelter. Terra sews all of our old clothing together while I gather branches for the posts. She definitely spearheads the project, but I do most of the grunt work.

By 4pm, we've created a shelter that's twelve feet tall and seven feet long and wide. Terra even weaves a door from yucca plant leaves since we ran out of material to build the walls with. It fits all of our stuff and leaves room for firewood, food and a sleeping area. The fire pit has two logs for sitting and the living room has an animal pelt rug.

By the end, after I pack everything into the shelter and Terra's putting on the finishing touches, she comes over to me, smiling. I hold her in my arms.

"Maybe this will work out," she says, quietly.

"Atta girl. That's what I want to hear."

I hear her groan, but we take in what is going to be our new home.

Home. It feels strange, even in my mind. But I can't say that I'd ever want to go back to the way it was. To the way I left my mother. To the person I was before.

And maybe that means staying in a tent in The Middle of Nowhere, Arizona for a while.

~

The desert noises are drowned out by the crackling, warm fire before us. Terra tosses leaves, fruit, and some cactus flesh into the pot of boiling water.

I play my harmonica, cross legged on the living room rug - weird.

"I always love it when you play the harmonica," Terra says, a sweetness hanging on her voice. She begins humming a harmony along with me.

"Why, thank you, because no one else seems to like it," I say, thinking of my mother.

"How does fruit and amaranth soup sound?" she says, flipping her hair.

I smile. "Absolutely delicious." The sun drips down the sky as the temperature drops and the flames bring heat into the air.

Looking down, Terra picks at a hangnail. "You know, I think this might actually work."

"What do you mean?" I ask, leaning forward.

"This," Terra says, gesturing around us. "We could actually live here, and quite comfortably."

"Now, did I tell you so or did I tell you so?" I say, smirking.

Terra smiles, glancing up at me, her gaze glittering with flirtiness. "You told me so."

Terra comes back over and sits next to me, holding two spoons that the Native Americans gave us. We spoon up the pungent mixture, which resembles soupy apple pie and cooked spinach, but the taste isn't bad - as long as you can get over the sight and texture.

After that, the fire in front of us burns brightly, and we go over and sit on the logs to warm our frozen fingers. But surprisingly, Terra sits right next to me and lays her head on my shoulder.

The awkwardness palpable, I wrap my arm around her shoulder and pull her in close. My thoughts waver and dance in my head like the ribbons of a fire, yet none ever take hold. For the first time since I can remember, no thought or emotion consumes me whole. For the time being, things are okay, and my mind can dwell on the good things.

But both of our heads perk up when we hear a deep pop in the distance, and see a scraggly trail of smoke leading off into the wind.

Just then, another one goes off, and as the light flashes before my eyes in a teeny shower of sparks along the horizon, I squint, realizing what these man-made explosions of light are.

"Fireworks," Terra verbalizes, her voice infectious with awe.

"Beautiful, huh?" I say, the unnatural yet vibrant lights flickering in my eyes.

The fireworks show lasts thirty minutes, and we soak up every second of it. Even though the pops are no louder than the clicks of the desert, our eyes stay trained on them because of their unnatural ring. If it weren't for the sound, I could stick my hand up at arm's length and cover the fireworks show with my thumb and you'd never know that such a spectacle was erupting.

But somehow, this display is not unsettling. It doesn't send us running and packing - because we know, it's worthless. We have truly wrapped our minds around reality, and have made embers of hope in this deep, dark pit of which we have been placed. And it's okay, because life is not about waiting for the storm to pass, but, instead, learning how to dance in the rain.

It's something Lilly would say.

"Don't give up hope, Terra."

"Never." She grabs her jacket and bunches it up under her head. "Goodnight, Wyatt."

"Goodnight, Terra." I lay down, across from her, facing the ravishing explosion that is the fire.

We watch the stars for a while. Then go into the tent and sleep.

Day 18 - August 22nd

I awake to see Terra over by the stream, staring out into the rushing water, on her knees. Curious, I stand, neatly rearranging our bed area.

With the wind at our backs, I come up behind her and massage her shoulders.

"Whatcha thinking about?" I ask.

She sighs and leans back into my embrace. "Too many things at once," she says, humoring me. "Actually, I keep seeing all these fish swimming by and wondering how we could catch them."

"We could get a net," I suggest, sitting on the rocks next to her, picking at a brushy plant with yellow flowers.

"And make it out of what?"

I shrug.

"I think a fish trap would work best. Maybe arrange sticks so the fish get caught but the water can go through."

"Sounds great," I say. "Would you need any help?"

"Probably not. But thanks for asking." She squeezes my hand.

While Terra works on gathering sticks for the trap she's making, I sit back against the tree, somehow exhausted.

~

It's been two days. Everything has been quite constant, and I feel a monotony of life settling in. While it feels natural, I don't like it. Like a loose tooth you just want to pull out already.

Or an itch you can't scratch. At times, I can't stand the silence, the normality and peace of it all, and that's when I have to go out and hunt even if it's at the worst time during the day and I make a shit-ton of noise just to scare the animals away.

The silence drives me crazy.

Day 21 - August 25th

Time passes. It's been raining for ages. A week, maybe. We forgot to make hatch marks on the tree during the rain. But like most rain, it comes and goes.

Terra and I spend most of our time inside our home, which gives us a considerable amount of shelter during the moments when it pours. We spend most of our time talking or playing games like Never Have I Ever, Three Truths and a Lie, and Rock, Paper, Scissors. One day, we even draw out a checker board and play checkers with sticks and small stones. We attempted chess, but it was too hard to remember which piece represented which.

We take turns venturing out and gathering food. We're cold. We're hungry. And we're bored.

At least we're not dehydrated. We couldn't be if we tried.

~

On the fourth day of the sky periodically vomiting down rain, the stream begins to extend its bounds. Having learned our lesson from last time, we packed up everything - even our shelter, and moved to higher ground, away from the stream. This higher ground, however, really just was further away from the stream. Because everything here is fucking flat.

Day 26 - August 30th

Actually, Terra says we're in more of a valley. The mountains start on either side of us, forming what was once a massive river basin.

The rain finally stopped. The ground has dried, the plants have been given their fill, and the stream washes away the impurities. And we finally pull our soaking, cold bodies back to our home.

It takes us nearly the whole day to reassemble our camp. And when we do, we cry tears of joy. Because we finally realize that this is home. Terra hugs me, and each time she does, it feels as wonderful as if it was the first.

Day 29 - September 2nd

Seemingly, the weather hates us.

Three days after the rainstorm hell, there is scorching heat. Every ounce of water not sucked dry by the plants is evaporated back into the air and blown far, far away. And with the wind comes a sponge-like dryness that sucks the life out of everything.

Terra calls this dust storm a haboob.

I spend about five minutes laughing at this.

We hole up in our tent again, having to tie the ends down and again, staying in our tent for 3 days straight.

Except, this time, it's different. There's no food. I refuse to let either of us wander further than the stream, which is running lumpy and slow. Air, something so essential and invasive, makes its way into the tent regardless. We are able to filter some of the parasitic sand out with cloth over our mouths and noses, but it claws over our eyes and gets under our fingernails. We endlessly cough and wheeze, as the sand builds up in our lungs. It affects Terra even more than it does me. Blood pools at her ribs.

And, one night, when the storm was at its worst and the wind ravages the landscape, when Terra and I are curled up in our bed, doing nothing but focusing on our breathing, I wonder for the first time in a long while if this is the end.

Day 34 - September 7th

Every day, we watch the skies for signs of civilization. We see airplanes regularly, but they're commercial flights or military jets. They probably couldn't see us even if we had a flare.

Terra thinks we haven't seen any low-flying planes is because they've stopped looking. That's usually when I tell her to shut up. We keep the signal fire going regardless.

We've lost a lot of weight. Even though most days we eat until our stomachs are full, I can count each of my ribs and my knees and elbows stick out at awkward angles. Terra has lost any trace of her feminine curves and is now hard and waif-like. Our teeth are fuzzy and brown, our fingernails are down to stubs and entirely black. Lips, cracked and textured. Hair, shaggy and matted, mostly tied back by something.

Emotionally, we're not doing too well. Days have become dragging and talks have become shallow. Hope is only a candle in an abyss. Love is only a star in the sky. Fear is as close as the grime ground into our skin.

Our thoughts of rescue are like the clouds drifting through the sky.

But we have this hope as an anchor for the soul, firm and secure. As unrelenting as the sun.

Day 36 - September 9th

Since there's not a whole lot to tell you anymore, I'll go through our regular day.

~

I awake. My eyes feel crusty and sticky, but I pull them open anyway.

I start the fire and begin boiling some water for our morning tea. Terra eventually emerges from the tent and puts the leaves and stuff in the water after it has cooled down. We let it steep.

After this, we put out the fire because it will just create heat in an increasingly warming day.

While drinking our tea, I read something from the Bible aloud, and we talk about whatever we read about. Today it was about selfishness. Then we separate for the rest of the morning, for alone time.

Around eleven, by the light of our makeshift sundial, we begin gathering food for lunch - checking the fish traps and snares, hunting if the conditions are right.

In the afternoons, we talk or do things that need to be done around our camp. Today's topic of discussion is about how the weather's been increasingly hot, chasing all of the animals underground. We stray away from emotional conversations now.

Later in the evening, we start the fire back up. Terra cooks dinner and I work.

Dinner consists of a small worship session on my harmonica. Today, though, it was hard to think of many songs we hadn't done a million times before.

The long nights are rarely spent sleeping. Our usual bedtime is ten or eleven at night and rising around dawn. If any discussion does get heated, it's then.

Tonight, it's my job to scrounge up a question for us to talk about: "If you could have any food in the world appear right in front of us, what would it be?"

Terra muses, twirling a matted lock between her fingers. "A nice cold, double chocolate milkshake with pieces of Reese's peanut butter cups. Definitely whipped cream, drizzled with peanut butter sauce and hot fudge."

I smile.

"How about you?" she asks.

"Probably a huge juicy steak. With steak sauce, of course. And steaming green beans. Mashed potatoes and gravy. Oh, and a peanut butter chocolate milkshake to share."

Terra smiles weakly. "Remind me when we get out of here to share that milkshake with you."

"Soon, Terra. I promise."

August 5th, 2015 - Wyatt

Early morning, I woke up. While the beds were comfortable, it wasn't home. The popcorn ceiling tells me otherwise.

Lilly and mom weren't up yet. I watched the sun leak through the openings in the blackout curtains. I heard the people above, below and around us get ready for their day.

Pretending to sleep, I listened as my mother gets up, showers.

"Wyatt. You up?" Lilly whispered from the other bed. Mom and Lilly had slept in the same bed, while I got one to myself.

I turned over. "Five more minutes, please!" I whined, immediately channeling a smile for Lilly.

She laughed, but then threw a pillow at me. "Shush, she'll hear you!"

From inside the bathroom, the blow dryer hissed on.

"Wyatt?"

"Hmm?"

"It's okay if I don't get to go on the plane ride," she said.

I sighed. "No, it's not okay. I'm sorry, the only person you can blame is our piss-poor planning mother."

"Take pictures for me, will ya?"

"Definitely. You can still probably come watch us leave."

Mom poked her head out of the bathroom. "Wyatt, Lilly! Get up!" she shouted.

"Sir, yes sir," I said, pulling myself out of the sinking bed.

"Don't treat me like that, Wyatt!" she snapped, hooking on her gold hoop earrings.

Sighing, I pulled on a shirt. And ugly striped one, but it was the nicest one I brought. "Like what? Like how you treat us?"

My mother sighed, shook her head of perfectly formed dishwater blonde curls. "I don't get you, Wyatt. I make all these sacrifices for you, and this is how you insolent children act."

I didn't say anything.

She scoffed, again. Why the hell was she dressing so nice? We were just going on a tour of the desert. It wasn't until I saw her push up her breasts and pucker her lips that I knew it was because of the pilot, Mr. Lombardi. Good God.

"You know, Wyatt, I don't know where you get this attitude from. The only place I can think of is your father."

That was it. "I'm leaving. If you need me, I'll be at the continental breakfast." I grabbed my pocket knife and stormed out, leaving Lilly wide-eyed.

August 5th, 2015 - Terra

Harper slept over, because she's awesome. In the morning, before the sun had even rose, we talked.

"Why were you so pissed off?" Harper said, from across my room.

"At who?"

"Your parents."

"Because they're being stupid and unfair and Christ almighty, I've never met worse customers than the Hartmans," I said through my pillow.

"You sound like you're ten."

I smiled. "Maybe I am."

"I think it's because you don't want to spend time in a cramped plane with that pompous ass," Harper said, shifting in her sleeping bag.

"Colorful language. And of course that's why. I just don't see why Dad wants or needs me there."

I heard her snort. "Because he wants you to take over the business since his delinquent of a son decided to be a doctor instead of a pilot."

"I can hear you, you know," his soft and dark voice resounded out through the house, and into my room.

Nick came in and leaned on the doorpost, smirking. I burst out in a smile and ran towards him.

"What's with the surprise visit?" I asked. He was usually away at college. This was his first year, so he came home a lot, but usually not unexpectedly.

He sniffed, rubbed his head. "It's, um, pretty close to the third anniversary of her death, so I figured I'd be there for everyone."

I pursed my lips. Somehow, I had forgotten. "Thanks, Nick."

He shrugged. "No problem. Hey, Harper, don't set anything on fire this time." Nick was referencing an actual time when Harper had set our house on fire. During a bonfire, she had accidentally set one of the posts on our deck on fire. And my dad, always being prepared, had put it out with a bucket of water, and Harper had to buy a new wooden post. But we still joke about it to this day.

"No promises!" she shouted as he closed the door behind him.

Even when things are going well, I still had to force myself out of bed, one motion at a time. Pushed off the covers, planted my feet on the ground, sat up, and stood. Once I've done that, I knew I could do anything.

It helped on the bad days.

~

Harper and I made breakfast - or, more accurately, I made breakfast because it was iffy whether Harper could even make a bowl of cereal.

I made two omelettes and bacon, and Harper poured the milk (she missed a bit). In our kitchen with the bar and the little round table, my mother wandered out of her bedroom.

Just seeing her reminded me of what I had to do today. I sat down, silent, my guts twisting.

"Morning, Terra. Good morning, Harper," my mom said, pouring herself a bowl of the fiber-rich cereal that only adults like. "How did you all sleep?"

"Well, once we actually got to sleep, which was at about two, we slept great!" Harper said.

I think mom laughed, or said something. After, no one spoke for a while. Nick and Dad were nowhere to be found.

I finally looked up at my mother, puffy eyed and wrapped in a bathrobe. Her eyes were rimmed in red. What was going on now?

"Mom, I don't want to go today."

"I know you don't. But you're going anyways."

"Why?" I nearly shouted. "Why, Mom, why?!"

"Because your father needs you there!"

"But-"

"Please, drop it, Terra! Why are you always like this?" Her spoon clattered to the table.

323

I dropped it. Harper watched like this is all a freaking soap opera.

The radio spewed music. Harper got some more bacon. In the near silence, we heard Nick open his door. I leaned back, and peered into the hallway. He met my eyes just for a second, before beelining it into our parents' room.

Our ranch house was old, and the walls were thin. The wallpaper was in desperate need of an update. You could hear just about everything through these walls.

Today, however, Nick's and my father's dialogue rose, piercing through the walls.

Suddenly, Harper stood up, looking at her phone. "I've gotta go. See you soon, Terra."

I stood. "Bye." But a part of me lurched out towards her, and I hugged her. Harper's not a hugger, but there I was, wrapping my arms around her, and holy hell, I'm glad I did it.

Her arms came up as well.

And then she left. I itched my cheek, angry that our outbursts made her uncomfortable and forced her to leave.

I sat back down, picking at my omelette. Through the walls, I heard buzzwords. *College, easier if you were a pilot, can't afford, Terra should, what I want, my girlfriend.* It all poisoned the air.

"When does the plane ride leave?" I asked.

"One," Mom replied, still stone-faced and cold and hurt.

I went back into my room, hearing the chaos around me, and wanted to scream.

CHAPTER TWENTY-ONE: Hope (And More Puncture Wounds)

DAY 37-38 - Terra; September 10th & 11th, 2015

Day 37 - September 10th

Everything is just motion after motion. I am a corpse trapped in an ecosystem of life.

It's early morning. So early that everything's still coated with dew and the air is still cold. Like every morning, I go and get breakfast. No fish in the traps, so I venture off into the wilderness, stepping over the occasional brush.

The sun peeks over the horizon, staining the purple sky orange.

I see Wyatt come out of our tent, starting a fire. I hope he makes tea, even though it never satisfies like morning coffee does.

I scan the desert floor. Sure enough, I have found some amaranth. I pinch them off and put them into my messenger bag.

I do this for a while, my mind wandering, crouching along and gathering when I step on something. It's thick and squishy, but when I put my weight on it, it clenches and yanks out from under my foot.

I lift my foot up just in time to see a Blacktail Rattlesnake writhe out from under a rock. The oily black tail and rattle rise in the air, above its orange-tinted body, wrapped in a distinctive pattern. Piercing yellow eyes with gaping black slits like gashes on Jaundice skin. Its black tongue flutters like paper as I step back slowly, as you're supposed to do when a snake is aggressive.

And like a snake shedding its skin, I emerge from a state of dormancy. Fear buzzes through me. I realize that I am alive again.

The snake shoots forward. I have no time to think before I jerk back, kicking my legs wildly. There's a flash of slimy pink gums like raw chicken as its jaws snap, thrashing like a whip.

With the sound of death ringing in my ears, I tumble to the ground. The amaranth leaves fly out of my shirt and blur my vision. I skid to a stop, flat on the ground, curled in the fetal position, still clutching my shirt in its cup-like fashion. I open my eyes, and see the snake a foot away from my face, hissing and erect.

Flinching and my entire body screaming with fear, I back away and stand up. "Wyatt," I say, the noise shaky as it escapes from my mouth. I look up, but he hasn't moved. Dammit. It's not worth it.

Rapidly, the snake slithers over the sand like water, chasing after me. Trembling like a leaf, I back away, but with each step I take, it cuts forward double the amount.

"Wyatt," I say, considerably louder, the sound crackling out of my throat. My eyes flit away for a second, but he still hasn't noticed.

The hiss fills me with liquid panic: throaty, high-pitched, and thick-sounding with saliva. Too afraid. I'm too afraid to breathe, to blink, to do anything other than have my voice teeter on the edge of screaming.

I back away, fumbling in my pocket for Wyatt's Swiss Army knife with sweaty hands. The Blacktail's neck is arched back, its head nearly levitating, in the perfect position to shoot forward and strike. If it had hackles, they'd be on end.

My heart slamming, raking against the bars of its cage, I walk backward slowly, trying to back away. But the snake just keeps gyrating, progressing towards me. And mostly because I have no real weapon. This little knife would only aggravate this tube of thick scales and coiling muscle. If only I had that machete . . .

"Wyatt!" I scream now, the sound tearing from my throat. My eyes jump from the snake to Wyatt, who has finally noticed. I flinch so hard my joints hurt when I back into a rock. "Wyatt!" I scream again, making an effort to keep the snake in my vision and get around the rock.

He grabs his machete and starts to run over. But I know it. He's not going to get there in time. I jump at every erratic motion the snake makes. It jerks forward again, the slimy and thick body grazing my leg.

I press my back on the rocks behind me, keeping the long, slender blade of the army knife poised. The two eyes on the sides of its head direct forward, trying to find a vulnerable place. The sound of it hissing is like a needle pressing into my skin.

Suddenly, Wyatt appears above me. He winks at me before saying. "I've got this."

Unfortunately, relief doesn't come running. Actually, any relief I still possessed scattered. This will not end well.

I stand up, slowly, and watch the exchange between Wyatt and the snake. Wyatt leans down and picks up a stone and flicks his wrist. The stone goes flying, hitting the snake in the neck, making it wobble like a ribbon. With a flaring urgency, it turns to face Wyatt, hissing mad at a new target. Something in my head whispers that this is a terrible, terrible idea. I creep behind the snake, fumbling for ideas how to disarm it. But I have nothing.

"Get the hell out of here!" he says, trying to deter the snake from where it had cornered me.

Moving slowly, I watch, paralyzed, as Wyatt and the snake engage in a perverted dance. The snake, analyzing, slithering, and lurching forward, but each time, the snake clamps its jaws around thin air. And Wyatt, nimble on his feet, swings the machete around teasingly, obviously not trying to hit the snake, but trying to scare it away and escape it. But - can he outrun it? Awful images flash through my mind, of venom and death and the end of it all.

Each time the snake lurches forward, Wyatt manages to jump out of the way in time, but the snake is getting better. It calculates Wyatt's moves, strikes faster, learning his behaviors, sensing his heat. Wyatt is weak and gregarious and slow; the snake is smooth and aerodynamic and faster than a bullet.

Stricken with fear, I crouch down. My mind races, trying to get us out of this, but the whole world seems to move too fast. "Just, run!" I scream.

The snake only whirls around to me in protest, rearing with anger, coming in stronger towards Wyatt, and cornering him now.

"Stop it!" Wyatt shouts between hacks of his knife.

Rotten with guilt, I back away, never taking my eyes off of the cruel dance. Only the fear for Wyatt's life compels me to continue watching as the snake's glistening fangs inch closer and closer to Wyatt's legs.

Wyatt glances up at me as he darts back, taking blind slashes at the writhing worm below, stumbling on a rock. And for a second, my chest jerks forward, for what he has done has killed him. He laughs, his eyes sparkling . . . and suddenly, they are filled with horror, the blackness of the realization clouding out his stupid glee. And in an instant, I look down to find the snake's head sticking out at an awkward angle on Wyatt's calf, the whole head buried deep in the folds of his pants.

It's one thing to be so afraid you scream, but it's another thing to be so inherently petrified that you can't breathe, can't think, can't move. And unfortunately, that's where I found myself in, suspended in time and space. I'm only dragged out of that stupor with the pain that perpetuates in Wyatt's eyes.

It all happens so fast - Wyatt slashing down on the machete, dislocating the wiry, slimy body from the wiggling, erect head. Me rushing over, just in time as he collapses in my arms.

I am thrust into overdrive, my mind reeling ahead of my body. Stupid, stupid stupid. I am so stupid.

I find myself cradling Wyatt's upper body, crumpled on the ground. His breathing heightens, rushing to a shrill cry squeezing out of his throat, and he writhes, kicking at the dirt with his good leg, acidic with pain. The black hole around me swells and swallows me whole. I must act, for this is my fault.

I set down Wyatt and rush over to the tent. I find the first aid-kit and run back over. Tears streak down Wyatt's face as he pushes himself up with his hands. Somehow, the things I need to do have already formed in my mind, so I just act - let the muscle memory fall over me like a shroud.

"C-can you stand?" I stammer, already helping him up, but an agonizing cry escapes his mouth when he puts weight on the leg with the still-attached snake head. Damn, I've got to get that thing out. Wyatt collapses back onto the sand. But I've also got to get him over by the stream . . .

"Wyatt, this is going to hurt," I say, walking around to the back of him and clamping my hands around his wrists. I pull and I drag and I tug, finally making it parallel to the stream. Each haul sends a shiver of pain up him, and he vocalizes in protest.

Wyatt lays prostrate on the sand, staring up at the sky, letting the sun cook his skin. His chest heaves up and down, sweat sticking his shirt to his body. I take out his pocket knife. Letting Wyatt's leg lay flat on the ground, I slash upwards on Wyatt's pant leg, avoiding the jagged circle of blood forming rapidly on his outer calf. The fabric tears until I've made it up to just below his knee, then, carefully, I put a hand under his knee and move it up, letting his leg bend naturally.

Grinding groans escape from his throat, but he doesn't resist, unfortunately assuming that I know what I'm doing. I move his leg upward until his foot is flat on the ground, and begin cutting around his leg, and eventually slip off the cylindrical piece of fabric.

I gasp in horror at the snakehead, locked hard around the fleshy part of Wyatt's right calf. Bright, dark blood drips from the snake's severed head and also streaks out of the holes where the fangs and head still remain. I have to get that fucker out of there.

Fear boils up inside of me and fills my lungs with steam. How the hell am I going to do this? I hesitantly reach forward, licking my lips, but I pull them back at the last second, craning to get a better view of the snake, embedded into flesh. I feel like if I don't do this right, it could release more venom and cause even more pain -

"Just take it out!" he screams, his brows knotted in pain. I jolt and look at him with uncertainty.

I reach forward and take two fingers and latch them around the snake's slimy jaws, cocked open wide. I begin to pull up and out, knowing that snake fangs are curved. A grisly cry grows from Wyatt's mouth as I slowly work the snake out of his leg, but it eventually becomes too much - I crack the jaws open and rip the thing out, causing blood to gush like a waterfall from the gaping wounds in Wyatt's leg.

He reels over, turning away from me and collapsing onto the ground, sideways, screaming and seized with pain. I fling the snake head onto the ground, the evil eyes glassy. Drawing back in horror, I watch as the snake's jaws still jerk and thrash, flopping the bloody head around on the sand like a fish out of water, spitting Wyatt's blood onto the sand.

I turn my attention away from the demon-snake and rush to Wyatt. He writhes on the ground, keeping his bad leg outstretched. Sobs rack his body. I glance down at the open wounds on his leg. With every beat of his rapid heart, the blood gushes out.

I kneel beside him, putting a hand on his back. "Hey, Wyatt, you have to calm down," I say, trying to get him to relax, but his muscles are clamped tight. I slowly pull him off of his side. Massaging his clenched hands, I slide my backpack under his head so he's lying flat on his back, but with his head and chest slightly raised. Anger boils up in me at his stupid reaction, but it doesn't surprise me, and I can't blame him. I continue to brush the hair out of his eyes until his breathing slows, and all the reaction he has is the occasional grunt and moan. "Just breathe."

Then I swallow my volcanic emotions and start working. I remove his shoe and sock because his leg is undoubtedly going to swell. I take off my black, dirty overcoat and place the cleaner side under his leg. Immediately, it soaks with blood. I take out my water bottle and begin to pour it out slowly over the wound. More blood travels out with the water. Wyatt grunts and begins to move, but I put a hand on him.

"Please stay still," I beg. I pour the water at an angle so the water flushes inside the two holes, and then overflows and comes out. After I've emptied the bottle, the puncture wounds continue to bleed, trickling but no longer gushing.

Wyatt's heart is still pounding - I can tell. I reach up and begin to stroke his hair away from his face, as he stares straight up at the sky. Sweat beads up on his face, and his jaw mechanically clamps and releases.

I try and make my voice as calm and soft as possible. "Wyatt, you need to relax. Everything is going to be okay."

"Shut up," he hisses. "Don't tell me that," he continues, his voice strained and clipped.

I sigh and grasp his hand. "Just breathe." Wyatt calms himself and takes deep breaths - in through his nose, and out through his mouth. I instruct him to breathe from his gut, not from his chest, and he looks at me like I'm insane. I reach up and place his other hand on his stomach. After further explanation, he proceeds to breathe deeply.

While Wyatt's attention is seemingly focused on this, I go back to work. I take the bandages and press them onto the bite. The bandages are soaked and dripping with blood in no time. I wring them out in the stream. The blood ribbons out of the cloth and down the flowing water.

I lay them on my leg to dry off. I take out new bandages and press them onto the wound. Wyatt jerks when the cool fabric touches his gouged flesh. I tape up the cotton to his skin, making sure the squares of cloth are big enough to encase the teeth marks. Wrapping the gauze lightly around his leg, I make sure it's not too tight and seal it with some surgical tape.

I move over to where Wyatt's head is, and I stroke his hair in order to calm the anxious convulsions of his face. He grabs my hand, squeezes it for dear life.

"It hurts," he groans. Sweat beads up on his face and it trickles down his dirty face, like rivers cutting through a forest, like a world of its own.

I press the back of his hand to my lips. "If it makes you feel any better, Blacktails don't have that potent of venom, and they don't usually inject something that's not their prey," I say, genuinely trying to make him feel better. He just rolls his eyes. "Do you think you can walk?"

"No," he says, his voice strained.

I sigh. "Well, you're going to have to," I say, my disdain seeping into my voice. "I can't drag you again."

Wyatt smiles at me, tight lipped and oozing sarcasm.

I find a smile pulling at my lips. At least he's got *some* sense of humor.

I lick my lips and sigh, standing. How the heck am I going to do this? "Okay, uh." I drop to my knees again. "Put your good leg under you, like this," I say, putting my hands under his left knee and bending his leg up until his foot is flat on the ground.

I put my arm under his back, locking under his armpits. "Push off of your good leg," I say, grunting as we both stand in a burst. Wyatt fumbles and groans when his right foot slams into the ground. I strain to keep him up as we hop over to our shelter. Every moment, the sun screams down, every second the pain, his cries, increase. It seems like an excruciatingly long distance, but we make it.

I settle him in, attempting to make him as comfortable as possible. He's shivering, even in the morning heat, so I wrap my bloody, tattered jacket around him.

I restart the fire and fill the pot with water. I let the pot boil. I then force Wyatt to drink.

"Terra," he says.

"Shh!" I hiss, putting a laser focus back on the simmering pot of water.

"Terra," he says, a bit calmer and more fervent this time around. "We have to get out of here."

I can't respond. His words strike a painful chord inside of me. I knew what he meant before he even said it.

"Terra," he says, this time the urgency in his voice scaring me. I slowly turn around, and he still sits, curled up under the tent, the evening sun shining off the sweat on his face.

"What?" I say, sitting back onto my knees, wishing he'd stop saying my name like that.

"*You* have to get out of here." His voice grates like pencil shavings.

The neurons in my brain fire off, but my mind refuses his words, refusing to acknowledge the weight they hold.

"I'm not leaving," I say, the words caustic in my mouth. I couldn't leave.

Wyatt rolls his eyes. It seems that he's already accepted death. However, I haven't, so he's just going to have to deal with that. The fire's heat burns my skin, and I pull my arm away viciously.

"I'm not leaving," I repeat, dropping the subject. "Brunch is ready."

With the tail of my shirt, I grab the pot handle and set it down in the sand, along with some pain pills. Wyatt takes the pot in his shaking hands, covered by his shirt, blows, and slowly sips.

I watch him eat.

I sit back on my knees again and stare at the ground, gnawing at my nails. It's only now, in the lull of events, that I feel the anxiety slowly clawing off the outer layers of my psyche. I'm not sure how much longer I can hold out, for I am gripping with bleeding hands at threads to keep dry eyes. I throw a handful of sand at the ground and stand. Immediately, my vision turns spotty like static and my head wavers like a helium balloon. I focus on sucking air in through my nose, and out my mouth. Eventually, the enveloping terror subsides.

I focus on organizing my shit in my backpack.

Wyatt finishes off the soup with ease and hands me the pot. I rinse it out in the stream. The smell of the fire is reminiscent of barbecues and meat and chips and baked beans. I slam the pot down onto the rocks, physically driving that thought away.

Wyatt perks to attention a few yards behind me, but I wave him off. Dragging my fingernails across my scalp, I walk back over and sit, criss-cross under the tent.

In the noon sky, Wyatt lies halfway upright, with his head strewn on the trunk, shivering beneath my cardigan, which has long ceased looking like any item of clothing. A soft feeling punches through my mechanical numbness, and I have a pulling desire to reach out and comfort him.

I pick at a dry spot on my lip. "Try to sleep, if you can."

He nods.

I stand and pull myself out of the tent, leaning on the wood and tarp in the lethal heat. I stomp over to the stream and stick my face in the water, pushing past the plants poking up through the rocks. Everything disappears under there, and I can finally think clearly.

I pull myself up, dripping. I rub the cool water on my arms, face, and neck.

What the hell am I going to do? Wyatt's got a fucking snake bite, for goodness sakes. I have basically no medical supplies, and even if I did know what to do out here in the fucking wilderness, I would still have nothing! I don't know if the snake bite is infected. I don't know if it will get infected. I don't know if the snake even injected any venom. If it did, I wouldn't know how to get it out. I don't know what kind of venom it is, what it would do to him. I don't know how to treat him. I don't know what to do next. I just . . . . don't know.

If I could give up anything to just know . . . I would in a second. If that would mean we lived but never got back, then I would. If that would mean my demise and his survival, then I would.

I can feel the anxiety rising up in me, pushing against my diaphragm, threatening to crush my heart. So, I close my eyes and press one thought into my mind. God, what do I do?

I can feel the tears pricking at my eyes. Hot, they streak down my face.

My heart bleeding, I push them down. Kick at my feelings until they cower in the corner.

Back at our shelter, I clean in my perpetually anxious state. Hours pass. A pang runs through my hollow gut, and I realize I haven't eaten lunch. Or breakfast.

I eat some leftover meat and fruit by the stream. But inside my bag, I find the canteen. I pop open the top, and the potent, acidic smell wafts into my nose. The alcohol - tequila with some kind of wine-like, fruity mix. I have to give him some of this. It's the only thing I've really got to make a significant dent in his pain. Mine as well, I think, referring to my side. And other things.

Bracing myself, I open my throat and take a few swigs of the alcohol, and immediately come up for air coughing and choking. But when I take my hand away from my mouth, the alcohol is down and safe in my body. I can already feel it seeping into the lining of my stomach.

Silently, I make my way back around to the front of the tent. Wyatt is there, safe, if not sound. The first thing I do it check his bandage. I pull up the loose fabric. Blood obscures everything, and the bandage is almost soaked through. Obviously swollen, but no pus that I can see. At least, not yet.

I flinch when the leg I am inspecting twitches violently, tearing my hand away from the wound. Now, however, Wyatt's legs are spread apart, the wound lying flat on the dirt, being compressed. He moans, cries out in his sleep. I cringe, and work quickly and move his leg back to where it was, the snake bite open.

I look over at the snake corpse, baking in the sun. Shuddering, I reach up and feel Wyatt's soft neck, and a pulse thumps erratic against my fingers. I put the back of my hand up to his nose. Warm, weak air flows over my skin, tickling the tiny hairs on my hand.

Suddenly, Wyatt's hands twitch, causing his arm to falls from where it was to the ground. Odd.

I feel his face: warm and sweaty, but then I feel my own. Slightly less hot, but not noticeably different. This could be because of a fever, or just this scorching heat. Lifting up his shirt, I feel his stomach with the back of my hand. Warm, abnormally so. My insides writhe. Suddenly, his hands come up and grasp mine, still touching his bare stomach.

"Mornin', beautiful," he murmurs.

The corners of my lips stretch out, but mostly for courtesy's sake. I don't have it in me to smile much more.

I pull away, running my fingers through my hair nervously. "It's 3 in the afternoon. Or something."

Turning away, I work on gathering a meal for us made of the food we have left. I press some plants and fruit into Wyatt's hands, and he sits up, adjusting himself, and eating. He continually leans against the trunk of the tree.

While he's distracted - not like he was fully aware in the first place - I decide to check his wound fully. I get the medical kit and a water can, full of fresh water from the stream. I reach, for the bandage, but his leg twitches away from my fingers, and a shiver runs up and down his sweaty body. I reel back, cringing again. With one swift motion, I cut off the bandage from his swollen calf with the scissors from the Swiss army knife. I keep an eye on him as I pour straight hydrogen peroxide over his two puncture wounds.

Suddenly the awful sound tears out of his mouth, a mix between a scream and a groan. I immediately yank back, my face unconsciously scrunching up. Fuck, maybe that was a bad idea.

"Oh, my God, don't do that!" he exclaims, gripping his upper right calf and clawing at his own flesh, getting dangerously close to his wound.

"Sorry," I hiss, feeling caught between a rock and a hard place. "I have to clean it, Wyatt."

"I know," he says through his teeth.

"Just . . . hang on. Grab my hand," I say, swallowing hard, and going back in with the water.

It's like a punch to the face again and again with each awful cry that he makes. But I manage to clean it off.

I sit back, breathing hard, every muscle in my body ready to clench. I sigh hard, and genuinely wonder what to do next. It is obviously swollen and there is a bright red halo around it unlike his sunburn. The blood hasn't clotted at all, and the wound remains wet and open, deep and burgundy. Bracing myself, I lean in and lightly press on it - and immediately, Wyatt reacts - he pulls back and cringes in pain.

"Holy shit, stop!" he says again, screaming. Cries tearing from a deep, primal place in his being that sends pangs through me.

"I have to," I say, apprehensive.

"Well, please don't."

I scowl at him, but sit back. I force myself to breathe for a few seconds. With my hand, I feel the crusty blood under my bandage, from the cactus spines long ago. Pain invades my lungs the longer I breathe, killing me from the inside out.

I make some more tea over the fire, holding the canteen of alcohol between my legs.

"Terra, you have to go," he says, a pained expression carving lines on his face.

Turning around, I know what he means, but I refuse to let it permeate my mind. "What?"

"You have to leave, find help." His eyes are like lasers, cutting right to the core. They fill up with tears, so hot and heartbreaking I might actually punch him. "You know damn well what I mean."

"I'm not leaving you," I say dismissively.

Wyatt sighs, heavily, but we can feel it in the air. I don't have a choice. Again, his face is unsympathetic, but he squeezes his eyes shut. Tears cut trails on the blood and dirt on his face. "You have to go, Terra. You have to find people."

I stare at him, one emotion not prominent enough to rise to my face. "I can't leave you."

"Yes you can," he says, swallowing hard. "You have to."

I breathe, taking a moment for pause. "You're not making any sense," I say, giving him some water. "Just, rest. I'm making you tea."

He complies, and again, he twitches, blood still seeping through the bandage.

My hands shake as I pour the alcohol into the dark tea. I swallow hard, because I know that this will be good for him. Even if it's bad for his body, it will ease his pain.
Wyatt tosses and turns in the tent, his brow crinkling, pained. I rest a hand on his arm, quieting his fits.

"Don't move so much. You'll spread the venom around," I say.

Wyatt grimaces. "It's already spread. It doesn't matter."

I sigh. "Just, please listen to me." I lean down and press my lips on his cheek, rest my face in his neck.

Sighing heavily, I let my eyes slide shut. I drink up the sound, but somehow, fear begins to fester within me. And the thought flicks on involuntarily: Wyatt's going to die. The fear boils like syrup - hot, sticky, and ensnaring like sap. And I'm going to be all alone out here. His soul will be pinned to my conscience for the rest of my life. The sounds out here are deafening, but even they cannot overcome the screams of my thoughts.

"Here's your tea," I say, sitting on the ground under our shelter.

"Thanks," he says, with nearly no voice inflection. He sighs heavily as well, sipping at the tea slowly. "You know, you don't have to do this. Care for me."

"Yes, I do," I say, wondering where this conversation is going. Apathy creeps into my body like a worm, like a parasite.

"No, you don't, Terra. You could let me die, you could kill me, and no one would know," he says, his voice growing in intensity at an alarming rate.

I swallow hard. "But I would know."

"But that's not the point. I . . . I'm dead already," he says, looking down at my sad excuse for tea.

I sigh and pick at a hangnail. "You're not dead yet." I inwardly groan. It's happening again, all of it, the pain and the suffering from my grandma's death is right here.

Wyatt runs his tongue across his teeth under his lips. "You're bad at lying, Terra."

Gazing at Wyatt up and down, I finally lean into his embrace. He wraps his arm around me. His budding fever heat seeps into my own body. Somehow, it's comforting.

"Everything's going to be okay, Wyatt," I say, and this time, I believe it more.

"Stop lying," he says softly.

I breathe, trying to calm the mounting anxiety. He's not helping one bit. Hysteria vibrates inside of me, like an earthquake shaking my very core. I sit up, looking right at Wyatt. But then, I pull away, receding into myself. Rubbing my fingers on my forehead, I say: "I'm not lying." Maybe if I say it a certain number of times, it will be true.

"Please drink, Wyatt," I groan.

It's surprisingly easy for him to drink it because he sucks down the mix no problem. I give him two more doses of the stuff, and he's out like a light.

Dinner fast approaches. The sun hangs low in the sky, orange and bright like it was early this morning.

I don't eat. I can't. The alcohol makes my eyelids heavy, and the world blurs like a vignette.

I just sit in front of the fire, my back to Wyatt, listening to his irregular breathing and the way he rustles in his sleep. Every breath resounds throughout our little home. My heartbeat pounds under my fingernails.

And the pain has come back. The deep quivering in my gut.

I turn to face Wyatt. Cheeks hollow, face perpetually smeared with dirt and blood. But under it all is freckles and a strong nose. Lively eyes.

The pain is so tactile, I can almost feel it grabbing me around the neck and shaking me around like a rag doll. Tears squeeze out of my eyes, and sobs expel out of me in undulations, like the cracking of a whip. The fear has been bottled up all day, it swallows me from the inside out, choking me. As if I let it go, it will already be so large it will just come back and tear me open again.

I sob and I sob and I let it all go because there's nothing left. No reason to keep holding it in.

The pain, it falls like snow on parched earth.

~

I hiccup the remnants of raw and tearing sobs.

Something inside me explodes like a firework, touching each part of me and searing me with the flames of loss, of love, of grief. Tears squeeze out of my eyes again, and I bat them away angrily. The thread of connection, of foreign angst, swells like a balloon inside of me, ready to pop. Fear grips around my neck, and my only fleeting thoughts are *why*. Why did this happen? Why do I feel this way?

Wyatt's pained face is carved into my mind, and it flashes before my eyes. And it suddenly dawns on me and sucks every wisp of breath out of me. I've seen that expression before, marred with a terrifying sort of peace only found on dead people's faces. I've seen that look before. On my grandmother seconds before her death and in my father's cold, silver eyes. And the fear, so electric and all consuming, I let it in. I let it ravish my insides and burn the skin off my eyes as hot tears boil out.

I'm so afraid. I'm so terribly afraid of the next moment that's going to eventually come and take away everything that I hold dear. It's going to take away my happiness, my family, the things I love - it's going to take me away from me.

It's going to take Wyatt away.

As soon as this stream of thoughts runs through my mind, intense sobs like never before run through me like electric shocks, because I finally get it. I know why I'm afraid and angry and frustrated. Because I'm so incredibly scared that what happened to my grandma is going to happen to Wyatt. History is going to repeat itself.

And this fact, however flooding me with relief, sends my violent sobs into soft, sad tears. I beg to God to not let him die.

But through my pain, through my tears, I see it.

I am incompetent. There's not much else to it - I can't fix Wyatt. I can't save him. The only things that will save him are strong antibiotics and antivenom.

Despite hating his vile words, Wyatt is right. I have to leave, because if I don't find help for him, he'll die, and I could no longer live with myself. I'd go crazy with guilt and fear and shame. I'd go crazy with trauma. I'd go crazy because he'd be dead.

Dare I say that fate has forced me into a corner - do or die, of sorts. Throughout this whole thing, there has always been some other solution to a problem - if we couldn't find water, we could wait or drink our own urine. If we couldn't find food, well then we'd wait because we still had some fat reserves to keep us going. If one of us got hurt, we'd compensate. But now, there is no compensating. There is no negotiating. There is only doing. Or dying.

I have to do this. I have to leave. I refuse to be passive, I refuse to let what happened with my grandmother happen again. This isn't about me - it's about him. There is no other option, no other way to save us. Though it pains me to admit it, Wyatt is right. I will do this.

~

I guess that it's about 9 pm when Wyatt finally awakes. I hear him the first second he moves. I push myself to my feet, rubbing my swollen eyes. I rush over to him and stroke his hair until he awakens fully.

He's already scowling at me when I press my finger to his lips.

"I put the alcohol in your tea."

His eyelids flutter. "I figured," he sneers, still half-asleep.

Gritting my teeth, I fix him up. I unwind the bandage and am appalled at the sight. Thick, gloppy pus spills out of the wound - and yet it's still leaking blood like a rusty faucet, and red streaks run up and down his leg like an old, haggard woman took her nails and started scratching like a rabid cat. His leg is discolored black, purple, blue, and yellow like a perverted bruise, and I compare his two calves. The affected one is swollen to nearly twice its size, with the skin stretched shiny and tight like a drum. The horrid leg is also taut and rigid like a pathetic wooden plank. I swallow down my vomit and tears.

Suddenly, I can't breathe. What has this come to?

"I have to leave," I blurt.

"I've been tellin' you that this whole time," he wheezes, some inkling of inflection in his voice.

I swallow hard again. "Please listen and take this seriously for once. There's no way you'd survive if I stay - and I've made the decision to leave. I hope you're okay with that." I guess if I repeat it to myself enough times and in the right way, it will make it better in my own, twisted mind.

Wyatt sighs, long and hard. "It's always been okay with me, Terra."

His words force it to a head. I melt myself into his embrace, holding him in the rapidly cooling night.

"I'll leave in the morning."

"Okay."

"Just, let me have this. For now."

"Okay."

Day 38 - September 11th

I awaken long before Wyatt does. Feeling his fevered skin, I sit up. The sun still hasn't risen, but the sky is painted in light.

Wyatt wakes up and smiles at me. We eat one last meal together - of hare and desert raisins. We sip warm water out of a pot, which I then put in my bag.

He forces me to pack everything I can into my backpack - even my tattered pockets.

But while I am filling up the two water bottles we have by the stream, self-hatred arises. It's nothing like I've ever felt before - and I've felt self-hatred before - but this is caustic and foreign. Like I'm doing something terribly wrong, by leaving him. But consciously, I know that I'm not, because, like burying my father, I have to do this.

Emotions swirl inside of me like the little black foreign object that somehow got in my water bottle. I groan and dump the thing back in the stream.

I eventually make my way back over to Wyatt and our tent. Sweat has built up on his face, so I take a cloth and dip it in the lukewarm pan of water and dab it on his face. He pushes me away and sits up.

"Stop it, dammit!" I say, slapping the wet cloth onto the ground.

Wyatt blinks and purses his lips at me, unfazed. "I know that you're doubting this."

I sit back and stuff more shit that I might need into my backpack.

"I know that this is going to be hard, and I know that you don't want to, but please. Do it for me," he says, a lacing of soft, yarn-like urgency in his words that I've never heard before.

I sigh, looking away. "I'm doing this, Wyatt."

"I know."

"Then stop talking."

The sun sits, perched in the white sky. Everything around us is like a tornado of calm, and we are the eye.

"Are you ready?" Wyatt says, his voice scratchy.

"No," I say, swallowing hard. I heave my backpack over my shoulder and wobble on my nervous legs at its weight. "But I am as ready as I'll ever be."

I sit back down, feeling an odd impulse inside of me for one last goodbye. I cannot believe that this is actually happening. The very thing I feared from the moment the plane collided with the sand is staring down my neck. Losing everything. Being truly, and utterly alone.

We sit there, reluctant, the tension building up, yet going nowhere.

"I . . . all I want to say is that I'm sorry," I push out. Dammit.

"For what?"

"For having it come to this," I say, the itchy feeling of emotions working through my body.

"It's not your fault," he says, but I want to hit him. I want to hit him so badly, I can feel the tingling anger on the palm of my hand.

But instead, I lean forward and kiss him. At this point, my demeanor has been worn to a tissue paper, so my impulses come thrusting out, burning and raw.

I pull away, but look down, feeling Wyatt's abnormally hot breath tickling my forehead and running down my nose. He reaches up, presses his lips to my forehead.

As I sink further and further into him, feeling drained of all worthy words, he begins to speak. Strained like rubber bands and cracking like hot lightning.

"You have to promise me. Promise that when you find people, you'll come back for me," he says, his voice thin and strained like the hissing of water out of a barely-on faucet.

"Okay," I say, sniffing angrily, and pulling away. "I promise."

Wyatt looks at me with one last oomph of spunk he's got left in him. A thousand feelings, memories, flash through me. "Now get the hell out of here and save the day, Sparkles."

I push up on my feet and breathe. Not daring to look back, I start walking west.

~

I walk for what seems like hours, but when I look backward, I can still see the cracked arthritic finger of a tree where Wyatt remains. Dragging one foot in front of the other, I try not to focus on the weight on my back. One thought, I realize, has permeated my consciousness, and sticks there like a sore thumb. I left Wyatt behind. I left him behind to die.

Guilt creeps up on me, weighing heavier than my backpack. But I hold fast to the promise we made - that when I found people, the first thing I'd do was come back for him. And now I realize: that was probably the most selfish thing I've ever seen him do.

I wheeze. My side grows wet with blood, and the old bandage sticks to my side like fat. I stop walking, but immediately when I do, my legs begin to buzz with ache. Inertia is a cruel thing, but I can't let it take me over.

Emptying my first bottle of water, I swallow hard and drop the bottle on the ground, the stainless steel piercingly bright in the sun. The sweat dripping down my forehead, off of my nose, in the canyon between my breasts, even in places like the creases of my elbows and knees, is all consuming. I'm so afraid I might melt away.

I take a breath and move on. But moving itself becomes increasingly treacherous. I find myself dragging my toes, forcing each individual muscle to move - first moving my hamstring, then moving the quads in my opposite leg, and then the pull-push motion of my calves moving my feet, and back again, and again, and again.

Take it one step at a time, Terra, I tell myself. But as one step becomes two steps becomes three steps, I find my mind still fixated on the thought of Wyatt.

Something in my head goes off, and I remember to periodically drop things, so I can find my way back. I take out the roll of twine and drop that. Next, I take out the flashlight, turn that on, and point it towards the ever-shrinking tree in the distance. Later I take out my broken compass. It's not like I'm going to need these things for much longer. Do or die, right?

While I'm distracted by leaving a trail, I trip over a rock and tumble to the ground. The sand grinds like gravel as I skid to a stop. My mind pounds, screaming against the inertia slamming down onto me like an elephant plopping right down onto me, snapping my bones and bursting my muscles. With every ounce of energy I have, I push up with my arms and turn my head so I can breathe.

A small lizard appears in my warping vision. It's green-tinted, thin, and scaly, like a rock, almost. It crawls over my hand, its tiny feet tickling the leathery skin on my hand. A small smile bubbles to my face. The lizard rests on my hand for a while, lifting its head against the setting sun and looking around, appearing like a humble king, ruling over his little domain. It eventually scuttles away, and a sad feeling washes over me. But it's more of a disconnected sad, like a deep, fuzzy blue light, seemingly so close, but when I reach out to grasp it, the light was never really there.

I let my eyes drift shut, thinking of this fuzzy blue light, far off in the distance, and I imagine myself wrapping my fingers around its cool light.

~

The harsh, yellow-toned sunlight pierces through my eyelids, giving my eyes the sensation of a muted scarlet.

I peel my eyes open. Why am I not dead? I thought I was dead. It seems as if I am just a head, for I cannot feel anything besides my face and the hot sand pressing up against it. But the light reflects off of the scrubbed color of sand, and I force myself to get up.

Wiping the sand off of my face - I don't bother with the rest of my body - I keep walking. By my judgment, I think I slept - or fell unconscious - for only a few hours, for the sun is bright and clear and climbing up the arc of the sky with its ray-like limbs.

I keep walking.

Eventually, I see something in the distance. It looks like a cluster of dusty boxes, like the ghost town. I immediately blame it on my delirium, but I keep walking towards it anyways since it's in the general direction I'm heading in.

I keep walking.

They are becoming closer, the details coming into focus. Something boiling and full of pressure rises up in me. My throat is sticky and like a wet tube of cardboard. I can't breathe. It's coming.

I keep walking.

The taste stings my mouth first. Then I feel the surge of blood coming up as I convulse and cough. Hacking and burning, I feel it right there. Right where those fucking thorns ripped my lungs to shreds. Gasping through sticky blood.

I keep walking.

Soon, it becomes to much. Blood streaks down my chin, my neck. Fumbling, I suck back water.

But it goes down the wrong pipe. Panic thumping in my chest, I keel over.

My mind screams. NO. Because if I stop, if I fall, then I won't be able to get up ever ever ever again.

I spit the water out, creating pinkish gloop as it mixes with the sand. Dragging my heavy limbs, my eyes burn with tears. With hopelessness. But I have no tears to cry.

Half a bottle left.

My soul screams that he'll still be alive when I get back. When people come for him. Because people *will* come for him. I'm going to make sure of it.

Life grinds my face into the groveling sand. My whole body shudders with sobs.

I have failed. I am going to fail. My entire life has been a series of fuck-ups, of failures, but no more. I believe that despite everything, it's going to be okay. I am not the summation of my broken parts.

My fingers rubbing over the sand, the endless sand that I have been trapped in for forty days, I cry out.

God. Save me from this hell. Save me from myself. Carry my weary body into glory. I believe.

Look up.

I look up.

And I see a sign in the far distance that says 'Welcome to Blythe, California!'

~

The city's skyscrapers glisten with glass, the metal on them winking in the afternoon sun. The organized orchestra of urban sounds swells in my ears. Low, fat clouds hang over the city, separating it from the rest of the endless expanse of desert. The Colorado River moves like a dancer across a stage, twirling with the ribbons of the wind. Cars whiz past me over the rustic bridge, with touches of new and old, connecting the primal with the advanced. Overwhelmingly beautiful and pristine and as sweet as honey, a smile peels across my lips.

Falling to my knees, tears begin to involuntarily stream down my face. We've made it. We've really made it.

Suddenly, a car horn jolts me out of my daydream. Sending electricity through my body, I sprint out of the road and straight into the divider of the bridge, my stomach collapsing in on itself. I stare down at the now menacing Colorado River, ready to swallow me whole.

And I stop. But I realize, that we haven't really made it. I've made it. This odyssey isn't over yet.

Shaking off the terror, I keep walking.

Except the car stops. Honks at me. The person rolls down their window with a mechanical hum.

With a soft look of confusion, a businesswoman peers at me. "Are you Terra Lombardi?"

I forget how to speak. "Uh, yes."

Her eyes sparkle. "You've been missing for forty days! Thank God you're okay! Your face has been all over the news."

Surging, I lean into her car, the mechanical sounds of the city whirring past. "Wh-what about Wyatt?"

"Oh, Wyatt Hartman, yes! He's on there too-"

"You . . . you have to take me back to him! He's still out there and he's injured and-"

"Whoa, whoa, slow down! It's okay . . . oh, Terra."

My eyes swirl around, swimming in tears that have finally shown up. I grip the metal door of the car, my knees trembling.

I see the woman lurch forward before my eyes roll back into my head.

~

I awake to a start, in the panic-ridden surge of car-motion. Clawing at the leather, I awaken just as she pulls into a parking lot.

The woman helps me, leans on me, as she pulls me into a building with red lights that say EMERGENCY, and they burn holes into my mind with nothing short of hope.

~

We make our way up to the doors with the red sign. It's got these thick double doors that are half glass, but they have no handles. I'm utterly confused as the doors open automatically and the woman nearly carries me in.

I blink hard at the artificial light. A curly haired older woman sits at a desk clicking at a computer. She looks up, and shock registers on her face, at me and the woman trying to explain my situation. Catching my own reflection in a stainless steel door, I draw back. My cheeks, sunken in. My eyes, wild with fear. My hair, my clothes, my entire demeanor like a shattered mirror.

I turn away, fast, and stumble toward the front desk. The lady keeps staring at me. I wish she would stop staring at me. She opens her mouth multiple times to speak, but nothing comes out.

I realize I should probably say something. The business woman's voice sounds tinny, far away. I can't tell what she's saying. Words escape me, as fluid as water and as fickle as smoke. I grip the counter until my knuckles are white. The lights are too bright and the smells are too sharp and the sounds are too cruel.

The sound of my breathing slowly overtakes my inner dialogue. I suddenly can't think of a damn thing to say. I know what I should be saying, but my thoughts are like one long shoelace, tangled and knotted with years of neglect.

I can hear the businesswoman trying to speak, trying to say "Help! She needs help!"

But no. The woman is wrong.

Pain creeps into my head like a parasite, and I blink at the secretary lady a few times, but then something else happens. My vision becomes spotty, like static on a television. Cotton balls seem to have been stuffed in my ears. My head feels like a helium balloon, and my neck the string. Against my will, my knees give and I crumple to the ground.

The secretary lady is slapping my face. I really wish she'd stop slapping my face. I wish she'd stop talking, too. The fluorescent lights come into focus above me, and their unnatural light scrapes the back of my skull. The worried face of the businesswoman appears above me as well.

I jolt, scramble away, like that stupid fucking snake is nipping at my feet again. This wasn't supposed to happen. Wyatt is still out there. He's still out there!

What the nurse is saying finally registers in my head, and every cell of my being fights against it. She keeps telling me in her soothing voice that I need to calm down, that everything is going to be okay.

I scamper away from her, kicking my feet at the open air, sometimes hitting the floor sometimes hitting her.

"No!" I scream. The words feel sweet and thick but rip from me like an explosion. "Don't touch me!" I make it to my feet just in time to slam into another patient in the waiting room.

Tumbling to the ground violently, hot tears burn in my eyes. I feel the nurse touch me again, and I whip around, not caring a thing if I smack her. Catching sight of the door, I scramble towards it, nearly tripping over a chair.

Angst burns in my chest like coal as the nurse actually body-slams me onto the ground. But nothing burns more than the tears pouring down my face. Because I got so close to saving him, and I am now watching it all dribble down the drain like his blood leaking from my hands.

The sobs rack my body like cracks of a whip. I find myself speaking words through the rounds of weeping. "We have to go out there! He's still out there! Please stop! You have to save him!" The sobbing makes my throat ache, but I don't care. Why should I? Because someday, someone is going to find Wyatt's rotting skeleton out there, and it's going to be all my fault.

It's going to be all my fault. I can't give up now.

Frantically, I pull out the Blacktail's rotting body and wave it around like a surrender flag, hitting the damned nurse with it, trying to communicate my distress to her.

When that doesn't work and she wrestles the snake out of my hands, I writhe and claw at her and at the ground, at anything, and she calls out to someone behind her. A male nurse appears in my blurry vision. When I see the syringe in his hand, I struggle against the nurse's grip, trying to tear my exposed arm away from his device of torture, another obstacle that is going to keep me from saving Wyatt.

"Stop it!" I screech. "There's still someone out there! You don't understand! I have to save him!" My body makes undulating motions, my bony figure slamming against the cold floor in an effort to escape the nurse. Suddenly, my arm is struck with a cold liquid, and horror strikes me like a blow to the chest. I fight against the strong relaxation seizing control of my being. I look the nurses one last time before my eyelids turn to lead. I say in my weak, anger-injected voice. "He's still out there . . . . ."

~

I awake to a start. The first thing I register is that I feel no pain. I also feel scrubbed clean. My hands wander over my body, covered in a thick blanket and a hospital gown. I feel a thick bandage around my ribs. My other cuts and abrasions have been stitched and bandaged as well. Needles run in and out of my hands. I notice a small tube around my face, and I suck in air through my nose. Artificially cool air rushes in, and I breathe with ease. Once I am sure that I am not dead, I focus my attention outwards.

Mom.

I am crushed by the weight. Words, infinite words dance on my lips as she and my brother, Nick, come into focus in front of me.

She cries as she rushes forward and hugs me. To smell her, to feel her warmth is something I didn't know I missed until now, and my chest heaves, holding her close because, above all else, she's my mother.

Finally, we part. But what truly reaches past my barriers, what truly breaks me from myself, is when I realize how much Nick looks like Dad.

~

An unfamiliar female nurse sits by my bed, with a plastered look of concern. I flinch, previously unaware of her presence. Words still seem to escape me, for he's is the only thing infecting my brain.

The second the nurse opens her mouth, words pop out of my own.

"Where's Wyatt?" I say, testing the waters of my scratchy voice.

"Now, we need for you to cooperate and listen," the nurse says. Surprisingly, I cannot detect an ounce of annoyance in her voice. "What is your full name, Terra?"

I swallow hard, wondering if the drugs let me talk. "Terra Lombardi."

"And how did you get here?" the nurse says, scribbling something down on a piece of paper.

I sigh and begin. "I . . . . I was one of the two survivors in a four person plane crash. We crashed forty days ago in the remote Arizona desert. Me and another sixteen-year-old boy survived for forty days, trying to find civilization. He . . ." I stop, for I can feel a lump swelling in my throat. "He was bitten by a snake . . . . a day ago, maybe. Then I . . . " Tears, cool, soft tears fall down my face. I can't move enough to wipe them away. "I left him behind and kept traveling. I then found this city, and tried to convince you that he was out there and that he was dying . . . and I guess you know the rest." Pausing, I lean over and wipe what I can of my tears on my shoulder. "Please go out and find him. I'd give anything."

The nurse purses her lips. She sighs heavily, so heavily that a blanket settles over the room. "Alright, tell me everything you know about where he is."

August 5th, 2015
Approximately 1pm

The incessant drone of the plane barely registered in Terra and Wyatt's ears. Their heads were so teeming with their own self-centered thoughts that they didn't grasp onto the sound of the yammering engine. Disgust filled Terra - she really did not want to be here. The boy next to her reeked of coconut sunscreen. *City-folk,* Terra thought, smirking to herself. Interestingly enough, Wyatt was thinking nearly the same thing. But, the opposite, of course.

Terra looked out the window, longing to be on the ground. She tried to tune out her father, giving his usual spiel to the passengers. He droned on and on about the plants, animals, and mountains - this, however, all looked familiar to Terra.

Wyatt glared out the window, his eyes burning against the mind-numbing sand. He tuned out this girl's father - Wyatt didn't really care what he had to say. Wyatt should be back at the lodge, with Lilly. But his mother had dragged him on this damn plane ride anyways.

A low rumble spurted out from deep within the engine, snapping everyone back to attention - at least the two kids in the back. Terra sighed, pulling herself away from the beautiful desert, painted like an artist's palette. Wyatt wrote something on the plastic part of his Converse shoes with a black Sharpie.

"The third place we'll land is a place rich with wildlife, just far enough away from the city that they can live in peace," Terra's father said, twisting around to look at his daughter and her reluctant counterpart. Terra knew exactly the spot they were going to land - it's where they always landed.

The plane jostled just a little, visibly jerking everyone back to the present. Terra's father quickly corrected himself, laughed nervously, and kept his eyes on the sky.

The plane landed promptly, and Terra waited for her father to turn off the engine, but no such thing happened. Wyatt pushed open his door and hopped out. The sun beat down like a reflective ball of spikes. Wyatt shielded his eyes and kicked at the dusty rocks on the ground. After getting out, Terra rolled her eyes in disgust at the ignorance and audacity of this boy. *That good-for-nothing asshole.*

~

Wyatt didn't pay attention much to the tour Terra's father gave, but his mother jabbed her elbow into his side and forced him to look at all of the plants with unpronounceable names and apathetic lizards that basked on dusty rocks. He rolled his eyes and looked for a while, but still crossed his arms and kicked at the weeds.

Then, of course, Ms. Hill scolded him like a small child. More rolling of the brown sugar eyes.

After Mr. Lombardi finished rambling - he was quite an intelligent man - everyone loaded back up in the plane. Terra, having had refused to get out, now refused to move over as Wyatt had to climb over her long legs.

More flying.

Terra looked over and saw the sheen of sweat on Wyatt's face. Turning back, she breathed out into the hot, soupy air that made the cabin of the plane stuffy, as if she would be suffocated by their stupidity.

"Dad, can we turn the air conditioning up?" she whined.

"Sure, honey," he said, taking his eyes off of the sky to turn a few dials and push a few buttons. Cool air blasted out of the vents, filling the stifling silence with some white noise.

Suddenly, the plane jerked, flopping like a pancake on a skillet. Terra gripped the seat's armrest. "Jeez, Dad. What's going on with your flying today?"

Mr. Lombardi sighed from the front seat. "Terra, I know you're mad because your mother forced you to come on this ride, but please don't be rude. You can do that later."

"Thanks, Dad," she said, sitting back in passive aggressive defeat.

Even more flying.

~

Wyatt continued mumbling to himself and writing on his shoe. Terra rolled her eyes in distaste, snorting at his insanity. Then she heard the harsh guitar music and his white earbuds.

Ms. Hill leaned back in her chair and whacked Wyatt's leg, making everyone in the whole plane jump. "Take those earbuds out."

He reluctantly complied as Mr. Lombardi readjusted the plane.

Terra pressed her hands on the glass, looking out at the strangely unfamiliar desert, and immediately pulled them back - the glass was burning hot.

"Hey, Dad?" Terra said, pulling out her phone to check the temperature.

"Hmm?"

"You do know that it's like 120 degrees out right now?"

"Really? That's nowhere near what the forecast said," he said, his voice suddenly grave and panicstricken. He whipped around to glare at his daughter.

"Yeah."

"Like how hot exactly?" he said.

"Uh." Suddenly, Terra couldn't speak. "One twenty-two. Uh, Fahrenheit."

"Oh my God. That's . . . not good," Mr. Lombardi said, gripping the steering wheel with astounding strength.

Terra sat back in her seat, her jaw slack.

"Uh, what?" Wyatt burst out, finally pulling out his earbuds. "I did not fucking sign up for this."

"Language!" Ms. Hill snapped. Terra rolled her eyes.

"Please stay calm. This is nothing I can't handle."

Just then, a red light blinked and a small ding went off.

"Dad . . . " Terra said warily and craning forward to look in the front seat.

"Be quiet, Terra!" Lombardi shouted, letting all of his panic out in one burst. Then he breathed and wasted no other second to take action.

He pressed a button on his headset and began rapidly talking into his headset. "This is Captain Lombardi speaking. This is passenger tour flight eleven-one at eight thousand feet and climbing. The engines are overheating, and I've gotta put her down. My beacon is on. Can you get a clear on my location? Over."

Static.

Then, a voice broke through the gray, and a man with a dapper and clear voice said, "Hey, Lombardi. We can't quite find your location, but the nearest safe landing spot is about 10 miles southeast of Loop B. Can you make it? Over."

"Uh, we're already twenty miles west of the regular rounds-"

"What?" Terra burst out, gripping her father's seat, seeing the craggy rocks below. Ms. Hill hissed at her to shush. Terra sneered. Who does she think she is, anyway?

Pause. More static.

"Well, that's all I can do for you. Best of luck to you at the landing site. Over."

Lombardi sighed. Then, a hollow feeling snapped Wyatt to attention. The fluttering, surging feeling when one drives down a steep hill or rides the descent on a roller coaster.

He looked out the window and saw the ground fast approaching. His stomach was lodged in his throat. He couldn't for the life of him describe it any other way.

"Uh, Mister...?" he started, forgetting the captain's name.

"Yes, we're stalling. I'm working on it," he said, pressing pedals and pulling on the steering wheel and throttle.

"We're stalling? What?" Terra exclaimed.

"Uh, yeah. Get with the program!" Wyatt snapped at her.

"Everyone quiet please . . . " Mr. Lombardi said, sounding less agitated than he actually was.

Terra's breathing quickened, Ms. Hill's face was completely pale, and Wyatt nervously tapped his Sharpie on the armrest of his chair.

~

Still falling. The feeling rose and rose in everyone's stomachs. The plane grated against the air, trying to slow, like ripping off fingernails. Mr. Lombardi flipped switches, checked instruments, did everything he could. But even Rome fell.

"Uh, Dad?"

"I'm kinda busy, honey," he said.

"Dad?"

"Terra - "

"Dad!!" Terra screamed, finally.

"What?!" He shouted, still trying to reign control of the aircraft.

"The engine - it's smoking," Terra said, pointing out the window with a childlike finger. She was right - the left engine was vomiting out thick black smoke.

"Holy sh-"

Suddenly, the left engine exploded, sending a rocketing shutter through the cabin. The mood turned grim and dark like a prison cell - they could all feel it. No more shouting in a panic. No more anxious tappings. Just silence. Just fear.

~

"Mayday mayday, the left engine is out on the Cessna 310. Extreme damage on the left wing of the plane. I am sending out a beacon so you can pinpoint our location. Send help. Over. Repeat. Mayday . . ."

Everyone's faces grew pale with fear. The plane cabin filled with thin smoke, suffocating everyone silently.

Static. Nothing.

The plane lurched and tilted downward with alarming steepness. Terra grabbed her arm rest and strangled in her seat belt, kicking at the rugs on the floor, panic flooding through her, fearing that she would fall over and down, down down into the endless desert floor.

The world spun around them as the plane lurched into a tailspin nosedive, sickeningly throwing everyone into paralyzing panic again and again as the plane made a smoking spring in the sky.

Alarms and buzzers went off and screamed in their ears, only adding to the panic. Wyatt wanted to scream back at them,

"YES, WE KNOW THAT WE'RE GOING TO DIE." But he didn't. He couldn't.

~

"Brace for impact!" Captain Lombardi shouted over the screaming noise, and the face masks shot down. Terra and Wyatt snapped them over their mouths while Lombardi did it himself, but Ms. Hill had already passed out, so Wyatt reached forward and strapped the mask around his mother's mouth.

How cute.

And the barren ground came closer and closer until the blue sky had completely disappeared. One last surge of terror ran through Terra and Wyatt, turning their agitated blood cold.

And then there was the impact. Alarming and shattering and resounding through their bones.

And then there was the blackness. Encroaching and gripping and resounding through their souls.

And then the silence.

CHAPTER TWENTY-TWO: Lost and Found
DAY 38-39 - Wyatt; September 11th & 12th, 2015

The figure of my last hope walks, stumbles, away into the misty distance.

And I am alone.

Pain, constant, lacerates through me. With every beat of my heart, the venom and the infection, moves further and further throughout my body.

And less and less I can feel of my leg.

The wind kicks up, dragging reluctant grains of sand with it.

I turn my head into the distance, but Terra is gone, masked in the layers of the desert.

Something hard catches in my throat, but I'm too dehydrated to release it into the stale air. My leg like a wooden log, I struggle to lean over, ripping tired muscles. Grab for the water she left me.

Watching the sandstorm hiss and roar, I huddle under our shelter, sipping water. Hoping, waiting, for the moment when the venom, the infection, reaches my heart.

~

I awake. Slowly, but the pain pulsing, growing, ribboning up my numbing leg yanks me out of it. Shoving through what little supplies she left me, I grab two more painkillers and some fruit. Down those.

My stomach swollen, I lean back onto the tree. Breathe.

I can feel night falling, even though I can't lift my head so much as to look outside.

Black balloons burst in my vision. Little bright lightning bugs come from inside my head and fly around in front of my eyes. This is it.

As a last ditch effort, I lean down and drag the jacket towards me. Drape it over my chest.

The wind beats against our haphazard walls. The sand always finds its way in. My eyelids flutter.

I pull out my wallet, suddenly consumed with the last ribbons of emotion. With guilt. With sorrow.

My fingers slick with sweat and trembling, I slide out the photo of one of the people whom I care about more than my own pathetic life.

Lilly.

Involuntarily, I feel tears rise to my eyes. God, I hope she makes it. I hope both Lilly and Terra have wonderful lives. I hope they marry handsome and kind men. I hope they have adorable children. I hope they are successful and have everything that I never could.

But still, part of me believes that this is all going to be okay, despite this, despite myself, despite the venom within me. Barely able to breathe, I sob, painful cracks erupting from deep within my chest. I am not the summation of my broken parts.

God. Save me from this hell. Save me from myself. Carry my weary body into glory. I believe.

Look up.

I look up and see the sun just laying down its weary head into the night. The light, it's never ending. But it comes from inside, from behind my eyes.

The photo slips from my fingers as the blackness swallows the last of my vision.

~

All of a sudden, air is sucked into my lungs. Almost not my by own volition.

Panic forms as a boil in my gut. But the environment swirls around me. Cool, starchy sheets. Chilling liquid flowing into my veins.

My fingers running over the lumpy mattress, I open my eyes. Sticky, like peeling up tape.

A warm, soft body flops against me, grasping my hair.

My senses rising to a scream, I flail, grabbing the bedside railings on either side of me.

But then, the soft blonde hair comes into focus, and I feel her familiarity on top of me.

Lilly.

~

She's here. She's really here.

And my first thought is that I am dead. I can't feel a good portion of my legs, anyway.

But she's here. Real, so real, and slipping through my fingers like sand.

Sand.

Kicking at the suddenly binding sheets, yet bound by medical equipment, familiar disorientation grips me by the neck. "Where am I?" I say, my voice ripping like sandpaper.

Swirls of white, blonde, gray. I am falling forever and ever, towards a black hole.

"You're safe! Wyatt, it's okay! It's me, Lilly!"

Lilly. Her voice drags me out of a deep muck. And from places I once knew, the aged and kind voice of my sister brings slamming reality.

"Lilly?" Like friction, the words come out and I can hardly believe them. A sob catches in my raw throat. Thin and weak and crying and alone, yet alive. All of the times I thought, I *believed* that I'd never see her again come flooding back. I release every ounce of anxiety and fear, every notion that we wouldn't make it back, and I just live. Just live in the undeniable fact that my sister is safe and is right here in my arms.

"I'm so glad you're back, Wyatt," she says, her warm breath creating something in me. Something large, something throbbing. Something that breathes life back into my tired bones.

She's here, and I cry. Each sob hurts my weary chest like a bitch, but she's here and that's all that matters. I have something, someone to live for, someone to die for.

Lilly holds me as I cry, for the infinite times I've held her in times of need. She holds me, small and fits perfectly like the hollow part of me.

I'm alright.

But still, something reaches past my pain, past my relief.

Terra. She saved me. She's alive. She made it.

Suddenly, I can't breathe. I push away the covers, only to be hindered by my legs that feel like lead.

I turn towards Lilly, my face carved in desperation. "Where's Terra?"

"Who?" Lilly asks, her face genuinely concerned.

I grasp at the sheets, my cracked skin peeling at the tension. "The . . . the girl I came back with."

She shakes her head, her eyes widening at my disheveled and frantic appearance. "No . . I, I don't know where-"

My breathing freezes in my chest. I have to find her. I push off the hospital sheets, only to see a massive bandage around my leg, from my knee down.

A machine next to me beeps erratically, and I feel Lilly's worried eyes on me. Something cold flows into my veins, and I kick at the cloudiness tugging at my vision. But it's not enough. It's never enough.

I see Lilly, gazing at me with a deep pain in her young eyes.

~

Cold. That's all there is.

Pain digs into my leg like a hot, metal spike. I push air in and out of my lungs. I sit up and see that I'm alone. My chest aches for Lilly, for someone.

I stare at the ceiling. Where will we go? Who will take us in? My first thought is Aunt Angie and Uncle Judd, but if so, where are they?

A nurse pokes her head in, waving a clipboard. I recede into myself as she checks my machines, takes my pulse, temperature, blood pressure.

I roll my head across the pillow. "On a scale of one to dying, how close am I?"

A young, pretty woman, she laughs, throwing back her head. Her hair shines auburn, but it looks like it's from a bottle."For being bitten by a snake, remarkably well."

I smirk. Doesn't feel like it. "You look like a lady who likes favors. Could you do something for me?"

She smiles, exasperated with me. "Mm?"

"You know, the girl I was rescued with. Terra. Could you take me to see her?" I ask, feeling the drowsiness pulling at my burnt skin.

"Ah," she stutters. "I'm not sure, I'll have to ask if you're ready to go in a wheelchair."

"You do that for me, sweetheart." I feel like vomiting.

She purses her nude, pink lips. "What, are you like seventeen or something?"

"I think you should be able to check on your little chart there," I say, winking. If only I could be doing this with Terra.

The nurse cocks her head at me. "I'll see what I can do."

"Thanks, sweetheart."

She leaves, taking all of the lightheartedness with her, and shuts the door behind her.

I lean back. Maybe if I freak out again, the machines will go off and give me some of those knock-out drugs again.

I pull the sheets up close, trying to mimic the feeling of warmth, of closeness. My chest aches, like my ribs and lungs are falling forever towards a single point. My heart.

Squeezing my eyes shut, they sting. And truly, a part of me wishes my mother was here to see it. Here to see the person I've become.

Salty tears leak into the cuts, the splits in my face. The endless desert sun peeks through the blinds, coating my face with a familiar heat.

My hands sweat, and I rub them against the starchy sheets. Lost - found? Are they all two sides of the same coin? For my soul, my heart, still feels like it's stuck out in that damned desert, walking circles around rocks and shrubs.

Fuming and trapped within a cage of myself, I kick off my sheets, my right leg swollen and twice its size. I can't stand it in here. Where the hell is Lilly?

A sea of white, that's what this room is. The walls, floor, ceiling, all ebb and flow like water over my parched mouth.

Reeling, I rip the wires and cords from my body. Crawl out of my bed.

But the second my bad foot touches the floor, pain rockets up my side like lightning, and I crash to the ground.

My raw skin burns against the tile. Each muscle rippling like cords, I drag my ass to the bathroom. The world swirls like I am being flushed down a toilet into an endless abyss.

Everything is dead. The blood of animals, of humans, coats my arms up to the elbows, and who I am entirely floats away into the wind and setting sun.

Pain in its many cruel forms cracks me open like an egg. My legs turn to spaghetti as I hold myself up, willing my spotty vision to stay. I am a shell of a person . . . my soul is a kite in the wind on a cloudy day.

My knobby elbows bang against the porcelain sink, but I pull myself up, force myself to look at my face in the mirror. Disheveled hair, bandages and sharp bones. Cracked skin.

My chest, abdomen contracts with a fresh pain, one that washes over me, drowns me. Gripping the sink until my knuckles turn white, the pain pushes its way out of me until I see stars, until black holes open up in my vision.

And the pain is that of a release, of the fact that there is no more. No more to be said, no more pain to be felt. The rope that I have reached the end of has shriveled up into threads that I grasp onto for dear life.

Slowly, I sink to the floor, one joint at a time, and let the cold of the floor seep into my flaming body.

Darkness. Like the endless, endless hole forming right in front of me.

Light. It goes on forever, and I can finally touch it.

~

A scream. And one I know all too well.

Hands touch me, move me, but I am trapped in a haze that doesn't allow me to protest. So I let them. I let them fuss over me and stab things into me and wrap me back up like a child.

I am stuck in limbo. A blackness surrounds me, encases me, but I can sense that Lilly's by my side. My soul fights, grabs at the darkness, wrestles with it.

There's no pain. But there's also nothing good.

Sometimes I feel the sun again, the sand. And sometimes I feel her so clearly that I almost reach the surface of reality again.

But most of the time, it's just me and my thoughts and the blackness.

CHAPTER TWENTY-THREE: At Last
DAY 39 - Terra; September 12th, 2015

I awake again, but this time, it's slowly, my consciousness being dragged like taffy. Aches pierce my body. My sheets feel crinkly and clean, like parchment paper, but I push them off, panic fluttering in my gut. The fluorescent light above is piercing before my eyes adjust. The buzzing sound of the long bulbs slowly comes into focus.

I am alone.

I begin to explore the tubes and wires coming in and out of my body. There's an IV - I rip that out. Blood leaks out of my arm and a clear liquid drips out of the exposed needle.

I take off many other odds and ends, my hands trembling. Suddenly disconnected, I feel odd, alone, a Frankenstein's monster of sorts.

I lean over the side of the bed, planting my feet onto the cold tiles. My bare feet make soft, sticky noises as I wander into the bathroom.

I draw back at my own appearance. My face is a nearly translucent pale, but cracked and dry, and the hair I have left greasy and matted into clumps. My hair has been fastened back with a thick headband to keep oil out of the four stitches in the fleshy part below my eyebrow, but just above my eyelid.

My cracked and peeling lips are nearly the same color as my skin. I tear my lips into a grimacing smile, just a tad, and blood peeks through the openings. I look away and lick my lips. As I do, my eye catches on the long gash on my forearm, from ages ago. That has also been reopened and stitched up. I can still

hear the glass clattering in the plane, see the shards scraping across my skin, and the sunlight pouring in through the sunroof . .
.

I feel a tightness on my right side, one of the deeply aching spots. I lift up my hospital gown until my entire side is showing in the mirror. A massive bandage encases my ribs. Peeling up the tape from my cracking, leathery skin, I see what's below.

Four long surgical sutures, including two smaller ones on my upper arm, see-saw across my right rib area, below my breast and a little to the right. They bulge and tear across my tissue-paper flesh and my bony rib cage. Sallow and bursting with infection-pink. Clawing at the flesh around the puncture wounds, I continue to stare, horrified at my own appearance. I swallow hard, breathing in and out, feeling the tightness and pain that bites at my side.

A small hole, about the diameter of a pencil eraser, is among the wounds on my right side. I breathe in deeply, feeling my tissue-paper lungs. It hurts like hell, but I can breathe all the way in and out, no problem. They must have had to reinflate my lung.

I look away and drop my hospital gown back to where it should be, thick, hot emotions coursing through me. I abruptly walk out of the bathroom.

As small as a mouse, I venture into the hallway and find it mostly empty. The doctors and nurses, however, immediately turn at the sound of me coming out of my room. I swallow hard, but it feels as if a roll of sandpaper has been stuck down my throat. Suddenly, all of the doctors flash plastic smiles and start striding over to me, speaking in a language so foreign to me that it hurts.

I panic. A balloon explodes in the center of my chest, threatening to seep out of my rubbery ribs. My heartbeat rises, screaming in my ear and under the most delicate layers of my skin. In a swirl of people, I find myself at the center, desperately alone.

And then I find myself running. Running as fast as I can. Pumping my weak and spindly legs. The hospital tile strikes cold beneath my feet, but the air slices cleanly between my legs and under my gown. The air whips past me as the stench of death pools in my nose. I dash past room after room, doctor after doctor, until I don't know what I'm doing anymore.

I don't know what I'm doing anymore.

Suddenly, I lurch forward, tumbling over my two left feet. I feel every knock, every bump that goes through me like lightning, until I skid to a stop, on my side on the unforgiving floor. Wincing in pain, I struggle to get up.

Breathing hard, I feel a sharp pain coming from the cluster of puncture wounds around my right side. So much for those painkillers.

I stumble over and clutch the corner, as I realized I have come to an intersection in the hospital. I lean back onto the wall and let my eyes slide shut. The moment I do, thoughts begin to infiltrate my mind, swirling like toy ships in an endless, stormy sea. Where am I? Why am I here? What happened to get me here? Where's my family? Where's Wyatt?

I slide down the hospital wall, slowly, letting my feet slide out from under me, and clatter to the floor. It hits me. He's dead. I'm dead. My father's dead. We're all fucking dead.

Yet I'm all alone.

Tears stream down my numb face, but I don't realize it until they leak into a peeling gash on my chin. Sobs fester inside of me, racking my body like jolts of electricity, but it can't find a way out because it hurts. It hurts too fucking much to let my pain explode into the air. Because it's over. It's all over. I'm drowning from the inside out.

Everything shiny and cold and smooth strikes me with disorienting terror. I grasp at burning threads of sanity. I'm not here . . . I can't be here.

Because, still, I am lost in the searing, endless desert that is my own mind.

~

Someone kind comes and eases me upward. They even hoist me up into their arms and begin to carry me. The rectangular, fluorescent lights above pass by silently. They lay me down softly back into a bed and shove something up my nose. Cold, clean air floods my lungs, and the knife in my side eventually goes away. I'm pretty sure they inject me with something, but I can't feel it. I slowly descend into a state of semi-consciousness. I am half-aware of the things swirling around me, but I can't react to them, I can't process them. Vibrating anger burns me from the inside out, until I am a failed paper lantern, crashing into the ocean to its drowning death.

~

Eventually, like all things, I emerge from this state. But another, constant, cold, medicine flows into my veins, and I fall under the blanket of blackness again. And again. And again.

I float in and out of consciousness. Nothing matters.

All bodily functions seem to stop. I don't get hungry, thirsty, I don't have to go to the bathroom. Sometimes I forget that I'm breathing. But oh well, I assume that the people here at this hospital are taking good care of me.

In these periods of unconsciousness, however, I hear my mother's voice. Occasionally, I hear Nick's, but, like always, he never has much to say. But when I bob back up into consciousness again, the plastic, cushioned chair is always empty. I dream of a day when I will awake and someone . . . anyone will be sitting in that lonely old chair by my bed. Nick. My mother. Harper. My father. Wyatt.

But there's never anyone there. The chair just sits, indifferently, as if it too is waiting for someone to comfort it, as well.

I stay, suspended, in this state, for who knows how long. But eventually, like all things, someone shows up. I recognize her first by her short cropped, shiny black hair, just skimming below her chin. Her rosy lips are pulled into a cocked smile, and her pale skin glows with life.

"Hey," Harper says, her voice soft, but coated with a thin layer of her usual spunk.

I wait a moment, to see if the drugs will pull me back under. When nothing happens, I roll my head over the pillow to look at Harper full on. She looks good, but I notice her eyes are swollen, creased with pain and lined red. My eyes flit down to her hands, where they rest in her lap, clenched together hard, twiddling her thumbs. I've only seen Harper cry twice, and I guess now I can count her shining eyes as thrice.

"Hi," I say, my voice scratching like a record. "How long have I been out?"

"Only maybe a day." Harper clears her throat and flits her eyes away from me a few times. Her demeanor immediately changes, her face brightening. "But, um, the story's everywhere! You are famous! Everyone's covering the story about the courageous Terra, who survived 40 days in the desert and traveled over 100 miles."

Instinctively, I smile. "Really, huh?"

Harper smiles, sadly. "Yeah. Everyone wants to interview you, but ... "

She doesn't continue, and I'm thankful.

Harper scratches her head, tousling her glossy, straight hair. "But, I, uh, do have something to show you." She half smiles, and suddenly, my heart floods with something old. Something powerful. Oh, how I've missed her. If there was anyone else who I'd be stranded in the desert with, it would be her. And all of those nights, thinking, knowing I'd never see her again come slamming back to me. All of that longing is displaced, is banished, because my best friend is sitting here. I so badly want to reach out to her. To touch her. Just to confirm that she's really here.

But I swallow hard and stuff it down. I have to wait for the right time. She's not ready.

After a moment, I find myself smiling back. Harper helps me unhook my IV and things, however, I try to stand up for myself. The drugs obviously haven't all worn off yet, evidenced by the tingly feeling in my fingers and toes and the constant swaying I find uncontrollable. Harper just laughs stiffly at me and throws my arm around her.

But I stop. I pull away from her and lean on the bed, my elbows shaking. Harper's soul can be viewed only through the glassy marbles with deep, hazel rimmed holes. "Harper, you don't have to hide from me. I'm okay."

These few, simple words brush away Harper's cool exterior like particles of dust on an antique ready to be restored. And through her eyes, I can see every ounce of pain.

I've seen Harper cry three times in our thirteen-year friendship. She's just much more emotionally reserved than I am. But tears mar her face more than she'd like. And finally, these tears come streaming down, like water from an endless well.

We immediately embrace. Harper's back trembles with sobs, and slowly, but surely, my knees give. As does Harper's, and we slide to the floor, a tangle of arms and legs and tears and love. As my best friend melts in my arms, tears prick at my own eyes. And eventually, I let go as well. I let go of the fear of never seeing her again. I let go of the fact that she is actually here. I let go of the fact that I am alive. I let go, and after I let go, I find that I can just be - I can just exist. The entirety of my soul exists in the present, and even though the past scars me and the future terrifies me, I am blessed with a tranquility that washes over me and drowns me. But it's a pleasant death, to be drowned by a peace that passes all understanding.

~

"I have something to show you," Harper eventually whispers in my ear, after our messy and hiccupy sobs subside.

We pull ourselves up - more accurately, Harper pulls me up - and she leads me to the right down the hallway. Confusion tugs at me, but it is only a passing star in the sky compared to a glowing moon of serenity that still lingers.

I see Harper visibly checking the numbers on the doors, and we finally come to one on the right, quite a ways down the hall.

Harper pushes the heavy door open.

A bright light comes from within the room, and from the angle and the quality I can tell that it's sunlight streaming in through a large window. One lonely hospital bed resides in the medium sized room.

That curly, blond hair meets my eyes, but it doesn't register. And so does that strong nose and those familiar lips. Wyatt.

My fingers barely skim the doorpost for purchase when I break out running. Awake or not, I throw myself onto his hospital bed and wrap my arms tightly around his neck. Softly, he awakes, his hot breath tickling my ear. His arms come up around me like he'll never ever hug me again. And I hug Wyatt tightly, thanking God with every breath I have that he's alive.

Ecclesiastes 3:1-8, NLT

[1]For everything there is a reason, a time for every activity under heaven.

[2]A time to be born, a time to die.

A time to plant, and a time to harvest.

[3]A time to kill and a time to heal.

A time to tear down and a time to build up.

[4]A time to cry and a time to laugh.

A time to grieve and a time to dance.

[5]A time to scatter stones and a time to gather stones.

A time to embrace and a time to turn away.

[6]A time to search and a time to quit searching.

A time to keep and a time to throw away.

[7]A time to tear and a time to mend.

A time to be quiet and a time to speak.

[8]A time to love and a time to hate.

A time for war and a time for peace.

Epilogue

December 24th, 2015

Dear Terra Lombardi,

First of all, Merry Christmas! I hope you have a wonderful celebration of Jesus's birth. Or the Winter Solstice. The details are a bit shoddy. Everything is well here in Los Angeles, in case you were wondering. If you weren't, that's too bad, because I told you anyways. It sucks that we couldn't be together on this holiday. Maybe during spring break. I know things between us are estranged, and have been for a few months now, but please listen to what I have to say. I want to work this out - with you.

Now, I'm no writer, but I am going to tackle the elephant in the room that we haven't talked about lately: There are parts of me that wish that this never happened. That the plane never crashed. That our parents never died. That we never had to survive out there. That the things we went through never happened.

But they did. And the other part of me is glad they did happen, because if they didn't happen, then I wouldn't have met you. I wouldn't be the better person I am today without having that experience in my life.

And even though it was hard, and I relive those moments every single day, I thank God every single day because it happened, and because of the immense fruit that it has yielded in me. I didn't realize until now the impact we had on each other, the impact the whole experience had on us individually.

But there's a reason for me saying all of this. Now, you know I am not a very encouraging person, but this has been on my mind for quite a while now. First, I want to thank you for saving my life out there many times. Despite my physical strength and willpower, I wouldn't have survived out there without your creative and caring hands.

But there's something else I want to let you know. I want to let you know that this isn't the end. Nowhere near it. That you, that we, are meant for so much more than surviving every day, barely scraping by. We are destined for greatness. Why? Because He that is in us is greater than he who is in the world. And so now, I want to remind you of something you said to me when I asked why we were out there, stranded and dying:

Romans 5:3-4 'We rejoice in our sufferings, knowing that suffering produces endurance, and endurance produces character, and character produces hope.'

So, Terra: This is not the end; this is only the beginning. Because you and I, we are just a cactus in the valley. A raindrop of hope in an endless desert. Life bursting forth where life should not. We are strong and resilient. We have been saved by grace through faith, dragged out of the miry clay into a glory we could have never imagined.

And whatever happens: don't you ever forget that, Sparkles.

Much love,

Wyatt Hartman

THE END

<u>acknowledgements</u>

First of all, all glory be to Christ. Couldn't have done any
of it without the big man upstairs. Secondly, I thank my parents,
Robert and Cathy Bennett, for always believing me and
supporting me in anything I do. You're my biggest fans. And my
brother, Andrew, too. I thank my beta-readers, who put up with
me nagging you and not replying to critique and all that stuff. You
were the flames that turned this ore into gold. Kate Kerr, Grace
Allaman, Matthew Sporrer, April Hoover, Sarai Monda, Chase
Sonnemaker, Sloan Huffman, and all of my other children in my
high school's Creative Writing Club. Josh Ringle, my eighth
grade English teacher, who told me that I could write a novel and
then made me write that said novel. You are one of the reasons
I'm the writer I am today. Lastly, I thank my readers. You're part
of the reason I wrote this, to reach all of you.

about the author

Olivia J. Bennett, more commonly known as Olivia J, The WordShaker, is a writer, artist, and creative extraordinaire. She is a professional nerd and occasional dabbler in the culinary arts. The companion novella to *A Cactus In the Valley*, entitled *A Panther In the Snow*, is coming Summer 2018!

Follow her blog for writing and life insight:
   oliviajthewordshaker.blogspot.com

Follow her on social media:
   Instagram: @olivia.j.the.wordshaker
   Facebook: /oliviajthewordshaker

Made in the USA
Monee, IL
11 April 2023

31128721R10216